ROMANCING THE EARL

DARCY BURKE

ZEALOUS QUILL PRESS

ROMANCING THE EARL

Major Elijah Hollister never wanted to be an earl, particularly not when it meant losing his brother. When a bold adventuress shows up at his door seeking a treasure map, Elijah suspects his brother's death may not have been accidental and that the lady knows more than she's willing to share. Whether she's a friend or foe, Elijah plans to keep her close—and hope the temptation of her kisses doesn't ruin them both.

Miss Catriona Bowen can almost taste the fruits of her years-long quest to find one of Britain's greatest treasures. The discovery will deliver the recognition and respect she deserves as an antiquary, despite the fact that she's a woman. However, to find the map that will lead her to success, she must ally herself with a stoic, yet provocative earl with a different goal. And when a villain threatens their lives, she realizes too late that love is the greatest treasure of all.

For Rachel

*A terrific author, a loyal and beautiful friend, and
the best chocolate martini-maker ever.*

CHAPTER 1

Wiltshire, July 1819

"$\mathcal{M}$ Y LORD, YOU have a visitor."

My lord. Would he ever get used to that? Like as not, he supposed, particularly after being called by a military rank nearly all of his adult life.

Major Elijah Hollister—rather, Lord Bloody Norris—looked up from the ledger he was studying. The enormity of inheriting an earldom when he had never planned on doing so weighed on him, almost as heavily as the shocking death of his brother Matthew, the previous earl, last year.

"Who is calling, Garber?"

The butler, a rigid, somewhat austere man who appealed to Elijah's desire for order, stood in the doorway, his dark blue costume plain but immaculate. "She did not present a card, my lord, but says she is Miss Catriona Bowen. She is accompanied by someone called 'Grey.'"

Elijah arched a brow, but said nothing.

"Would you like me to inform her that you are busy?"

Elijah glanced down at the ledger and decided an unexpected visit would be more diverting than trying to make sense of these numbers. Besides, he'd yet to make the acquaintance of more than a handful of people since arriving in Wootton Bassett just a fortnight ago. "No, I'll come. Where is she?" He stood up from the desk and walked around it.

"The Egypt Room, my lord."

Elijah fought a grimace. That was his least favorite room. The entire house was overdecorated and stuffed to the brim with antiquities the former earl—that is, the cousin who'd held the title before Matthew had inherited it two and a half years ago—had collected. However, the Egypt Room was particularly offensive and, frankly, disturbing, with a pair of sarcophagi flanking the massive fireplace and an array of paraphernalia that had no doubt been stolen from someone's tomb.

Elijah left the study, which he'd already begun to simplify by removing much of the former earl's collection. The ballroom was quickly becoming a depository for the excess of artifacts, which Elijah planned to sell at the earliest opportunity.

A medium-sized saloon, the Egypt Room was located at the back of the house with a view of the gardens. The day was overcast and mild, a far cry from the burning Australian summers he'd become accustomed to over the past five years.

His guest, a young woman with striking dark, nearly black hair turned from the windows where she stood with the second woman, a much taller female wearing a wide-brimmed hat, which he couldn't help but notice she'd failed to remove, and a stoic expression. Elijah had no trouble discerning who was Miss Bowen and who was "Grey."

"Good afternoon," he said, striding into the room.

Miss Bowen moved forward and smiled at him, her dark

pink lips curving up and forming dimples in her cheeks. She was quite pretty, though in an unconventional way, with her dark hair and eyes and a complexion that could be described as the color of tea with a spoonful of milk. In a room of flaxen-haired, blue-eyed, pale-skinned debutantes, she would gleam like a vibrant jewel.

"Good afternoon, my lord. I must beg your forgiveness for our presumption in visiting. I hope you won't mind. I am Miss Catriona Bowen and this"—she gestured to the other woman who angled her body toward Miss Bowen—"is Grey."

Elijah glanced at the single-monikered woman and decided she'd make a good soldier. She was tall and stoic, with an air of self-discipline about her. Something about the way her gaze followed Miss Bowen yet seemed to still fix on him invoked a sense of fierce protectiveness. "Your visit is not presumptuous," he said. "As I am new to the district, people have come to extend their greetings and I expect them to do so."

Her smile faltered a bit and she blinked. "Yes, well, I am not from the district. My apologies. I *am* imposing. You are new to town—to England, from what I hear—and are likely trying to find your way as the new earl. Yes, I'm being quite presumptuous," she said firmly, almost insistently, as if she would argue with him about her cheek. He fought the urge to smile at that. Miss Bowen not only didn't look the part of the typical young miss, she didn't act it either. And that made her . . . interesting.

"Then do tell me why you've come," he said.

"Certainly." She walked to a dark blue settee. "Shall we sit?" Grey moved to stand next to the piece of furniture.

"Of course." His hosting duties required some refinement. But then, what about him didn't? He'd spent the last five years on the other side of the world. Nothing was less refined than dwelling in a penal colony.

Her smile returned as she perched on the settee, and Elijah decided she wanted something. Why else would she behave so boldly—and be proud of doing so—and continue to smile at him as if he could make all of her dreams come true?

What a ridiculous notion.

"I'm visiting my friend, Lady Miranda Foxcroft. I think you've met her?"

He had, as well as her husband. "Yes, I'm surprised she didn't accompany you."

"I'm afraid I didn't inform her of my intention to call on you. You see, my errand today is rather . . . secret."

What sort of game was she playing? He didn't have time for nonsense, not when he was drowning in estate business and overwhelmed with creditors demanding to be paid for the bills his brother had run up during his brief time as the earl. "Miss Bowen, how can I help you?"

Her face brightened. "Yes, that's precisely it. You *can* help me. I'm an antiquary and I'm looking for a small tapestry that Lord Norris—the previous"—she shook her head—"that is, the previous-previous, maintained in his collection."

Blimey, another antiquary. Perhaps she'd be interested in taking some of this lot off his hands—provided she could pay for it. He had creditors to satisfy and an entire estate to overhaul. He looked at her intently. "Have you any idea how many tapestries Norris—the 'previous-previous'—kept in his collection?"

Her eyes were warm as she nodded. "I do. I've toured Lord Norris's collection on multiple occasions. It's exemplary."

It was bloody obnoxious. "I couldn't say."

"No, of course not. You're a soldier, not an antiquities expert. I can describe the tapestry for you. It's a medieval battle scene, about three feet square." She gestured the size with her hands. "I believe it's the only tapestry of that dimension. It's a bit of an oddity. Lord Norris used to display it in the upstairs gallery; however, he liked to move his treasures around from time to time, and of course who knows what's happened in the years since he passed."

"While my brother was the earl."

"Right." Her eyes filled with sympathy. "I'm sorry for your loss."

"Thank you. However, I haven't seen the tapestry you describe and I'm afraid I wouldn't know where to look. I've only just arrived a fortnight ago and I'm still trying to find my footing."

"Of course you are, and this is why my presumption is terrible." Her forehead creased into attractive little pleats. Attractive? "I'm so sorry for bothering you. However, I'm afraid my need for the tapestry is quite urgent. I should like to buy it."

"I wouldn't know what to charge you for it. I will, in fact, be selling the entire collection, but I need to consult with an antiquary before I do so." He'd received a letter from a Lord Septon, an antiquary who'd offered to assist him with cataloging and evaluating the collection, and he planned to respond to him with haste.

Her face split into a beatific smile. "That is where I can help you. I can tell you precisely what the tapestry is worth, and I can pay you for half of it now."

Oh yes, this woman had cheek to spare. "That's a bit dubious, isn't it? You telling me the price for something you clearly desire most fervently."

Her expression dimmed, but only slightly. "I'm a trustworthy sort."

He leaned forward in his chair. "So you say, but I don't know you at all. You're here on a secret errand so that I can't even verify your identity with Lady Foxcroft. In my situation, would *you* trust someone such as yourself?"

He chanced a quick look at Grey, who still lingered beside the settee, to gauge her reaction. Her gaze was steady, confident. If she took issue with his question, she didn't reflect it. And why should he care? Was she Miss Bowen's bodyguard? He realized that was precisely what she seemed.

Miss Bowen blinked at him. "Of course I would. I know myself to be quite honest and ethical."

He couldn't help it—he laughed, and she looked a bit startled by his reaction. "I'm still skeptical—perhaps it's the soldier in me. However, it's a moot point since I don't know where the tapestry is and I don't have time to find it. I will, however, contact you after I've located the piece and ascertained its value from an objective source."

She scooted forward and squeezed her hands together on her lap. "I understand your hesitation, but perhaps I haven't made my *need* for this antiquity plain. I require this tapestry immediately, my lord."

Her insistence and passion—passion?—was most curious. He might not have time for her nonsense, but he was intrigued. He sat back and set his hands on the arm of the chair, then speared her with an intense stare. "Why?"

She glanced at her maidservant or chaperone or whatever-she-was, who seemed to slightly nod her head as if they'd silently communicated something. When Miss Bowen returned her attention to him, her gaze was frank. "Because I need the tapestry to find something."

That made no sense whatsoever. "How?"

She stared at him and he could almost see her mind churning. "It contains a . . . map."

Just like that, Elijah snapped to attention as if his commanding officer had just stalked into the room. He leaned forward once more and slitted his eyes at her. "Like a treasure map?"

Her eyes widened. "I didn't say anything about treasure."

No, but he could tell from her reaction that treasure was precisely what she was looking for. Suddenly, the note Matthew had penned just before his death took on a whole new meaning. Instead of the drunken ramblings of a man who'd always dreamed of a grander life, it now seemed like something far more disturbing.

"What do you know of this map?" Elijah asked.

"It's a medieval battle scene and was likely stitched in the early to mid-fifteenth century."

"How is it a battle scene *and* a map?"

For the first time, uncertainty crept into her gaze. "I don't know. It only ever seemed to be a battle scene to me. And don't ask how I know it's a map. I'm afraid I can't disclose more than I already have. As I said, this is a secret endeavor. I shouldn't have even told you this much, but you must understand how important it is that I obtain this tapestry."

"What I understand is that you are likely trying to fleece me of something that is already quite valuable and possibly represents even greater value."

Grey shifted her position, moving a few steps toward Elijah's chair and lessening the distance she'd have to cover should she decide to launch an attack. He shook his head, wondering why he'd assumed she was on the offensive. He'd likely thought that because though he'd left military life, he simply couldn't ignore his military sensibility.

She shook her head. "I'm not trying to fleece you at all. The treasure it leads to is not monetarily valuable. It's only important to the study of history. My brother is the Keeper's assistant at the Ashmolean Museum at Oxford and I plan to give it to him for display. The amount I would offer you for the tapestry is more than fair."

Yet she hadn't stated it as of yet. Elijah's wariness intensified. Matthew had indicated the treasure *was* valuable. Had he been mistaken, or was she lying? "How much?"

"Two hundred pounds."

Good Christ, where had she gotten that kind of money? "You actually have a hundred pounds with you to give me today—you did say you had half?"

"Yes." She darted a glance at her indomitable companion. "I am prepared to pay you a hundred pounds. But first we have to find it. I know Lord Norris kept an inventory. Perhaps that will reveal its location. Might we review it?"

There *was* an inventory and Elijah had given it a cursory overview. However, it wouldn't help them. Not with this. "I'm afraid that won't be necessary. I'm fairly certain the map is gone."

Her eyes widened and her mouth dropped open for the barest second. "No," she breathed. "It can't be. You said you didn't know where it was; you didn't even know what I was talking about."

"I didn't until you called it a map. My brother wrote a letter to me shortly before he died. In it, he mentioned a treasure map, but not a tapestry. I discounted it as the product of his fanciful imagination, something he was prone to."

"Then it's still here." Her tone carried hopeful excitement.

Surprisingly, he sympathized with her plight. He might not share her enthusiasm for this tapestry-map, but he knew what it was like to want something most desperately and realize you'd likely never have it. "It is not, I'm afraid. Several people offered to buy it, and someone attempted to steal it, prompting my brother to hide it. I now wonder, however, if one of those buyers was as eager as you to find the map." Had she been one of the interested parties?

Miss Bowen lifted her hand to her chest. Her eyes widened with concern. "Whatever do you mean?"

"Tell me, Miss Bowen, what do you know of my brother's accident? Given what you've revealed about the importance of this tapestry, I find I must ponder whether it was an accident at all."

~

ate tried to mask her inhalation and failed miserably. She needed to work harder to be guarded, like Grey. But if he was saying what she thought he was saying . . . "You can't think I had anything to do with his death?"

Lord Norris's stone-blue eyes hooded briefly. "Forgive me, Miss Bowen. I am merely trying to understand this situation, now that I know my brother's ramblings were true. There *was* a treasure map, which someone tried to steal, and which Matthew subsequently hid. And then he died. I have no proof it wasn't an accident and yet I am suddenly struck with the troubling apprehension that it was not."

Troubling was perhaps an understatement. "You think someone killed your brother because of the map?"

"I don't know. But I find the timing of these incidents disturbing."

The back of her neck chilled with dread. Despite what she'd told the earl, the treasure she sought *was* extremely valuable and desired by many. Perhaps even by those who would resort to violence to obtain it. That thrust her quest into a new light, one she would discuss with Grey later.

She glanced at her companion, who gave her a subtle nod of encouragement. Squaring her shoulders, Cate returned her attention to Lord Norris. "What do you intend to do?"

He tipped his head to the side. "I'm not certain, but I'll make some inquiries. It's neither here nor there, however, as it doesn't affect you. Unless you are somehow involved?" He peered at her with a hint of suspicion to his gaze.

She fought to keep herself from becoming angry. The man had lost his brother . . . over a year ago, but it was still a loss. "I am absolutely not involved. This is the first time I've tried to purchase the tapestry. I only recently learned it was a map."

He leaned back in his chair and contemplated her for a long moment. "A map to an historically-important, but not valuable, treasure. My brother indicated to the contrary in his letter. He said it was incomparably valuable. Yes, I believe those were the words he used."

His tone and the gleam in his eye said he knew she'd lied before. Or, more accurately, misled him.

More vexing than his annoyance, however, was the fact that others—at least his brother and whomever had tried to purchase it—were aware that the tapestry was a treasure map. Cate should be one of very few people with this knowledge, which she'd uncovered without intellectual assistance. She planned to find the treasure the same way, though she would require Grey's help with the logistics. Then she would surprise and impress the antiquarian world with her astounding discovery.

"I apologize for misleading you, but this *is* an important artifact. Yes, I suppose the treasure might be considered valuable but I desire it for its academic worth. Did he say what the treasure was?" She held her breath waiting for the answer.

And she had to wait, because Norris was taking his time, likely weighing how much to divulge. She wanted to demand complete honesty in exchange for the same, but she couldn't do that. Not right now. Maybe not ever.

"No," he said finally, causing her to exhale softly. "His letter did not reveal the nature of the treasure, nor did he mention the fact that the map was a tapestry. He wasn't very good with details." Norris's tone was resigned. "As I said, he had a tendency to be fanciful, which is why I discounted the entire letter as a drunken farce. He was also fond of playing jokes in our youth, and I wondered if this might be an adult version of the same."

She could feel the tension between the brothers as if the previous Lord Norris were in the room with them. Though she'd just made this Lord Norris's acquaintance, she would wager *he* was very good with details. His pale blue eyes were alert, intelligent, which made him exceptionally attractive—to her. She was far more impressed with a man's intellect than his appearance, although Lord Norris certainly boasted a handsome exterior as well. He was perhaps the tallest person she'd ever met—standing well over six feet and taller even than Septon—and held himself with the sharp, imposing bearing of an officer. His blond hair kept him from looking completely fierce.

She internally shook herself. Now who was being fanciful? "Did the letter mention who the potential buyers were?"

He frowned. "Unfortunately, no. Pardon me for repeating myself, but he wasn't good with specificity."

"And you have absolutely no idea where the tapestry might be hidden?" He'd said as much, but she had to consider the possibility that he was lying. Except he'd declined knowing its whereabouts before he'd learned it was a map to a valuable treasure.

"I do not. And that is the truth—on my honor." His stare was direct, and she could tell his honor was very important to him. She couldn't help but believe him. "So, you see, I can't help you."

Believing him didn't ease her frustration, however. "You mean you *won't* help me. He didn't destroy the map; you said he hid it. What is hidden can be found. That's what we antiquaries *do*. And I am a skilled antiquary." She scooted forward on the settee. "I should be delighted to help you find the map, and I'll still pay you two hundred pounds for it."

He chuckled softly and like his earlier laugh, it was a warm, delicious sound that caressed her senses. "You'd give me the benefit of your *skill* free of charge? How magnanimous of you."

His sarcasm nearly provoked her to laugh in return, but she didn't. She needed to keep her mind on the task at hand —obtaining the map before someone else did. "I won't pretend I don't have a vested interest in finding this map. You already know I want it and I'm willing to pay a tidy sum. Your lack of desire to help me is most baffling."

"Desire?" His eyes were cool, but there was something burning in their depths—it gave her that same icy-hot feeling as after she'd spent too much time outside in the snow as a child. "What I *desire* is to learn how you know this tapestry is a map or that it leads to treasure—a treasure you have yet to reveal, I might add."

This was a complicated chess match. Neither of them wanted to share too much, but they each had to give something in order to obtain a sliver of information. She sent a conspiratorial glance at Grey, who again nodded in support.

"Have you ever heard of the sword Dyrnwyn?" Cate asked.

His forehead creased. "Should I have?"

"It is also known as 'white-hilt' or the Sword of Rhydderch Hael. It is one of the thirteen treasures of Britain. Surely you've heard of those."

"Can't say that I have."

"They are ancient artifacts of Welsh origin, perhaps even magical in nature."

"Magical?" he asked in disbelief. "It sounds like a myth. Like Arthur and Excalibur."

She ought to have expected him to be dubious. Anyone outside of the antiquarian world would be. "It's exactly like Arthur and Excalibur. Dyrnwyn belonged to one of his knights. There are many documents that purport the existence of all of these things."

He looked unconvinced. "There are many documents that proclaim a virgin bore a child, but I don't believe those either."

Grey let out a decidedly unladylike snort. Cate threw her a suffering glance. "That's rather blasphemous, isn't it, my lord?"

"I've spent the last several years in a rather blasphemous place. You must forgive me," he said unrepentantly. "You think this tapestry map leads to"—he paused a moment—"Durnwin?" He did a fair job of pronouncing the Welsh name.

"I'm confident it does, yes."

"And this confidence is based on what? What is your evidence that this is a map leading to Dyrnwyn?"

She borrowed his tactics for evasion. "Forgive me if I don't disclose that information. It would spoil the academic paper I plan to publish."

He crossed his arms over his chest. "You think I might steal your ideas? I assure you, I have no academic designs on your research. Or whatever you call it."

She scowled at him, her anger rising. As a female antiquary, she fought against prejudice. This quest would give her the credibility and respect she deserved. Her gender ought not matter to the antiquarian community, but women were not admitted to the London Natural Society of Antiquities, nor were they allowed to present their ideas. "And I assure *you*, my research is sound. My father, Mr. Rhys Bowen, is a renowned scholar in the realm. His personal library of medieval manuscripts is unparalleled. Many of his documents appear in the Ashmolean Museum, where my brother works." She was, unfortunately, quite used to invoking her father and brother's names in order to recommend her own integrity. It was, overall, a galling circumstance.

Norris lifted a shoulder. "A fine pedigree, I'm sure, but you must understand that all of this means next to nothing to me. I've inherited an apparently remarkable collection of antiquities, but it may as well be a warehouse full of farming implements. On second thought, such tools would perhaps be more useful."

Cate tried not to gape at him. "I assure you that your collection of antiquities is far more important and at least more valuable than farming implements."

"I shall have to take your word for it. As a *skilled* antiquary."

She couldn't tell if he was being facetious, but her ire was fully pricked now. "I've been searching for Dyrnwyn for years. I've pored over every document I could get my hands on, and I recently found one that indicates the tapestry is a map that leads to the sword depicted upon it." She was revealing far too much, but he'd called her abilities into question.

His eyes rounded briefly. "*That's* your evidence? Unless the document was written by King Arthur himself, I'd say it's ambiguous at best."

She worked to keep her tone even. This was precisely why she hadn't shared her theories with anyone besides Grey. Not that her brother and father wouldn't have listened to her with considerably more interest and credulity than Lord Norris. But she hadn't told them because this was going to be *her* discovery. Hers alone. "The document was authored by a reliable medieval source—Edmund de Valery. Perhaps you've heard of the de Valery manuscripts?"

His blank stare said he hadn't.

She charged forward, warming to her topic. "They're a pair of books by a medieval scribe detailing stories of one of the Knights of the Round Table—Gareth—as well as other tales involving Arthur and his knights. My mother owns one of the manuscripts, so I'm quite familiar with de Valery's work. I immediately recognized that his hand had created the document regarding the tapestry."

"I'm sure it's fascinating. I can see that you're quite passionate about the subject." His tone suggested a *but*. "However,"—*and here it came*—"you're using a document written by a storyteller as your 'evidence.' Pardon me if I remain skeptical."

Cate was used to opposition and refused to let his bother her. "More like bull-headed," she muttered. She inhaled deeply and tried again. "My father has a poem—a copy, actually—written by a sixth-century scribe who was a contemporary of Gareth. He documented the exploits of Arthur and his knights and their acquisition of the thirteen treasures of Britain, one of which is a sword: Dyrnwyn. That this information was recorded during or shortly after their lifetimes is proof enough for me. I'm afraid I can't offer you a birth or death notice for any of them, but perhaps you'll credit my research instead."

He listened to everything with apparent interest, but she couldn't be sure what was going on behind his distractingly attractive eyes. "If proof exists that Arthur actually lived, why hasn't that been publicized? Or did I miss that while I was in Australia?"

That was actually a question she shared. She'd found the poem hidden away in her father's study and since he openly shared all of his documents, she had to imagine he'd kept it secret for a reason. Even from her. "I don't know, but I don't see how that matters."

"So you say, but perhaps your father's poem isn't authentic. You did say it was a copy. It could be an outright fabrication."

In her father's handwriting. He would never contrive such a thing. The normally tight control she kept on her temper snapped. "Oh, for heaven's sake, you are an infuriating person, aren't you?"

His brows shot up briefly. "In fact, I have been accused of that on occasion. Just ask my mother," he murmured. "My apologies. I am only trying to ascertain the facts. Like you, I prefer evidence and logic."

That he recognized her as a logical mind soothed her ire considerably. She inclined her head. "Indeed. Please take my word that this poem authenticates the knights' existence. Would it help to know that one of the thirteen treasures has already been found—that it's in the Ashmolean Museum?"

She held her breath, hopeful that she'd finally broken through his stubborn skepticism.

He exhaled softly. "Miss Bowen, I sympathize with your plight, but I am, quite frankly, too busy in my new role to provide assistance. I'm afraid you'll have to conduct your quest elsewhere." He stood.

She scrambled to her feet, frustration rioting through her. She cast a glance at Grey, who glared daggers at Lord Norris. "My lord, if you would only let me search the estate, I promise I won't be a bother." At his incredulous look, she rushed to add, "And of course, I would notify you the moment I found it. I shan't take the tapestry away from Cosgrove without your knowledge."

"Steal it, you mean? How comforting. Perhaps I failed to mention that my brother indicated in his letter that the map was no longer at Cosgrove." He massaged the bridge of his nose with this thumb and forefinger. "Miss Bowen, I have many business matters to attend. I do thank you for stopping by." He turned his body so that the angle indicated a clear path to the door.

Cate gave Grey a resigned look and strode toward the door. "Thank you for your time today. It was a pleasure to make your acquaintance."

"Indeed. Garber will see you out."

The butler appeared and showed Cate and Grey to the door. Cate held her head high and tried not to be discouraged.

And failed miserably.

CHAPTER 2

*O*nce they were outside, Cate tightened the ribbons of her bonnet and tossed a glare at the imposing façade of Cosgrove. "What an imperious, arrogant man."

"He's a major and an earl. What did you expect?" Grey asked.

"I was hoping for someone more . . . amenable."

They turned and strolled down the drive. It was only a two-mile walk back to Bassett Manor and neither one of them was a stranger to exercise. In fact, they enjoyed it, particularly Grey, who was fond of all manner of manly pursuits, such as boxing, riding astride, and swordplay. She was also a crack shot and had taught Cate to fire a pistol with considerable accuracy.

"It wasn't a pointless errand," Grey said, her long stride demanding that Cate walk briskly beside her. "You at least learned that the map is hidden somewhere and not simply lost."

While that was true, Cate was disappointed Lord Norris wasn't going to be of assistance. "It may as well be. It could be anywhere. The former Lord Norris sounds as though he was a featherbrain. Who knows what he might have done with the tapestry?" The notion that it was gone forever made her stomach turn.

"This may not be the only way to find the treasure. Perhaps there's another clue."

Cate appreciated Grey's optimism. She always tried to find a way around things—it was one of the traits that had drawn them together when Cate had been just twenty. She'd been traveling with her parents and wanted to sneak out of the inn to see a bawdy play. She'd almost made it when she'd run into Grey who'd been working at the inn as a maid. Instead of turning Cate in to her parents, Grey had helped her to escape and they'd gone to the play together. After that, Cate had convinced her parents to hire Grey as her personal maid. "And how would I find this supposed clue?"

"Back in Lord Septon's secret library would be a place to start," Grey said with a touch of irony.

Where Cate had found the document about the tapestry being a map in the first place. Septon, a close friend of her father's, was one of England's premier antiquaries and had taught Cate much of what she knew about antiquities. If Lord Norris thought Cosgrove's collection was overdone, he'd be completely overwhelmed by Septon House. A veritable museum, it also contained Septon's secret library, which Cate had seen once as a child.

After Cate had found the poem in her father's study, she'd renewed her quest for information about the thirteen treasures, particularly Dyrnwyn. She'd thought of Septon's library, and she and Grey had contrived to find their way inside. "You're willing to sneak back in?"

Grey shrugged. "Getting the key was the hardest part, and I can do that again."

Cate wasn't even exactly sure how Grey had obtained the key. She'd asked, but Grey hadn't ever directly said. Cate had long ago learned to trust Grey to do what needed to be done. "Yes, but will I be so lucky in finding something a second time? Assuming another clue even exists."

"I think you can find anything you put your mind to," Grey said.

Cate appreciated her companion's confidence. It was nice to know that at least one person in the world believed in her completely. "Norris knows more than he's saying."

Grey glanced at her as they crested a small hill. "You want another crack at him."

"I do." Cate's boots scraped over the dry earth. The day was warm, and perspiration gathered at the small of her back. "It should be easy to persuade Miranda to host a dinner party and invite Lord Norris."

"Certainly. Lady Miranda is always eager to entertain."

Cate's hostess was also Septon's goddaughter and, as such, an old friend of Cate's. Unlike Cate, however, she'd been raised a Society miss and though she'd come to adore life in the country, she never missed an opportunity to open up her home. And Cate knew Miranda was looking for a reason to invite the new Lord Norris to Bassett Manor. "My thoughts exactly. I'll speak to her as soon as we get back."

"What do you think Norris is hiding?" Grey asked.

"I can't believe that he has no idea whatsoever about where to look for the tapestry. I think it's fair to assume he was genuine in his surprise at learning his brother's claim was true—that there is a map to a treasure. And I think it follows that he's now considering all he's learned and perhaps trying to determine where it could be."

"If he finds it, what makes you think he'll tell you?"

"He said he plans to sell the entire collection. Why wouldn't he sell it to me? I offered him a fair price."

"Until someone offers him more," Grey said darkly, echoing the thoughts seeping into Cate's mind. Someone had already approached the previous Lord Norris about the tapestry, and she imagined that Septon would want to obtain it as well. He could offer a far greater sum than her two hundred pounds.

Cate stepped through a gap in a four-foot-tall hedge. "I'm simply going to have to persuade him to sell it to me and no one else."

"How are you going to do that?"

"I'm not sure." Cate tried to think of something he might want, something with which she could barter. If she could offer him something in return, something beyond money, perhaps he'd let her buy the tapestry. A knot of frustration formed between her shoulder blades. None of this mattered if he didn't actually *find* the tapestry in the first place. She could only hope he would look for it.

They walked in silence for several minutes, Cate's mind churning with thoughts and contingency plans.

"What about the previous Lord Norris's death?" Grey asked. "If Lord Norris suspects it may not have been an accident, shouldn't we do the same?"

This was one of the many concerns weighing on Cate. Yes, the previous Lord Norris may have been prone to an excessive imagination, but he'd known the tapestry was a map. How would he have learned that? "Do you suppose whoever tried to buy the tapestry told him it was a map? How else would he have known?"

Grey frowned. She looked over at Cate, her green-brown eyes squinting against the bright afternoon, despite the brim of her hat. "But why would they have told him? It makes more sense to let him think it's just an old tapestry."

"Agreed." She pressed her lips together and kicked at a small rock, sending it bouncing across the uneven ground.

"My brilliant plan to find Dyrnwyn and surprise the world with my discovery just became a good deal more complicated."

❧

From the comfort of his leather desk chair, Elijah stared out at the sloping lawn. The visit from Miss Bowen had thrown him into a bit of turmoil, and he wasn't yet certain if that was good or bad. The good was Miss Bowen. She was an unexpected acquaintance and one he thought he might like—if he'd wanted to make the acquaintance of a young woman, which he hadn't. He wasn't in the market for a wife and never planned to be. He'd been forced into his current role and he'd be damned if he'd change everything about himself to suit it. He'd envisioned and accepted a lonely life. Given his own experiences, he would be far happier that way. The alternative was pain and misery.

On second thought, perhaps Miss Bowen wasn't the good after all.

The bad were the questions he now had about this tapestry-map and any role it might've played in his brother's death. He'd gone from simply mourning his brother to wondering if there was something nefarious afoot. He'd told Miss Bowen he didn't have time for such things, but in truth, he found this puzzle far more intriguing than learning how to be a bloody earl.

After she and her companion had left an hour or so ago, he'd sent for his valet, Wade, and shared everything he'd learned. Barnabas Wade had been Elijah's batman in Australia and had accepted Elijah's invitation to accompany him to England. He was both servant and friend—the only one Elijah had.

"My lord?" Wade had gone to fetch Garber, the butler who'd been at Cosgrove for going on fifteen years.

Elijah tried not to wince as he turned his head toward the doorway. He was so used to "Major," especially from Wade.

"Yes, Wade, come in. And Garber." Elijah didn't bother inviting the butler to sit since he knew the man would refuse such familiarity. "I hope I'm not disturbing your duties?" Elijah was still growing accustomed to having such a large household. Hell, he was still growing accustomed to having *any* household.

Garber was of medium height and his thick, dark hair was peppered with gray. He presented a rather elegant figure and could easily have passed himself off as a gentleman— probably better than Elijah could. The butler stood behind the pair of chairs that faced Elijah's desk and inclined his head. "I am always at your pleasure, my lord. Is there something you require?"

"Only information." He flashed a look at Wade, who'd taken up a post near the bookcase. They'd discussed what Elijah ought to ask the butler. "Earlier, my guest came in search of a tapestry. It's notable in that it was small, only about three feet square, and was perhaps a . . . treasure map?" It sounded ludicrous even with knowing that multiple people believed it to be just that.

"I know precisely which tapestry you mean. His lordship —that is, the prior earl who wasn't your brother—once told me there were those who believed it was a treasure map, though he believed that was utter nonsense. It doesn't resemble a map at all. One gentleman, obsessed with the tapestry and the fact that it could be a map, annoyed his lordship so grievously with his incessant interest that his lordship stowed the item away in a storeroom." Garber scoffed. "I can assure you it was a dusty old tapestry and nothing more. It wasn't even particularly well stitched, if I might be permitted to observe. The back should have looked as pristine as the front, but there were several imperfections."

Pieces began to fit together in Elijah's mind. "Did you tell Matthew it was a treasure map?"

Garber clasped his hands behind his back. "I did, and I must admit I regret doing so. He believed it immediately." Clearly, Garber didn't share that belief, but would his opinion have changed if he'd known that someone had tried to steal it?

"Are you aware someone attempted to steal the tapestry?"

Garber looked aghast, as if one of the footmen had just dropped a serving dish. "I don't know anything about a theft. Are you quite certain this occurred?" The butler perhaps thought that if he hadn't been informed of something, it hadn't actually happened. In his short time here, Elijah had deduced that Garber demanded order and excellence. He likely didn't tolerate being ignorant of anything.

But *was* Elijah quite certain? His brother had said so, but until Miss Bowen's visit today, Elijah had ignored the entire account, given Matthew's propensity for telling exaggerated tales.

"It's unfortunate, my lord, that you cannot query Mason, his lordship's valet," Garber said.

Elijah sat straight in his chair. "Where is he?"

"He left, my lord, immediately following your brother's demise." Garber's typically austere brows pitched low over his dark brown eyes, which narrowed with disapproval. "His abrupt departure caused quite a stir."

"Why is that?" Elijah asked.

"He traveled with his lordship to Bath to visit your mother. They left Cosgrove together, but Mason wasn't with his lordship on the return trip. He arrived here the day after his lordship's accident."

Could Mason have been part of the plot to steal the tapestry? If indeed there had been a plot. "The coachman disappeared from the scene of the accident. Is it possible Mason also abandoned the wreckage and then arrived here as if he hadn't traveled with my brother?"

Garber took on an alarming pallor. "I hadn't considered that, my lord. I honestly couldn't say."

"Of course you couldn't. I didn't mean to imply you knew anything of what transpired regarding the accident." Elijah needed to find and speak with Mason. "Have you any idea where he is now?"

Regaining a bit of his color, Garber said, "I'm afraid I don't, my lord."

"Surely someone on the staff knows where he's gone. Conduct a thorough inquiry and report back to me. Wade will assist you."

"Very good, my lord." Garber hesitated. "May I offer another piece of information that may be helpful?"

Elijah nodded. "Please."

"Your brother had a visit that precipitated his search for the tapestry. A pair of men—I daresay they weren't gentlemen despite their manner of dress—called asking after the tapestry, which prompted his lordship to query me about its location."

"I see." These had to have been the other interested party, aside from Septon. "Do you recall their names?"

"I do not, my lord." His back straightened, making him appear even more rigid, which Elijah wouldn't have thought possible. "My apologies, it was over a year ago."

"Don't concern yourself, Garber. You've been quite helpful."

"Thank you, my lord." The butler turned and flicked a glance at Wade as he made for the door.

"A moment, if you please, Wade," Elijah said. "He'll find you later, Garber."

With a final nod, Garber left.

Elijah looked at Wade, who moved closer to the desk. "I want you to ascertain whether Garber is certain the tapestry is no longer at Cosgrove. I've no reason to doubt what Matthew indicated in his letter, but I wonder if we ought to search for it nonetheless."

"I'll see what I can learn." He gave Elijah a determined look. "And we'll track down this Mason chap."

"I hope so. We'll need to add discovering the identity of these men to our growing list."

"We'll do that too," Wade said confidently, with his ever-present amiable and earnest disposition.

Elijah appreciated the man's company more than he would ever know. He'd forecasted a lonely existence, and the entrance of Wade into his life had been a welcome addition. "Thank you, Wade. I shall be eternally glad you saw fit to follow me to England."

"Aside from the weather, it's not a bad place." With a quick smile, he turned and left.

Matthew's letter sat before him. Elijah had located it in the desk after Miss Bowen had left. He'd read through it three times to detect any clues he might have missed, but there was nothing. Two pages that included a weather report, an update on their mother—of that pair of topics, Elijah couldn't decide which was drearier—and an in-depth description of some of Matthew's livelier antics since becoming earl. Parties. Racing. Gambling. Women. Matthew had aspired to such a life, and that he'd been able to live it for even a short time made Elijah smile, even if he didn't understand it the slightest bit.

Buried near the end of the missive, Matthew made brief

mention of the treasure map, saying only what Elijah had shared with Miss Bowen. Well, not *only*. Matthew had also revealed the identity of one of the parties who'd been interested in purchasing the tapestry: Lord Septon, the very antiquary whose letter offering to assist with Cosgrove's collection had arrived just two days ago. Was Septon somehow involved with Matthew's accident? And what of these two mystery men—had they been involved?

If it had indeed *been* an accident. Carriage accidents weren't unusual—Matthew's coach had been found wrecked at the bottom of a ravine near the road about ten miles from Cosgrove—but the absence of his coachman and his valet or any other retainer had been dubious. The coachman had never turned up, and the authorities had deduced that he'd run off in fear. Nothing had been stolen and Matthew's injuries were commensurate with an accident of that nature. However, now, after learning of this map and the attempted theft of it, the event took on a far more suspicious tone.

Had the coachman caused the accident for some reason? Was the accident somehow connected to the map? Perhaps the person who'd attempted to steal the tapestry at Cosgrove had tried a second time, thinking Matthew had carried it with him to Bath. Had he?

Elijah supposed he should visit his mother and inquire. Thinking of her pulled forth an involuntary shudder. He hadn't seen her in years, and he didn't miss her. That he'd grown to appreciate his brother and miss him meant Elijah was able to forgive, but then his mother's offenses had been far greater. Matthew had simply gone along with her treatment of Elijah, and why shouldn't he? She'd bestowed love and affection on her first son and to him, she was the world and the sun and the moon combined. While to Elijah, she was . . . Hell.

Even so, he'd call on her if it would help his current cause. He owed it to Matthew.

In the meantime, he definitely needed to locate Mason. And hope the valet could provide some illumination into this increasingly curious affair.

CHAPTER 3

*E*lijah surveyed his appearance in the glass in his dressing chamber. He looked odd in civilian clothing, particularly for an event such as the dinner party he was attending at Bassett Manor. He'd only ever worn his regimental costume for such occasions.

"You look just as you should," Wade said, brushing something off Elijah's shoulder.

Elijah tugged at the bottom of the coat, adjusting the fit, which was already superb thanks to Wootton Bassett's accomplished tailor. "I suppose."

"Would it help to wear a sword?"

Elijah's mouth curved up. "Perhaps, but I think that's frowned upon." He turned from the glass. "Thank you, Wade. You did an excellent job with the cravat."

"I did practice, my lord."

Elijah strode from the dressing room into his bedchamber, with Wade following close behind. "Still nothing about the elusive Mason?"

"A bit of news, finally. I was able to speak with the last

footman today—he's been ill, but was back at his post. He said Mason hailed from Bradford on Avon."

Elijah paused and turned. "That's just outside Bath. I'm surprised he isn't a weaver."

"Apparently his father and elder brothers are just that. Mason, on the other hand, chose to go into service."

"I see. I hope you thanked the footman for his assistance."

"Profusely, my lord."

Elijah pivoted and continued toward the door. "Hopefully our trip to Bath will prove fruitful on both fronts—locating Mason and tracking down the tapestry's hiding place." After discussing the tapestry with Garber, Wade had determined it wasn't at Cosgrove. This naturally begged the question of where it could be. They'd concluded the likeliest place was Elijah's mother's house in Bath, and he planned to visit in the next few days. Summoning the patience necessary to tolerate her company would take at least that long.

Wade followed him as they exited the bedchamber to the corridor that spilled into the upper gallery. "Indeed, my lord. Will you be sharing any of this with Miss Bowen this evening?"

Miss Bowen. Elijah suspected she was behind his invitation to Bassett Manor tonight. She was a guest of the Foxcrofts and undoubtedly wanted to plead her case for the tapestry again. He looked forward to seeing what other information she might divulge about the entire affair, such as the identities of the other potential buyers of the tapestry. Since she was involved in the antiquarian world, it seemed logical that she would be able to provide assistance.

"I don't know," Elijah said. "I suppose I shall see how the conversation goes."

Elijah passed the large, gilt-framed portrait of Lord Norris—the previous-previous, as Miss Bowen had referred to him. He'd been Elijah's father's cousin, though Elijah struggled to see any family resemblance. His father had been tall, fair-haired, athletic, where this image of Lord Norris portrayed the former earl with thinning brown hair and a burgeoning girth that had only expanded over time. Elijah had learned the latter from the staff, along with the fact that Norris had also been rather short of stature. Clearly, they came from opposite ends of the family with regard to physical appearance.

The same was apparently also true of their temperament, given Norris's obsession with antiquities and his utter lack of concern for anything else. Garber had informed Elijah that the earl had overseen a scheme in which he'd defrauded the district's residents—collecting tributes, or really bribes, and using the local MPs as his personal puppets in Parliament. He'd died shortly after being exposed by Montgomery Foxcroft, the very fellow hosting tonight's dinner party.

They reached the grand staircase. As Elijah began his descent, he tossed a glance at Wade. "We'll travel to Bath in three days."

"Will we stay with your mother?" Wade asked.

"Good God, no." Elijah's lips twisted with distaste. "We'll stay at an inn." Or set up camp somewhere. Anywhere was preferable to residing under the same roof as his frigid mother.

Wade nodded. "The coach is waiting."

"Thank you." Elijah turned toward the foyer.

"Good luck!" Wade called after him.

Elijah made his way outside to the landau, the top of which was open. Elijah had requested it so that he could enjoy the night air. After so many years of spending a great deal of time out-of-doors, he found his new role poring over accounts and ledgers to be constricting. He looked forward to the day when he was well-versed in his duties as the earl, so that he could return to some of his previous pursuits.

He settled himself into the landau, and the driver took them on their way. What had his previous pursuits included, exactly? Riding, which he still did every day. Building, which had been a necessity in the expanding Australian colony. Hunting, though that truthfully wasn't his favorite activity. What he really ought to do was spend some time with his tenants. He'd taken a tour last week, but overall the people had been aloof. Could he blame them? They'd apparently suffered a criminal and then Matthew, who'd visited the tenants exactly once.

The pastoral countryside passed by, in some ways familiar and in others completely foreign. After two several-month voyages across multiple oceans, and years in an isolated locale, his "home" felt like anything but. The grandeur of his bedchamber made him ill at ease, the fussing of the servants was unwelcome, and the responsibility he now bore as earl suffused him with restlessness. He told himself the situation would improve once he grew acclimated, but he wished the adjustment would happen faster.

He found the mystery surrounding the hidden tapestry and possibly his brother's death considerably more engaging. He thought of little else beyond all of his unanswered questions. And of Miss Bowen. He thought of her far too much.

The trip was brief, and soon they were passing a newly repaired gatehouse as they drove up the lane. Bassett Manor rose before him, the early evening midsummer sun shining upon the mullioned windows, casting the house in a warm, inviting glow. The impressive façade was equal parts medieval castle, Tudor hall, and Restoration manor. It was a bit convoluted in design—it looked as though it had been enlarged several times—but it held far more character than Cosgrove.

He exited the landau without waiting for the coachman's assistance, something his retainers were learning to accept, and made his way to the front door. A footman opened it and held it wide as Elijah stepped into the massive foyer. Soaring three stories, the space seemed cavernous, likely because it wasn't stocked to the brim with *stuff*. In fact, it was rather austere, with a simple, thick carpet covering the stone tiles. Large rooms opened off the hall, and a wide, grand staircase ascended the far wall.

Another footman approached. "This way, my lord." He led Elijah to the room at the right side of the foyer. Like the entry, this room was huge, with exposed, arching beams. Despite its size, it felt comfortable, as though people actually lived here. Elijah realized just then that he resided in a museum, not a house. He couldn't wait to get rid of the antiquities cluttering it up.

He immediately recognized Miss Bowen and his hosts, Mr. and Lady Foxcroft. There were four other occupants— two couples—but he didn't know them.

Mr. Foxcroft came forward with a welcoming smile. "Good evening, Lord Norris. It's our pleasure to have you in our home this evening."

Lady Miranda joined him. "Indeed. I'm so glad you accepted our invitation. Allow me to introduce our guest, Miss Catriona Bowen."

Though they'd already met, it hadn't been a formal introduction—that much Elijah recalled from his brief time in English Society—and it had also been *secret*, at her request. Miss Bowen inclined her head and dipped a brief curtsey. "Good evening, my lord."

Lady Miranda gestured toward a settee where a red-haired woman, her belly rounded with child, perched. The man standing next to her carried an air of authority that Elijah recognized. Had he also been in the military? "And this is my brother, Lord Saxton, and his wife, Lady Olivia. They are visiting on their way to Saxton's home in Yorkshire."

Saxton stepped forward and offered his hand. "Pleased to make your acquaintance."

Elijah shook his hand, appreciating the man's direct stare. "As am I."

"Finally, this is my steward, Rob Knott, and his wife, Felicity," Foxcroft said.

Knott, a muscular fellow, came forward and offered his hand with a firm grip. "Glad to see Cosgrove inhabited again. Sorry about your brother."

His wife nodded with a warm smile. "Indeed. Lord Norris —that is, your brother—was a charming fellow. I met him on a few occasions."

She had? Had all of them? Perhaps the Foxcrofts had hosted a similar dinner party for Matthew. "I'm a bit surprised," Elijah mused. "I would've expected Matthew to spend most of his time in London." He preferred to be where he could engage in the most debauchery.

"He did," Lady Miranda said. "However, he also enjoyed his time in Wootton Bassett. He hosted a few, ah, gentlemanly parties. And, of course, we entertained with him here."

Elijah imagined Matthew enjoyed socializing with the daughter of one of the most powerful dukes in the realm. "I hope you found him well-behaved."

Lady Miranda's blond brows drew together briefly until she realized he was joking. She smiled, which only enhanced her classic English beauty. "Compared to the prior Lord Norris, he was positively perfect."

"Ah yes, but then the previous earl was a criminal, wasn't he?" Elijah said.

"Indeed he was," Foxcroft said darkly.

"Fox was a criminal too," Lady Miranda said with a grin. "Two years ago, the orphanage was in such dire straits that he had to resort to highway robbery. That's how we met."

She beamed at him and curled her hand possessively over his arm.

Elijah blinked, looking between them. He couldn't begin to think of how to respond.

Knott laughed and shook his head, defusing any tension that Lady Miranda's declaration had aroused. Miss Bowen took that moment to move toward Elijah. "I'm glad you came tonight," she said softly.

He looked down at her and tried not to notice how lovely she looked with her ebony hair swept into an artful style, an intriguing silver pendant gracing her slender neck and dragging his gaze lower. He snapped his attention to her face, which was as alluring as the rest of her, with her pert but lush lips and too-strong chin. "Why, so you can interrogate me further?" He arched a brow to indicate he was teasing—though it probably wasn't too far off her intentions.

Her gaze lingered on his. "Perhaps."

A footman announced dinner, and Foxcroft led them from the great hall. The couples paired off, leaving Elijah to guide Miss Bowen. "I suppose I have you to thank for tonight's invitation."

She tucked her arm over his. "Why would you think that? Miranda loves to entertain, and as the social leader of the district, she feels it's her duty to welcome you."

"I see." And he did. Lady Miranda surely would've invited him sooner or later, but Elijah was certain that Miss Bowen had ensured it was the former. "How long will you be staying with the Foxcrofts?"

"I suppose that's up to you." She flashed him a beguiling smile as they entered the dining room.

Elijah managed to pull his attention from his captivating companion and take in his surroundings. Obviously from the same era of the house as the great hall, the dining room boasted a massive fireplace, whose wood mantel was decorated with carved deer, foxes, and other woodland creatures. The table was impeccably set with crystal and fine bone china. Elijah briefly wondered if he'd ever host such an occasion at Cosgrove, and found he couldn't imagine it.

Lady Miranda took her chair at the head of the table, opposite her husband at the other end. "Lord Norris, you're over here by me." He vaguely recalled how formal seating arrangements worked. "And Cate, you're next to Lord Norris."

Elijah guided Miss Bowen to her indicated seat. "I take it you also arranged to be seated beside me?" he murmured.

She looked at him over her shoulder. "You're a suspicious fellow, aren't you?"

"Suspicious *and* infuriating. It's a wonder you speak to me at all, given your lofty opinion of me."

She laughed softly and her eyes sparkled with mirth. *Yes, captivating.*

Elijah took his seat and wine was poured. "Pardon me for raising this subject again, Foxcroft, but are there any reparations that need to be made for the prior earl's crimes?"

Foxcroft shook his head. "No. Repayments were made and may have been what sent Norris into the apoplexy that caused his death. And please, call me Fox. Everyone does." He sipped his wine. "I know he was your relative, but I can't apologize for my lack of remorse. He was a thoroughly reprehensible man."

Elijah now recalled the ledger entries detailing the money that had fled the coffers two and a half years ago—those had been the repayments. And they'd started his brother at a bit of a disadvantage. *If* he'd been paying attention to the accounts, which Elijah doubted. But pair that with Matthew's extravagant expenses and it was no wonder the earldom was in financial disarray. However, selling off the ridiculous antiquities collection should repair matters. Add a valuable treasure into the mix, and Elijah could see turning the situation around completely and bringing a new level of honor to both the title and the estate.

He contemplated Miss Bowen briefly as the first course was served. Could he find this treasure without her? Since he didn't particularly want to share it, he supposed he'd have to try. Wait, he *wanted* to find it?

"Did you determine where your brother hid the tapestry?" she asked. Conversation had sprung up all around the table and no one heard her question but Elijah.

"You assume I even looked into the matter."

She paused in lifting a spoon to her mouth. "Never say you didn't, for I shan't believe you."

He resisted the urge to smile at her cleverness. "No, I haven't found it yet."

"But surely you have a notion as to where it might be?"

Not that he planned to disclose. He liked Miss Bowen—he did?—but he didn't yet trust her. Trust was something he gave sparingly. "Miss Bowen, I realize you desire to purchase the tapestry, but for now, I'm not interested in selling it. Which is entirely moot since I've no idea where it is."

She leaned toward him. "You must have *some* idea. If you just think about—"

"Whether I think about it or not, find it or not, is none of your concern." He enjoyed the pretty flush that rose in her cheeks, but he wasn't purposefully trying to aggravate her. He simply wanted to be honest and forthright about his intentions and as of now, he had no reason to include her in any of his plans.

She pulled back and scowled at him. "Is it too late to add stubbornness to your list of attributes?"

~

*N*orris's warm laughter rankled Cate even further. She considered *accidentally* spilling her soup bowl in his lap, but that would likely send him directly home, and she wasn't finished with him yet. He joined the conversation about improvements to the orphanage that Fox owned and she was content—for now—to simply watch him interact with the others.

He was annoyingly confident and intelligent, with a hint of dry wit. How was she going to persuade him to help her? She was pleased to learn that he'd at least considered the tapestry. That was better than him doing nothing. Presumably, he would find it, and she'd be watching. She'd talk to Grey and they'd come up with a plan to get the tapestry, one way or another.

As the final course wound down, Miranda glanced around the table. "Do you gentleman want to stay here for brandy or shall we all adjourn to the hall?"

The men exchanged looks and gentle shrugs. "Let's all go to the hall," Fox said. "Young Albert from the orphanage has consented to play the pianoforte for us this evening if anyone would care to dance."

Cate looked over at Norris, who slid her a curious glance. Did he think she'd organized that too?

"I had nothing to do with the entertainment," she whispered.

He stood and helped her from her chair, then offered his arm. "I didn't say you did."

"You were thinking it plenty loud enough."

"I wasn't, actually." He led her from the dining room, following the other couples. "I was merely trying to determine if I recalled how to dance. It's been an age. And since we seem to have been paired off this evening, it occurred to me that I should partner you."

She blinked up at him. "There was no dancing in Australia?"

"Very little. There weren't many social occasions."

She cocked her head to the side. "What did you do for entertainment?"

"I read, though finding books was sometimes a challenge. I rode my horse and explored the area."

"Did you bring your horse back with you?"

"No." Was there a touch of regret to his tone? She rather thought so, but didn't remark upon it. "Just my batman, who is now my valet."

They strolled into the great hall where Fox was pouring brandy for the gentlemen and Miranda was giving directions to the boy at the pianoforte. "Reading and riding? That sounds a bit dull. You had no other pursuits—a hobby, perhaps?"

"A hobby?" Something flickered over his features. "I was quite busy leading a regiment, Miss Bowen."

She withdrew her arm from his. "I saw something there. You're a secretive gentleman, are you not?"

"I might say guarded." He gazed down at her, his blue-gray eyes probing. "Adding to my traits again?"

"Oh, I'm not adding to them. I'm identifying them." She ticked off her fingers. "Infuriating, suspicious, stubborn, secretive—sorry, *guarded*."

He blinked at her in mock affront. "Have I no features to recommend me?"

"I'll let you know after the dance."

Albert started to play a country dance and they formed a square. With Lady Olivia, who wasn't particularly spry given her pregnancy, and Norris, who was clearly out of practice, it wasn't the most accurate of endeavors, but it was terribly fun. By the end, they were all flushed and laughing, even Lord Norris. Then Albert started a waltz. Everyone paired off, save Cate and Norris. He offered a courtly bow and she curtseyed in formal response.

His hand clasped her waist and he swept her into the dance. "I'll try not to step on your toes."

"I'm sure you'll be quite adept."

He arched a blond brow and gave her the skeptical stare she was coming to expect from him. Suspicious indeed. "You saw me during that cotillion, did you not?"

She chuckled. He'd made a few missteps, but overall appeared a good dancer, particularly for someone who hadn't done it in a long while. "The waltz moves much slower." She looked up at him in alarm. "Goodness, do you even know how to waltz? You were on the other side of the world when it came to England."

Given how he'd taken her into his embrace and now steered her through the steps, he clearly did. "Just as books came to us on ships, so did new dances and clothing and other items and activities from home."

"So you *did* dance?"

"I never said I didn't. It's just been a long time. I left Australia last September." His fingers dug lightly, *pleasurably,* into her waist as he turned her.

A tremor rippled through her, but she refused to consider the possibility that it was because of him. "That must be a harrowing journey. And you've done it twice."

"I don't know that it's harrowing, but it's certainly boring."

She gave him a knowing look. "You see, you should have had a hobby."

His lip lifted in a half-smile. "Such as searching for antiquities?"

She didn't think he meant his comment as an affront, and didn't take it that way. But she wanted him to understand what most people didn't—that she was passionate about being an antiquary and considered it an occupation. "It's more than a hobby to me. I have an affinity for all manner of artifacts. I like to hold an object and imagine the care and skill that went into crafting it. Such as my necklace."

His gaze dipped to her pendant. "What is it?"

"A silver piece from a trove that was found in Somerset a few years ago. It's from the ninth or tenth century, based on its design and the items found with it."

"You knew that just by looking at it?" He sounded genuinely interested, unlike most gentlemen she met.

"Somewhat, but that's after years of reading books and papers, viewing antiquities, and discussing such topics with other antiquaries. Well, those who will talk to me," she added without bothering to hide her derision.

He twirled her expertly, and she decided he wasn't as rusty at dancing as he'd said. Or at least, he was better at waltzing. "Why won't they talk to you?" he asked. "Do you pester them as you do me?"

"No, I do not." They'd fallen into a pattern of teasing each other, and she enjoyed it more than she probably ought. "They don't talk to me because I'm female. Some antiquaries think I have no business nosing about in *their* interests."

"I admit I find your—vocation . . . is that an appropriate word?—surprising. Most women of your station would be married by now and managing their own households."

She couldn't tell what he thought of that. Most men were disdainful of her work. "I can't think of anything more tedious than managing a household."

"Now, that is an opinion we share. Does that mean you have no interest in Society?"

"I haven't even had a Season." She hadn't wanted one, and her parents hadn't encouraged it. Her mother and father had found each other in an unconventional fashion and fallen deeply in love. In their experience, a Season wasn't only unnecessary, it was perhaps a hindrance to truly finding your love match if you weren't interested in adhering to Society's rules. Which her family was not. They were scholars, explorers, antiquaries.

"Fascinating," he said softly, perhaps even admiringly.

The music drew to a close and he brought her to a halt. His hand dropped from her waist and she reluctantly removed her hand from his shoulder. Reluctantly?

Miranda clapped, thankfully drawing Cate's attention from Norris. "Thank you so much, Albert," Miranda said. "Wasn't he wonderful, everyone?"

Others joined her applause and Albert stood, blushing. He bowed smartly before departing.

"There are some refreshments here if you're inclined." Miranda gestured to the sideboard, where Fox had poured out brandy earlier. There was also sherry for the ladies.

"Would you like anything?" Norris asked politely.

"A glass of sherry wouldn't come amiss," she said.

He took himself to the sideboard to fetch their beverages, and Cate moved to the side of the room, to a pair of chairs. She didn't intend to sit, just to move out of the center of the hall.

Miranda sidled up beside her. "Lord Norris seems interested in you."

Cate watched the earl talk with Fox at the sideboard as their host poured the drinks. "He doesn't either. We're just the only two unmatched people here."

Miranda exhaled. "That's true. I'm afraid I'm a hopeless matchmaker."

Cate patted the back of her hair, unused to wearing it in such an intricate style. She typically wore it in a simple knot or, on occasion, even loose. "As I've told you before, I don't need a match."

"So you say, but trust me when I tell you that you're missing out on one of life's best pleasures."

Cate wasn't sure exactly which pleasures she referred to and didn't want to ask, lest it invite questions as to why an unmarried miss like her was versed in such matters. Instead, she steered the conversation in a more seemly direction. "Marriage, you mean?"

Miranda's aqua eyes lit. "Love, silly."

"Yes, love *is* silly." Cate didn't necessarily believe that, but she didn't concern herself with love at all. She subscribed to what her parents had told her—that it would happen in due time if she was meant to find it. Their pragmatism appealed to her logical mind.

"You only say that because you haven't felt it." Miranda looked over at Norris, who had scooped up their drinks and was now heading toward them. "I still contend Norris is interested."

Cate wholeheartedly disagreed. Yet they'd managed to enjoy their dances and even converse rather genially . . .

Miranda floated away as Norris arrived with Cate's sherry.

"I didn't mean to drive Lady Miranda away," he said, handing Cate the glass.

Cate took a fortifying drink. "You didn't. She was trying to play matchmaker, but I set her straight."

His brows shot up for a brief moment. "You did?"

"I'm not interested in making a match, and I have the sense you aren't either."

"You are correct," he said quickly. "I'm far too busy learning how to be a bloody earl." He winced at his language. "Forgive me, it's a difficult adjustment from my previous life to this one."

"I can imagine." Cate behaved differently in social settings like this than when she and Grey were out searching for antiquities, so she understood what he meant. "For what it's worth, that sort of language doesn't offend my sensibilities."

He peered at her with an odd expression. Curiosity? Disbelief? Respect? Perhaps all of them. "You're an interesting female."

She looked at him over the rim of her glass. "Does this mean I'm to have my own list of characteristics?"

"It seems only fair." He sipped his brandy. "I'd add persistent."

She laughed. "Very astute. Lest I disappoint you, permit me to carry on. I won't allow you to ignore my quest for the tapestry. I intend to find it."

"How, if I don't help you?"

"I'm not certain, but I'll find a way. It would, however, be far simpler—and more charitable—if you would deign to offer assistance."

He took another pull on his brandy, his gaze never leaving hers. As at Cosgrove, she felt a shock of icy heat as she bore his perusal.

Shoving the bothersome sensation away, she plodded ahead. "I understand your brother spent a great deal of money and that you're likely trying to refill the coffers. It's why you want to sell the antiquities collection, isn't it?"

"Not entirely." His tone was guarded. "I find it a dust-collecting jumble of nonsense."

She longed to show him how wrong he was. "I should love to walk through Cosgrove with you and show you just how incredible some of those pieces are."

His gaze dropped to her pendant once more. "Your passion for them is almost persuasive."

His use of the word "passion" provoked another stirring response, but this one carried more fire, blooming inside of her and spreading warmth to her extremities. "I could help you determine which items would garner the most money and you could sell those first."

He tipped his head to the side, considering. "In exchange for my helping you to find the tapestry?"

"Of course—keeping in mind, I'll still pay you for it once it's located."

"I already have another antiquary who's offered to help with the collection."

Bollocks. "Who?"

"Lord Septon. Do you know him?"

Bollocks again. Septon had contacted Norris? Had he mentioned the tapestry? He'd seen it at Cosgrove for many years and Cate had to wonder if he he'd ever tried to buy it. But of course the previous earl was notorious for never parting with his treasures.

Or—and this was a far more troubling thought—had Septon puzzled out the map and gone on to find Dyrnwyn already? Cate swallowed against a rising sense of unease. "Yes, I know him quite well. You didn't inform him that I came to see you?"

His lips curved up slightly, displaying a rare bit of humor. "No, I thought that was a secret."

"It is. Thank you for keeping it as such." She took a drink of sherry to try to quell her tumultuous nerves. "What can I do to persuade you? You need money. What if I offered you five hundred pounds for the tapestry?"

Surprise flickered in his eyes. "Five hundred pounds for a magical sword? I'm not sure that's enough."

"You don't have Dyrnwyn." She fought to keep her voice low.

He leaned close. "I'm probably closer to it than you are."

"You wouldn't know what to do with the map if you found it."

"Now it's an 'if' I found it? I thought you were convinced I would find it."

She sensed he was provoking her on purpose. "Very, very infuriating," she said under her breath. "I'm a generally optimistic person, and as such, yes, I choose to believe you *will* find the tapestry."

"Or it could be gone. What if someone else found it first?"

Now she was all but certain he was taunting her. The unease rolling around inside of her became full anxiety. "You're a beast."

"I'm pragmatic," he said softly, moving subtly closer. "I don't wish to cause you concern, and I can see from the creases in your forehead that I'm doing just that. There's no telling where my brother hid the map and whether it's still there."

She stood her ground, unsure if he was even aware that he'd crept toward her. While she was completely aware of every breath he drew. "You said your brother spent time in London. What about his house there?"

"It was leased, so I'm afraid I no longer have access."

"Bollocks."

His eyes widened. "Pardon?"

She cast him a disbelieving look. "Oh, you heard me." Catching an unsettling amount of his unfortunately delicious scent of sandalwood and pine, she took a small step back.

"Maybe I just wanted to hear you say it again."

"*That* I believe." She lifted her chin and gave him an unflinching stare. "You didn't respond to my offer of five hundred pounds."

"You don't have five hundred pounds."

"You don't know that," she said crossly.

He glanced up at the ceiling as if he were trying to find some patience from on high, but he'd given her the impression he was somewhat of a heathen, so she really had no idea what he was doing. When he looked at her again, his gaze was clear and bold. "I'd stake the tapestry on it."

"The tapestry you don't have."

"The tapestry you'll likely *never* have."

She sucked in a breath. "Now you're just being cruel."

"Still being pragmatic, actually."

She took a long drink of sherry. It heated her throat and coated her stomach with a delightful warmth that she wished would soothe her rioting nerves. But with Norris standing there staring at her with his imperious blue-gray eyes and taut lips, she only felt frustration. And maybe a touch of desire.

Desire?

Now she was being foolish, and she blamed Miranda for bringing up love and matchmaking in the first place.

She leaned forward and spoke in a low hiss. "I will deliver five hundred pounds to you, and you'll help me find the tapestry."

"You won't, but I admire your tenacity. I'll add that to your list of attributes."

"Isn't that the same as persistence?"

His gaze warmed and her body responded in kind, heating in a most betraying fashion. "I think you've earned synonymous characteristics on that front, don't you?"

She turned from him. "I daresay we've spent more than enough time together without appropriate chaperonage."

"Amusing, given your uninvited visit last week," he said.

She looked at him over her shoulder. "I brought a chaperone."

"Is that what she is?"

He'd moved beyond provoking into the realm of outright vexing. "You've just earned 'aggravating' in addition to 'infuriating.' Careful, lest I include 'exasperating' as well."

"I wouldn't want that," he murmured.

She turned back toward him. "Do you know what you *should* want? Dyrnwyn. And I can help you find it. Forget five hundred pounds. Just what do you think that sword could be worth?"

"Enough to kill a man?" The question was soft, but held menace. "Tell me, Miss Bowen, do you know who tried to buy the tapestry from my brother?"

She tried to relax the tension rioting through her shoulders. "I do not."

He eradicated the distance between them, coming closer than he had yet. Closer even than during the waltz. "You know Septon and countless other antiquaries. Doubtless you could find out."

That's what he wanted to bargain. Her assistance in determining what happened to his brother in exchange for his help with locating the tapestry. She looked up into his determined countenance. "You're certain his death wasn't an accident?"

"The only thing I'm certain of, Miss Bowen, is that you're the only person of my acquaintance who knew what my brother knew. For that reason alone, I've just decided to keep you close."

CHAPTER 4

*E*lijah drew his mount to a halt. He missed Chester, his faithful horse in Australia, but he hadn't wanted to subject the poor beast to the journey. It was hard enough on a man, let alone a creature who needed to run and jump.

"But we're getting to know each other, aren't we?" Elijah patted Devon's ebony neck and glimpsed two riders approaching. *Good, she was punctual.* He added that to the growing list of Miss Bowen's attributes. He'd come up with several more in the days since he'd seen her last—chief among them was enticing. He'd looked forward to seeing her again far more than he cared to admit. He didn't remember the last time a woman had occupied his mind for more than an evening. Never, he realized.

Miss Bowen rode up beside him, demonstrating an excellent seat. Her companion, absent from the dinner party the other evening, stayed a few dozen yards distant. "I was surprised to receive your note this morning," she said coolly, holding her reins with a loose grip.

"I'm not sure why. I said I wanted to keep you close."

"I thought you meant under surveillance. I had the

impression you suspected me of some manner of involvement in your brother's death." Her dark brows pitched low over her even darker eyes. "I assure you, I had nothing to do with the previous Lord Norris's death and your presumption that I did is an egregious insult."

She was in high dudgeon. He fought to stifle an ungentlemanly smile. He enjoyed sparring with her more than he'd ever imagined was possible. He'd never met a woman who could give as good as she got—or was even interested in doing so. "My apologies. You are, however, much better acquainted with the antiquarian world than I. As such, I require your assistance to determine who offered to purchase the tapestry from Matthew."

She looked moderately mollified. At least, the pink in her cheeks faded. "I surmised as much the other night."

They'd discussed it briefly, but had been interrupted before they could continue the conversation. Hence his invitation for her to meet him today. "A pair of men visited Cosgrove in search of the tapestry. I should like you to help me identify them."

Her brow furrowed. "You don't have their names?"

"That would be too easy, wouldn't it?" He ought to tell her that Septon had also inquired, but he was still assessing how to proceed on that front. Right now, Septon was a person of suspicion, and since she knew him "quite well" he wasn't sure he wanted to confide in her.

"Perhaps." She smoothed her gloved hand over the side of her mount's sleek neck. "They could have used aliases in any case."

"I hadn't thought of that." He continued to be impressed by her intellect. "My, but you are well versed in surreptitious behavior."

She turned her head briefly to look at her "chaperone."

"Grey and I have had occasion to use false identities. To protect my reputation, usually."

Perhaps her behavior surpassed surreptitious. "I see. Should I be concerned about mine? Reputation, that is."

Her eyes widened. "From me? I didn't mean it like that. I sometimes go places a young, unmarried woman ought not. I do not behave inappropriately."

Did she not realize how that sounded? "Save being young and unmarried in unacceptable circumstances. What do your parents think of this?" Did she have parents? He knew she had a father, but did she also have a mother? And if she did, was their relationship any better than Elijah's with his mother?

"I do, and they fully support my antiquarian activities." She looked as though she might make an addendum to that statement, but ultimately just pressed her lips together firmly and lifted her chin.

Part of him wanted to pursue this rather provocative line of conversation, but it didn't signify. Flirting with Miss Bowen, and bloody hell, he'd just realized that's what he was doing, was the pinnacle of unacceptable. "Whether these men used aliases or not is moot since I don't have a record of their names at all. My butler only said they were young gentlemen —perhaps in their middle twenties—but that was all he could recollect given that it was over a year ago. Now you see why I require your assistance."

"I'm not sure what I can provide. Such a description doesn't bring anyone to mind. Most antiquaries I know are older—on the other side of fifty. The only people I know of that age are a few friends of my brother's and, well, never mind."

"These men couldn't be your brother's friends?"

"No." She waved her hand. "His friends aren't terribly serious about antiquities in any case. They sometimes follow

Penn around because, well, never mind that too . . . Anyway, they've started to go their own ways, to see to their obligations."

He nodded, understanding that's what men of a certain station—his new station—did. "You're 'never-minding' a lot. Please elaborate."

She cocked her head to the side. "I would argue that twice isn't 'a lot.'"

"You're leaving information out, and it might be helpful to me."

"I highly doubt knowing that Penn attracts a following because of his success with women is important to your investigation."

Elijah couldn't help himself. "Success with women?"

She made a sound of abject disgust. "They trail after him like kittens mewling for their milk. He's attractive, I suppose, and exceptionally intelligent. He has a certain . . . air. Or so they say. Obviously, I don't notice. To me, he's a bothersome older brother."

"I see. And the other 'never mind'?"

She glanced away, and he wondered if he ought to have pressed her. "Equally as unhelpful to you. The only other younger antiquaries I know are women."

He couldn't mask his surprise. He'd thought her a singular female. "Like you?"

She shifted in her saddle. "Yes. As you can see, I don't know the men who came to see your brother."

Curiosity about these female antiquaries nearly overrode his thoughts, as had her description of her brother. Further proof that he found her too interesting by half, and ought to establish a greater distance lest they become something more than acquaintances. Hell, they were likely past that, weren't they?

He forced himself back to the topic: determining the

circumstances of Matthew's death. "Is it possible they were agents for someone else?"

She considered this. "Anything is possible. What is it you want me to do? Interrogate the handful of antiquaries who will talk to me?" She looked to the side and muttered, "That'll elevate my reputation."

He didn't wish to cause her any problems. "I'll interrogate. Just point me in the right direction." A thought occurred to him. He could, perhaps, use this as an opportunity to get to Septon. "Is it possible Lord Septon could help? You did say you knew him."

Her gaze, dark with apprehension, jerked back to his. "You need to be careful about what you say. Most people don't realize the tapestry is a map, and you'd do well not to reveal that you know."

Her sharp reaction was a bit perplexing. "I thought Septon was a friend of yours."

"He is." She fidgeted with the reins and he suspected she wasn't telling him everything. Not that he expected her to, since he wasn't revealing everything either. Would they ever reach a point where they would trust each other? He wasn't confident their association would endure that long, but he had to admit it had already outlasted any of his expectations.

She looked at him in grave concern, her forehead creasing and her gaze direct. "It's important to me to be the one to find the sword. If other people know, my chances diminish."

Maybe trust wasn't as far off as he'd thought. He heard the passion and determination in her voice and couldn't help but admire her zeal. "I understand." He also understood she didn't want Septon to know about her activities. This affair only grew more curious with each passing moment.

"I'll be traveling to Bath tomorrow. Septon doesn't live too far from there, so I'll plan to visit him as well. Perhaps you could write a note of introduction?" He didn't need one, but perhaps his cause would be aided by her relationship with Septon.

She sat straight in her saddle. "I've a better idea. Why don't Grey and I accompany you? You did say you wanted to keep me close."

He had said that, damn it. "No, you don't need to come."

She sidled her horse closer to his. "Are you looking for the tapestry there? Doesn't your mother live in Bath?"

"How do you know that?"

She lifted a shoulder. "Miranda knows everything."

He was not surprised. "Do what you will, but we're not traveling to Bath together. I'm trying to establish myself as a bloody earl. The last thing I need is to be aligned with a young, unmarried lady." He said this to persuade himself as much as her.

She nodded. "We'll meet you there." She turned her horse and looked over her shoulder at him. "How else am I to help you discover the circumstances of your brother's demise?"

She had a point. She was the best chance he had for his investigation given her experience in the antiquarian world, and for that reason alone he would suffer her company.

Suffer? Was it really a hardship?

He frowned as he watched her ride to her companion and then the two of them galloped away. No, it wasn't a hardship; it was vexingly . . . interesting. Damn, there was that word again. She was also charming, intelligent, and attractive enough to be a hazard to his bachelorhood.

With a muttered oath, he turned Devon about and rode back toward Cosgrove. He *was* a bloody earl and he had no interest in finding a countess. What's more, he didn't need to. He had an heir—a distant cousin. Two heirs, actually—that cousin's son was nearly twenty.

Elijah had long ago decided a wife wasn't necessary.

Becoming an earl hadn't altered his opinion one bit, and neither would the dangerously captivating Miss Bowen.

~

"C ate!" Lady Andromeda Spier stood from her favorite chair in her sitting room in Sydney Place in Bath, her full lips spreading into a warm smile. "I'm so glad you're here." She came forward and hugged Cate, then turned to Grey and did the same. "And you too, Grey. Come, both of you, sit. Blessing will bring tea before we go in for dinner."

Indeed, the butler had already disappeared from the doorway, to be replaced by Andy's younger sister, Cassiopeia. Her red-blond hair was loose around her shoulders as usual, and her gold spectacles were perched on her nose somewhat askew, also as usual. "Cate, Grey, what a lovely surprise." More reserved than her sister, she didn't come toward them, but she reciprocated the hug Cate offered.

"I hope it's not too much of a surprise. I did send a note ahead," Cate said, untying her bonnet. In truth, though, she'd just dispatched the letter yesterday after her horseback meeting with Lord Norris.

"Not at all," Andy said, resuming her seat in the floral-patterned chair situated near the gilt-edged fireplace. "We always love your spur-of-the-moment visits. Your note said you would explain the purpose when you arrived, so do sit down and tell us why you've come." Andy leaned slightly forward, always eager for information.

Cassie took the chair near her sister's, while Cate and Grey arranged themselves on the generous settee facing them across a low table.

Cate removed her bonnet and drew off her gloves, setting both on the settee beside her. She always behaved as if she were at home when she visited Andy and Cassie. "I wish Selina was in town." Selina Ashcombe was the fourth and final member of their group.

"As do I," said Andy, "but she's still in Scotland with her husband. I received a letter from her a couple of days ago. She's made some excellent discoveries."

"I should love to read it." Cate knew she probably had a similar missive awaiting her at home, but right now she wasn't sure when she would be back in Wales.

"Shall we call the meeting of the Ladies' Antiquities Society to order?" Cassie asked, looking between them.

"Informally," Andy said. "There's no need to record our activities." She snapped her gaze to Cate. "Is there?"

"I don't believe so. Not yet, anyway." These women were the only people aside from Grey who knew of her determination to find Dyrnwyn. "Unfortunately, I don't have much to report. Lord Norris is not in possession of the tapestry. Furthermore, he says he has no idea where it is."

Cassie frowned. "Your note said you were coming to Bath as part of your quest. I took that to mean you were on the hunt?"

"Norris's mother lives here—Mrs. Hollister, if you're acquainted with her. It's possible his brother hid the tapestry at her house." Cate hoped that was the case, but had to admit to feeling more than a bit of trepidation. "He's not terribly keen on helping me. In fact, the only reason he's sharing information is because he's on his own quest to determine if his brother's death was accidental or somehow related to the tapestry."

Andy's eyes widened. "Does he really think so?"

"He's suspicious." Cate fought back a smile as she recalled the list she'd crafted with "suspicious" at the very top. Or maybe it should really be headed with "infuriating" . . .Or "bone-meltingly attractive." *When had that joined the list?* "His brother died in a carriage accident after several parties sought to purchase the tapestry and someone attempted to steal it."

Andy leaned her elbow on the arm of the chair as she pitched forward with unabashed interest. "Indeed? Does Norris suspect murder?"

He hadn't used that word in particular, but the suggestion had been there, just beneath the surface. "I'm not entirely certain, but it seems so, yes."

Andy settled back in the chair, her expression contemplative. "I don't like this one bit. Are you sure you shouldn't just give up on this entirely?"

"She can't," Cassie said crossly, her eyes tossing daggers at her sister. "And she shouldn't have to."

"No, I'm not overly concerned yet," Cate said. "To be honest, I'm not sure how much I trust Norris. Our goals aren't in alignment—I want to find the treasure and he wants to investigate his brother's death."

"But you believe him when he says he doesn't know where the tapestry is located?" Andy asked, her pale brows slashing low over her gray eyes.

"Yes." She also trusted that he was eager to learn the truth about his brother's alleged accident. "He's asked me to help him try to identify the men who came to Cosgrove to purchase the tapestry."

"I see," Andy said. "Given your contacts in the antiquarian world, it makes sense that he would. At least he isn't stupid."

No, stupidity was definitely not one of the attributes she'd add to her Norris List.

Cassie cleared her throat and adjusted her spectacles, settling them straighter on her nose. "How does he even know these men are from that community?"

Grey scooted slightly forward as she addressed the question. "When Cate inquired about a tapestry, the current Lord

Norris had no idea what she was talking about. However, when she said 'treasure map,' that garnered his attention. His brother wrote him a letter that mentioned a map, not a tapestry."

Cassie sucked in a breath and exchanged excited glances with her sister. "How would his brother have known it was a map?"

"Those men likely told him," Cate said. She and Grey had discussed this countless times. How had those men known the tapestry was a map? Was Cate mistaken in believing she'd stumbled onto some centuries-old secret when she'd found that de Valery document in Septon's hidden library? Were there a number of antiquaries who were already aware that the tapestry was a map to Dyrnwyn?

Andy tapped her chin with her forefinger then stopped abruptly as Blessing entered with the tea tray. They all fell silent while the butler set everything out on the table. With a nod, he departed, knowing they preferred to pour out themselves and, more importantly, that they preferred privacy. The business of the Ladies' Antiquities Society was for their ears alone—and Grey's, as she was an adjunct member.

Grey, also adept at serving tea—really, there was very little she couldn't do—poured and doctored everyone's cups according to their taste.

Once everyone had their tea, Andy finally spoke. "For a long time now, we've suspected that Septon has been involved in something more than just hunting for antiquities. We know he has a singular passion for Arthurian artifacts. He's known that this tapestry was a map—he had to have, since he was in possession of the de Valery document regarding the tapestry—and he also knew it was in Norris's possession. He's been a frequent guest at Cosgrove over the years."

"My thoughts exactly," Cate said. She set her tea down

without taking a drink because her insides had pitched into an anxious riot. "It seems an unlikely coincidence. I'm afraid Septon must be involved somehow, and I'm even more afraid Dyrnwyn might already be found."

"And yet we've heard nothing about it." Cassie shook her head. "No, if it was found, we'd know."

Cate didn't agree. "What about the Anarawd poem in my father's library? The one that all but confirms Gareth and his contemporaries, including Arthur, actually lived." She'd shared this information with them when she was last in Bath a few weeks ago, just before she'd worked her way inside Septon's secret library. "I had no idea it existed until recently. My father kept it secret for some reason."

Andy's gaze turned shrewd. "And your father is known to work closely with Septon on occasion. As I said, I think Septon has other objectives beyond just finding antiquities." Andy sipped her tea.

Cate wasn't sure she agreed, and she couldn't imagine her father, whom she admired and respected more than any other person, having ulterior motives of any kind, but it certainly appeared he and Septon were keeping secrets. Had they already found Dyrnwyn? Was that why they'd dissuaded her from searching for it? She'd talked about it for so long, saying she would find the sword and present it to the Ashmolean Museum, where it could reside next to the Heart of Llanllwch.

"What's your next move?" Cassie asked, disrupting the troubling direction of Cate's thoughts.

Cate and Grey had also discussed that at length. First, they'd see what happened with Lord Norris and his mother. Cate had a tenuous agreement with the earl that each would help the other, him with finding the tapestry and her with uncovering the circumstances of his brother's death. He was doing his part—supposedly. She had no choice but to trust him.

"I need to talk to Septon," she said. "I've sent him a note—as has Norris. I hope to coordinate our visit, tomorrow or the day after."

"Norris has contacted him?" Andy asked.

"Yes, Septon has already initiated a correspondence. He offered to help liquidate the Cosgrove collection."

Cassie swore in a most unladylike fashion. "Never say Norris is *selling* the lot?"

"He finds it a nuisance." Cate didn't bother hiding her disdain. She understood his need to replenish his coffers, but he could likely be back up to scratch after only selling a handful of treasures. "I offered to help him, but he wasn't interested since Septon had already contacted him. In fact"—Cate's blood began to simmer—"I think he might have something against me because I'm a woman."

"Typical." Cassie scoffed. "No man thinks we're worth anything. It's why we have our own society, after all."

Cate didn't categorize her father and brother in that manner, which Cassie knew and pointedly disagreed with. "Not all men, but yes, the vast majority," Cate said. She'd rather hoped Norris was different and was disappointed to realize he likely was not. Why? She shouldn't care what he thought. Except she needed his cooperation, and it would be easier if he attributed her at least some value. Surely he did, since he'd shared his plans to come to Bath with her. Her head was beginning to hurt. She took a sustaining drink of tea.

Andy set her teacup on the table. "We do in fact know Mrs. Hollister. Not well, but she's active in Bath Society and we've run into her on occasion. I do believe she spends most Wednesday evenings at the Assembly Rooms. Should we go tomorrow so that we can speak with her about the tapestry?"

Cate appreciated their assistance, but she wanted to see if Norris would simply share with her what he learned. "I need to find where Norris is staying so that I may send him a note." She wanted to arrange a meeting to discuss their joint investigation and their findings. Or lack thereof. She also wanted to coordinate their visit to Septon House, which was only eight miles outside Bath.

"You don't think he's staying with his mother? She lives over on Green Street," Andy said.

Cate didn't think so. "I'm not certain if his relationship with his mother is cordial. It's possible he's lodging elsewhere."

Grey stood with her hat in hand. "I'll find out. Don't hold dinner for me." She turned and left.

Cassie lifted her cup to her lips. "Grey will run him to ground."

"Is he like the old Lord Norris?" Andy asked with a moue of distaste. "The antiquary?"

Lord Norris the previous-previous. "No. In fact, if you told me they were related I should think you were lying. Or mad. He's taller than Septon, if you can imagine. Fair-haired, rigid, but then he was in the military. In Australia of all places. His skin has a sun-kissed quality that must be permanent since he left there some ten months ago."

Both sisters' movements arrested. "Sun-kissed?" Andy asked, exchanging a curious glance with Cassie, who shrugged.

"Oh, stop." Cate made a noise of disgust. "You're as bad as Miranda. She was trying to pair us off. It was appalling."

Cassie pursed her lips. "Because he's a woman-bashing cretin."

"Maybe," Andy said judiciously. "Cate barely knows him. And they have to work together. You never know what might happen. Not all men are philandering, woman-denigrating cretins like Selina's husband."

As they went in to dinner a quarter hour later, Cate couldn't help but wonder what sort of man Norris really was. Could he be trusted? Time would tell. Unfortunately, Cate had never been a very patient person.

CHAPTER 5

*E*lijah glanced up at the cloudy sky as he stepped out of the coach before his mother's house in Bath. Yesterday had been clear and pleasant, perfect for their journey from Cosgrove, but today looked as though it would storm. It seemed an appropriate herald to seeing his mother after so many years away. It also went hand in glove with their acrimonious history.

Within an hour of his and Wade's arrival last night, he'd received a note from Miss Bowen requesting a meeting at his earliest convenience. Occupied with steeling himself—which had taken a larger than average course of whisky—in order to visit his mother, he had not yet responded to Miss Bowen.

Reluctantly, he made his way to the front door and rapped sharply on the wood. After several moments, the door opened. Elijah didn't recognize the butler. He was rather young, maybe not even as old as Elijah's twenty-nine years.

"Yes?" What the butler lacked in age, he made up for in haughtiness. He somehow managed to look down his nose at Elijah, despite being far shorter.

"I'm here to see Mrs. Hollister."

The retainer gave Elijah a thorough perusal, but didn't reflect any judgment as to what he saw. "I'm afraid she doesn't receive visitors until noon."

Elijah offered a humorless smile. "Please inform her that her son is here." He strode forward, giving the butler no choice but to open the door wider and move out of the way.

Time hadn't changed the interior of the house, which they'd moved into after the death of his father thirteen years before. Elijah noted the landscape painting of the Somerset Levels, the area from where his mother hailed, its vibrant colors somewhat overshadowed by the bright blue paint with which she'd insisted on having the walls of the entry hall painted.

"This way," the butler said, gesturing Elijah into the front sitting room. Much of the furnishings were familiar, but there was a new carpet—vivid yellow and bronze. Elijah's eye was drawn to the portrait of him and his brother hanging over the fireplace. Matthew's mischievous ten-year-old face stared back at him, while Elijah, just eight and wearing a timid look, stood somewhat behind him, as Mother had arranged them.

Timid? Yes, he'd grown up in his brother's shadow and under the brunt of his mother's displeasure, but his years in the army had completely changed him. Would she even notice?

The butler interrupted his thoughts. "I'll see if Mrs. Hollister is able to receive you."

Elijah didn't think she'd turn him away. That her son was an earl had to give her endless satisfaction—even if it was Elijah and not Matthew—and he couldn't imagine her ignoring his call. Would she, however, be forthcoming with any information she might have regarding his search for the tapestry and with any information about Matthew's death?

After a good quarter hour, she finally came into the sitting room. She wore a glaring fuschia morning gown. Her dark blond hair was swept simply but tidily atop her head. Elijah detected a few more strands of gray since he'd seen her last, but she wore it well. Her dark blue eyes pierced him with curiosity. "I must own I'm surprised to see you, Elijah."

Because the last time he'd left, he said he'd never return. And at the time, he'd meant it. Elijah fingered his hat, which he'd removed while he'd been waiting. "I'm surprised as well, but then there have been many surprises, haven't there? I never imagined I'd be back in England as an earl."

Mother moved into the room and sat in a chair the color of the Australian sun in midsummer. She arranged her skirts and gestured for him to sit. "Yes, it was unexpected enough for Matthew to inherit, but then for him to die so suddenly . . ." She looked up at the portrait and blinked.

Elijah knew her grief was real and was sorry for it. He might not like her, but he didn't wish for her to suffer. He also wasn't comfortable discussing it. "Matthew visited you just before he died."

"Yes." She returned her gaze to his. "Aren't you going to sit down? I'm getting a neck ache looking up at you. I'd almost forgotten how unnaturally tall you are."

Unnatural, yes. She'd always found so many traits and behaviors to criticize about him. He dropped onto the settee, setting his hat down beside him, but didn't relax. "Did he bring anything with him?"

She looked at him blankly. "Such as his valet?"

That she mentioned the valet piqued Elijah's interest, but he'd discuss that in a moment. "I'm looking for a tapestry that he may have brought here for safekeeping."

Mother shook her head. "No, he didn't bring anything like that. Is that why you're here? You're looking for some tapestry? I suppose just paying your mother a visit didn't occur to you."

Elijah stared at her, dumbfounded she would say such a thing. "Are you going to pretend we have that sort of relationship?"

Her answering look was cool. "That was a long time ago, Elijah. I expected the army to have eased your frustration."

"It did." But he'd never forget the way she'd abused—not physically, but with words and demeanor—him and his father. She'd hated everything Jerome Hollister had done— the way he'd dressed, the manner in which he'd eaten, the amount of time he'd spent with his horses. That Elijah had taken after him, particularly in his love of animals, had ensured she'd all but hated him too. "Do I not seem changed to you?"

She perused him at great length. "Yes, you do. You're quite handsome, more so than I would've thought."

The backhanded compliment didn't surprise him, but the fact that she'd given him a compliment at all did. It also wasn't shocking that she noted only his physical appearance. He didn't expect her to glean a sense of how he'd matured, not within the span of brief minutes since she'd come downstairs, but even if he spent a fortnight in her company, he doubted she would. However, now that he was the earl, perhaps she would treat him differently—maybe try to acquaint herself with the son she'd always disdained. But he didn't want that. He was content with their mutual disregard.

"Back to my reason for being here," he said, avoiding her gaze as much as possible. "What was the purpose of Matthew's visit?"

"Purpose?" She cocked her head to the side as if she were an exotic bird, many of which he'd seen firsthand in Australia. "He came to see me. He was a good son." She sniffed.

It seemed Matthew hadn't told her anything about the tapestry. That in itself was curious, since he'd been an overly effusive fellow. If he'd been excited about the prospect of a treasure map, he would have found it difficult to contain his enthusiasm, especially from their mother. That he did spoke volumes about his desire to keep the map secret from those who were desperate to obtain it, perhaps by any means necessary.

"You mentioned his valet. He accompanied Matthew?" he asked.

"Of course." Her mouth puckered. "This is an awfully strange visit, Elijah."

Would she not call him Norris? He would've thought his title would be too alluring for her to resist. But maybe she couldn't quite accept him as the earl. It was far more than she ever would've expected for him. She'd been shocked enough when he'd found success in the army.

He knew the precise way to gain her assistance, if not her interest, which he'd prefer to do without anyway. "I'm troubled by Matthew's death," he said, waiting for her reaction. She leaned forward slightly, suddenly engaged in a way she'd hadn't been since entering the room. "Someone tried to buy this tapestry from him. It's very valuable. After he declined their offer, someone tried to steal it. He then hid it, and I wondered if it might be here."

Her manicured hand fluttered to her chest. "What are you saying, that Matthew was involved in something dark? Because I don't believe it."

Elijah worked to retain his patience. "No, I'm not saying that. I merely want to find this tapestry before someone else does. It occurred to me that his death might not have been an accident."

Mother's sharp intake of breath filled the room. "You don't think he was killed?"

"I'm not certain. The circumstances are somewhat suspicious. Right now, I'm merely trying to gather as much information as possible."

She put her fingers to her lips and looked up at the portrait again. When she turned her attention back to Elijah, her mouth was tight, the flesh around her lips pale. She clasped her hands in her lap. "Shortly after . . . he died, there was a robbery here."

Elijah sat forward, anticipation coursing through him. "What happened? Tell me everything."

"There isn't much to tell. It happened while everyone was out, save the cook. She didn't hear a thing, but Denkins found several pieces of silver missing."

Elijah frowned. "How do you know it wasn't one of your retainers?"

Her gaze turned positively frigid. "Because I do. Denkins also found a broken vase in my upstairs sitting room, and the carpet near the back door was wet—it was drizzling that day —and no member of the household had used it."

"Did you report the theft to the authorities?"

She gave him a supercilious glare. "Of course I did. They determined that it was simply a burglary."

"Were there any other thefts in the vicinity?"

"No, I recall the constable saying there weren't."

It wasn't much, but it was something. Elijah felt certain it was related to the tapestry. The theft of the silver was puzzling, however; why take that if you were searching for a treasure map? Unless you wanted to cover up what you were really looking for. Ice pricked his spine. He was growing more and more unsettled by the entire bizarre affair.

"Do you think the robbery was somehow related to Matthew's death?" she asked. "How can that be possible?"

He didn't want to share more with her. The less she knew, the better, and not only because he didn't wish to prolong this interview. However, he was still no closer to finding the tapestry. If the villains—and he was beginning to think of them as such—hadn't found the map here, did that mean Matthew had hidden it elsewhere? Or did it mean they simply hadn't found it and it was perhaps still somewhere in the house? And if it wasn't here, Elijah was no closer to where it could be. "You haven't suffered any other intrusions since then?"

"Not to my knowledge." Her face bore more lines since he'd last seen her, and now they deepened with alarm. "You don't think someone has come into the house on more than that occasion?"

"Don't concern yourself over it." For more than a year, she'd been safe, and he had no reason to expect circumstances would change. "If you think of anything else, will you let me know?"

"I suppose." She sounded resigned and a little bit callous. But then, she usually did, in his experience. "I'm afraid I must return to my chamber."

As she stood, he leapt to his feet, eager to be on his way, but disappointed that he was no closer to finding the tapestry. However, there was still the issue of Matthew's valet. "You said Matthew's valet was with him. Did they leave together?"

"How odd that you should ask. In fact, they did not. They arrived on a Tuesday and his valet left Wednesday morning. Matthew stayed until Thursday." Her features softened. "I remember the days because he accompanied me to the Assembly Rooms where I play cards with my friends on Wednesday evenings."

They'd left separately. At last, a kernel of helpful information. "Do you know why his valet left alone? Or where he went?"

"I do not. But perhaps Denkins might recall something."

She smoothed her hand over her hip. "I'm afraid I really must return upstairs. If you'd like to call at a more respectable hour, I'll receive you." *How kind.* "Or perhaps I'll see you at the Assembly Rooms this evening."

"Thank you. I'll consider it." Like bloody hell. This short engagement was about all he could endure, and he was quite ready for another seven- or eight-year separation. At the very least.

For the first time she looked at him with something akin to interest. "I'm sure you'll be an excellent earl. Your father always thought very highly of you. He'd be very proud to see how you comported yourself as an officer." No mention of how she felt, but he supposed this was as close as she'd ever come to praising him.

With a gentle nod, she moved past him.

Elijah cleared his throat. "I'm sorry Matthew died. I would've preferred for things to remain as they were."

She turned to look at him. "You were happy across the world?"

He thought of his simple life in Australia—his small house, his horse, his mistress. "I was."

She said nothing, just blinked at him and left.

Elijah wondered if Denkins would return or if he'd have to go in search of the butler. After a moment, he went toward the door, but then Denkins appeared.

"Mrs. Hollister said you wished to speak with me."

"Yes. When my brother visited, he brought his valet, a chap called Mason. Do you recall why he left before Matthew?"

"Let me think, my lord." Denkins stared at the window while he pondered. "It was some sort of errand, but I don't know the details. His lordship put him on a post chaise to Worcester."

Worcester . . . They'd grown up near there . . . A thought

sparked in Elijah's mind. Could Mason have taken the map and hidden it? *Don't get ahead of yourself.*

Elijah was more keen than ever to speak with Mason. Bradford on Avon was a short ride southeast of Bath. Finding Mason there would be a boon, but Elijah doubted he'd be that lucky. At best, he hoped to speak with Mason's family and hopefully run the valet to ground.

"Thank you, Denkins, you've been most helpful." Plucking his hat from the settee, he dashed from the house. And stopped short at the sight of Miss Bowen and her ever-present companion awaiting him on the sidewalk.

~

*C*ate tensed as she watched Norris come toward them. She couldn't exactly read his tight expression, but he looked somewhat anxious. Like as not, he was annoyed to find her and Grey waiting for him. She summoned her most charming smile in an attempt to soothe any discontent. "Good morning, Lord Norris. Did you receive my note?"

He stopped, eyeing them deliberately. "Yes. I've been busy. Come, let us not stand in front of my mother's house." He said this with such distaste that Cate assumed he was even more irritated by her arrival than she'd thought.

"Shall we take a walk?" Cate suggested.

Norris glanced up at the steel-gray sky. "It's going to rain."

"Not for a bit." Cate had spent enough time outside to anticipate the weather with a good amount of accuracy.

"A short one around the block," Norris said. "I've things to do."

She cast him an inquisitive look as they started out along the sidewalk. "Things you plan to tell me about?"

Grey followed behind them, close enough to probably hear most of what they said. If not, Cate would fill her in later.

Realizing he didn't mean to answer her question, which she took as an answer—*no*—she attempted a hopefully informative conversation. "How was your visit with your mother?"

He spared her a brief glance. "Blessedly short."

"That's all? Have you nothing else to share?"

He looked over at her as they strolled. "What about you, Miss Bowen? What have you to share?"

She wished he wasn't so irritable. "Nothing yet, but then I didn't just come from an interview that may have yielded information about our objectives."

They'd reached the end of the street and the river. He paused and turned to face her. "And just what are 'our' objectives?"

She stopped with him and pivoted so she could look him in the eye. "You wish to determine the circumstances of your brother's death, and I wish to find the tapestry."

"I also wish to find the tapestry."

Did that mean he wouldn't allow her to buy it? She pretended to be obtuse. "So you can sell it to me."

His mouth flattened into a grim line. "That remains to be seen."

Frustration eroded her attempt to remain pleasant. She'd been foolish to think they were perhaps working together with common interests. "I don't appreciate your tone or demeanor this morning. I've done nothing to warrant your disdain."

"Am I being disdainful?" He looked beyond her for a moment, then exhaled. "My apologies. Visiting my mother is a stressful occasion."

She felt instantly contrite.

"I'm sorry to hear that." She loved her parents more than anything and couldn't imagine having a cool relationship, as it seemed he did with his mother. This made her unaccountably sad for him. "Why is it stressful?"

He looked at her in surprise. "It . . . it just is."

She touched the sleeve of his coat. "I should be happy to listen. Perhaps that will ease your stress." She curved her lips into a gentle smile.

He stared at her as if he couldn't quite make sense of her offer. "I . . . thank you. I'd rather not speak of her, if you don't mind. Let us focus our energies on things that matter."

His mother didn't matter? Her heart ached for him and whatever had caused such cold feelings toward the woman who'd raised him.

She didn't wish to make him uncomfortable and so she dropped the topic of conversation—for now. She made a mental note to pursue it at a later date. She always felt better after unburdening herself to her friends. He would undoubtedly feel the same. "I've arranged for us to visit Septon House today. As it happens, Septon is hosting a gathering at present, not quite a country-house party, since the focus is on the discussion of antiquities, but there will be typical amusements such as picnics and dancing. We shall have ample time to speak with him about the men who visited your brother."

His brow furrowed. "I'm not entirely sure I wish to do that. I'm afraid I don't trust anyone at the moment. The situation has become a bit more complicated."

Had he learned something new? "Because of your meeting with your mother? I do hope you'll share what you discovered. You *can* trust me. We want the same things."

His gaze was skeptical, as it often was. "I'm not certain we do."

"We do," she said firmly. "I want to identify the men who sought to purchase the tapestry as much as you do. I need to know who else is aware of this map and the fact that it leads to Dyrnwyn. I'd also like to know if there is danger. No, I *need* to know that too."

He exhaled as he turned and retraced their path. "There was a robbery at my mother's house after Matthew died. Some silver went missing, but I don't think that's what they were looking for."

"You think they were after the tapestry." Alarm spread through her, tightening her frame. "Did they find it?"

"It's impossible to know, unfortunately. I do, however, plan to make another inquiry this afternoon."

He did? "Where?"

He cocked a brow at her. "I do not recall that we agreed to share every bit of information with each other." He continued toward where her coach was parked, just beyond his mother's house. "I believe I felt a raindrop."

A fat droplet landed on Cate's arm. "Perhaps Grey and I will follow you on your errand this afternoon."

"You would, wouldn't you?" He seemed to have lost a bit of his irritability as they lapsed back into their habit of provoking each other. "Very well. Wade and I will be journeying to Bradford on Avon to speak with the family of Matthew's former valet. I believe he might know something about the tapestry, if not its location."

Cate was relieved to hear the trail wasn't completely lost. "We'll accompany you."

"I didn't offer an invitation. Wade and I will conduct the inquiry on our own, and I *promise* to share the results with you when we reach Septon House."

She preferred to go with him, but she wouldn't press the matter, not in his current agitated state. Perhaps she and Grey would stop in Bradford on Avon on their way to Septon House. They might become thirsty after all . . . "Thank you. Who's Wade?"

"My valet." He glanced back at Grey walking behind them. "Think of him as my version of Grey, minus the chaperone part."

They'd arrived at Cate's coach. The drops began to fall more frequently, but it still wasn't full-out rain yet. Cate's footman opened the carriage door.

Norris looked at Cate. "I'll see you at Septon House later, then, and we'll continue our investigation."

He'd said *our*. Maybe they were working together after all.

Cate blinked against the rain. "Are we a team, then?"

He looked at her, and the heat of his blue-gray gaze warmed her. He was familiar now, not quite a friend, but something more than a mere acquaintance. "You aren't going to leave me alone until you obtain that map."

It was a statement of absolute certainty. He sounded as if he appreciated her tenacity, which only heated her further. Something pushed her to move just a hairsbreadth closer. "Do you want me to?"

His nostrils flared slightly, but it was his only visible reaction. The other response was his delayed exhalation, as if his breath had just caught. "I haven't decided. I'm concerned about the well-being of anyone in pursuit of this tapestry."

"Yet another reason for us to band together." A huge raindrop splashed against her nose as she looked up at him.

"You should go," he said, reaching out to swipe the moisture from her face. Though his gloves kept the touch from being flesh to flesh, it still felt intimate.

Quickly, before she could think too long about her reaction, she climbed into the coach, swiftly followed by Grey. "See you this evening."

The footman closed the door and the rain began to fall in earnest, hitting the roof of the vehicle with a steady pit-a-pat. Cate caught sight of Norris jogging back to his own coach, which waited in front of his mother's house. She settled back against the seat as they moved forward.

"You looked friendly with him." Grey's voice was carefully monotone.

Cate glanced at her and made a noncommittal noise.

"You like him," Grey said.

"I *need* him. There's a difference."

"The last time I saw you behave in this manner was with Iscove."

Cate scowled. "Don't say his name." He'd been a fortune hunter, not that she'd known it straightaway. She'd been taken in by his silver tongue and gilded looks. He'd encouraged her antiquarian activities and hadn't cared that she was a woman. In fact, that had inspired and attracted him—or so he'd said. Cate had been utterly foolish to fall for him, even for a short time.

Grey held up her hand. "What kind of friend would I be if I didn't tell you what I saw?"

"Norris is nothing like him. He's autocratic"—though perhaps less so than when they'd first met—"suspicious, secretive . . . The list goes on."

"Does he still seem secretive? He did tell you about the robbery and his brother's valet. He appears to be trustworthy."

Cate fixed her companion with a perturbed stare. She wanted to argue, but was afraid Grey was right. With a resigned sigh, she looked back out the window at the falling rain. "I have to trust him, and it's in his best interest to trust me. But if we can find our way to the map, I won't have any further need of him."

"But you'll still like him."

"Oh, do stop, please. Why does everyone insist on trying to pair us off?"

Grey shrugged. "I wasn't. Just observing."

Cate was past ready to change the subject. "I wonder if we should try to get back into the secret library tonight?"

"I'd wondered the same thing. I'm up for it, if you are."

Cate nodded. "The single page of information by de Valery is suspect—I have to think there are more like it. Perhaps something that would tell us how to read the map." Once they found the tapestry, they had to figure out how it was a map. It looked like a battle scene and nothing else. She'd never seen the back, however. It was possible the map was there.

"We'll go after dinner, while everyone is surveying Septon's latest acquisitions."

"And what about Norris?" Grey asked, her gaze probing across the dim interior of the coach.

"What about him? He's not invited to join us in our search."

Grey nodded and turned her attention to the window.

Cate frowned. She was awfully touchy about Norris. She couldn't deny that he was attractive or that her heart had sped like a runaway horse when he'd touched her nose. He'd been so close that she could smell his masculine scent, see the faint freckles along his upper cheeks.

Grey was unfortunately correct. Cate could imagine Norris drawing her in, as Iscove had done. But Iscove had been charming and irresistible, where Norris could be quite frustrating.

And maybe that made him even more fascinating.

CHAPTER 6

*O*nce they'd arrived in Bradford on Avon, Elijah and Wade had obtained directions to the Mason home from the vicar. During a brief visit with the former valet's mother, they'd ascertained that Mason was currently employed as a footman at a coaching inn in town and went by his mother's family name of Swinson.

Wade spoke as the coach pulled into the yard of the Brass Pony. "An odd situation, what with him working at an inn under a different name."

"Indeed," Elijah said. Why wasn't he working in a house as a valet? "Hopefully our questions will be answered shortly."

"I wonder if I ought to hunt him down," Wade said. "An earl asking around for him might attract attention he doesn't want. Especially since he's seen fit to use an alias."

"I quite agree. I'll just go into the common room for a pint of ale." Though it had rained that morning, the air was warm and cloying.

"Very good, my lord." Wade took himself off, and Elijah went into the dim interior of the inn's taproom.

He'd just situated himself on a bench with a mug of ale when a feminine voice interrupted his thoughts.

"What a coincidence to find you here." Miss Bowen sat down opposite him while Grey carried two pints of ale toward the table and joined them.

He frowned at Miss Bowen. "I find nothing coincidental about this. You knew I was coming to Bradford on Avon."

She accepted her mug from Grey. "While it's true I knew you were coming to Bradford on Avon, I had no notion you were coming here to this inn. We were on our way to Septon House and fancied a bit of refreshment along the way. Finding you here doing the same is the very definition of coincidental." She cheerfully held up her ale and took a hearty swallow.

He drank his own ale in silence.

"Where's Wade?" she asked, glancing around. "I was hoping to meet him."

"He'll be along." Elijah purposefully didn't elaborate.

"It's turned into a rather fine afternoon, after this morning's rain, hasn't it? Perhaps we'll take a picnic tomorrow at Septon House if the weather holds."

He set his mug down. "I don't plan to participate in the party's amusements. You agreed to help me question Septon and that is all I wish to do."

"Actually, we didn't ever discuss specifics, but yes, I shall help you question him." She cocked her head to the side. "What specifically do you wish to ask?"

Elijah narrowed his eyes at her. "I think I shall start with querying his opinion on your inquisitive nature and perhaps risqué behavior."

She straightened. "My behavior is not risqué."

"Calling on me without an invitation, following me . . . No, you're quite right. Those are the activities of any well-bred young lady."

She scowled at him and he nearly smiled. "I'm . . . exuberant," she said. "You can add that to my list of traits."

"I shall." And it suited her perfectly. He wasn't being particularly gentlemanly, but then he wasn't accustomed to answering to anyone. Her invasion into his life was like Australia when he'd first arrived—absolutely unknown territory, but exciting and fascinating just the same.

Sunlight streamed inside as the door opened and Elijah turned to see that it was Wade who'd come inside. He raised his hand to draw his valet's attention.

Wade came to the table, his gaze lingering on Grey before taking in Miss Bowen and then settling on Elijah. "My lord?"

"Miss Bowen, this is my valet. Wade, this is Miss Bowen and her . . . maid, Grey." Elijah stood. "I'll come with you to fetch an ale from the barkeep." Elijah picked up his mug and followed Wade to the small counter where the tap was mounted.

As soon as they were out of the ladies' earshot, Elijah asked, "Success?"

"Found him, but he didn't have time to talk. He wanted to speak directly to you, in any case."

Elijah looked at him askance as they arrived at the bar. "When?" He glanced at the barkeep. "An ale, please."

"Said if we could wait a bit, he'll come find us." Wade inclined his head toward the two women who were watching them unabashedly. "What about them?"

"We need to persuade them to go on to Septon House. Any ideas?"

"Leave it to me," Wade said, somewhat mysteriously. He quaffed a bit of ale, set the mug down on the bar, and strode toward Miss Bowen and Grey. He said something and Grey stood. Then he escorted her over to the corner and spoke to her for a few moments. Miss Bowen, appearing perplexed, glanced between them and Elijah, who merely offered a bland smile. At length, Grey returned to Miss Bowen, said something near her ear, and Miss Bowen stood. With a smile and a raise of her hand toward Elijah, she and Grey left the taproom.

Wade rejoined him at the bar and picked up his mug for another long drink of ale.

"What on earth did you say?" Elijah asked, never more impressed with his manservant.

"I explained to Mrs. Grey that their presence was hindering our investigation, but that if they would continue on to Septon House, I would inform her of what we learned."

Mrs. Grey? Was she married or a widow? The latter seemed more likely, particularly in the absence of a wedding ring. "That's it?" If Elijah had tried the same tactic with Miss Bowen, she likely would've argued. In fact . . .

He crossed to the window and peered outside. They were just climbing into their coach. A moment later, it departed the yard.

Elijah turned. Wade had followed him to the window. "I don't know how you did it, but thank you."

"Perhaps I'm merely more adept at speaking to the gentler sex."

Elijah clacked his mug against Wade's. "I have no doubt."

Halfway through their second helpings of ale, a footman —who had to be Mason—approached their table. Elijah motioned for him to sit down. "Join us, Swinson. Please."

Mason was perhaps five or so years Elijah's senior, but his timid expression made him seem far younger. "I only have a few minutes before I need to get back to work."

"I shan't take up much of your time." Elijah smiled at him. "May I ask why you're working here and not as a valet?" He purposely kept his tone low and even, hoping to put the man at ease.

Mason looked down at the table. "I didn't have a reference, my lord. His lordship—your brother—was my first post as a valet."

"I see." Elijah chose his words carefully. It wouldn't do to scare the man off, not when he likely possessed valuable information. "You traveled with my brother to Bath to visit our mother just before he died. Why did you leave before him and go to Worcester?"

Mason's head snapped up, his dark brown eyes widening. "It was an errand for his lordship. I . . . hid something for him."

Elijah's pulse quickened. "A tapestry? Yes, I know all about it."

Some of the tension left Mason's rigid frame. "I figured I could trust you, my lord. His lordship—your brother—spoke very highly of you."

Elijah's heart squeezed, surprising him. He wasn't a man of strong emotions. Indeed, he hadn't even wept when he'd heard of Matthew's death. However, since he'd returned to England, he'd missed his brother. Being home was strange and somewhat unfamiliar, and he realized it was because Matthew wasn't here. "Thank you for saying so, Swinson. Where did you hide the tapestry?"

"In a small cave—a hole really—near a folly that he said you played at as children."

Elijah knew precisely of where he spoke. It was on an estate near their childhood home outside Worcester. Discovering the location of the tapestry loosened something inside of him, made him feel . . . hopeful. Miss Bowen would be inordinately pleased.

"Why did Matthew ask you to hide it there?"

Mason shrugged. "After the footman—Dalby—tried to steal it, his lordship wanted to get it away from Cosgrove. He considered stashing it at your mother's, but decided someone might try to steal it from there. So he sent me off on my own to hide it. He thought no one would pay notice to what I was doing, whereas he might've been followed."

"You said a footman tried to steal it?" Elijah exchanged glances with Wade. "What happened to him?"

"His lordship let him go without a reference."

"His lordship didn't report him to the authorities?" Wade asked.

Mason shook his head. "Dalby was a blubbering mess. Pathetic, really. Said he'd been taken in by villains and tempted with coin. His lordship felt sorry for him."

Elijah wasn't surprised to hear this. Matthew had always been easily taken in. It was what made him a terrible gambler. "Did he say who these villains were?"

"No, though his lordship did ask. We suspected it was either the baron who'd written and asked to purchase the tapestry or the pair of men who'd visited and done the same."

Septon and the mystery men. "Yes, Garber told us of these men," Elijah said. "Do you remember who they were?"

Mason thought for a moment but ultimately shook his head again. "I'm afraid I don't, my lord. But I think Dalby was lying."

Elijah splayed his palm atop the table and pressed his fingers into the wood. He glanced at Wade. "I'd like to find this footman."

"That shouldn't be a problem, my lord," Mason said, drawing Elijah's interested gaze. "He's employed at Stratton Hall near Hereford. He told one of the maids where he went. I think he tried to persuade her to join him, but she didn't want to leave." Mason glanced anxiously toward the windows. "I need to return to my post."

Elijah nodded. "Of course. I'm nearly finished. Do you know anything about the accident that caused Matthew's death?"

Mason had seemed nervous throughout the duration of

the short interview, but now he crackled with tension. When he finally spoke, it was with hesitation. "When . . . When I returned to Cosgrove and learned what had happened, I immediately went to the site of the accident. The wreckage was still there, so I had a look." He swallowed and looked about, then lowered his voice to barely above a whisper. "There was a box beneath one of the seats. It had a lock and was meant to hold valuables. It had been smashed open, but I could tell it had been done with a tool and wasn't a result of the accident."

Elijah forgot to breathe for a moment. "You think someone was looking for something."

"I do. And I'm sure you know what that was." He took a deep breath before continuing. "I returned to Cosgrove directly, packed my belongings, and went home." His dark gaze connected with Elijah's. "I adopted my mother's name in case someone decided to come looking for me."

He was afraid. Elijah hated that. "You think someone killed my brother, that it wasn't an accident."

"Since Dalby had been lured to steal the tapestry, I figured the coachman could've been corrupted too. They didn't find him. What if he caused the accident and leapt from the box before it went off the road?"

Elijah's entire body went cold. "Mas—Swinson, you've been more helpful than you can possibly imagine. I should be happy to provide a reference for you as a valet—under whatever name you choose."

Mason blinked at him, looking surprised and . . . pleased. "I would appreciate that very much, my lord."

"It's the least I can do."

Mason stood. "I really am sorry about your brother. I say a prayer for him every night and wish that I would've been with him. Mayhap I could've prevented it." His voice broke at the end, evidencing his affection for Matthew.

"Let us keep in touch," Elijah said, standing and offering his hand.

Mason shyly took it and gave him a quick shake. "Be careful, my lord."

"You do the same, Swinson."

Elijah watched the man leave the taproom and felt a surge of rage. As soon as he finished with Septon, he'd go directly to Stratton Hall to interrogate this would-be thief. But what if Septon was involved? What if he was the one behind Matthew's death? Elijah didn't know if he could keep himself from cornering the man and asking—and potentially making an utter fool of himself. He grimaced. Entering a baron's home and accusing him of murder was perhaps the wrong way to enter Society.

"What is it?" Wade got up from the table.

Elijah turned toward the door. "I'm trying to determine how to suffer this evening without demanding Septon tell me everything he knows regarding my brother and this infernal tapestry."

CHAPTER 7

ade put the finishing touches on Elijah's cravat. "Are you prepared for this evening?"

Elijah surveyed himself in the glass. "If you mean, do I intend to maintain my composure with Septon, the answer is yes. However, if you mean am I ready to demonstrate my social skills as the realm's newest earl, the answer is also yes. I comported myself quite well at Bassett Manor, didn't I? I even danced."

"Yes, that was a sufficient rehearsal."

Elijah arched a brow at Wade, who knew him better than probably anyone on this earth. "Your faith in me is encouraging."

"Just making an observation, my lord. I know you aren't terribly fond of these types of events."

Elijah brushed a speck of lint from his coat and turned from the glass. "Which makes being an earl rather difficult."

"Well, at least it's only one night then we'll be off for Worcester."

To find the tapestry. The only reason he planned to find the map first was because it was on the way to Stratton

Hall. Elijah hadn't yet told Miss Bowen about discovering the map's location because he expected she'd want to leave for Worcester posthaste. And he wanted to talk to Septon first.

He'd tell her later. She'd be annoyed with him, but knowing that she was on the path to finding the tapestry ought to ensure her irritation was short-lived.

Did he care that she'd be angry with him? *Yes.* The answer surprised and rattled him. He wasn't going out of his way to cause her grief. He simply had his own agenda, and it took precedence over hers. But for the first time, he wondered if that was the right course of action. Wait, he'd put her desire for treasure above his brother's death?

He shook his head, frustrated with himself for letting his emotions—emotions!—get the better of him. They'd go after the tapestry tomorrow, and that was soon enough.

"What will you do once you find the map? You can't mean to let Miss Bowen and Mrs. Grey take off with it."

Elijah pivoted to look at Wade. "What do you suggest?"

Wade shrugged. "I wondered if you might want to help her find the treasure. If there are others looking for it and they're not above killing to find it, I don't think Grey is going to offer sufficient protection."

"You met her—she's larger than you and possesses a fierce demeanor. She looks as if she could hold her own with any one of my regiment."

Wade's lips curved into an appreciative smile. "You might be right about that."

Elijah wondered at Wade's odd reaction, but didn't say anything. "Your point is well taken. I do worry over Miss Bowen's safety, but ultimately it is not my concern." He said that partially to convince himself. He could very easily take on the role of her protector. Not because Grey wasn't capable, but because Elijah wanted to be sure Miss Bowen didn't come to any harm like his brother did. Just thinking of her finding the same end sent a chill down his neck.

"You have no interest in helping her to find this sword? You must admit it's quite a lure."

And then there was the sword itself. Was he interested? He wasn't certain, but he smiled at Wade. "Spoken like a thief." Wade had been transported for stealing when he'd been just ten and six, and had completed his sentence before becoming Elijah's batman. "*If* it's Dyrnwyn, which I can't believe that it is, it would be a great treasure. I already have plenty of treasures cramming Cosgrove to the brim."

Wade looked at him as if he were cracked. "None of them are the legendary sword of one of King Arthur's knights, but I won't press the matter."

"I never knew you to be the fanciful sort, Wade." Elijah turned and left the chamber.

He made his way to the large drawing room at the back of the house. The guests were to gather here before dinner. There were already a good number of people milling about and also spilling onto the terrace to enjoy the pleasant summer evening.

Their host, Lord Septon, approached Elijah. He was an angular man of exceptional height, one of only a few people Elijah could look straight in the eye without pitching his gaze down even a fraction.

"Good evening, Lord Norris," he greeted, extending his hand. "I'm pleased to make your acquaintance."

Elijah clasped the man's hand for a moment and couldn't help but wonder if he were shaking the hand of a murderer. "Thank you for including me."

"If I'd known you were ready to accept invitations, I would've invited you. I wanted to give you plenty of time to readjust to life in England."

"Yes, it's quite different from what I'm used to, particularly the title."

Septon chuckled. "I can imagine it must be for someone who never planned to inherit. I came into my baronetcy when I was just twenty, but I had at least been prepared for it. If there's anything I can do to help, I hope you'll let me know. Your cousin, Lord Norris the antiquary, was a close associate of mine."

Elijah noted he didn't say "friend." Was that because Septon, like everyone else Elijah had met, hadn't cared for the man? "I understand he was a criminal." Elijah saw no reason to mince words, and he preferred to get right to the point, especially tonight.

Septon frowned. "Yes, it turned out that he was. I had no idea. It was most disturbing. We shared a common interest in antiquities. I was gravely disappointed to learn he was fleecing money from his district."

Did Septon's disdain for Norris's criminal activities indicate his own nature? Could Elijah deduce the man hadn't been involved in Matthew's death? Not yet. "At least reparations were made, though that didn't leave the earldom in the best financial state. You offered to assist me with the antiquities collection, and I would like to liquidate it."

The color seeped from Septon's face. "All of it?"

Elijah nodded. "I've no need for it. Or interest, to be honest."

"My goodness, it's a veritable museum. In fact, I know that Oxford would love to acquire several items. You should write to Mr. Penn Bowen at the Ashmolean and invite him to visit. I should prefer to see some of those items in a museum instead of someone's private collection."

"Mr. Bowen is Miss Bowen's brother?" Elijah asked.

"Yes. He's what I like to call an adventuring antiquary. He travels all over Britain obtaining artifacts."

That sounded somewhat like what his sister might do. Elijah made a mental note to ask her about that. "I'll write to him when I return to Cosgrove. I don't think I'll have any trouble finding homes for the collection. Indeed, my brother was approached about selling some items." Elijah was purposely vague in order to gauge Septon's reaction.

"That's not surprising, given its value. I know many people were keen to purchase items once Norris died. However, the length of time between his death and when your brother arrived back in England was so great, that I wondered who had actually contacted him, if anyone."

Elijah gave him an unflinching stare. "Well, you did, of course."

Septon gave a nod. "I did, and though he responded, he never seemed interested in accepting any of my offers of help or to purchase items."

That sounded like Matthew. He would've been too busy spending money to consider how he might replenish it. "You offered to purchase multiple items? Which ones?"

Septon stroked his chin. "My goodness, the list is terribly long." He laughed. "When you invite me to Cosgrove, I'll bring it. I hope you'll give me first crack—after you speak with Bowen."

"Of specific interest to me at present is a tapestry. Do you recall offering to purchase that particular item?"

Septon's eyes narrowed slightly. His gaze became more fixed, and his curiosity was clear. "Yes. What of it?"

"In addition to you, there was a pair of men who also demonstrated interest. It's apparently quite valuable and they wanted it most desperately." Time to see what Septon was capable of. "In fact, someone tried to steal it. Since these men and you are the only people I know of who offered to purchase it, I find myself wondering if one of you was behind the attempt."

Septon's eyes widened briefly and then narrowed again. His gaze darted to the left where a small group of gentlemen stood talking, but Elijah couldn't determine whether he was looking at one of them. Septon frowned. "I can assure you I did not attempt to steal anything from the Cosgrove collection. I am more than happy to pay for the items I wish to own."

Elijah sensed the man's reaction was genuine, but it brought him no closer to solving this mystery. He was about to ask if Septon might know the other men who'd tried to purchase the tapestry, but the question died on his tongue as Miss Bowen entered the drawing room. Dressed in vibrant blue, with her hair swept into an elegant style—had Grey accomplished that? Elijah couldn't imagine her skills stretching to such feminine achievements—Miss Bowen gleamed like a jewel amidst a pile of rocks.

"Ah, one of my favorite people." Septon smiled as he greeted her. "Cate, you look lovely. And you're wearing your favorite pendant, I see."

Elijah, having followed him, glanced down at the familiar silver necklace kissing her flesh. He envied that piece of metal and its claim on that particular bit of Miss Bowen.

Septon gave Miss Bowen a quick hug and dropped a kiss to her cheek. "I'm so pleased you could come."

"I'm glad I could be here after all. I see you've met Lord Norris." She looked past Septon and when her gaze met Elijah's, he tried to ignore the rush of awareness that crested over him again.

"Indeed," said Septon. "He was telling me he wishes to sell the entire Cosgrove collection. I can't fathom it."

"Yes, he told me the same when we met in Wootton Bassett. I am equally shocked. But only think of the opportunity you now have." She patted his sleeve.

"Too true." His answering smile was positively gleeful. "To

be fair, however, I did recommend he contact your brother first."

"How magnanimous of you." She looked toward Elijah. "You ought to know that you'll garner more if you sell to Septon—his pockets are deeper than Oxford's or my brother's."

"I hope you'll both join the antiquities discussion after dinner. We'll be gathering in the front hall." Septon looked between them. "I see Lady Stratton beckoning me. Please excuse me." He offered them a warm smile—that might have cooled a degree as he glanced at Elijah—before taking himself off.

Elijah watched him cross the room to an attractive woman of middle age with dark hair. Something about her reminded Elijah of one of the gentlemen in the far corner—in the group Septon had looked at. Elijah cast a surreptitious glance in that direction and again noted the similarity. The gentleman looked to be around Elijah's age. Perhaps he was her son.

Miss Bowen touched Elijah's sleeve, drawing his swift and singular attention. "What did you and Septon discuss? We never did strategize how I was to help you with him."

Elijah motioned for her to follow him to the corner. They stood near a medieval—at least, he guessed it to be of that age—suit of armor.

"He assured me he had nothing to do with the attempted theft of the tapestry. I was asking him about the other men who sought to purchase it when your arrival interrupted us."

Her brow creased. "My apologies. Although, I daresay you were going to lose him to Lady Stratton anyway. She will always be his first priority."

Elijah's ears pricked up like those of a dog on the hunt. Stratton as in Stratton Hall where Dalby, the corrupt footman, was now employed? "Lady Stratton is Septon's paramour?" At Cate's slight nod, he continued, "And is there a Lord Stratton?"

"Yes, but he's not here. He would never set foot in Septon House or anywhere Lord Septon would be."

Elijah slid a glance toward his host and Lady Stratton. "I take it her husband is aware of their affair?"

"Quite. They've been together for years. She left Stratton when I was very young." Though they spoke in low tones, Miss Bowen leaned closer. "Lest you think I'm a gossip, they are actually my family. Stratton is a cousin of my father's."

Elijah's chest puffed with satisfaction, for he'd been wondering how to gain entrance to Stratton Hall since he was not acquainted with its owner—he hadn't even known who it was. "Indeed?"

Her gaze narrowed at him in an assessing manner. "Why are you so interested?"

"Because I need to question someone employed at Stratton Hall. After you and Grey left the inn in Bradford on Avon this afternoon, we learned from my brother's former valet that the footman who'd attempted to steal the tapestry is now in service at Stratton Hall. I mean to speak with him in order to determine who put him up to the task, and you are perfectly positioned to help me. You'll arrange for us to visit."

Her lips curled into a distasteful moue. "I did say I would help you, but I must admit I'd rather not. Stratton is universally regarded as an awful person. He's a philanderer and a drunkard. I've never met anyone with a lower opinion of women."

Derision weighted her tone. This was not the first time she'd made an observation regarding the status of women. As a female antiquary, he knew, she fought a near-impossible battle to gain attention, let alone respect. "Since he is a relative, I assume you've met him."

"Yes, a few times, and I must say that I don't blame Lady Stratton for leaving him. In fact, I think she deserves a knighthood—if women could receive them—for staying with him for nearly ten years." Her features softened. "But then I know she only did it to be with her son. Who can blame her for that?"

Who indeed? Elijah wondered if his own mother would've done such a thing. Not for him, certainly, but would she have suffered such a husband for Matthew's sake? Judging her behavior, one would have thought she'd suffered the husband she had, but Elijah's father—though fond of drink—had never treated her poorly.

Shoving his own disappointing childhood to the recesses of his mind, Elijah scanned the room for the gentleman he'd seen earlier, certain that he was Lady Stratton's offspring.

"Who are you looking for?" Miss Bowen asked. "I thought you didn't know anyone."

"I don't, but I believe I saw Lady Stratton's son. He bore a striking resemblance . . . "

"Kersey's here?" Miss Bowen joined him in searching the room. "Ah, yes. There in the other corner." Her lips curved down ever so slightly.

"You don't care for him?"

She looked at Elijah. "It's not that. I actually have fond memories of spending summers together when we were children. He's cut in the image of his father, unfortunately. I often wonder if he would've turned out differently if Artemesia hadn't left him at such a young age. Alas, we'll never know."

Elijah surveyed the gentleman from across the room. Kersey was engaged in conversation with a portly fellow who was gesturing enthusiastically with his hands. "You mean he drinks too much and has a low regard for women?"

"The term 'rake' comes to mind, but I fear that may be too

tame of a description. He did marry, but his wife died just six months later and he fell right back into his bad habits. Artemesia hopes remarrying will calm him down again, but I doubt we'll ever find out. No decent woman will have him because the rumor is that his wife killed herself to escape him—something his father's first wife is also said to have done."

Elijah's head swam. "Stop. Please. I can't possibly retain all of this information, nor do I want to. Unless Kersey has something to do with the men who visited my brother, I couldn't care less about his romantic situation."

She stared up at him. "I couldn't agree more. How refreshing. Can you imagine"—she leaned closer as if to impart a secret, not that any of their conversation ought to have been exchanged in full voice—"Stratton actually hoped for Kersey and me to *marry?*"

Elijah shot a sharp glance toward Kersey. "But he's your cousin."

"Not that closely related by blood, but yes, I do share your dismay since we somewhat grew up together. Stratton liked the union because it would combine his meager manuscript collection with my father's massive medieval library. He fancies himself some sort of collector, though I don't think he has the faintest notion of how to go about it."

"I take it your father is more competent at collecting?"

Her dark gaze simmered with pride. "My father is a scholar. He acquires medieval manuscripts to study them. His father before him was the most renowned medieval manuscript scholar in all of Britain." The love and admiration she felt for her father was palpable, and Elijah felt a surprising stab of envy. He'd loved his father, but there hadn't been much to admire about either of his parents, though he supposed his father deserved credit for enduring his wife's frigidity and verbal abuse.

"Should we talk to Kersey about the men who tried to purchase the tapestry?"

She pulled her gaze from her cousin and looked up at Elijah. "I doubt he would know anything. Let me talk to Septon. Never fear, I'm confident we'll learn something."

He didn't share her confidence, but didn't say so. He ought to tell her about the tapestry, but he would wait until after dinner.

At that moment, the butler announced that dinner would be served. Elijah offered his arm to Miss Bowen. "May I escort you?"

She slipped her hand over his sleeve, the contact giving him another jolt of awareness. "Thank you."

As he guided her to the dining room, he decided it was good that their association would be over soon. The more time they spent together, the more he was drawn to her. The last thing he had time or inclination for was a wife, and when it came to someone like Miss Bowen, he couldn't have her any other way.

∼

After a pleasant dinner during which Cate was able to observe Lord Norris discussing his assignment in Australia, she suffered the requisite post-meal gathering of ladies in the drawing room while the men enjoyed their port in the dining room. Cate was usually bored during these times as the conversation typically focused on the latest scandal or, even more tedious, the prospects on the Marriage Mart. If only one of her comrades from the Ladies' Antiquities Society were present, she could have enjoyed the event. Instead, she smiled and nodded and thought about whether Grey had been able to obtain the key to Septon's library.

At last, Lady Stratton—the de facto hostess—led them

from the drawing room. As they neared the front hall, where Septon housed a great deal of his collection, Cate was intercepted by her host.

Septon took her hand and gave it a warm squeeze as people walked by them on their way to the hall. "How long do you plan to stay?"

"I'm not sure." She didn't want to commit to a specific duration. "A couple of days. At least."

Septon's familiar gray eyes crinkled at the corners as he let go of her hand. "Does it depend on Norris? Is there a chance he's courting you?"

"Goodness no, why ever would you say that?" She realized she'd responded with great haste and perhaps a tad too much enthusiasm, but it was true.

Septon's gaze took on a curious glint, which Cate recognized from nearly everyone else who'd interrogated her about Norris. Why was everyone bent on matching them together? "I only want to see you happy."

Which could be said of all who'd inquired about Norris. "I know. And I appreciate your concern. However, I'm not in any hurry to marry. Love will find me when it's time, or mayhap not at all. That isn't what guides my life. I'm not like most females."

He laughed softly. "No, you are not, by the grace of God. However, you are still of the fairer sex and the world can be harsh for an unmarried woman."

Cate clenched her teeth. She loved Septon and supposed he couldn't help his archaic views since they were shared by the vast majority. "I assume you don't give Penn these same lectures."

"Of course not. I'm not sure he'll ever settle down. That boy—not that he's a boy any longer—has far too great a taste for adventure."

Did no one recognize that Cate did too? She and Penn

weren't actually blood-related, since he'd been adopted by their parents when he was nine. Despite that, and their ten-year age difference, they shared a love of excitement and thrilling experiences that most people would never dream of. "Girls like adventure too," she murmured.

"Yes, yes, I understand," he said somewhat condescendingly. "You aren't Penn, however." His gaze turned shrewd. "Just how long do you think you can go gallivanting around with your Ladies' Antiquities Society friends?"

Cate bit back her gasp. "How do you know about that?" she whispered. It was supposed to be secret. People would actively try to stop them or discredit their work. And they were on the cusp of publishing their first set of papers.

"I know everything that occurs in the antiquarian community. It's not common knowledge—yet. But you can't have expected it to remain secret?"

"In fact, we did," she said tartly. They'd planned to publish their papers under male pseudonyms and fabricate a false name for their organization—something without "ladies" in its title. "How did you learn of it?"

His gray brows pitched low over his eyes, which held a sheen of regret. "I'm afraid I can't say, but I'll keep everything you told me inviolate."

Septon seemed to harbor a wealth of secrets. She thought about what Andy had said, that she'd long suspected Septon of something more than antiquity collection and research. But what more could it be? "Since you're privy to all things antiquarian-related, can you tell me who else might have wanted to purchase the flaming sword tapestry from Lord Norris's brother? They were younger men, no one that made me think of anyone in the antiquarian community. Have you any idea who they could be?"

"None." His answer came more quickly than she would've liked. "Cate, I have to ask about your association with Norris.

You aren't courting and yet you seem to share at least some level of intimacy."

Intimacy? The word sparked a fire deep in her belly. She couldn't deny they'd shared a . . . friendship, but it was nothing more than that and it was *temporary*. "When he learned that I am an antiquary, he sought my assistance in trying to identify these men," she said.

"He told me someone tried to steal the tapestry. Did you know that?" Septon asked.

Though it would only underscore their close relationship, Cate answered in the affirmative. "I did."

"And it truly can't be found?" He sounded a trifle alarmed, likely because he understood the true value of the tapestry and what its loss would mean. His reaction, though subtle, perhaps indicated that the tapestry was the sole link in finding Dyrnwyn.

Cate kept her response deliberately mysterious—if he could be secretive, so could she. She offered a slight shrug. "I really can't say. And since you don't know who these men could be, I suppose it's safe to assume you don't know quite everything that happens in the antiquarian world."

His lips pursed briefly. "I misspoke. I'm aware of *most* things." His eyes narrowed and he lowered his voice to barely above a whisper. "Do you have any idea why these men would want that tapestry?"

It was quite obviously a coded question: Did she know the tapestry was a map? And yet, he didn't ask her outright, and that told her that if she didn't know, he preferred to keep it that way. Yes, Septon was a man of many secrets.

She blinked at him, suppressing the surge of triumph rising in her chest that came from knowing the secret he didn't think she knew. "Of course. It's an incredibly valuable piece of Arthurian art."

The lines around his eyes and mouth faded a little—

something she wouldn't have noticed if she hadn't been paying very close attention. "Just so."

The crowd in the corridor had completely dissipated as everyone had made their way into the hall for Septon's lecture. "My goodness," Septon said, "I must attend to my guests. Please forgive me, dear." He flashed her a smile and ducked inside.

As Cate watched him go, she tried not to tap her foot in irritation. She'd always trusted Septon as much as she trusted her own parents, but it certainly seemed that Andy was correct, that there was more to Septon than met the eye. And speaking of her parents, what of her father's keeping that poem from her? Was all of this secrecy due to the fact that she was a woman? Was her mother also kept in the dark? She wished Mother wasn't so far away—at home in Wales.

Cate stepped away from the door as Septon began to speak at the front of the room. She had no desire to hear a presentation when she had other objectives, especially not when the speech was to be delivered by someone who sought to keep her misinformed. Now more than ever she wanted to find that sword. She'd show all of them that she was as good an antiquary as any of them—better, even. Who else would be able to claim the discovery of something so history-changing?

Time to find the library and hope that Grey was waiting there with the key.

Making her way from the hall, she rounded a corner and stopped short as she came face-to-face with her cousin, Lord Gideon Kersey. "Kersey, good evening."

"Cate, what a delight to see you. It's been too long." He took her hand and dropped a kiss on her glove.

Again, she thought of their childhood summers together and how abruptly the visits had stopped when his mother had left his father, much to Cate's father's chagrin. Rhys

Bowen had worked hard to have Penn, Kersey, and Cate together for at least a few weeks each year. Family was very important to her father, which she understood because he didn't have very much of it.

"I'm surprised to see you here. Isn't one of Septon's house parties a little tame for you?"

His stone-gray eyes flickered with exasperation. "Don't believe everything you hear."

"My apologies." And she was suddenly sorry. It wasn't fair to assume the rumors about him were true, even if they had been at one point. "It just seems as though you've picked up where you left off when you wed Rose."

"Yes, well, I haven't." He sounded beleaguered, as if he'd mounted a defense on many occasions. "But I don't really care what anyone thinks. You, however, are a different story."

"Because we're family."

He inclined his head slightly.

Cate wasn't sure what to say. Kersey had never been particularly . . . familial. In fact, she was most surprised to see him here because as far as she knew, he avoided his mother and Septon at all costs, despite their repeated attempts to include him in everything they did. He was angry with her for leaving him all those years ago, and with Septon for luring her away. At least, that's what Cate surmised.

"Have you decided to become more involved in antiquities?" It was the only reason she could think of for him being here.

"Yes." He sounded surprised. "Septon's been trying to persuade me to come for years. I thought it was about time."

"I'm sure your mother is very happy."

"I believe so." If there was a lack of warmth to his tone, Cate didn't remark upon it. She needed to extricate herself from this conversation.

"If you hurry, you'll just catch Septon's presentation. I

understand he's introducing a handful of artifacts from a site in Northumberland. Viking coins and such." She took a step to move past him.

He didn't move. "You aren't coming?"

"I'm afraid not." She touched her temple and winced for added effect. "Bit of a headache. I'll see you tomorrow."

He stepped to the side at last. "I hope so. It really is good to see you."

"You too." She smiled before heading for the staircase. When she risked a look back, she saw that he was still watching her. She tried not to let the curiosity in his gaze burn her spine as she continued on her mission.

CHAPTER 8

*E*lijah stepped out from the shadowed doorway as soon as Lord Kersey moved into the front hall. While Elijah knew there was no courtship between the two cousins, he'd still felt a stab of jealousy, which infuriated him to no end. He didn't wish to be jealous regarding Miss Bowen. She was a means to an end, not a diversion.

And just where was she going? He stealthily made his way to the staircase and followed her trail. At the top, he paused, wondering which way she'd gone. He stood very still and listened, something he'd grown quite skilled at doing when hunting in Australia. Detecting the faint swish of a skirt, he turned left and followed the gallery to a branch of corridors. Again, he became a rock and focused his senses. Sure that he was on the right path, he veered right.

A few minutes later, he turned a sharp corner and had to stop himself before he overtook her. Pressing himself back against the wall, he kept as quiet as possible. With care, he peered around the corner and watched as she slipped into a room.

What the devil was she up to? And why hadn't she told him?

Intent on discerning her motives, he strode around the corner without being properly alert. Which caused him to run straight into a brick wall.

Named Grey.

"My lord," she whispered urgently. "Go back downstairs."

"I think not." Good God, the woman *would* make an excellent soldier; she was built like a warrior.

"I won't allow you to cause a problem." The dark threat in her tone was unmistakable.

He stared down at her unflinchingly—not as far down as he was used to, but it was enough to convey his point. "I understand and even appreciate your protectiveness; however, I don't think you'll be able to stop me from my objective."

She must've recognized the steel in his promise—he didn't make threats—because she stepped back. "You won't sound the alarm?"

"Of course not. I don't wish to cause Miss Bowen any trouble." Particularly when it seemed she could likely do that very well on her own, given her behavior.

Grey glanced behind her. "You must hurry. We only have a few minutes before the guard returns from making his rounds. Go behind the largest painting in the room."

Behind a painting? Elijah went into the room, an office. Though it was dimly lit, with just a pair of wall sconces flickering on either side of the fireplace, he quickly located the massive portrait. It depicted a gentleman from the last century surrounded by his hunters. He tried to peer behind it, but there was just a wall. A slight draft tickled his neck. Curious, he pulled at the frame, to no avail, and then pushed . . .

He practically stumbled inside as the wall, more accurately a door, gave way, and was immediately smacked in the arm by a dark-eyed virago.

"You scared me," she hissed.

The small, windowless chamber was little more than a closet lined with bookshelves and a solitary locked trunk that was tall enough to act as a table one could stand at. A lantern hung from a hook on the wall cast a swath of light around the cramped space.

"How did you get in here?" she asked. "Why didn't Grey stop you?" The edge of panic in her voice told him she was worried about her bodyguard.

"She tried, but I convinced her that I could help." It was a reasonable enough explanation. "I would've helped from the beginning, had I known what you were up to. Just what *are* you up to?"

She had the grace to look discomfited. "This is where I found the document that states the tapestry is a map."

"That fails to explain what you're doing here and why you didn't inform me of your plan." It occurred to him that he was perhaps being unfair, since he was also keeping information from her. The difference, however, was that he'd planned to tell her about the location of the tapestry later this evening. Perhaps he ought to rethink that plan.

She pursed her lips, a frequent occurrence when she was frustrated, he noted. He tried not to also note that it made her mouth look utterly kissable.

"I'd hoped to search for more clues, perhaps something that might point to the location of the sword, since the tapestry may very well be lost to us." She went to a bookshelf and began investigating its contents.

"I see." And he did. He could stop this right now, but he was curious to look around. "What is this place?"

She didn't turn from her task. "Septon's secret library. A retainer regularly patrols it, but he's currently checking other areas since Septon's valuable collection is so vast. We don't have much time before he returns."

Elijah went to a different shelf and pulled out a tome. It was very old and written in a language he didn't recognize. "Where did you find the document about the tapestry?"

She looked over her shoulder at him and pointed to a cabinet he hadn't noticed behind the door. "There. It's between those two books on the top shelf."

Elijah wanted to see this "proof" for himself. He went to the cabinet and easily found the parchment.

"Be careful to put everything back exactly as you found it. We can't risk Septon knowing someone was in here."

The document was beautifully decorated, particularly the likeness of the tapestry in the center of the page. It was also written in an unknown language. "I can't read this," he said.

"It's medieval Welsh."

Elijah couldn't even read modern Welsh. "You can read this?"

"Yes. I told you, my father is a medieval manuscript scholar."

Impressed, he looked over at her. She stood her toes as she tried to reach something. Closing the book, he set it on the locked trunks and went to help her. "Let me." His arm brushed against hers as he reached up. "This one?" He rested his fingers against a slender volume.

"Yes."

He pulled it down and handed it to her. "Why that one?"

"The symbol on the spine. It's a pictograph that repre-sents flame. And since the tapestry is known as the 'flaming sword tapestry,' it seemed worth investigating."

"It's a bit of a stretch, isn't it?"

She tossed him an exasperated look. "Feel free to search elsewhere. And don't leave that parchment there!" Though her voice was barely above a whisper, her irritation was plainly evident.

He plucked up the loose page, frustrated that he couldn't read it. Did that make it any less true? If it said what she claimed—and she'd no reason to lie . . . For the first time, anticipation swirled in his gut as he contemplated the sword actually existing.

He wasn't sure what made him do it, but he folded the document, coughing as he did so to cover the crinkling sound of the paper, and slid it into his coat.

"There's nothing here." She closed the book he'd pulled down for her and held it out to him. "Will you put it back?"

He did as she asked. "How much time do we have?"

She pulled a watch from a pocket in her dress. "Damn. We're nearly out of time." She looked at the locked trunk. "I wish we could open that."

"Just what are you hoping to find?"

"I don't know." She lifted her dark eyes to his, and he saw desperation in their depths. "The tapestry is all but lost. I can't give up. I won't. I don't know what else to do."

"Well, then it's good I do. Come on, we can go." He turned toward the door.

Her hand on his arm halted him and sent a vexing shock of desire rioting through him. "What do you mean?"

His years of training brought the sound to his ears. It was faint, but it was human-made. He clasped her hand and pulled the handle on the portrait door. She resisted him, but only to quickly extinguish the flame in the lantern. He dragged her through the doorway and spun around, holding his finger to his lips as he eased the painting closed.

She held up her free hand, but he tugged on the one he still held. "Wait," she whispered tensely. She withdrew a key from her pocket and slid it into a keyhole hidden in the eye of one of the dogs. He wondered how in the hell she'd even found this bloody library in the first place.

He'd ask later, because right now someone was coming into the room and they sure as hell weren't supposed to be there. "We're about to be caught."

She grabbed his other hand and pulled him into the dark corner. "Kiss me, and make sure whoever it is can't see who I am."

~

*N*orris stared down at her, his pale eyes flickering with disbelief. Exhaling a whispered curse, she pulled his head down and put her lips to his.

She'd kissed two other men—a long-ago experiment with a boy in Monmouth and the treacherous David Iscove—and suddenly she felt as though she'd never been kissed before in her life. Norris's lips were warm and firm, but so gentle. If he was shocked, he was hiding it well. His hands clasped her waist, their warmth seeping through the layers of her clothing until she felt as though she might combust.

When his thumb grazed the underside of her breast, she opened her mouth in an involuntary gasp without thinking that he'd consider it an invitation. But thank heavens he did. His tongue grazed past her lips and met hers. She opened further, never expecting that this necessary action would become something so delicious.

A man's cough drew Norris to pull back. "Turn," he whispered, guiding her to pivot toward the wall.

"What are you doing in here?" the retainer asked.

"What does it look like?" Norris replied coolly. She'd heard him employ that tone before and imagined it must make his soldiers snap to attention. Hearing him use it to keep her safe was surprisingly arousing.

"I beg your pardon," the retainer said, sounding a bit uncertain. "This is a private area."

"I had hoped so, but apparently it's not." Norris's tone now carried a tinge of irony and she had to fight to keep from giggling. *What was wrong with her?* This was not a time for laughter.

"I'm afraid I have to ask you to leave." Yes, he definitely sounded unsure. Cate could picture what Norris must look like, his icy gaze fixed arrogantly on the retainer.

"Would you mind giving us a modicum of privacy? I'd prefer to obscure my companion's identity. I'm sure you understand."

"Of course. I'll just turn."

"Thank you." Norris took her hand and tugged her from the corner. "Keep your head down," he murmured.

They moved quickly and didn't stop once they reached the corridor. He guided her away, retracing the path he'd used earlier. After a minute, she pulled him to a stop. "Where's Grey?"

"I didn't see her." Norris let go of Cate's hand. She glanced down at her now lonely appendage, sorry to see him go.

"Here." Grey came from a room across the hall looking pained. "I had to dash off when the guard came back."

"I thought we had a little more time. Was he early?" Cate asked.

Grey's expression was grim. "I think so. Did he find you?"

"We improvised," Norris said.

Cate gave Grey a look that she hoped would be interpreted as "don't ask."

"I need to return the key." Grey held out her hand as Cate withdrew the key and dropped it into her upturned palm. Grey glanced between them. "Is it acceptable for me to leave you alone?"

"We've *been* alone," Norris noted wryly. "We shall go our separate ways."

Grey nodded before taking herself off toward a set of servant stairs to deliver the key to wherever she'd obtained it. Cate had asked last time how she'd acquired it, but Grey would only say that it was her job to take care of the difficult details.

Norris looked down at her. "Can you find your way back to your room?"

Cate tried not to stare at his mouth, but the imprint of his lips lingered on hers and the heat in her body didn't dissipate. In fact, the longer she looked at him, the more her desire smoldered. She averted her gaze. "We are *not* going our separate ways—not yet. You still owe me an explanation about what you meant in the library. You said you know what to do. Tell me."

He glanced up and down the hallway. "Not here."

She grabbed his hand, heedless of the attraction sparking between them. "My chamber is this way."

He pulled her to a stop and dropped her hand again, quickly, as if she might burn him. "We can't go there. Your reputation is already at risk. Where is your sense?" His tone was stern, but there was an underlying heat. She'd never heard him sound like that, as if he wasn't completely and utterly in control.

"Everyone is in the front hall listening to Septon. He'll go on for quite some time."

"You don't know that *everyone* is there," he said quietly, but with urgency. "And the servants are not. I may be somewhat new to my role, but I'm aware that servants talk and are often the source of gossip and rumor."

Cate rolled her eyes. "Just come with me. There's a sitting room we can use and we'll leave the door open."

"On second thought, a private situation is preferable." He

went to the door of the room Grey had vacated and carefully opened it to reveal a small, unlit storage chamber. "This will work." He beckoned for her to follow.

Once she stepped inside, he closed the door and plunged them into darkness. Only a strip of light from the illuminated corridor broke into the pitch black. She didn't like that she couldn't see him. On the other hand, she was intensely aware of his scent, his heat, and his proximity.

As if he'd read her mind, he took a step back.

Cate forced herself to focus on their mission. "Now talk."

"You're a bit of an autocrat," he said softly. "I'll add that to your list."

"Add anything you like, just tell me what you meant." She fairly growled the last, her impatience taking over.

"You needn't worry about not finding anything because I know where the tapestry is located."

He did? "Where?"

"Worcester, near my childhood home."

"How do you know?" And *how long* had he known?

"Mason hid it there. He told us this afternoon."

He'd known about it for hours! He'd known about it when they'd met before dinner. He'd known about it as she'd furiously searched the secret library. She reached out to find where he was standing. Her hand connected with his chest. She'd meant to lightly smack him—he more than deserved it —but as soon as she touched him, the manner of her contact changed. She snatched her hand away before she did something foolish, like kiss him again.

"I didn't wish to tell you until tonight. I was certain you'd want to go after it directly, and it was important to me to visit Septon."

He was right, drat it all. She *would* have wanted to pursue the tapestry straightaway. "It made sense that you wanted to talk to Septon since you were so close, and Worcester is a day away." *She* could already be in Worcester. Except they were working as a team and that wouldn't have been fair. "I wish you would have told me earlier. If we're to work together, I want to know that I can trust you to be honest."

"You can. As I said, I planned to tell you this evening. I was never going to keep it from you. Whereas I have to wonder if you would've shared this evening's excursion to Septon's secret library if I hadn't followed you."

He made another valid point, but like him, she'd planned to disclose any information she'd learned—*if* she'd found anything. "I didn't know if I would discover anything helpful. If I had, I would've told you about it."

"I shall have to take your word for it."

She couldn't tell if he was being genuine or if there might be a thread of sarcasm. This inability to see him only made him even harder to read. "I spoke to Septon just before he started his presentation," she said. "He doesn't know the men who tried to purchase the tapestry."

Silence greeted her revelation. She could almost feel his disappointment. "I'm sorry he didn't know anything to help you. But you still have this footman at Stratton Hall to interrogate."

"Yes, and I plan to do just that after we retrieve the tapestry," he said.

They were going to find it! She allowed herself to feel a rush of excitement and impending triumph. Working to contain her jubilation, she asked as casually as possible, "Do you wish to leave tomorrow?"

"Yes, the earlier the better. Will Septon be offended that we aren't staying for the duration of the party?"

Cate frowned into the darkness. "No, but he'll question why we're leaving together."

"Then we won't leave together. I will depart at first light, and you will depart later."

It grated on her that he would leave first, but that was silly. She could trust him. She had no other choice.

"There is an inn in Worcester—the Black Hound—meet me there. I'll arrange for a room for you and Grey."

"Thank you," she said, appreciating his thoughtfulness. They were now most definitely a team. "We'll see you in Worcester, then."

She reached for the door as he did the same, and their hands collided. Instead of jerking back, she hesitated, inviting the rush of sensation that took her back to that surprising kiss.

He withdrew his hand. "You go ahead."

Cate's heart pounded. He was so close and in the darkness was so . . . anonymous. *Secret.* Who would know if she kissed him again? She pivoted, bringing her body nearly against his just in front of the closed door. "Norris," she murmured, setting her palm against the front of his coat and sliding it up.

His head bent—she felt the movement and sensed his closeness. "Miss Bowen."

She stood on her toes, but couldn't find his mouth. He hadn't come down far enough.

His hand stole along her waist, sending a shiver up her spine. The latch of the door clicked and light spilled into the room from the corridor behind her. "I'll see you in Worcester." He spoke very near her mouth, the whisper of his words gliding over her with promise.

But it was to be unfulfilled.

He stood back and ushered her into the corridor. Then the door snapped shut, and she was alone.

The light from the sconces and the sudden drop in temperature—or was that merely her imagination?—cooled her ardor. She put a hand to her temple and admonished herself for being foolish. This was going to be David Iscove all over again if she wasn't careful. Steeling herself, she strode away from the room. Norris wasn't Iscove, and she wasn't going to lose her head. She was closer to her dream than she'd ever been, and there was no way she was going to let a man, no matter how attractive or alluring, stand in her path.

~

*E*lijah leaned back against the door, his pulse thudding through his body, and listened to her walk away. *Blood and bones,* that had been a near thing. He stood there in the dark, willing his erection to stand the hell down so he could leave the bloody room.

What the devil had she been thinking? Kissing him? Nearly kissing him a second time? What sort of woman of her station did that? Granted, he had next to no experience with women of her station, but he had to assume that a young, unmarried miss shouldn't know how to kiss. Yet Miss Bowen had. She'd claimed his mouth with an expertise that had practically melted his bones. It wasn't as if he'd gone *that* long without a woman. There'd been a few stops on his journey home, and upon arriving in London, he'd visited an elegant brothel where he'd been serviced quite well. It had reminded him, in a bittersweet fashion, of Lily, his mistress, whom he'd left in Australia. She'd offered to come with him, but he'd declined, knowing that she loved her homeland— she was the daughter of a woman who'd been transported— and preferring to maintain an unfettered life. Indeed, Lily was the only woman he'd ever kept and he couldn't imagine doing so again. And certainly not Miss Bowen.

Elijah massaged his forehead. Finally judging himself fit, he turned and left the closet. Thankfully Miss Bowen was nowhere to be seen.

He strode purposefully for his chamber, hoping that Wade would be there. He wasn't disappointed.

"You're in early, my lord," Wade said.

"All in all, it's been a bit of a frustrating evening." He didn't plan to tell Wade about the kissing business. "Unfortunately, Septon doesn't know who these other men who wanted to buy the tapestry are."

"I'm sorry for that, my lord. But we still have the footman at Stratton Hall."

Elijah unknotted his cravat. "Indeed we do. And as it happens, Lord Stratton is a distant relation of Miss Bowen's, so we have an entrée."

Wade held out his hand to take the cravat from Elijah. "That is an excellent turn of events, my lord. Below stairs, I heard that Lady Stratton is Septon's lover."

"Yes, I heard that as well," Elijah said.

"And her son is here, Lord Kersey. It's the first time he's come to Septon House. Apparently Lady Stratton is delighted by his presence. They've been estranged for many years."

"So Miss Bowen informed me. She is Kersey's cousin, if you can believe it."

Wade's light brown eyes flickered surprise. "Is there some connection, do you suppose? With the footman at Stratton Hall?"

"To Miss Bowen? I doubt it." Elijah tried to puzzle how Dalby might have made his way from Cosgrove to Stratton Hall, but couldn't figure it out. "I admit I find it odd that she has a connection to the place where this footman was able to find a position after being turned out without a reference."

Wade eyed him curiously. "But you think it is merely coincidence?"

Elijah blew out a breath. "I don't know what to think. I can't believe Miss Bowen was involved with trying to steal the tapestry or with Matthew's death." Was that because he liked her and found her attractive? None of that held any consequence in the larger scheme, and he'd do better to remember that. As he'd indicated before they'd left for Bath —he meant to keep her close until he figured it all out.

"Is your plan still to travel to Worcester tomorrow to find the tapestry?"

"It is. Miss Bowen and Grey will meet us at the Black Hound in Worcester. Once we have the tapestry, we'll continue on to Stratton Hall."

"A sound plan, my lord. Are we to leave in the morning, then?"

"At first light." Elijah shrugged out of his coat, and the paper he'd taken from Septon's library fluttered to the floor.

"What's that?" Wade asked, bending to pick it up.

Elijah watched as Wade opened it. "Something I thought might be a good idea to borrow."

Wade perused the document. "Is this a drawing of the tapestry? Can't read a word of what's written beneath it."

"Neither can I, but Miss Bowen says she can. She's not aware I've taken it, though. For now, let's keep this between us."

"Very well." Wade refolded it. "Shall I pack it in your case?"

"Actually, I prefer to keep it on my person. Tuck it under the pillow for now. Did you by chance see Grey? At dinner, perhaps?"

Wade stashed the parchment as Elijah asked. "I did, though she disappeared immediately afterward."

"Yes, she was otherwise engaged in assisting Miss Bowen with her sleuthing activities."

Wade arched a brow, but didn't pose a query. "We didn't have a chance to discuss our meeting with Mason."

"Miss Bowen will enlighten her." Elijah moved into the

dressing chamber and removed his waistcoat, handing it to Wade.

"She's rather pretty."

Elijah shot him a disbelieving glance. "Grey?" Elijah tried to think of how he would characterize her. She wasn't *not* pretty, he supposed. He thought her hair might be brown in color, but it was always pulled back in a rather severe knot. She had blue eyes if he wasn't mistaken, and yes, they were clear and . . . pretty.

Elijah slipped his shoes off and nudged them toward Wade. "You realize she has a good five inches on you?"

Wade flashed Elijah a look that said he was not amused. "More like four."

Elijah tried not to smile. "Let's keep our focus."

Wade picked up the shoes and tucked them into the traveling case in the corner. "Does that include you and Miss Bowen?"

"There is no 'me and Miss Bowen.'" He tried not to think of her kiss or her almost kiss or his ragingly inappropriate reaction to both.

"I understand." Wade's tone said he didn't believe him, but Elijah didn't wish to debate the matter. Best to put it from his mind entirely.

"Before you turn in, will you inform Septon's butler that we're leaving? Tell him . . ." He blinked at Wade. "I don't know what to tell him."

"I shall inform him that you have a previous engagement, my lord."

"Wade, you are astonishingly efficient at this new position. Tell me again, why did you fall into crime?"

He shrugged. "Because that's what we did when there were too many of us to feed. Some of us are lucky and find our way, align ourselves with people who help us along." He gave Elijah a meaningful, appreciative glance as he folded the clothing and packed it away.

Elijah knew he'd communicated with the siblings with whom he still had contact—two younger sisters who'd found their way and were now married. The rest of his family was unfortunately lost to him. "It takes a particular fellow to rebel successfully against circumstance."

"I'll run down and inform the butler. Will there be anything else?"

Elijah felt restless. Though he planned to rise early, he didn't think he could yet sleep. "Perhaps some brandy or better still, whisky. And some cards. If you're of a mind." They'd passed many nights in Australia and on board the ship playing cards and drinking.

"Sounds about right." With a nod, Wade took himself off.

Elijah wondered briefly what Wade would do if he encountered Grey. Would he steal a kiss, or exercise the same control Elijah had barely managed? And if it were the latter, would he regret it as bitterly as Elijah did?

What happened to putting this from his mind?

Swearing under his breath, he strode back into the bedchamber to await Wade. The sooner he delivered the tapestry to Miss Bowen, the sooner he could exorcise her from his life. He needed her family connection to visit Stratton Hall, however.

Bloody hell, tapestry or not, it looked as though he'd be saddled with Miss Bowen—and her kissable lips—if he had any hope of unraveling the circumstances of Matthew's death.

CHAPTER 9

*T*he journey to Worcester had taken several hours, ample time for Cate to relive the kiss with Norris at least two dozen times. Give or take a dozen.

She both regretted not kissing him a second time and counted herself fortunate. There was no telling how much farther a second kiss might have taken them. And now that she was about to see him again, the memory of his lips seemed even more present than it had all day.

Put the kiss from your mind!

Straightening her shoulders, she stepped into the private dining room at the Black Hound.

Norris stood from the table and offered her a bow.

She dipped a brief curtsey in return. It felt formal after the intimacy of the night before, but she found it was necessary if they were to maintain an appropriate association. "I received your kind dinner invitation. Thank you."

"I trust your journey was pleasant," he said. "The weather was especially fine."

"Quite. And yours?"

"It was long, but pleasant enough."

The inn's footman held out her chair so she could sit. Norris retook the chair he'd vacated.

She'd had enough of the awkward, stilted conversation. They were business associates—partners even—and they could move past a silly kiss. She draped her napkin across her lap. "Now that we're here, will you tell me where we'll find the tapestry?"

Norris frowned slightly and shook his head. He darted a glance at the footman, who served their soup from the sideboard. Once the bowls were placed before them, Norris looked up at the young man. "Would it be possible for us to serve ourselves?"

"I'll have to fetch the rest. It won't be quite as hot." He appeared concerned about this.

Cate smiled at him to ease his anxiety. "It's all right."

The footman nodded and left. Cate helped herself to the soup while they waited for the food to be delivered and the footman to leave them alone.

Once he'd gone, she gave Norris a pointed look. "Here we are, alone again." Did she need to draw attention to it? She wasn't doing a very good job of moving past anything.

"Indeed we are." He arched a brow at her. "I know it doesn't bother you, given the way you and your companion traipse about, barely adhering to the confines of your station. I've decided to try to not let it bother me."

"But it does." She wasn't sure how she felt about that. On the one hand, she found his condescension regarding her "station" infuriating, although expected. On the other, she appreciated the care with which he handled her reputation.

He lifted a shoulder and sampled the soup. "I've arranged to borrow mounts for our excursion tomorrow."

"Three of them?" She was nearly certain he'd include Grey, but wanted to make sure.

"Four, actually. Wade will be joining us."

That made sense. After all, he'd described his manservant as his "Grey," which in retrospect made her want to smile. Everyone should have a Grey. "And where are we going exactly?" Cate asked.

"Not terribly far—maybe three miles. I was raised near here."

"Not in Bath?"

"No, my mother moved there after my father passed. She sold his house, which had been my grandfather's, and bought the town house in Bath."

She couldn't determine how he felt about that, but then Norris was quite careful with his personal expressions. She suspected his mother troubled him, given that he'd characterized their meeting as "stressful," and that his relationship with his brother had perhaps been tense due to Matthew's penchant for fancy. Beyond that, his emotions were difficult to discern. "How sad to lose something that had been in your family. How old were you when your father passed?"

"Six and ten."

He could be frustratingly economical with his speech, and she was beginning to understand that he was most brief when the topic likely made him uncomfortable. Perhaps his father's death had been difficult. "Were you and your father close?"

He snapped his gaze to hers. "Yes. May we get back to the matter at hand?"

Definitely uncomfortable. "My apologies. My mother says I'm too intense."

"What an odd word choice, but I have to agree. I'll add that to your list."

She smiled at that, enjoying their absurd lists. "The tapestry is at your childhood home, then?"

He shook his head as he set his spoon down and dabbed at his mouth with his napkin. "No. Thankfully it's nowhere that will require us to interrupt anyone or ask to gain access. We'll have to intrude on someone's land, but that won't be difficult. The location is somewhat removed. We shouldn't have any trouble."

Was he being purposely vague? She understood his desire for secrecy about their mission, but did he really think someone was standing outside the room trying to hear their conversation? "Is there a reason you aren't just telling me where it is?"

"I'm suspicious and secretive, remember?"

She gave him a wry look. "How could I forget?" She didn't press the issue. There was no need. Tomorrow she would have the tapestry and she'd be another step closer to Dyrnwyn.

They finished their soup and stood to help themselves to the next course. Norris waited until she was seated before he sat.

She watched him eat for a moment. A mistake, for it brought her attention to his lips. They looked as firm and soft as they'd felt. Blinking, she returned her attention to her plate before he could catch her staring.

"I find it odd that the footman who attempted to steal the tapestry finds himself employed at Stratton Hall," Norris said between bites.

Cate looked at him in surprise. "Do you?"

"It all seems strangely connected. The footman going without a reference from Cosgrove to Stratton Hall. Lady Stratton's connection to Septon. Your connection to both Septon and Stratton."

Her chest squeezed with agitation. "I'm not certain what you're implying."

"I don't think you had anything to do with the attempted theft or Matthew's death," he said. She relaxed at his words. "But you must agree it is odd."

"It is indeed. It's as if Fate wanted you to find this footman."

Norris scooped a spoonful of parsnips. "I don't believe in such nonsense."

"Like you don't believe in the Bible—didn't you say something to that effect?"

"I don't believe there's a puppet master deciding what happens to us. We make our own lot in life, for better or worse."

"A pragmatic view, but does that mean you have no faith whatsoever?"

"I have faith that Wade will awaken me in the morning and that my saddle will remain secure around my mount. But if you're asking whether I believe some invisible person or power will cure my ills and answer my prayers, the answer is no."

"Why?"

"Suffice it to say that none of my prayers were ever answered. After a time, you have no choice but to stop believing." The frigidity and conviction in his tone chilled her. She wanted to ask about his prayers, but doubted he'd tell her. They'd already veered into an uncomfortable topic and she was all but certain he'd said more than he'd intended.

She wanted to banish some of the ice from his eyes. "It sounds as if you lost faith in something—or someone—a long time ago. But as you say, you have faith in Wade. I should feel privileged if you would also have faith in me." She lifted her wineglass and studied him over the edge.

He said nothing, but his gaze seemed to warm. "We've lost track of our subject, I'm afraid." His attention reverted to his plate. "I should like to visit Stratton Hall after we attain our objective. Are you able to secure an invitation?"

She exhaled, unaware that she'd held her breath. Like him, she returned her focus to her meal and took a sip of wine. "Certainly. Stratton is always delighted to entertain male guests. It gives him an excuse to have a libidinous party, not that he needs one. I do believe he keeps at least two or three women on staff whose sole purpose is to pleasure him."

Norris, who'd also taken a drink of wine, now coughed and sputtered. "Good God, Miss Bowen, have you no guile whatsoever?"

She grinned. "Why would I have need of that?"

He swiped the napkin over his mouth again, but not before she glimpsed his smile. "I begin to wonder what manner of woman you actually are. You are aware of . . . *things* I would think you ought not be aware of, and you kiss as though you've done it before—and not just once or twice. Has behavior changed so much since I left England?"

Hearing him mention the kiss caused heat to pool in her belly and rush to her face. She prayed her cheeks weren't flaming scarlet—not from embarrassment, but from the completely inconvenient desire she felt for him. "They have not. However, I believe I've explained to you that I am no ordinary female. I have no interest in Society or making a match on the Marriage Mart. I do care about my reputation in that I don't wish to bring shame to my family. Beyond that, I don't care what people think of me—you included." She gave him a saucy look. It seemed she couldn't help but provoke him.

His eyes had widened briefly as she'd spoken. Now he looked at her with something akin to curiosity, as if she were a conundrum, and she supposed she was. "You are the most unusual female I've ever met."

"I shall take that as a compliment."

"Please do."

She froze for a moment, wondering if she'd heard him right. He *had* just complimented her. The warmth suffusing her intensified.

After several minutes, he set his utensils down and took another drink of wine. "I should like to know how you came to kiss like that."

The air crackled with their mutual attraction. At least she thought it was mutual. He'd responded to the kiss, hadn't he? And he was currently looking at her as if he wanted to do it again.

A tremor went through her, and she set her own silverware down. Unlike him, she wasn't opposed to sharing revelatory details. "I was . . . in a courtship."

"And what happened to this despicable fellow?"

She bit back a laugh. Iscove *was* despicable, but Norris couldn't know that. "Why do you characterize him like that?"

"Because he kissed you and didn't marry you."

"You've kissed me."

His eyes narrowed. "On the contrary, *you* kissed *me*. If you recall, I prevented you from kissing me a second time."

His words stung, which was foolish. He was behaving like a consummate gentleman, the absolute opposite of Iscove. She should feel relieved and happy.

"It doesn't matter, because I didn't wish to marry him." She might've. Once. For a very short time. But she didn't admit that to anyone, even to herself.

"Yet you kissed him."

If she were a man, this would be an altogether different conversation. "Why not? Just because I prefer to remain independent shouldn't mean I can't enjoy myself. A lifetime without romantic entanglement sounds horribly dull, does it not? I enjoyed kissing you, and I don't regret it."

His eyes seemed to smolder before he looked away. "Forgive me. I shouldn't be asking you such personal questions. I quite forgot myself."

"It's all right," she said softly, not wanting him to feel

awkward. She liked talking to him, sharing with him. "For some reason I am rather comfortable in your presence."

"For the sake of propriety, we should stick to our mission."

Yes, they should, but she'd never been terribly interested in propriety. "May I ask you a question?"

His eyes narrowed again. "You may, but I don't promise to answer it."

"When do you plan to take a countess?"

His answer came surprisingly fast. "I don't."

"Ever?"

"No."

Fascinated, she leaned forward. "Why not?"

His lips lifted in a half-smile, and his eyes gleamed enigmatically. "I beg you to forgive me for not answering."

She was more curious than ever, but now wasn't the time to pester him.

When they finished dinner, he stood and held her chair while she got to her feet. "What is the name of that loathsome reprobate?"

"Why?"

"I should like to know in case I encounter him in the future."

She doubted that would be possible. Iscove had cheated several gentlemen in a card game and had disappeared. He wouldn't likely show his face in Society anytime soon, if ever.

She didn't mean to tell him, but the icy promise in his gaze was too magnetic to ignore. "David Iscove."

"Mr. Iscove had better hope he doesn't cross my path. In the military we dealt with reprehensible men in ruthless fashion."

Cate shivered. Not from the threat he offered, but because of what it meant. She had somehow become important enough to him that he would guard her honor. There was no way he could be Iscove all over again. He could be something far worse—someone who could steal her heart.

~

*E*lijah should have been exhausted after rising early the day before and traveling, but he'd awakened several times in the night. Every time, he'd had some dream involving Miss Bowen. In one, she'd read to him from the Bible and he'd hung on her every word. In another, he'd challenged the faceless knave Iscove to a duel and shot him in the chest. And in the last, he'd taken control and been the one to kiss her. Only he hadn't stopped there.

He watched her mounted the borrowed horse with the aid of a block in the yard, and had to avert his gaze from the enticing swell of her hip encased in a riding habit that allowed her to ride astride.

"Rough night?" Wade asked quietly as he checked the bridle on Elijah's animal.

Elijah gave him a perturbed look, which earned a smile from the valet. They took to their mounts in the yard of the inn.

"Ready?" Miss Bowen asked from atop her horse, standing next to Grey and her beast, who danced uncertainly. Judging from her seat and hold on the reins, Elijah suspected riding might be the one vulnerability in Grey's armor.

Elijah looked to Wade and inclined his head toward Grey.

Wade nodded. "I'll keep an eye on her."

Satisfied that all would be well, Elijah rode from the yard. Miss Bowen kept good pace with him as they traveled out of town along a slender road in the direction of his childhood home. They wouldn't go that far—their destination was before that—and Elijah felt a pang of regret. He was surprised to find he wanted to see the old place, to recall the happy times he'd shared there with his father and with Matthew.

There had been no happy occasions with his mother. She preferred to stay with friends in Bath, but during the infrequent times she spent at home, she'd been irritable and demanding, practically impossible to satisfy. She'd always left in a huff, causing Elijah to wonder what he'd done wrong. His father, ever the calming element in the household, had eventually convinced him that it wasn't his fault, that his mother was simply a frigid woman. The damage, however, had been done. She'd ensured Elijah wouldn't trust a woman to treat him with generosity, respect, and definitely not love.

Lost in memories for the duration of the ride, Elijah was surprised when Miss Bowen rode up beside him and asked if they were nearly there.

"Yes." He led them toward a copse and slowed, guiding them around the trees. As the outcropping of rock from the hillside came into view, Elijah could practically hear his brother's laugh as they played chase and scaled the rock, taunting each other about who could climb faster.

Miss Bowen walked her horse up beside him. "You're smiling. Why?"

He gestured toward the hill rising past the trees. "I spent a lot of time climbing that as a lad."

"It looks a bit dangerous with all of that exposed rock."

"Perhaps, but children don't think of such hazards." He looked at her riding astride, heedless of propriety. "But then, you aren't a child and I'm not certain you think of such hazards either."

She glanced down. "This isn't dangerous, just unacceptable."

"You and Grey traveling around Britain on your own isn't dangerous?" He looked behind them to see how far back

Grey and Wade were. She was having difficulty with her horse, but Wade looked to have the situation in hand.

"We're quite careful. I do appreciate your concern." She said the last a little too sweetly, maybe with a touch of sarcasm.

As they fully rounded the copse, Miss Bowen let out a surprised gasp. "There's a folly!"

The structure, built by their eccentric neighbor, Mr. McConley, to mimic a Roman temple, was the largest of four different follies his property boasted. For a time, McConley had even allowed a hermit to inhabit one of them, but he'd moved on after a year.

This folly, however, had been Elijah and Matthew's favorite. It was the first McConley built and as such had been a good fifteen or twenty years old back then, giving it a wild, natural quality they'd loved. Now it was even more over-grown, with vines climbing the walls and shrubbery combatting for space inside the open-air structure.

He brought his horse to a halt outside the building and tethered the beast before helping Miss Bowen to dismount. He touched her as little as necessary, preferring that they keep their distance after the lurid images that had filled his dreams.

She looked at him as she brushed at her skirt. "This is a rather good hiding place. I can't imagine anyone looking for it here."

"Yes, it's not surprising when I think about it. Matthew enjoyed hiding objects when we were children, and he hid any number of my toys in this exact spot." Elijah pictured him laughing and rubbing his hands together with glee, his blue eyes sparkling with mischief.

Miss Bowen's gentle touch on his arm startled him. "I can see how much he meant to you. I'm so sorry he's gone."

Elijah strode forward into the folly.

Miss Bowen followed him and tugged on his elbow when she caught up. "Why do you do that?"

He moved away. "What?" He was being purposefully obtuse, and he didn't care.

She exhaled. "Never mind. Where is this special spot?"

"This way." He went out through the back and stalked toward the hill, to the rock exposed at the base.

The morning sun beat on his back, reminding him of summer days with Matthew. Shoving the memories away, he reached the rocky area and pushed through the shrubbery.

He saw the opening in the rock and knelt. Could he still fit inside?

No. The opening was too narrow. He turned his head and looked up at Miss Bowen, blinking at the bright sky behind her. Wade and Grey approached from the folly.

"Is it in there, do you think?" Miss Bowen indicated the small cave. "I can fit through the hole."

"It'll be pitch black inside."

She shrugged, appearing fearless. "It can't be very large."

"No, just big enough for two boys to escape a torrential downpour."

"You and your brother?" she asked.

He nodded as the specific memory filled his mind. Mother had been at home and had become furious when they'd returned soaked and filthy. Matthew, who'd affected a sneezing fit to garner sympathy, had been ushered directly into a warm bath. She'd blamed Elijah for the entire event, heaping admonishments and scorn upon him until he'd cried, which had only further provoked her anger. She'd dunked him in a cold bath and sent him to bed without supper. Long-buried hurt scalded his insides and he couldn't speak any further.

She squatted down beside him. "Move aside."

Elijah pulled himself from the past and scooted over to let

her pass. Her backside, a welcome distraction from his dark memories, drew his grateful attention as she wriggled into the opening.

She disappeared into the hole and Elijah's gut clenched. What if some animal was currently using it as a home?

He stuck his head into the void. "Miss Bowen?"

"I'm here. You were right, it's very dark. I'm just feeling around. I hope there isn't anything dangerous in here." She laughed, and it seemed she didn't feel any of the apprehension currently tightening Elijah's shoulders.

"Oh!"

Elijah jumped, hitting his head on the rock. "What is it?"

"I found something. Here." A solid object came at him through the opening. He withdrew his head and pulled out the long box.

His apprehension turned to excitement. He set the case aside and turned back to Miss Bowen, who appeared in the hole. She reached forward and he clasped her hand, tugging her out as he'd done the box.

She blinked in the sunlight and then fixed on their discovery. "Open it." She sounded as anxious as he felt.

Wade and Grey knelt down beside them, creating a circle around the box.

Elijah glanced at them. Everyone would be exceedingly disappointed if the tapestry wasn't inside . . .

He unlatched the top and carefully opened it. There, rolled up, was the flaming sword tapestry.

Miss Bowen reached in and gently picked it up. She held the tapestry toward Elijah. "Take the end."

He did so and she unrolled it, exposing the intricate needlework to the bright summer day. It was exquisite, the detail impressive and the colors vibrant—a true piece of art. "The drawing on the paper didn't do it justice," he said.

"It's just as I remembered." Miss Bowen lightly touched

the sword, almost reverent in her attention. "Turn it over." She sucked in a breath as they flipped it . . .

He watched her scan the reverse, noted the enthusiasm slipping from her expression to be replaced with frustration.

"There's nothing here," she said.

Elijah recalled what Garber had said about the backside and saw what he meant. There were a few places where the stitching was uneven or perhaps tangled into a knot. "You were hoping for an actual map."

She looked at him, her brows pitched at a furious angle. "Or a clue. *Something*."

"Turn it back," Grey said gruffly. "Maybe there's something we're missing."

They flipped it back over. Elijah wanted to look at it from the same angle. "Here, take this corner," he said to Wade as he moved closer to Miss Bowen so they could both look at it straight on.

Miss Bowen gave her top corner to Grey so that both she and Wade held a side. They all studied the image for several minutes.

Miss Bowen made a defeated sound. "I don't see anything, just a regular depiction of a battle scene."

"I rather doubt regular battles include flaming swords," Wade said with a touch of humor.

Grey's mouth ticked up, but Miss Bowen tossed him a glare.

"What battle is this?" Elijah asked.

"No one is certain," Miss Bowen said. "It could be any one of the battles Arthur and his knights fought."

Elijah pointed at the man wielding the flaming sword. "This is Arthur?"

"More likely Gareth, if de Valery's *Ballads of Gareth* are to be believed, and given the contemporary poem in my father's library, that's what I'm inclined to think."

"What is this on his shield?" The design was a quartered block with two red lions rampant against a gold field and two gold lions rampant against a red field. "Would it tell you with absolute certainty who this is?"

"No, because it's Owen Glendower's banner, which at the time the tapestry was created was simply a popular symbol of Welsh identification."

Elijah couldn't quite recall who Glendower was, but he didn't understand her certainty. "Is it possible this is Owen Glendower instead of Arthur or one of his knights?"

"This tapestry was created shortly after Glendower disappeared—he was the last true prince of Wales. He led the Welsh rebellion in the early fifteenth century. It's likely that whoever crafted it was a Welshwoman and chose to use his banner to signify the tapestry's importance to Wales."

"Or it could actually *be* Owen Glendower and one of his battles."

Miss Bowen jerked her head up, her lips parted. But she snapped them closed and stared off into the distance for a moment. When she looked back at him, her lips were pursed and her gaze was skeptical. "That would be a significant departure from the previous line of thought."

"That doesn't mean it's wrong."

"No." She shook her head. "It's just . . . I have to think about this. Grey, will you?" She relinquished the tapestry to Grey and stepped away, brushing the dirt from her dark green riding costume.

Grey took possession of the tapestry and Elijah stood, following Miss Bowen.

"What's wrong?" he asked, walking alongside her.

"Nothing's wrong. I'm just trying to think this through. If that's Owen Glendower in the tapestry, is that really the sword I think it is?"

Elijah thought about everything she'd told him. "I thought

that document said it was the sword, that the tapestry was a map leading to it?"

She froze in her tracks. "Yes." She swung to face him. "I wish I'd studied that document more closely, or better yet, taken the time to write it down word for word."

"You're in luck." He pulled the parchment from his coat and held it out to her. "I thought it might be a good thing to have."

She took it from him, her dark eyes wide. "You folded it? I realize you're not familiar with historical documents, so I shan't blame you. However, in future, never *ever* crease a valuable piece of history such as this." She opened it carefully.

"My apologies."

Staring at the parchment, she shook her head. "I can't believe you took this. When Septon finds out we took this, he'll be livid."

"How will he know who took it?"

She looked at him in admonishment. "He won't—he doesn't even know I'm aware of the library—but that doesn't excuse your stealing it."

"*Borrowing* it," he corrected. "You never did tell me how you knew about his 'secret' library."

"I'm very clever." Her tone was haughty, angry.

"Not clever enough to figure out that was Owen Glendower."

Her eyes sparked as she glared up at him. "We don't know if that's true. Now, if you'll be quiet for a moment, I'd like to read this."

Elijah silently chided himself for provoking her. She wasn't angry with him; she was angry with herself. He'd seen something she hadn't and that grated on her pride, something he now understood was incredibly important to her. Yes, she was a most unusual—and exciting—woman.

He waited patiently while she reread the document. When at last she looked up, she no longer appeared upset. Instead, she looked eager.

She pointed to the words. "It says, 'Tapestry depicting sword of flames, stitched early fifteenth century.'" The timing fit Glendower if he was an early-fifteenth-century leader. "'The sword exists. One need only use the tapestry to find it.' That's how I determined it was a map."

He comprehended why she'd made that assessment. "There's more," he said.

She moved her finger to below the drawing of the tapestry. "It's just a description. I admit I didn't pay close attention when I found it—the part I just read to you drew my focus. 'The tapestry was stitched by Alice,'" she read. "'It measures twenty-two inches by twenty-two inches and took seven months to complete. The castle, situated atop a rock with a proximity to water, with mountains in the distance, could be any number of strongholds, though it is believed to be Welsh.'"

"Is that a clue?" he asked.

"I have to consider it is. It was foolish of me not to read it carefully when I first found it." She pursed her lips again. "Is it directing us to a specific castle?"

He wasn't sure if she was asking him, or merely musing aloud. He chose to answer. "It seems that way."

"A Welsh castle next to water and mountains . . . " She looked up at the sky with a contemplative expression. "I've seen so many of them."

"I've seen none." A bead of frustration lodged in his chest. He wished he could contribute more. He'd somehow been pulled into this mystery and currently found himself unwilling to disentangle himself. Or perhaps it was more accurate to say that he didn't wish to disentangle himself from *her*.

She turned and stalked back to the tapestry, squatting down again. He followed her, but remained standing.

She ran her fingertips over the castle stitched in the upper right corner. "If you're right, that this is Glendower, then it could be Harlech Castle. It was the final stronghold of Glendower's rebellion. It fell back to the English in 1409 after a siege, during which Edmund Mortimer died."

He wasn't surprised that she knew the history, but he was still impressed. He couldn't tell if she'd reached a conclusion or if she was merely thinking it through. "Does this look like Harlech? I presume you've been there."

"I have. And yes, it does bear a resemblance." She shook her head. "I will take better care in the future when I look at artifacts."

She stood and faced him, her eyes animated and her lips curving into a smile that held a barely suppressed excitement. "I think you *are* right—that this *is* Glendower. We need to go to Harlech."

Elijah felt a burst of elation at having made a significant contribution after all. "Harlech is on the coast?"

She nodded. "It's at least a two-day journey."

"Especially since we plan to stop at Stratton Hall."

She exchanged a glance with Grey that provoked an unsettling feeling in Elijah's gut.

He lightly touched her shoulder and inclined his head away from Grey and Wade. She stood and followed him out of earshot of their companions.

"You do still plan to accompany me to Stratton Hall?"

"Yes."

He didn't like the hesitant quality to her one-word answer. "What aren't you telling me?"

She fidgeted with her skirt. "I wonder if Grey and I might continue ahead after we stop with you briefly."

Disappointment sprouted in his chest, and he *despised* that emotion. He gritted his teeth against the unwelcome feeling. "I had thought you would assist with my portion of this endeavor."

Her brow creased. "Isn't getting you into Stratton Hall helpful?"

"Yes." It was his turn to inject that single word with a wealth of doubt.

Her dark eyes held a sheen of uncertainty. "Will you join us when you've completed your interview with the footman?"

Was that an invitation, or was she merely being polite? He could see her wanting to obtain the treasure on her own, particularly without male involvement. "I'm not sure you need me to. My primary goal must be determining the circumstances of Matthew's death." He'd lost sight of that as he'd become caught up in Miss Bowen's quest, or more accurately—caught up in Miss Bowen. "If I'm able to join you at Harlech, I will do so. In the meantime, let us be on our way. We'll arrive at Stratton Hall by midafternoon, and you should be able to complete at least part of your journey to Harlech."

He turned to go, but she touched the front of his coat briefly before snatching her hand away. "Thank you. I don't know if I would've puzzled this out without your keen powers of observation."

Is that why she wanted him to join her at Harlech? Not because she wanted to share the experience with him, but because of what he could provide? *Hell*, what did he care about experiencing something with her?

He turned on his heel and strode toward the horses, lifting his hand to beckon Wade to follow.

As they rode back to the inn, he welcomed the irritation their impending separation wrought. They'd become far too friendly during this association and now that it seemed she was on her way to finding her precious sword, he could be rid of her at last.

Yes, he welcomed the frustration even as it bothered him to feel it in the first place. He'd much rather do what came naturally, which was to feel nothing. Why, then, couldn't he?

CHAPTER 10

ate shifted in her seat. Her coach was well-sprung, but she'd spent a great deal of time bouncing around the countryside in it of late and had many more miles —nearly a hundred—in front of her.

"It's the worst part of our endeavors," Grey muttered, noting Cate's movements.

"Yes," Cate agreed, "a necessary evil. But we'll arrive at Stratton Hall in a few miles. We'll stop for a bit and take some refreshment before continuing on our way."

Grey peered at her from the rear-facing seat. "I'm surprised you're abandoning his lordship."

Cate was surprised at Grey's surprise. "Why? I've done what I said I would. I took him to Septon House so that he could speak with Septon, and now I'll introduce him to Stratton so he can continue his investigation."

Grey shrugged. "He's been very helpful to you. You must admit, his taking you to where the tapestry was located suggests that you obtained more out of the bargain."

Cate crossed her arms over her chest. "I don't have the tapestry, however. He still hasn't consented to sell it to me."

"You don't need it to find the sword—assuming it's at Harlech."

"And if it's not, I may need to consult the tapestry again, which will be difficult since it's not in my possession."

"At least he gave you the de Valery document."

To return to Septon's library. Surreptitiously. She couldn't be irritated with Norris for taking it, not when it had proven so bloody necessary to puzzling out the location of the sword. Cate didn't answer, instead choosing to direct her attention out the window.

"Mayhap you'll change your mind once we arrive at Stratton Hall," Grey said.

Cate looked at her friend with a narrowed gaze. "Why do you care so much? Wait, have you and Wade developed a *tendre* for each other?" Cate had noted their riding together both to and from the folly. Grey wasn't an accomplished horsewoman, but she also wasn't terrible. Still, she'd hung back with Wade, or so it had seemed to Cate.

Grey returned her stare with another shrug.

"It's all right if you have," Cate said, uncrossing her arms.

Grey's brows dipped briefly. "I wouldn't need your permission."

"I didn't mean it like that." Cate massaged her temple, mentally admonishing herself for sounding like an employer. While she *was* Grey's employer, their relationship was completely egalitarian.

They were quiet a few minutes before Grey said, "Do you plan to dispatch a letter to your parents from Stratton Hall?"

Cate nodded. "I'll let them know I'm traveling to Harlech." She was careful to communicate with her parents frequently, both for their peace of mind and to ensure that someone knew where she was going for safety and propriety's sake. She'd originally told them she was going to Wootton Bassett to visit Miranda, saying nothing about

Dyrnwyn or the tapestry or approaching Lord Norris. Then she'd sent a letter saying she was going to attend Septon's party in order to see his new acquisitions. Before leaving for Worcester with Norris, she'd sent another note indicating that she was helping the earl track down a missing piece of his antiquities collection. It was the truth, even if she'd left out several key details.

"Norris could've insisted on going to Stratton Hall first." Grey apparently wasn't ready to abandon her attempt to persuade Cate to change her mind. "But he stopped in Worcester to find the tapestry for you."

In growing frustration, Cate glanced up at the roof of the coach. "Our objective has to be obtaining the sword. Every moment we waste is a moment that someone else could find it."

"Do you really think someone has figured out the tapestry?"

"I don't want to assume they *haven't*. Finding the sword is the most important thing." Saying it out loud made it somehow sound hollow. Yes, it was important—*to her*. But the most important thing? Worth disregarding the man who'd gone out of his way to help her fulfill a lifelong dream?

Cate tipped her head back against the cushion and pushed out a heavy sigh. "You're right. We'll stop with them at Stratton Hall. Does that satisfy you?"

Before Grey could answer, the coach came to a swift and tumultuous stop, tossing Cate forward and then jerking her back so that she slid to the floor in an ungainly heap of skirts.

Grey, still perched on her seat, reached down for Cate. "Are you all right?"

Cate stumbled to her feet and fell back onto the seat. "I'm intact. What the devil happened?"

Grey threw open the door and froze.

Cate leaned forward and looked over Grey's shoulder—

straight into the eyes of a masked highwayman with a pistol pointed directly at them.

Grey clapped the door shut and turned to pull two guns from beneath her seat. She handed one to Cate as a booming voice overtook the interior of the coach.

"Stand and deliver or I'll shoot yer coachman!"

"I'm going to open the door and shoot him," Grey whispered calmly.

Cate peered out the window and winced. "Don't. There are two of them. One is standing and he has a pistol—and it's pointed at Wood."

Grey swore softly. "We're coming out," she called. Then she turned to Cate and spoke quietly again. "Hold the pistol low; try to disguise it among your skirts."

Cate nodded and Grey opened the door. Wood, the coachman, dashed forward under the watchful eye of a second masked highwayman, and lowered the step. Grey descended from the coach and Cate made to follow her. But the sound of a gunshot drew her to turn her head.

Norris's coach had been trailing a bit behind them, and they'd clearly caught up. Unfortunately, there was another pair of highwaymen waylaying their coach too.

~

*E*lijah cocked his pistol and looked at Wade. "Ready?" Wade picked up the pouch of gunpowder and shot from the seat and nodded. "Two that I can see, but we ought to presume more."

Elijah agreed, and he also presumed the "more" were at Miss Bowen's coach. And that made his blood fairly boil. "I'm going to fire as soon as I open the door. Then give me your pistol and I'll shoot the other."

"Yes, sir."

Wade had lapsed into his old address. Nothing could've satisfied Elijah more—save these highwaymen going straight to the devil. *Momentarily*, he told himself.

With a final look at Wade, he pushed open the door, set his sights on the horseman to the right and fired. The bullet struck the man in the shoulder and he fell from the horse. Elijah thrust his used weapon at Wade and took the next one, which Wade had already cocked. Spooked by the first shot, the other highwayman's mount danced beneath him. The rider tried to train his pistol on Elijah, but the horse jostled him too much. Elijah fired. The shot only nicked the man in the arm. The second report was enough, however, to send the horse racing down the road, with the rider desperately clinging to his mount to remain astride.

Another highwayman rode toward them, coming from the direction of Miss Bowen's coach. Wade swiped the pistol from Elijah's hand and replaced it with the reloaded first one.

Elijah lifted the weapon and leveled it at the approaching horseman. "Keep coming and I'll shoot you as I did the others," he called out. "Turn tail and run and I'll likely let you go."

The sound of a pistol shot from the vicinity of Miss Bowen's coach drew Elijah's attention just long enough for the advancing highwayman to fire. Elijah's carelessness nearly cost him an ear as the bullet whooshed by his head and lodged in the side of the coach. Refocusing, Elijah shot at the masked highwayman, but he turned his horse and evaded the bullet.

Uttering a vicious curse, Elijah exchanged the pistol with Wade once again, but the highwayman was already riding away. No, not away, but back to Miss Bowen's coach, where another masked man was clutching his arm. Grey had presumably shot him. Elijah ran toward them with his pistol raised.

Grey stood outside the coach, a pistol—presumably spent —dangling from her hand, while Miss Bowen held her own weapon pointed at the wounded highwayman.

The brigand who'd nearly uneared Elijah reached them first. He pulled a second pistol from his saddlebag and aimed it at Miss Bowen. "Lower yer pistol or I'll shoot 'er."

"Not before I shoot you," Elijah said, his finger itching to pull the trigger. "What do you want?" He was nearly certain they were after the tapestry, which was safely stowed in his coach.

He turned to see a small, slight figure stealing into the vehicle.

Hell.

"Wade, Timmons!" Elijah called out to his valet and coachman, whose attention was fully focused on what was happening outside the ladies' coach.

Timmons pivoted immediately, but Wade was slower—as if he couldn't bring himself to turn away from the women, or more accurately Grey. Timmons ran to the coach and leapt inside only to fall back out again clutching his side.

Elijah went into full battle mode. He refocused on the highwayman threatening Miss Bowen and shot him in the vicinity of his collarbone before the man realized what was coming. Without sparing a glance for the women, Elijah quickly spun about and ran toward his coach, where Wade had just reached Timmons.

"See to him," Elijah barked at his valet as he pulled a small blade from his boot and launched himself into the coach. The flash of a knife greeted him, but he'd expected that and met the villain's thrust with a swift parry. He caught the man's sleeve and rent the fabric.

The villain lunged forward, driving Elijah back onto the

seat and into a defensive position. The knife slashed into Elijah's waistcoat, but didn't reach his flesh as he managed to flatten himself back against the seat. Elijah brought his legs up and kicked the man in the gut, sending him sprawling. Then he leapt up and grabbed the man's wrist, squeezing to force the knife from his grip.

The man howled with pain and dropped the weapon. "Don't hurt me, my lord."

"What do you want?" Elijah rasped. He arced forward until he knelt over the man. He held his wrist and poised his blade near the man's throat.

The man's gray eyes were wide with fear, and his pock-marked face was pale. "I was jes' told to fetch a box from inside the coach." *The tapestry.*

"Who 'told' you this?"

He shook his head. "I don't know. Jes' a bloke down the pub earlier."

"Where?" Elijah pushed the word through his clenched teeth. He pressed the knife snug against the brigand's flesh.

"Worcester." The single word squeaked from the man's lips.

"Major!" Wade's call pulled Elijah off his captive. He didn't relinquish his grip on the villain's wrist however. He merely dragged the man with him as he emerged from the coach.

"What is it?" Elijah looked down the road, but the only people he could see were Miss Bowen, Grey, and their coachman rushing toward them. He turned his attention to Wade and Timmons.

"We need to get Timmons to a doctor," Wade said.

"Let's get him in the coach." Elijah pulled the criminal out, heedless that he tumbled to the ground. "Grey, do you have a weapon you can train on this miscreant?"

She raised a pistol and pointed it at the villain. "I do, my lord."

Elijah relinquished the quaking man to Grey's custody and replaced the knife in his boot. He and Wade lifted the bleeding Timmons into the coach.

"Let's take him into Leominster and find the doctor there," Elijah said. "And we'll turn the would-be thief in to the magistrate."

"My lord, I beg of you to let me go." The pitiful whine of the criminal's voice wafted into the coach.

"Stay here with him," Elijah directed Wade before leaving the coach once more. "I'll take over, Grey. You ride with Wade and Timmons. Miss Bowen, if you don't mind, I'd like your coachman to drive them. I can drive your coach."

Elijah stripped his cravat from his neck and went to the criminal. "Turn and put your hands behind your back."

The man whimpered as he complied. Elijah quickly bound his wrists.

"You'll ride in the other coach." He glared at the man. "Go."

The criminal tripped as he started toward Miss Bowen's vehicle.

Elijah looked up at Miss Bowen's coachman, who'd climbed up into his driver's seat. "Go on now. We'll see you in town."

The coach started down the road as Elijah followed the bound miscreant toward Miss Bowen's coach. She fell into step beside him.

"Miss Bowen, you'll sit up beside me."

She nodded. "Timmons will be all right."

Elijah kept his gaze fixed on their captive's back. "Proba-bly. The wound didn't look as though it was bleeding enough to be mortal."

"Have you seen that before?" Her question was soft, tentative, and quickly followed by a brisk, "Never mind. I don't wish to know."

Good, because he didn't wish to tell her. He looked around the road and was surprised to find all of the highwaymen and their horses were gone. They'd each been injured, but Elijah had seen wounded men achieve feats they ought not to be able to accomplish. The human body worked in mysterious ways, especially when one's life was at stake

Elijah quickened his pace and opened the door to the coach. "Get in." He grabbed the man by his right arm and pushed him up and inside.

The man scrambled to the rear-facing seat, his face ashen. "Please, my lord. You don' have to take me to town. I've learned me lesson."

"Are you certain you don't recall who recruited you for this ill-conceived attempt at theft?"

"'E didn't tell me 'is name. But 'e was big, with a scar on his nose."

That information was better than nothing. "If you hadn't stabbed my coachman, I might have been inclined to leniency, but as it is, I'm afraid you have an appointment with the magistrate. And I suggest you pray my coachman doesn't die."

The man began to sob as Elijah shut the door. He helped Miss Bowen climb up in to the seat and clambered up beside her. A moment later they were on their way to Leominster and Elijah's pulse finally began to ebb.

"Are you all right?" She stared at his chest.

He glanced down and saw the rent in this waistcoat. "Yes, the blade didn't get through."

She exhaled. "I'm relieved to hear it."

She was? Of course she was. Just as he was relieved that she'd emerged from that encounter unscathed. Watching that highwayman train his pistol on her had provoked a deep and bruising rage. Even now, he felt unsettled about the entire thing. He imagined she was at least equally disturbed. "Are *you* all right? I can't imagine you and Grey are used to such peril." He gave her a hard look. "Please tell me you aren't used to such peril."

"No."

He let the tension flow from his shoulders.

"And I must thank you for your quick thinking. I can hardly believe how rapidly you dispatched those villains."

"I had some help from Wade—and from Grey, I believe."

"Yes, she made a remarkable shot. I'm only sorry I didn't have a chance to demonstrate my ability."

He looked at her askance. "Are you as good as Grey?"

"No, but I'm always improving. I'm confident I could've shot that man, perhaps not as squarely as you—"

"Stop, I don't want to think of you shooting someone." Killing a person was life-altering for trained soldiers. For a woman like her, it could be devastating. Not that Elijah knew personally. He hadn't killed anyone while he'd been in the army, and he wondered if he'd mortally wounded any of those highwaymen. Possibly the one he'd shot near the collarbone—Elijah was surprised the man had been able to escape—which the man deserved for threatening Miss Bowen. Elijah would do it again to protect her.

Perhaps it wasn't as life-changing as he'd thought. That he wanted to go to such lengths to protect Miss Bowen perhaps was . . .

"Do you have any idea who those men were?" Cate asked.

"No. I asked our captive who hired him and he claims he doesn't know. For now, he appears to be a hireling."

"You believe him?"

"I find it odd that he was not masked while the others were."

"An excellent observation." Her tone held a note of admiration.

"I'm hopeful he'll reveal more to the magistrate once he realizes his situation is dire."

"Will you remain for the interrogation?"

"I need to see to Timmons first. We'll drop this bloke at the magistrate and continue on our way. I'm sorry your journey will be delayed. In fact, I believe it should be completely postponed. Once we deliver Timmons to a physician, you and Grey should return to your home."

She flashed him a surprised glance. "I appreciate your concern, but I don't think that's necessary. I'll accompany you to Stratton Hall and then we'll go to Harlech as planned."

Elijah frowned. Her life had been in serious danger. A gang of murderous thieves had been in pursuit of them and the tapestry. Though they'd all been wounded, Elijah couldn't be certain the threat had been mitigated. For all he knew, there were even more villains waiting to pounce. "You and Grey could have been killed today. I must insist you return home."

She smoothed her skirt with her gloved palm. "Again, I appreciate your concern, but we'll continue on. You are not my keeper."

"No, but you're sorely in need of one," he muttered.

Her brows rose, giving her a haughty expression. "*That* is why I choose not to marry. I am not 'in need' of anything that I can't provide for myself."

And that is why *he* chose not to marry—women were far more trouble than they were worth. If she were his wife, he'd have to keep a rein on her risky excursions. That was a problem he didn't want. He gritted his teeth. "It's good that you prefer to save some poor man's sanity by choosing to remain unwed. You are an infuriating female."

"So we've established," she said wryly. "Nevertheless,

Grey and I will be going to Harlech to find the sword. If you'd prefer not to travel with us—"

"You couldn't stop me from doing so now." He might not want to be saddled with her, but for now he was. Knowing what he did about this entire situation, he simply couldn't let her and Grey continue on by themselves. He looked at her and she turned her head as if she felt the intensity of his stare. "I expect you to stay at Stratton Hall while I interrogate the footman, and then we'll all go to Harlech together."

She pursed her lips. "You needn't be so dictatorial. That's what I meant. Even before the highwaymen showed up, I'd decided to remain with you at Stratton Hall."

She had? A bolt of pleasant satisfaction burrowed through the apprehension still lingering in his bones. "I'm glad we agree on that at least." He still preferred she went home, but remaining in his presence would have to suffice, apparently.

Perhaps he ought to write to her parents and inform them of the danger surrounding her quest. Surely they could put a stop to her behavior. Actually, he wasn't certain that was true. Furthermore, he knew how important it was to her to find this sword and to do it on her own. She'd somehow won him over. Had he done the same to her with regard to his investigation?

"Why did you change your mind about staying with me at Stratton Hall?"

She plucked at her skirt, fidgeting. "I . . . changed my mind, that's all. You took me directly to the tapestry and I'm incredibly grateful."

"I see. So this is reciprocation."

She sighed. "Must you characterize it like that? I'm staying because we're in this together." She glanced backward and down at the coach where their captive was housed. "Now more than ever."

Clearly their relationship had progressed to something beyond acquaintance and now they were aligned in this mission—each with their own goals, but apparently each invested in the other's. "You care about finding out what happened to Matthew?"

She looked over at him, her lips parted in a thoroughly enticing fashion. "I do. I particularly care that it doesn't also happen to you."

For the briefest moment, he wondered what it might be like to kiss her. In the middle of this beautiful summer day. Where anyone could happen upon them. He mentally chided himself for such ridiculous thoughts. He couldn't dally with someone like her. And even if he could, she was a distraction he didn't need right now. Obtaining answers about Matthew was his primary goal—nothing was more important.

CHAPTER 11

$\mathcal{B}$y the time they reached Stratton Hall, Cate was overheated and tired—both mentally and physically. After delivering the weeping criminal to the magistrate, they'd gone directly to the physician's home, where Grey and Wade had taken Timmons. The physician had stitched him up and proclaimed him well enough to be moved to a nearby inn, where Norris paid for a caretaker. Norris had also arranged for someone to drive his coach back to Cosgrove with Timmons inside, when the physician deemed him fit for longer travel. That meant that they would now all ride together in Cate's coach.

Cate had felt surprisingly calm during the highwaymen's attack and even for quite some time after. But the stress of it was finally beginning to catch up with her, and she'd be the first to say she was relieved that Norris and Wade would be accompanying them to Harlech.

She was beginning to worry that Norris's brother's death really might have been murder. It certainly seemed someone was going to do whatever necessary to obtain the tapestry. Or more accurately, the sword. Cate wanted so badly to find it, but it wasn't worth risking her life. She hoped Norris could obtain answers from his brother's former valet. She glanced over at the earl as they walked into Stratton Hall. He'd been brooding since the attack—his eyes like crystal and his features set in granite. Except for that moment on the coach when she'd said she didn't want him to die like his brother. Norris had stared at her mouth . . . Her gaze was riveted to his lips as she remembered the feel of them against hers.

He looked at her then and she forced herself to turn away and greet the butler.

"Good afternoon, Colman. It's a pleasure to see you again." Cate hadn't been to Stratton Hall in a few years. It wasn't a terribly fit destination for young, unmarried ladies, even if they *were* relatives and brought their own bodyguard. She glanced at Grey, who'd entered behind them with Wade and now stood in the background.

"Welcome, miss, we received your note earlier today." They'd sent a missive ahead of them from the inn to give Stratton time to prepare for their arrival. "His lordship is delighted to have you and Lord Norris as his guests." Colman flicked a glance at Norris. "His lordship is sorry to hear about the difficulty you encountered. He hopes your footman will recover."

"Thank you. His prognosis is good," Norris said.

Colman gave a nod. "His lordship will be pleased to hear it. We've prepared rooms for you." He gestured for a footman to come forward. "Smith will take you up. I regret to inform you that his lordship is currently indisposed, but he hopes to see Lord Norris for dinner. Unfortunately this evening's entertainment won't be suitable for you, Miss Bowen, and you'll need to dine in your room. His lordship prays you understand."

"Understand" was perhaps not the best word, but she

summoned a placid smile. "I appreciate his lordship welcoming us on such short notice. Of course, I wouldn't wish to disrupt his plans."

"It's no disruption. He is quite enthusiastic to host Lord Norris."

"Tell his lordship I'll see him later then," Norris said. "And thank you for handling the coach."

Colman inclined his head and it seemed they were dismissed to their rooms. Cate couldn't wait to have a bath and wash away the heat and grime of the road.

As the footman led them up the stairs, Cate shot Norris a sideways glance. "Do you have any idea what sort of dinner you'll be attending?" she whispered.

"One at which I eat and drink?"

She suppressed a smile. "Likely with feminine assistance. Stratton is notorious for his debauched dinners. I've heard some of the food is actually served *on* the women."

Norris muttered a curse. "How in the world do you know that?" He kept his voice low, but the footman—and Wade and Grey—could probably hear them anyway.

She shrugged as they started along the upper gallery. "Everyone knows that. Everyone who's been in England, that is," she amended.

"Even when I lived here, I hadn't heard of that, unless it's a new development."

"No, he's always been an utter reprobate. It's why Lady Stratton left."

"I see."

Neither his statement nor his expression reflected whether he found the idea repulsive or enticing. Thinking of him participating in Stratton's lurid entertainments set her teeth on edge. Was she jealous? She was attracted to Norris, but she had no claim on him whatsoever. And wanting to exchange another kiss or two didn't mean she desired anything more.

She ought not care how he spent his evening. But she did. Even so, she couldn't bring herself to ask.

The footman guided them toward a distant corner of the house. "You're here, miss." He opened a door to a small but well-appointed chamber.

Grey entered first as Cate turned to Norris. "If I don't see you later . . ."

His gaze bore straight into her. It felt almost . . . intimate. But that had to be her own fancy. "You'll see me at some point."

With a nod, Cate went into her room and wondered where he would be lodging. Would it be in the other wing, where Stratton and his friends' chambers were located?

Cate closed the door and joined Grey, who'd located their luggage and set about unpacking the bare necessities for their stay.

"Do you think it will be just one night?" Grey asked.

"I don't know. I hope so."

After a bath and a short nap, Cate felt much improved, at least physically. She was still bothered by what Norris might be doing and how he planned to spend his evening, but strove to expel such thoughts from her head. She had other concerns, such as how they would find the sword once they reached Harlech. She really had no idea what to look for at the castle. She only hoped something would present itself.

A knock on the door quickened her pulse. Was it Norris? He'd said he'd see her later. Had he conducted an interview with the footman?

Cate stood in front of the hearth while Grey went to the door. When she returned alone, Cate quashed her disappointment. "Who was it?"

"A note."

"For me?"

Grey shook her head. "For me. From Wade. He's invited me to dine with him."

Annoyance pricked Cate's insides. It seemed everyone was to have an enjoyable evening while she was going to spend hers alone. "Will you go?"

Grey shrugged. "Mayhap, but I don't wish to leave you."

Cate pushed out a breath. She didn't want to deprive Grey of a pleasant occasion, particularly if something was developing between her and Wade. "I'll be quite well ensconced here in my chamber. Are you going to respond to my inquiry now about what's between the two of you?"

"I'll let you know later." Her lips briefly curved into the most charming smile Cate had ever seen on her. But it was gone almost as quickly as it had appeared, indicating Grey hadn't wanted her to see it.

"I need to get out of this room," Cate said. "I'll be back in a while." She left the chamber and made her way downstairs to Stratton's library. He kept the handful of medieval manuscripts he owned on display, locked under glass.

She'd seen the books on multiple occasions, but she never tired of looking at the illuminations. And every time she came, he had them opened to different pages. Once, she'd been allowed to look at a few of them out of the glass, but that had been years ago under her father's supervision. She doubted Stratton would allow her to touch them without her father present. He was the expert and she was just a silly woman.

"Miss Bowen."

Cate turned at the sound of Norris's voice. He'd changed his clothing and appeared fresh and handsome, his blond hair waving back from his temples. "How are you feeling?" He certainly looked good. Spectacular, in fact.

"Better, thank you. A hot bath can do wonders."

"Yes, it can."

He came to stand beside her at one of the cases. "What is this?"

"This is the de Valery manuscript. It's the companion to the *Ballads of Gareth*, which my mother owns."

"The fellow who made that paper I took from Septon's?"

"Yes, though please don't advertise that." The words came out more sharply than she intended. She didn't apologize, however, because to do so would draw attention to her prickly mood and she didn't want to acknowledge it. Instead, she changed the topic. "Have you spoken to Dalby?"

"Not yet, but I hope to shortly."

"Before or after you have dinner with Stratton?"

He jerked his gaze to hers. "Before, I should hope."

"So you are having dinner with him? Even after what I told you?"

His eyes narrowed slightly, but with something akin to confusion, not anger. "I think it's only polite. I'm certain I can dine without . . . indulging."

"It's really none of my business."

He looked down at the manuscript encased beneath the glass. "No, it isn't."

Cate resisted the urge to make a truly unladylike sound. Maybe a growl. It was so unfair that men were free to pursue their sexual needs, while women had to temper their desires until a man deigned to take them to wife. Unless she wanted to risk her reputation. Yet a man could satisfy himself without censure. Mostly—she had to admit that Stratton's proclivities had cast him into the shadows of Society.

"I see the resemblance to the tapestry document," he said, surveying the de Valery manuscript. "The writing and the illustration."

"You've a good eye." *And an unfortunately lush mouth.*

She really needed to stop looking at him. How was she

going to do that for the next few days? They would be traveling in closer proximity than they had been thus far in their association and as a result would spend far more time in each other's company. And the more time she spent with him, the more attracted to him she became.

Would she feel this way if she hadn't kissed him? It didn't signify, because she *had* kissed him and she couldn't take it back. Nor did she want to. In fact, she longed to do it again. But for far longer. Maybe even more than just a kiss . . .

Tamping down the desire rushing over her, she moved to another case. Yes, this was better. The air was cooler here and she couldn't smell the soap he'd used in his bath—sandalwood and pine.

But then he followed her, damn it.

"It seems as though my valet and your companion have struck up a friendship of sorts."

She decided to be a tad saucy and pretend to be obtuse. "Like our friendship?"

"Er, no. A . . . *tendre* perhaps."

He saw their association differently. But then it had to be. Their station demanded it. How freeing it would be to be Grey and Wade—able to explore their impulses and feelings.

"They are to have dinner together," Norris continued. "Wade is being cagey, but I can tell he likes Grey."

She turned toward him. "Indeed, how?"

He considered the question a moment. "The way he looks at her, I suppose."

"Do you suppose he's fallen in love with her?"

Something lurked in the depths of his pale blue eyes, something she suspected he kept deeply buried. "I wouldn't begin to know what that looks like."

"Love doesn't interest you." She wasn't sure that was true, but she wanted to see what this man was made of. "Just as marriage doesn't. Since you don't plan to marry, will you take a mistress?"

He sucked in breath and promptly choked on it. "This isn't an appropriate avenue of conversation, Miss Bowen."

She swayed toward him, shocked by her boldness, but not enough to stop herself. "It is if I'm interested in the position."

~

*E*lijah just barely kept his jaw from hitting the carpet. Had he heard her right?

"I beg your pardon?"

Swaths of pink flagged her cheeks. She turned from him and he lost the dark intensity of her gaze. "Would you mind forgetting I said that?"

He didn't think he could, not in ten lifetimes. "Why *would* you say that?" And why in the bloody hell would he not do as she asked and immediately forget what she'd said? Apparently his brain wasn't fast enough to contradict his body, which had flared to awareness the moment he'd walked into the room and found her here.

She moved around the case, putting it safely—and agonizingly—between them. "I was thinking of Grey and Wade and how lucky they are to be able to pursue . . . whatever it is they're pursuing. I'm a lady. I'm not allowed to . . . feel."

Bloody hell.

She wanted him. That had to be what she meant. She'd all but propositioned him. But she *was* a lady and he shouldn't think of her in a sexual way. His gaze dipped to her lips and further south, to the delectable curve of her breast.

Too late.

She gave her head a quick shake. "Please, let's forget I said anything. I'm going back to my room. Do let me know if you discover anything with Dalby."

She stalked from the room, her feet carrying her faster than he'd ever seen her walk. And his legs itched to go after her.

Because he wanted her too.

Blood and bones, he couldn't have her. He turned from the door and willed his cock to stand down. He was half bloody aroused just thinking of her as his mistress. Mistress? He couldn't put her in the same category as Lily. His former mistress had been the daughter of a convict, a free-spirited woman two years his senior who knew how to obtain her own pleasure as much as give it. She'd possessed a wealth of experience, and confidence had fairly over-flowed from every part of her. Actually, he saw a similarity between her and Miss Bowen. What Miss Bowen lacked in experience, she more than made up for in confidence. And that was just about the most damned attractive thing about her.

For a moment he indulged his lust, imagined what it would be like to have her in his bed. She'd be adventurous, he was sure, and guileless. His cock did the opposite of what he needed it to—hardening at the thought of her pleasuring him, for he'd no doubt she would be a fast and eager student.

What the hell was he doing even thinking about this? He cast his head back and inhaled, working to cool his body.

After several agonizing minutes, he'd reined his body under control. He needed to keep his focus: Dalby. He left the library and went in search of the footman. After speaking to Colman, he found the man in the silver closet below stairs.

Dalby was a year or two younger than Elijah, with light brown eyes, thick, dark brown hair, and a rather soft-looking face. His nose was wide, his chin ample, and his mouth flaccid as he worked at polishing a silver ladle.

Elijah lightly cleared his throat as he approached. "Dalby?"

The man looked up from his work. He studied Elijah, perhaps thinking he was familiar but not able to place where they'd met. "Sir?"

"Norris."

Dalby's eyes widened and it was impossible to miss the shock and perhaps fear in his gaze, though he did try to settle his features into impassivity. Too bad the attempt was an abject failure.

"My lord." Dalby inclined his head. "I'm sorry for your loss. His lordship—your brother—was a good man."

Elijah moved into the small space, but didn't close the door. "Is that because he only turned you out without a reference instead of taking you directly to the magistrate? I want you to understand that I would have done the latter. I still might."

Dalby nearly dropped the ladle he was cleaning. He snatched it to his chest before it could tumble to the floor. "Please, my lord, I didn't mean any harm. I made a poor decision." He turned a ghastly shade of gray.

"You were caught trying to steal from my brother." Elijah injected just a bit of menace into his otherwise soft tone. "That is a punishable offense. Did you know I recently returned from Australia? They'd likely send you there for your sentence. Should you survive the journey, I'm sure you'll find the backbreaking work beneath the blistering sun to be quite a departure from polishing silver."

The man went from stone gray to snow white. "Please, my lord, I beg you, don't turn me in."

Satisfied that he'd put Dalby into a malleable state of fear, Elijah launched his interrogation. "I'll consider it. However, first, I should like to know how you came to work here without a reference."

Dalby swallowed audibly. "I was told to come here for a position, my lord."

Elijah clasped his hands behind his back in an attempt to contain the energy coursing through him. "By whom?"

"Crane. He's the fierce-looking bloke who recruited me."

At last, a name. "Tell me what else you know of this man. Where did you meet?"

"He approached me at the pub on my afternoon off." Dalby's voice carried a slight tremor that revealed his anxiety. "He knew I worked at Cosgrove. He told me about the tapestry and offered me three pounds to nick it for him." Dalby clutched the silver ladle in his hands. "I needed the money, my lord. I owed someone," he muttered, glancing away.

Elijah had no sympathy for the man. "Your problems are not mine. You say Crane found you at the pub. What happened when you didn't procure the tapestry?"

Dalby winced. "He wasn't pleased, especially when I told him I'd been sacked."

Elijah realized he was squeezing his hands together behind his back almost painfully and loosened his grip. "If he wasn't pleased with you, how did you end up here?"

"He asked me if I could find out where the tapestry was kept."

None of this made sense to Elijah. "And how were you supposed to do that from here, so far from Cosgrove?"

His cheeks flushed, bringing some much-needed color to the man's face. "My lady love is one of the upstairs maids at Cosgrove."

Elijah suddenly recalled what Mason had said—that Dalby had invited one of the maids to join him, but she'd refused. He wondered if the woman would actually help the pathetic footman. Elijah would need to determine her loyalty at some point. "Which maid? Remember what I said at the start of this conversation, Dalby, before you attempt to shield her identity."

"Becky Chambers, my lord." *Another name. This was excellent progress.* "Please don't blame her. She didn't know anything about this. I only asked her questions from time to time when I wrote her. I'd hoped she could provide information about the tapestry, but she doesn't know anything—she's innocent in this, my lord." At least the miscreant had the spine to protect the woman he loved. Elijah's opinion of the man improved slightly. "Do you . . . never mind."

Elijah felt certain he'd been about to ask whether Elijah possessed the tapestry, and of course he had no intention of revealing that information. "Tell me more about Crane. Do you know how to find him?"

"I don't, my lord. He contacts me periodically here."

"In person?"

Dalby shook his head. "By letter."

"Show me." Elijah wished he had the correspondence Matthew had received from the men who'd offered to buy the tapestry—assuming he'd received a missive before they'd shown up at Cosgrove. Elijah suspected they'd been drafted by the same hand and longed to compare the two.

"They're in my quarters, my lord."

"Later this evening, after you conclude your duties, you will fetch them and provide them to my valet."

Dalby nodded. "Yes, my lord."

"Can you tell me anything else about Crane? Did he work alone or with others?"

"He mentioned his 'associates,' my lord, but I never met any of them. He also referred to his employer, but never used a name. I had the sense the tapestry was for him."

Unsurprisingly, Crane was a hireling. "Have you any idea who his employer might be? Any bit of information could help—whether he's titled or where he lives."

Dalby thought for a moment, but ultimately shook his head with regret. "I can't help you there, my lord. I sincerely wish I could. You'd be able to recognize Crane on sight, however. He's a large bloke—broad." Dalby puffed up his shoulders to demonstrate. "Dark, nasty eyes, if I'm being honest, and a scar along his nose that makes him look down-right terrifying."

A scar on his nose? Could it be the same man the thief from that afternoon had mentioned? It had to be. Crane was still after the tapestry. Or more accurately, the man Crane worked for. Could it be Septon after all? Had Elijah allowed himself to be blinded to the man's guilt by his warmth and close relationship to Miss Bowen?

"My lord . . . Are you going to report what I did?"

Elijah noted the return of the man's pallor. "I have just one more thing I need to ask you. What do you know of the carriage accident that killed my brother?"

Terror filled the footman's gaze. "Nothing, my lord, I swear it."

Did his reaction mean that he knew it hadn't been an accident? "Do you think he was killed?"

Dalby frantically shook his head. "I couldn't say, my lord."

Elijah would wager Dalby had wondered if Matthew had been murdered. "You described Crane as a fearsome fellow. Has he threatened you or in some way led you to believe that he was capable of violence?" Elijah knew that he was— assuming he was the same man behind today's attempt at highway robbery, he was at least comfortable with menacing.

Dalby's gaze darted behind Elijah to the open door and he lowered his voice to barely above a whisper. "He said I was lucky I received this position instead of a beating, that if it were up to him, I would've had a few broken bones."

Elijah had squeezed his hands together again without thinking, and now feared he might break his own bones. He released his grip and flattened his palms against his outer thighs. "I want those letters." He doubted there would be anything useful, but he wouldn't know for sure until he looked.

"You'll have them, my lord. I . . . I need to return to my work."

"For now, I'll let you be at your post. But Dalby, I'll be keeping an eye on you and I expect you to notify me if you hear from Crane again. My valet will instruct you on how to contact me."

Dalby nodded. "Happy to, my lord." As scared as he'd been of Crane, Dalby seemed more frightened of Elijah having him arrested. Or perhaps he was simply most upset by whoever happened to be in front of him. He appeared a weak-minded, self-serving sort.

With a final cold stare, Elijah turned and left the closet. By the time he arrived in his bedchamber, his body was teeming with pent-up energy. He wanted to find Crane and thrash him soundly. And then have him arrested for murder.

Wade eyed him as he strode into the chamber. "You look agitated. Did you learn something from the footman?"

"Yes, although I'm no closer to finding the men responsible for Matthew's death."

Wade went to a table near the bed and poured a glass from the whisky bottle he'd procured after they'd arrived. "You're certain then that it was murder?"

Only because his gut told him so. He still had no proof that Matthew's death was anything other than an accident. "Yes, but proving it will be another matter." Elijah accepted the glass and took a hearty swallow, then proceeded to tell Wade everything Dalby had disclosed.

"What is our next move, my lord?" Wade asked when he was finished.

"Studying the correspondence Crane sent to Dalby.

Hopefully there will be some clue as to how we might find him."

"What of the sword, of Harlech?"

"We'll leave tomorrow as planned, unless I'm able to discern something useful from the missives." God, he hoped that would be the case. He despised feeling this helpless. Restlessness drove him to walk to the fireplace and back again.

"You're in a dudgeon, if I may say so," Wade said, sounding concerned. "Perhaps dinner will soothe your temper. Shall I prepare your clothes? You have just under an hour."

The bloody dinner. Where his host and the handful of men visiting would apparently take their meal from atop female flesh. "Do you suppose they lay the women on the table and put the food on their chest or stomach?"

"Either one. Or perhaps both. But what do I know of it?" His brow furrowed. "What about the soup?"

Elijah paused in drinking his whisky, feeling a bit more relaxed with the turn of the conversation to something more . . . absurd. "I can't imagine they put that on—or in—her."

Wade grimaced. "Ouch, no." He flinched before continuing. "So you're going, then?"

He really *should* go. The idea of losing himself in a woman, of relinquishing his stress, was incredibly alluring. "I think I'd like a good shag."

Wade went into the dressing room, but spoke loudly. "It may very well do you some good. It always has in the past." A more inane statement had never been made. What man didn't feel better after a satisfying screw? "I'm hopeful my own evening might go in that direction."

"Grey?"

Wade peered around the corner. "How did you know?"

"I'm not an imbecile." Elijah sipped his whisky. "Forget I said anything. It's none of my affair. Best of luck to you."

"Thank you, my lord. I'm encouraged by her interest." He disappeared into the dressing room once more. "It all depends on whether she's comfortable leaving Miss Bowen alone."

Miss Bowen. *Alone.* Had there ever been a more alluring picture? Not in his present state of mind. Perhaps he should dine with her instead. That way Wade and Grey could conduct their assignation without concern.

Which would leave him and Miss Bowen to . . . *no.* He had to stay away from her. He needed a woman, but not her. He needed a woman to drive *her* out of his mind and body.

He followed Wade into the dressing chamber, intent on joining Stratton and his merry crew.

CHAPTER 12

*C*ate pushed her half-eaten dinner away and stood up from the small round table situated in a corner of her chamber. Grey had departed a little while ago to meet Wade, which had left Cate alone, her mind tortured with images of Lord Norris intertwined with a faceless woman.

With a groan, Cate circulated the chamber, wishing she'd thought to take a book or two from Stratton's library to occupy her evening hours. She glanced down at her dressing gown, regretting her decision to prepare for bed. She didn't dare leave her chamber in this state, not when the house was potentially teeming with lascivious men.

Though, she wondered if encountering one would be so bad—one in particular, anyway.

Cursing her own foolishness at such thoughts, she flopped down on the bed and stared at the canopy. A pale blue thread dangled from the edge, looking as unfinished as she felt.

Unfinished?

She wasn't sure how else to describe it. Unfulfilled

perhaps. She didn't particularly wish to marry, but she longed for intimacy. For a feeling she couldn't yet name.

A knock on the door jerked her to sit straight up. She strained to listen, wondering if she'd misheard. Who would be calling on her at this hour? Had one of Stratton's guests become lost?

A second knock came, louder and more insistent than the first.

Tentatively, Cate inched off the bed and made her way slowly to the door. The third knock was sharper and accompanied by a male voice.

"Miss Bowen, I wish to speak with you."

Norris.

Exhaling her relief while at the same time feeling a burst of anticipation, she opened the door. "You're not at dinner."

"No. I tried, but I became distracted."

From the women likely draped across the table? Cate worked to stifle the pleasure that rushed over her. "What happened?"

"May I come in?"

"Of course." She stood aside as he passed into the chamber and closed the door. This was entirely inappropriate, but she didn't care. She didn't live her life by Society's rules and she didn't plan to start, well, ever.

"Dalby has disappeared." He turned to face her. His eyes looked a bit wild, with a glazed sheen.

"That's awful. I'm sorry you didn't have a chance to speak with him."

"I did, actually. Earlier, after I saw you in the library." Nothing about his demeanor indicated he'd been affected by what she'd said, or if he even recalled it. Whereas she'd relived the moment a hundred times in her head and wished desperately she could take it back. Or see it through. She really couldn't decide which.

"You did speak with him?" Why, then, was he upset?

"Yes, he told me the name of the man who enlisted him to steal the tapestry at Cosgrove and he bears a striking resemblance to the villain who also recruited this afternoon's would-be thief."

She inhaled sharply. "This man is quite committed to obtaining the tapestry."

"Yes, but not for himself. He has an employer, but Dalby didn't know his identity. He was to deliver letters written by Crane—the man who hired these thieves—to Wade later tonight, but now that he's gone, I doubt I'll ever see them."

"Why are these letters important?"

"Crane—or perhaps his employer—arranged for this position for Dalby. In exchange, he was to use his continuing relationship with a maid at Cosgrove to share any pertinent information regarding the tapestry."

"I see. You said he disappeared? He simply left his post?"

He set his hands on his hips. "Yes. Colman said he'd never done anything like this before. I must've frightened him off. Damn it, I should have made him fetch those letters right away this afternoon."

He didn't frighten her, yet in that moment, under the severity of his stare and the menacing curl of his lip, she believed he could intimidate anyone. She resisted the pull she felt to move toward him. "Are you certain he took the letters with him?"

"Quite. I excused myself from dinner—good Lord, what a ridiculous affair—to find Dalby and ask him to fetch the letters for me."

His opinion of the dinner pleased Cate inordinately. "That was when you discovered he'd gone?"

"Colman was unable to locate him, so I went directly to his quarters. His room was in disarray and the majority of his belongings were gone. It was clear to me—and later to Colman after I alerted him—that the bounder had fled."

"Do you think he left because you questioned him?"

He dropped his hand to his side and raised his head. "I do. Everything is bloody connected. I wanted those letters to try to discern the identity of whoever is in charge of this operation to steal the tapestry. Whoever it is was able to procure Dalby's position here at Stratton Hall. It's all too convenient."

Her brain halted and her emotions spun into apprehension. "You think his assignment at Stratton Hall is convenient?"

His hesitation pricked the back of her neck. "You have a connection here. You want the sword. The coincidence is disturbing." He spoke softly, but there was a thread of foreboding lacing his tone.

"You can't believe I had anything to do with your brother's death?" Her insides felt hollow.

"I don't want to, but I don't know what to believe anymore. All I know is that I was enjoying a perfectly fine existence on the other side of the world and now I find myself encumbered with an earldom, a murdered brother, and a woman who demands far too much of me."

He'd moved toward her as he spoke, his ire radiated from him, heating the space around her.

She didn't want to be the cause of his anguish. "I never intended to be demanding. If you'd prefer to part ways, I won't try to stop you."

"Of course you won't," he whispered harshly. "You know where to find the sword. You have precisely what you want."

The pain in his voice drew her in, kept her from rising to his anger. She suspected he wasn't truly upset with her, that he really didn't think she'd had anything to do with Matthew's death. But she had to be sure.

She took a step toward him, until they were just a breath apart. "I want this sword more than I've ever wanted anything, and I am prepared to do whatever it takes to find it. But I would never, *never,* sacrifice someone. And I would certainly never be able to look that man's brother in the eye and tell him that right now the only thing I want more than the sword is him."

"Miss B—"

"*Cate,* call me Cate."

"Cate, you can't . . . You can't speak to me like that. Not unless you want to be kissed. And not like that kiss the other night."

She laid her hand against his chest. "Perhaps you should not have invaded my bedchamber when I'm barely dressed. Not unless *you* want to be kissed."

"Hell and the devil," he breathed as his arm snaked around her waist and drew her against him.

"Please don't make it like the other night. Make it better."

His eyes gleaming in the candlelight, he lowered his mouth to hers and snatched her lips in a decadent kiss. One hand held her waist while the other cupped her nape, holding her absolutely hostage to his embrace.

His tongue swept into her mouth, claiming every bit of her that he touched. Cate grasped at his shoulders before curling her arms around his neck. She had to stand on her toes to reach him, which stretched her body against him in a devastating connection, one that was simultaneously over-whelming and not nearly enough.

She angled her head, hoping to deepen the kiss. He answered with a sound in his throat and his fingers digging into her waist, bringing her inexorably closer to his hard frame. Clad in just a nightrail and her dressing gown, Cate felt every contour of his body—and of his clothing.

She shoved her hands beneath his coat and pushed it over his shoulders. Without breaking the kiss, she tugged the arms down until the garment came free and she dropped it to the floor.

His mouth left hers, but traced along her jaw until he threaded his fingers into the back of her hair and tugged, elongating her neck. He kissed and nipped at her flesh, torturing her with his delicious lips and tongue, before reclaiming her mouth.

She tangled her fingers into his cravat and pulled at the silk until it came loose. With a merciless tug, she whipped it from his neck and threw it aside. Her hands dipped into his shirt and found the warm flesh of his collarbones. She clasped him, pulled at him, thrust her tongue deeper into the hot recesses of his mouth.

His hand moved up her spine and then forward until his thumb grazed her breast. Her nipple instantly hardened and again he left her mouth to kiss down her neck.

"Norris," she pleaded, not entirely certain of what she wanted, but confident that he could give it to her.

"*Elijah.* Norris is a name I never wanted and can't bloody stand." He pushed her dressing gown aside and kissed the flesh above her nightrail, his mouth open and hot against her.

She plunged her fingers into his hair and moaned as he kissed even lower, his lips moving over the linen of her garment. The feel of him through the light fabric was an exquisite tease and she longed to take it off. But to do so would sever the moment, and she couldn't bear for it to end.

She turned him so that the bed was behind her, her intent crystallizing in her mind. She *did* want him more than the sword. Her flesh burned where he touched her and smoldered everywhere he didn't. The ache growing between her thighs was all-encompassing, crowding out all other thought.

Finding the buttons of his waistcoat, she plucked them

free until she could push the garment open. She ran her palms up his shirtfront, eager to feel his bare skin.

"Cate." The word was a strangled whisper against her breast, a plea. *"Cate,"* he rasped. A curse.

She clutched at his head. "Don't stop. I don't want you to. And I know you want me. There's no reason to deny ourselves."

He lifted his head and looked at her with lust simmering in his gaze. The pull of that alone was enough to make her knees weaken. "There is every reason. You are not some trollop."

"Of course I'm not, and you're not treating me like one." She pulled his neck until his mouth was near hers. "Please don't think about propriety or expectation. Just think about this." She kissed him again, nipping his lower lip before plunging her tongue into his mouth.

His hand moved over her breast, dipping into the top of her night rail. When his fingers came into contact with her bare flesh, heat flooded through her, pushing her desire to an almost unbearable sensation.

The latch on the door sounded like the blast of a cannon. And just like that their spectacularly magnificent interlude came to a crashing and wholly disappointing end.

~

*E*lijah jerked away from her and snatched his waistcoat closed. He fumbled with the buttons, keeping his back to the door and whomever had just come inside. He swallowed a groan of frustration. There was no way he could appropriately clothe himself.

Echoing his thoughts, Cate whispered, "Don't bother. Grey won't care and it's not as if you can make this look acceptable. I'm in my dressing gown, for heaven's sake."

He glanced down at her attire as she pulled her garments back into place. Blood and bones, what had he nearly done? He'd been a scant moment from bending his head to her breast and suckling her, devouring her, claiming her.

"Good evening, my lord," Grey said from behind him. "Should I come back later?"

Elijah nearly choked. What the hell sort of chaperone was she? "No." He finished buttoning his waistcoat as Grey moved past them.

"I'll just give you a moment or two," she said, going through the doorway in the corner that likely led to a dressing chamber and her sleeping area, leaving them blessedly alone to compose themselves.

Hell, there was only one way he could rightfully compose himself and he wasn't about to do it here. He plucked up his coat and cravat, pulling the latter around his neck before donning the former. "That was a near thing," he said.

"Not near enough," she murmured, her voice heavy with regret. Her dark eyes lifted to his, and the stark lust shining there almost did him in.

"Stop looking at me like that. And stop saying provocative things. We are business associates until we find this sword and nothing more."

Her eyes narrowed. "How can you say that now?"

"Because someone has to regain their head. Let us not speak of this again." Really, if he didn't put it from his mind, he was going to embarrass himself. He struggled to change the subject to something more suitable. "We'll be on our way in the morning. Be ready to depart early." He turned to go, but she touched his arm and he had to clench his fists to keep from snatching her against his chest.

"What about Dalby?"

Damn, he'd completely forgotten why he'd come to see her in the first place. Why had he? To tell her that Dalby had run off. Wade had been busy and Elijah hadn't wanted to interrupt him. No, that wasn't precisely true. The first person he'd thought of seeing when he'd found out had been Cate. And *that* was a disaster. Elijah strove to find the control he normally employed, but that he'd utterly lost when he'd come into her bedchamber. *Her bedchamber.* He pulled away from her touch. "What about him? He's gone."

"We can go after him."

"What of the sword?" He couldn't believe she'd delay her quest even more. She hadn't even wanted to stop here.

"It will still be there." She didn't sound completely certain, but he appreciated her trying to.

"You don't know that. We'll leave for Harlech in the morning."

She made to touch him again, but he backed away and she dropped her hand. "I really do want to find out what happened to Matthew."

"We'll need to be careful going forward. I expect Crane to try again—unless he's too injured to continue." All of the highwaymen had been injured in some way, but there was no telling which one was Crane since they'd all worn masks covering their faces from hairline to mouth. Presumably, the mystery employer could simply hire more brigands, if he didn't already have an army of them.

Elijah noted the concern in her dark eyes. He still wanted her away from this danger.

She tipped her head to the side. "Don't even dare think of abandoning me now," she said, accurately guessing the direction of his thoughts. "I meant what I said—we're in this together."

Together.

In more ways than simply pursuing the sword, he realized. He took in her kiss-reddened lips and the strands of hair that had escaped the simple knot she wore at the back of her head. She was temptation personified and if he didn't leave now, he sure as hell was going to regret it. Spinning on his heel, he departed without a backward glance.

The corridor was blissfully cool and he finally felt as though his control was returning. He went to his room—it was neither near nor terribly far from hers—and was immediately greeted by Wade.

Elijah handed him his coat and cravat. "You cut your evening short."

"Had to. I heard some disturbing news and wanted to tell you at once. Dalby's gone off."

"I'm the one who discovered his departure. I left Stratton's obscene dinner to find him and obtain the letters from Crane."

"I wondered if you might." Wade turned to go into the dressing room, and Elijah followed him. "Have you any idea where he went?"

"None." Elijah was so angry he wanted to find a horse and ride until he felt nothing but the wind on his face and the speed of the animal beneath him.

Wade looked at him curiously, his gaze fixed on the rumpled cravat hanging around Elijah's neck. "Where did you just come from?"

There was no point in protecting Miss Bowen—Cate's—reputation since Grey would likely tell Wade what she'd witnessed. Or perhaps not. A lady's maid kept her employer's secrets inviolate. But was Grey a typical lady's maid? His head began to throb from a mixture of agitation and disappointment.

"I went to see Miss Bowen to discuss this development." "Discuss" was perhaps a generous term. He'd more accurately accused her of some sort of nefarious connection to Matthew's death and quite thoroughly and embarrassingly relinquished his tightly held self-discipline. "I don't believe she had anything to do with Matthew's death."

Wade's eyes widened slightly. "You suspected her?"

"I find the connection between her and Stratton Hall unsettling, but Septon also has a connection." Elijah exhaled. "She has no reason to remain with us now that she knows where to look for the sword. She could've easily left us here and continued on her way."

"Which she'd planned to do," Wade noted, as he took Elijah's waistcoat. "Grey said she had a change of heart, however."

So she'd said that afternoon. Wait, was he still suspicious? After everything she'd said to him, after what they'd just shared? He couldn't let their physical attraction interfere. Yet another reason he had no intention of touching her again. Or, hell, even being alone with her again.

Elijah kicked his slippers off. "Speaking of Grey, I'm sorry your evening was abbreviated."

Wade knelt to pick up the shoes. "Eh, it happens. We were searching for a cozy spot when I learned Dalby had left. Lousy timing to be sure."

Elijah coughed, thinking of his own interrupted evening. But in his case, it had been a stroke of good fortune. Despite her pleas, he couldn't succumb to her seduction. Her life might be unconventional, but he didn't bed ladies of her station. Especially not when doing so could land him in the parson's trap.

"We'll still leave in the morning?" Wade asked. "No sense in staying. I doubt Dalby will return."

"No." Defeat, something Elijah hated more than anything, curled in his chest. "I'd like to persuade a member of the staff to watch and listen for us. Give some money to whomever you trust most. I know you can scarcely have made a judgment since we just arrived today, but do your best."

"As it happens, the head footman is a bit of a kindred spirit. His father was transported when he was a wee lad and returned a few years back. He enjoyed meeting someone from the colony."

"Excellent."

Knowing they'd have a spy of sorts watching out for Dalby made Elijah feel moderately better, though his mind and body were still a mess of unsatisfied lust as he lay in bed. He calculated the time he'd need to spend with Cate. They'd have to stop and spend the night somewhere on the way to Harlech. Once they found the sword—and who knew how long that would take—he'd see her safely home. Where was that again? Monmouth. He'd take her there and deposit her with her parents, who hopefully wouldn't mind that she'd been traveling with him, with only their personal servants to act as chaperones.

On second thought, maybe he'd part ways with her some distance from Monmouth lest he find himself leg-shackled.

Either way, their time together was finite. Instead of filling him with relief, the notion made him feel just the smallest bit hollow, a sensation he'd thought long buried. And one that he wished had stayed that way.

CHAPTER 13

*E*xcitement thrummed through Cate's veins as she stepped into the morning sunshine filtering through the light clouds that dotted the sky. Today was the day she would find Dyrnwyn. Today she would solidify her place amongst the most respected antiquaries in the country. No, the world.

Not even Elijah's aloof behavior during yesterday's long journey could dampen her spirits.

"Here they come." Grey inclined her head toward the door of the small inn where they'd all spent the night.

Elijah had to duck his head as he came through the door. She caught a brief glimpse of his blond hair before he put his hat on. He glanced at Wade and said something Cate couldn't hear.

Cate smiled brightly as they approached, hopeful that Elijah would be more amenable today. She didn't want their encounter from the other night to completely destroy the friendship they'd developed. "Good morning, I trust you slept well."

Elijah looked at her only briefly before shifting his gaze to the castle atop a two-hundred-foot-tall stone outcrop. "Looks like a good walk."

"Not too long, but it's a bit of a climb," Grey said. She wore her most serviceable gown today, one that allowed her to move more freely, and her favorite walking boots.

Cate had chosen her attire in similar fashion, donning her most comfortable day gown and her oldest pair of boots, which were perfect for a rigorous walk. "Shall we be on our way?"

"Let's." Wade, carrying a small bag that held the tapestry, moved to Grey's side, and they started toward the castle.

Elijah fell into step beside Cate. "Did you bring the de Valery document in case we need it?"

Cate slid her hand into the pocket of her skirt, where she'd tucked the parchment. "Yes. I can hardly believe I'm this close. It's a dream come true."

He glanced down at her as they walked. "Most people don't ever realize their dreams."

"That's a rather cynical view."

He shrugged. "But probably accurate."

"I don't know if I agree. Why would you think that?"

He was quiet a moment, perhaps pondering her question. "In the military, most men are there because it's the only path open to them."

She cast him a sideways glance. "Was that how it was for you?"

"My father was a landowner, but not a very successful one. After he died, we had to sell the property to settle his debts. What was left went to my mother and my brother. I could've opted for a profession, but I was anxious to leave."

She thought of what he'd said outside his mother's house in Bath. "I sensed that you and your mother don't get on well. May I ask why?"

His answering silence made her tense, but he eventually

said, "There isn't much to say. She spared little time or thought for me. Consequently, I do the same for her."

Cate's heart clenched as she pictured him as a boy yearning for his mother's love. "I'm fortunate to have two wonderful parents, whom I love very much. I can't imagine my life without them. You said you were close to your father." *And then asked to change the subject.* Would he do the same again?

"I admired him as a lad, until I reached an age when I could see his faults."

"It sounds like he disappointed you."

"Not terribly. I was sad when he died."

It was a simple statement delivered with almost no emotion, and she suspected there was more to it than that. But she didn't press. She was amazed he'd shared as much as he had when he typically ignored her probing questions. "My mother says I'm meddlesome."

The look he cast her was tinged with humor. "Your mother is right."

Cate grinned as she thought of how her mother would love to hear that. They reached a steeper section of the hill and fell quiet as they climbed. Wade and Grey were in front of them, occupied in conversation, which Cate couldn't hear.

"They seem to be getting on quite well," Cate said as they reached a more level portion of the road.

"Yes. He thinks I'm not aware that he left in the middle of the night for a period of time."

Cate shot him a surprised look. "Did he? I didn't hear Grey leave."

"I think it's safe to assume she did."

They'd conducted a secret assignation in the tiny inn? Could Cate have done the same thing with Elijah if they'd stayed another night? As if it signified. He'd been clear about his intent to leave her alone.

They crested the hill, and the castle rose before them. What had been an imposing battlement rising above the town was now a breathtaking monument to a time long dead. Harlech Castle was in ruins, but still enough of a fortress to conjure battles of old.

"I can see Owen Glendower taking his last stand here." She hadn't meant to whisper, but she felt a reverence toward this ancient place.

"And I can see why it was his last stand. This would be a difficult castle to breach. Indeed, the innkeeper told me last night that it held for seven years during the War of the Roses."

She smiled at him. "Your military mind is at work."

He surprised her by smiling back. "It is. I admit the prospect is exciting."

"Did you ever see battle?"

"No, I did not. During the war, I was stationed here until I went to Australia in 1813."

"But you hoped to?"

"In theory, yes. The strategy of war fascinates me, but in truth, I doubt I would have enjoyed it."

Cate nodded solemnly. She was acquainted with a handful of men who'd returned from the war wounded and broken. She also knew a few who hadn't come home at all. "I'm glad you didn't have to fight."

Their eyes connected for a brief moment before he looked away. "I hope we won't see a battle today, but we must all be on our guard." They'd discussed the need for vigilance last night at dinner at the inn. Everyone had brought a pistol, and Cate was certain the knife that had been in Elijah's boot the other day was still there.

Grey looked at Cate. "Do you have an idea where to search?"

Looking at the massive castle constructed of sandstone,

Cate felt suddenly overwhelmed. A crumbling stone bridge led to the entrance, which was flanked by two towers that made up the massive gatehouse one passed through to reach the inner ward.

She *didn't* have a specific idea at all of where to look. "I suggest we go into the gatehouse."

Grey started over the half-ruined bridge, fearless as usual, and Cate followed her.

"Be careful," Elijah warned as he moved past them. He turned his head to look at them over his shoulder. "Walk where I walk. I don't want any of you to fall."

Cate went up second, with Grey behind her and Wade in the rear. Elijah waited for her to reach the top and gestured for her to go in first. Stone loomed above her as she moved between the two towers. She passed two sets of doors, a pair on either side of the corridor. Then she was in the inner ward. Ruined stone and wood from the building cluttered the periphery, and again she was struck with a burst of sadness for the grandeur this castle must have held.

"It's a shame to see it like this," she said.

Elijah moved into the center of the ward and turned in a half circle, his eyes scanning the four towers that guarded the fortress. "Magnificent."

As she watched the sunlight hit his upturned face, she had the same thought. Not about the castle, but about him. She averted her gaze lest he see her staring and assessed where to look first. The private quarters would likely have been upstairs in the gatehouse.

When Grey and Wade joined them, Cate suggested they split up. "I'll search the left side of the gatehouse. Elij— Norris, you take the other side. Wade and Grey, perhaps you can start in the towers?"

Grey nodded. "I'll take the northeast."

"I'll take the southeast," Wade said and they both departed.

"Do you really think you'll just find it tucked away somewhere?" Elijah asked.

The excitement at being so close had been replaced with anxiety that they were still too far. It was like searching for a pin in the grass. "We found the tapestry, didn't we?"

Elijah chuckled. "Your spirit is unmatched." He turned and went to the right side of the gatehouse.

Cate, feeling inordinately buoyed after his reaction, went into the opposite side. A pile of rotting wood sat in one corner, indicating the state of ruin. She surveyed the room briefly, but didn't see a place in which to hide anything. She climbed the circular stairs in the corner and moved into a chamber. It was empty, but offered a view of the grassy inner ward below via a massive window. She moved into the other room, which sported an enormous hole in the floor and nothing else.

Frowning, she retraced her steps and returned to the inner ward. Where next? Buildings that would've provided the heart of the castle—the kitchen, dining hall, granary, chapel—were laid out at the edge of the ward. Beyond that, encircling the towers and the inner ward was the outer ward, an important line of defense in castles from this time period.

She eyed the crumbling building against the back wall of the ward in the southwest quadrant and stalked through the doorway. The stone wall was intact, but the roof had caved in, leaving her to pick her way through the ruined timber. She searched through the wood as best she could on her way to the tower and then froze at the sound of boots against stone.

Cate dropped down low and tried to crouch behind some wood. Peering over the top toward the tower, she relaxed as a boy emerged. She stood, smiling with relief.

But he shrieked.

"Oh! I didn't mean to startle you," she said.

He looked at her strangely, as if he couldn't understand her. She remembered where she was and tried again, but in Welsh.

His shoulders released and his mouth ticked up. "It's all right. I like to play here."

Cate looked around her and thought of the mischief she would have found had she grown up near such a treasure. "What a wonderful place to play. I should like to be a child again here."

Elijah rushed into the room. "Cate!"

"I've met a friend." She turned to the boy and introduced Elijah to him in Welsh. "He doesn't speak English. He's here playing."

"Did you ask him if he's seen a sword?"

"No, but that's an excellent suggestion." Cate moved closer to the boy. "I wonder if you could help us. We're looking for something that's been here for a very long time, nigh on four hundred years. A sword." As soon as she said the words, she realized how foolish they sounded. If this boy had found a sword, he certainly wouldn't have left it untouched. But that didn't mean he didn't know where it was.

The boy's earth-colored eyes darkened. He shook his head. "I don't know anything about a sword."

Cate frowned and looked at Elijah. "He doesn't know anything."

"I gathered that from his demeanor, although I also gather he knows more than he's saying. He became guarded when you mentioned the sword."

She'd thought so too.

Wade and Grey entered then. "Haven't found anything yet," Wade announced.

Cate gestured toward the boy. "We did. He's just here playing, and no, he doesn't know anything about the sword."

"So he says," Elijah added.

"Perhaps we should look for a clue in the tapestry." Wade pulled the bag from his shoulder and set it on a rotting slab of wood that looked as though it had once been a table. He took out the map and laid it out flat.

They all moved closer to inspect it, except for Cate. "I've looked at that until my eyes crossed. I don't think there's anything more to be discerned."

The boy arched his neck to see what they were doing. "What is that?" he asked Cate.

"It's a special tapestry. It shows a battle that was fought here four hundred years ago. Would you like to see it?"

The boy nodded and Cate gestured for him to come forward.

They made space for him at the table. He inhaled, a sound of total awe, as he looked at the vibrant picture. "That's Glyndwr!" He pointed at the man wielding the sword.

Cate exchanged looks with Elijah. "Yes, we think so too."

"Oh, no, it *is* him! I've heard of this battle and this tapestry. His daughter made it."

Cate's heart froze in her chest. He'd heard of this tapestry? Glendower's daughter had made it? She squatted down to the boy's height. "How do you know of this?"

He shot her an innocent glance, all of his earlier caution gone as if it had never been. "It's an old story. My father tells it better."

"Would your father tell us this story?"

"I don't know. He only tells it to certain people."

Cate's pulse raced.

"What's he saying?" Elijah asked.

Cate looked up at him, eager to share what the boy had said. But the sound of a pistol cocking robbed her of speech.

"Cate." Elijah grabbed her arm and pulled her to his side.

The boy's eyes widened. He turned and ran for a window, vaulting through it to the middle ward.

"Don't ye move," a male voice called. Cate turned her head this way and that to try to find the source, but she didn't see anyone. "We're all around ye."

Wade and Grey stood back-to-back, pistols already in their hands.

"What do you want?" Elijah asked loudly as he slowly picked up the tapestry and carefully folded it.

"You know what they want," Cate hissed, nodding at the tapestry.

A single man walked around the corner from the direction of the tower, where this room flowed into another along the adjacent wall of the ward. As with the highwaymen who'd attacked them two days ago, a mask covered his face from hair to mouth. "I want that tapestry. Just put it back down and be on yer way."

"No," Elijah said.

The man sneered, his pistol trained on Elijah's chest. "If ye want to keep breathin', ye'll do as ye're told. This isn't goin' to be like the other day. There's more o' us than there are o' ye and the second his lordship puts his hand on a weapon, he's a dead man."

Fear curdled Cate's stomach. She would do anything to protect Elijah, but she also didn't want to lose the tapestry.

"We have to give it to them," Elijah whispered. "We already have what we need."

"Probably, but it's a valuable artifact. That boy said it was made by Glendower's daughter." Whether it led to a sword or not, it was now an important piece of Welsh history.

He looked down at her. "You expect me to safeguard it?"

She wasn't sure he could—and she didn't want him to be

in danger. "I do, but at the same time, I don't see how you can."

"Stop yer chatterin' and put the tapestry down afore I tell me lads to start shootin'."

Elijah looked at Wade and they seemed to exchange some sort of silent communication. He didn't look at Cate, but spoke in his quietest tone yet, his lips barely moving. "When I touch your shoulder, I want you to drop to the ground. Get as low as you can."

Cate's gut clenched and a cold sweat broke out on her neck. She didn't dare nod, didn't want to notify the villains of their plans. But she also didn't want Elijah to die. The tapestry wasn't worth that.

She turned, pressing against Elijah, intent on telling him they should just go, but he pushed on her shoulder, and her knees buckled, almost with a will of their own. She flattened herself into the grass and mud as a shot sounded over her head. Terror sliced through her, but she stayed down. And prayed.

~

*E*lijah whipped his pistol from his waistband and fired at the brigand who'd just missed him. The bullet pierced the man's shoulder, dropping him to the ground. Gunfire sounded around him, coming from the other villains lurking amidst the ruins.

"Get down!" Elijah called, turning toward Wade and Grey, who had already fired their weapons. They were down, but not by choice.

Wade bent over Grey, who grimaced in pain.

One of the brigands came from behind a pile of timber and raced for Elijah. Cate's head came up, but Elijah barked, "Stay down!"

He dropped the tapestry as the villain scrambled over the wood and launched himself at Elijah. He'd just pulled his knife from his boot when the brigand knocked him backward.

The man moved quickly, dodging Elijah's knife thrust and rolling to the side. Elijah shoved him off and caught sight of Wade engaged with another villain.

"Get the tapestry!" one of the villains yelled.

Elijah kicked at his opponent and tried to push himself up.

"No!" Cate's plea sent icy fear straight through his gut.

He turned in time to see a man rip the tapestry from her hands and then strike her across the face. She landed in a heap. Elijah growled as he sprang forward like a wolf on the hunt.

"Run!" the man who'd attacked Elijah cried from behind him.

Elijah felt a whoosh of air and stepped neatly to the left just as the blade of a knife scratched across his upper back, tearing his coat. Gripping the knife in his hand, he turned with an upper cut and sliced through the other man's coat from chest to shoulder. He barely managed to catch a bit of flesh, causing the man to lose his footing and fall back.

"Elijah, he's getting away!"

Turning to her, Elijah saw the brigand clutch the tapestry beneath his arm and flee the cluttered chamber. Elijah wanted to give chase, but he couldn't leave Cate or the injured Grey. The tapestry might be valuable, but it wasn't worth any of them dying. Losing Matthew was bad enough, and he was now irrevocably convinced that his death hadn't been an accident.

Elijah spun back to check on his valet. Wade stood heaving, his own knife at the ready. But the air had gone quiet.

Now that they had the tapestry, it seemed the villains had gone.

Wade turned and dropped to his knees to tend to Grey. Elijah went to Cate and helped her to stand. "Are you all right?" he asked, touching her reddened cheek. He shouldn't be so familiar, but he couldn't help himself.

She stared up at him, her eyes nearly as dark as pitch. Tugging herself from his grip, she pressed her lips together. "I hate that they have the tapestry."

He stroked his thumb against her flesh. "I know."

Her gaze shifted to something behind him and she gasped. She pulled away and rushed toward Grey. "What happened?"

Elijah followed, sharing her concern for the brave woman who'd likely captured his valet's heart. Cate knelt down beside her.

"She took a bullet to the leg," Wade said, his voice tense. He'd pushed up Grey's skirt and was investigating the wound. "Looks like a clean shot, but the wound needs attention." He smiled down at her. "Your complexion matches your name, love."

Grey scowled at him in response.

Cate looked up at Elijah. "How are we going to get her back to the inn? She can't walk."

"I can hobble," Grey said with an irritated tone. Cate looked at her with sympathy.

"Wade and I will carry her." Elijah could see that Cate was uncertain, apprehensive. "She'll be all right."

With a subtle nod, she turned and smoothed her fingers against Grey's brow. "You aren't supposed to be hurt."

"It's a bloody inconvenience. I barely feel it." Grey grimaced, disproving her words.

"Liar," Wade said. "Are you ready for us to move you?"

She pressed her lips together and gave a single nod.

A small voice drew them all to turn toward the window. The boy had come back and spoke to Cate in Welsh. Cate responded and they conversed for a moment. At last she looked at Elijah. "This boy's mother is a healer and their house is nearby. We passed it on the way. It's the dwelling closest to the castle."

"Let's go." Elijah exchanged looks with Wade and they worked together to heft Grey, who was no dainty flower. "Lead the way."

Cate spoke to the boy in Welsh and he led them from the castle, through the gatehouse and down a path that circumvented the steeper part of the hill, which they had climbed earlier. This boy knew his way around.

They had to stop twice, but they managed to arrive at the boy's cottage without causing Grey too much pain. The boy, who Cate said was called Berwyn, opened the door and ushered them inside.

A woman met them in the main room and immediately began barking orders. Elijah and Wade stared at her while Cate interpreted. "She says to take Grey through there." Cate indicated a doorway to the right.

They followed the instruction and went into a bedroom, where they laid Grey on the bed. Cate and the woman spoke for a few minutes and then the woman disappeared into the main room.

"She's gone to fetch some implements," Cate said, moving to the bed and offering a weak smile to her companion. "She's a skilled healer. It's good luck that Berwyn found us."

The woman returned a few minutes later. She spoke to Cate, who looked at Elijah and Wade and gestured toward the door. "She says to wait out there. I'll help her and come out when we're finished."

Wade frowned. He took a small step, then paused. Elijah nudged his arm. "Come on, then."

Out in the main room, the boy indicated they should sit at their dining table, which was situated at the back of the room in a kitchen area with a wide hearth. He brought two cups of ale and set them on the table.

"Thank you," Elijah said, lifting the glass and offering a smile of appreciation that the boy clearly understood.

He grinned in return and nodded, then said something in Welsh and left.

"What's he saying?" Wade asked, picking up his ale.

"No idea." Elijah took a long drink. "Cate said the boy told her that Glendower's daughter made that tapestry. It's a bloody Welsh treasure and I let it go."

Wade swallowed and set his cup down. "You didn't 'let' it do anything."

"I should've gone after them."

"One against at least five, assuming there actually were more of them than us?" Wade asked.

"Two of them wounded."

"Did you wound the other one? That'd be three if you count the one I stuck."

"Well done," Elijah said. "I only nicked mine, unfortunately. Did you land a good blow?"

Wade nodded. "Got him low between the ribs. He ran off, but he's hobbling by now."

They drank in silence a moment.

"Did you call her 'Cate'?" Wade asked.

Elijah set his cup on the table. "I did."

"That's familiar. I thought you a confirmed bachelor."

Elijah snorted. "I am."

Cate came out of the room a moment later. "Wade, if you'd like to go in, she's expecting you."

Wade was already halfway to the bedroom.

Elijah stood. "How is she?"

"In pain, but the leg should heal. She'll need to remain

here a few days, however."

"You say that as if you don't plan to stay with her." Elijah recognized the set of her jaw.

Her lips curved down. "I don't know what I plan to do." She glanced around the room. "Where's Berwyn?"

"I don't know. He said something unintelligible and left."

"I need to speak with his father. He has a story to tell me about the tapestry."

"You said it was made by Glendower's daughter. Is that a clue that will help locate the sword?"

"I hope so. I don't know anything about her. And if he doesn't either, I'll need to consult my father's library."

Elijah didn't know if he dared travel with her to her parents in Monmouth, which meant she'd have to stay here and wait for Grey to heal. Would he stay with them? He didn't know what he ought to do. He only wished he could get his hands around the men who'd taken the tapestry, and not because of the theft, but because he was certain they were behind Matthew's death.

He flexed his hands as rage spiraled through him.

The door opened and in walked Berwyn with a man. They bore a strong resemblance to each other with their dark, straight hair and slightly hooked noses. The man greeted them in Welsh. Cate responded as the boy rushed to fetch his father a cup of ale. He also refilled the two on the table. He turned to Cate and asked her a question. She answered and the boy obtained a fourth cup, so Elijah surmised he'd offered her ale as well.

The man quaffed his beverage and handed it to the boy for a refill. Then he spoke to Cate in a long string of what sounded like gibberish to Elijah's non-Welsh-understanding ears.

Cate looked at him. "This is Ifan. He's lived in the shadow of Harlech his entire life. In fact, his family has lived here for generations. He invites us to sit so that he may tell us a story."

Elijah fought the urge to scowl. He didn't want to hear a story. He wanted to find the men who'd killed his brother.

Perhaps Cate read his annoyance, because she cast him a quelling glance. "Sit, Elijah. He's going to tell us who stole the tapestry."

CHAPTER 14

*T*hey settled themselves around the table—Cate and Elijah, Berwyn, Ifan, and Rhona. She'd finished tending Grey, who was now resting with Wade at her bedside.

Cate sipped her ale, her body thrumming with anticipation. "I am anxious to hear your tale, Ifan." She spoke to him in Welsh and then turned to Elijah. "I'll translate, but please be patient."

His expression was stoic, his gaze cool. She could practically feel the frustration radiating from him. She touched his hand and registered the shock of desire that seemed ever-present when she looked at him now and which only intensified when they came into contact. She left her hand atop his. He didn't seem to register it, but neither did he flinch.

Ifan launched his tale, his dark eyes sparkling in the midday sun streaming through the small window next to the table. "I tell you this because you had the tapestry in your possession." He frowned. "Berwyn says it was stolen from you. I'm sorry for it. What did you plan to do with it?"

"I'm an antiquary," Cate said. "The discovery and preservation of antiquities is my life's work. And my life's dream is to find the sword depicted in the tapestry and share it with the people of Britain."

Ifan smiled and gave a single nod, appearing satisfied with her answer. "The tapestry belongs here in Harlech. It's a treasure that belongs to the people of Wales."

"Because Glendower's daughter stitched it?" Cate was unsurprised when he nodded in response. "I'm heartbroken it was lost. I'm hopeful we can get it back, and yes, I think it should be kept here in Harlech, perhaps on display in the church." She leaned forward, anxious, but not wanting to appear too desperate. Desperate, however, described precisely how she felt. "You were going to tell us who took it."

"Yes, yes, in time." His dark brows wiggled. In fact, they moved every time he spoke, as if they had a will of their own. It made his face very expressive and earnest. "First, I must start at the beginning. This is a story passed down through my family since the time of Owain Glyndwr." Some people found the sound of Welsh harsh, but Cate loved the lilt of it and she smiled at hearing him pronounce the Welsh hero's name. "As I said, we've always lived in the shadow of Harlech. Or inside its walls. We supported Glyndwr in the rebellion. My ancestors fought with him before the castle fell to the English." His lip curled as he said the last, and his eyes darted briefly toward Elijah. Cate gave his hand a squeeze, hoping he wouldn't take offense. Ifan wouldn't hold a grudge against Elijah personally, but he was clearly of the mindset that the English had stolen Wales's independence.

"The legend of the flaming sword is my duty to preserve. It is known amongst the people of Harlech, but we hold the tale dear as our treasure. The tapestry is the manifestation of it. It shows in picture what we share in word."

Cate nodded and asked him to pause while she translated

what he said to Elijah. She turned back to Ifan. "Please, continue."

"The sword belonged to a young man. What he lacked in experience, he made up for in courage. He rushed into battle, his sword bursting with white flame. It scared the English at first and he took many lives, but they rebounded and he was soon overcome. The English lifted the sword in victory, but it didn't flame. The fire only sparks for the worthy." Ifan grinned, sending another glance—this one tinged with superiority—toward Elijah. "They were not worthy."

Cate shared this with Elijah who suppressed a frown. "Please don't take offense," she said softly.

Elijah arched a brow. "This man clearly holds the English in low regard. And I'm an Englishman."

She gave him a pleading look and squeezed his hand again before returning her attention to Ifan. "This sword was Dyrnwyn?"

He nodded, his eyes gleaming with admiration. "Yes. The Sword of Rhydderch Hael. One of the thirteen treasures. Glyndwr refused to allow the English to take it. He attacked and regained the blade. And it burst into flames once more."

"Because Glendower was worthy," Cate said with more than a touch of awe. "What happened to the sword?"

"It disappeared with him. After the castle fell, Glyndwr fled."

Cate's stomach caved in. That couldn't be all. The sword couldn't be lost. "How did his daughter know to make this tapestry? Was she here?"

Ifan shook his head, a small smile curving his slender lips. "We don't know for certain, but she married Sir John Scudamore and lived with him at Kentchurch, where she made that tapestry. What's more, Glyndwr lived there with them."

Cate looked at Elijah, expecting to see the excitement unfurling in her chest reflected in his eyes, until she remembered that he didn't understand a word of what Ifan said. "The sword is at Kentchurch. It's where Glyndwr went after the battle."

Elijah's hand tensed and his eyes shone with enthusiasm. "He knows this for certain?"

He hadn't said it exactly. Cate turned back to Ifan. "Is the sword there?"

Ifan leaned back in his chair with a slight shrug. "It isn't here."

What did that mean? She let go of Elijah's hand and crossed her arms.

"What is it?" Elijah asked.

"He doesn't definitively say where the sword is located, just that it isn't here. Glendower took the sword and he went to Kentchurch with his daughter. It therefore follows that the sword ought to be in Kentchurch, no?"

He looked at her with an edge of skepticism. "I'm not sure I believe anything is that straightforward. Not after the chase this has become."

Cate worried he was right. She looked at their host intently. "Where do I look at Kentchurch?"

"That I cannot tell you because I don't know." He sounded regretful and Cate believed him.

"What of the men who stole the tapestry?" Cate asked.

Ifan's eyes gleamed with something akin to malice. "The Order of the Round Table. They seek to control the thirteen treasures."

Cate's neck pricked. "What is the Order?"

"What?" Elijah asked, leaning toward her. "You look concerned."

Cate uncrossed her arms and pressed her palms flat on the table. "Give me a moment."

Ifan finished his second cup of ale. "The Order was founded by the descendants of the Knights of the Round

Table. At first, their mission was noble—to protect the treasures from theft and misuse. Over time, they accepted members who were not descendants and some of them became corrupt. I am not surprised they stole the tapestry from you—they will stop at nothing to get what they want."

Those words chilled her to the bone. *They will stop at nothing.*

She glanced at Elijah and worried about his reaction. "Ifan, do you know who is in the Order?" She was afraid of the answer because she suspected she already knew. All of Andy's suspicions flooded Cate's brain.

"Not by name. As I said, they are mostly descendants of the knights, though I have heard that one of their current highest-ranking officials is not a descendant. They invite scholars to join their numbers—this is what perverted the organization."

Scholars.

Septon.

He had to be a member. His knowledge of Arthurian legend and the thirteen treasures was unparalleled. Cate's muscles tensed. Was her father also a member? She thought of the secret poem she'd found in his library and felt queasy.

"Cate, what's wrong?" Elijah touched her shoulder.

She looked at him, glad for his presence. "There is an organization—the Order of the Round Table—which seeks to protect the thirteen treasures, including the sword."

His gaze hardened. "This is who stole the tapestry and killed my brother?"

Cate swallowed. "Ifan said they'll stop at nothing to obtain the treasures."

Elijah withdrew his hand from her shoulder and his jaw tightened. "How do we find them?"

She looked at Ifan. "Is there a way to find the Order? To contact them?"

He shook his head. "Not that I know of. The best way to gain their attention is to pursue one of the treasures, which you are already doing."

Cate exhaled, her pulse beat a staccato rhythm through her veins. She turned in her seat to face Elijah. "He doesn't know where to find them, but I think I do."

His eyes widened then narrowed. "How?"

"I suspect Septon might be a member."

The flesh around Elijah's mouth turned white, and again, she felt his fury as if it might combust into flame like the sword. "He said he didn't know the men who visited Matthew. If they're all part of this Order, he lied."

Cate was afraid Septon had lied about a lot of things. Throughout her entire life. She felt hollow as she wondered if her own father was also a part of the deception. Did her mother even know? Cate was instantly torn between following the sword to Kentchurch and unraveling the mystery of the Order—and she only had to look at Elijah to know which he wanted to do.

"We're going back to Septon House." He practically growled the statement.

"I think we should find the sword first—before they do."

"How will they know where to look? The tapestry won't tell them. If you couldn't figure it out, they can't."

She warmed to his confidence. But she still wanted the sword. "I don't want to take the chance that they'll find it first, especially if their intentions are malicious. This sword belongs to history and the people of Britain, not some secret group."

He didn't soften. "I need to find the men who killed my brother. I will see justice done."

"Of course we will. I want that too." As much as she wanted the sword, she realized. How deeply had she come to care for this man? The thought rattled her, and she pushed it away for now.

"What will you do?" Berwyn asked, his dark eyes wide in his young face.

"We're not sure yet," Cate said honestly.

Rhona looked across the table at Cate, her sherry-colored eyes narrowing with worry. "Your maid needs to remain for a few days to recuperate."

Cate had figured as much. "You will allow her to stay here?"

"I think it's best. We could accommodate you and the Englishman as well, but it will be close."

Cate made a mental note not to tell Elijah they referred to him as "the Englishman" and wondered if that was also how they referred to Wade. "Lord Norris and I will be leaving; however, I believe his valet, Wade, would like to stay with Grey. Will that be all right?"

Rhona nodded. "He said as much. We may have to post the banns." Her mouth curved into a pretty smile.

"What are you talking about?" Elijah asked with a hint of irritation.

She quickly apologized, realizing he must feel completely excluded because he didn't understand what was being said. "She's invited us to stay, but I declined. Wade, however, will remain with Grey while she recovers from her wound."

"I realize they can't comprehend what we're saying, but may we speak in private?"

Wary at his crisp tone, Cate nodded slowly. "Yes." She turned to Rhona and Ifan and smiled. "Will you excuse us for a moment?"

She stood and Elijah joined her. After glancing about, she led him into a small room off the kitchen. It held a narrow bed and some toys. Berwyn's room, then.

Elijah closed the door and she arched a brow at him in question.

"We're about to embark on a journey alone together and you're concerned about a closed door?"

"I'm not, but I know how much you value propriety."

"Hang propriety just now," he bit out. "Will you come with me to Septon House?"

She desperately wanted to go after the sword first, but could she convince him? If not, she'd have to wait at least two or three days until Grey was well enough to travel. Her wound would heal, but she needed time to let it knit and ward off any fever. "I will," she said cautiously. "After we go to Kentchurch."

He swore, turning from her and going to the small window.

She came up behind him, but resisted the urge to put her hand on him. The desire to touch him was becoming more frequent. "What would we do when we reached Septon House? Accuse Septon of organizing Matthew's death?" Cate didn't think for a moment that Septon had actually done that. He was committed to antiquities, but not at the cost of someone's life.

Elijah turned from the windows, his eyes blazing with icy heat. "What do you propose we do? It's clear you have a plan. One that no doubt prioritizes your goal."

Cate worked to keep her ire in check. She understood his anger—he'd lost his brother. "I'd like to go to Kentchurch—and I know you think that's selfish, but it isn't. I don't want this Order to find the sword first. I don't know what they plan to do with it, but if they're willing to kill to obtain it, they must have a reason for their desperation."

"Your argument doesn't help your case. The risk of danger is now a reality, not a supposition. If we find the sword, this Order will track us and perhaps kill us." His jaw clenched as his eyes gleamed with something she could only describe as suppressed violence. "Or at least try to."

Cate decided right then that she was glad she'd never have to face this man on a battlefield. "But they don't know where they're going. We'll ensure we aren't followed. Something tells me you're probably skilled at such evasion."

"I am." There was no arrogance in his statement; it was a simple declaration of fact.

Excitement bloomed in her chest, and she couldn't help herself any longer. She took his hand in hers, felt how cool his fingertips were and rubbed her thumb across his knuckles. "Then come with me to find the sword. We can do this—together. Once we have it, we'll go to my father and talk to him about this Order."

His gaze turned skeptical. "Why?"

She glanced away, not wanting him to see how much this unsettled her. "Because I'm afraid he might be part of it too."

"What?" The single word was barely a whisper, but it carried the weight of iron.

"He would never, ever harm anyone, Elijah." She couldn't see past the hardness in his gaze. She looked at him imploringly. "Please, he's my father. Perhaps there are corrupt members of this organization, but he isn't one of them." She knew that as well as she knew herself. The alternative was unthinkable.

"I would have difficulty believing that your parent could condone such a thing, but be warned that while I trust you, I do not extend that sentiment to anyone else. Do you understand?"

It was all she could ask of him right now. That he trusted her was enough—it had to be. She nodded.

He took his hand from hers and set it on his hip. "This is what we will do." He spoke in an authoritative tone, one she was sure he employed with his troops. "You will stay here while Wade and I go to the inn. We will tell the innkeeper that we will be staying with friends—here—but that we need to keep our coach and team at the inn's stables. After we disguise ourselves, you and I will leave on horseback when darkness falls tonight. There is enough of a moon to guide our way."

Cate was amazed at how quickly he'd formulated a plan. "How will we be disguised?"

"I'm not entirely certain, but be prepared to dress as a man."

The corner of her mouth ticked up. "It won't be the first time."

His gaze dipped briefly to her legs. "Why doesn't that surprise me?" Finally, his gaze lost a bit of its fury. "It is imperative on this journey that you do exactly as I say. If you can't agree to that right now, we're not going."

"I understand. You're in command." She suppressed a shiver as she realized she had no trouble accepting this hierarchy, and normally she would bristle at the thought of answering to anyone, especially an autocratic earl. Except he wasn't being autocratic, at least not without reason.

Some of the tension left his shoulders as he went to the door. Pausing with his hand on the latch, he turned to look at her with an inscrutable expression. "I fear I'm going to regret this."

She locked her gaze with his. "I promise you won't."

∿

*E*lijah wiped a bit more soot on his face for good measure. Grime was an essential component of any good disguise, especially in the case of Cate, whose beauty would be difficult to conceal.

For the thousandth time since agreeing to this mad

adventure, he reconsidered his decision to pursue the sword. He ought to be riding straight for Septon House so that he could demand the truth from that lying prick, Septon. Elijah didn't care if Cate had known him her entire life—if he was guilty of arranging Matthew's death, Elijah would see him prosecuted.

And then there was her father. He didn't know the man at all, of course, but he couldn't accept that he could be involved in something so heinous. Unless Elijah was completely wrong about her, and he didn't think so. He believed her when she said she was committed to finding out how Matthew had died. He only hoped he wasn't blinded by his emotion.

He pressed his lips together and felt his muscles tighten. He wasn't certain how he felt about her, but he cared whether she found her blessed sword, and a shadow cast itself over his mood whenever he thought about what happened after that. When he thought of the end of their association.

Forcing the tension from his shoulders, he straightened his threadbare coat, with its missing buttons. Ifan had collected a ramshackle assortment of clothing for their disguises, which only helped their cause. The objective was to avoid notice, to fade into the background. Unfortunately, footwear had been a problem. Unable to find boots that would fit his large feet, Elijah had mucked up his own to the best of his ability—rather, to the best of Berwyn's ability. The lad had taken the task quite seriously while at the same time having a jolly time of it. Elijah was only glad they'd found suitable boots for Cate because wearing her own was out of the question.

As if summoned by his thoughts, she came out of the bedroom where Grey was convalescing. If he hadn't known of Cate's disguise, he likely wouldn't have recognized her. He smiled.

"Don't laugh at me." Her tone carried an edge of humor, and he suspected her warning came from a desire to remain sober as opposed to a sense of vanity.

"I would never."

She cast him a dubious look, but smiled. "You're right. I'm certain I can count the number of times you've laughed in my presence on one hand."

It might have sounded like a jest, but she was right. Elijah rarely laughed. He rarely had cause to, although he found levity more and more in her presence. Perhaps that's where this *emotion* he couldn't describe was coming from.

"Will I pass muster, then?" She turned in a circle. Thankfully her coat covered her backside, else Elijah was certain the entire charade would fail. There would be no mistaking her feminine curves outlined in the snug breeches.

"Not in my regiment, but that's precisely the point," he said. She looked just like a ragamuffin young man with her hair tucked up into a hat, her face caked with dirt, and her form clad in worn clothing that cloaked her sex. It was, without a doubt, a most successful disguise. Why, then, was he more attracted to her than ever?

"Are we ready?"

"Ifan is with the horses in the alley." In addition to procuring their clothing, their Welsh benefactor had performed a minor miracle and obtained a pair of beasts for them to ride. "You've bid farewell to Grey?"

"Yes." She frowned—at least, he thought that's what her mouth was doing. It was hard to tell beneath the dirt. "She is quite aggravated that she can't accompany us. I'm grateful to Wade for staying with her. I fear she'd insist on coming if it weren't for him."

"He's not terribly pleased with this turn of events, either.

He'd much rather be at our side." And Elijah would much rather have him. He hoped they'd be able to meet Wade and Grey in Monmouth at Cate's parents' house.

Rhona approached them, speaking in Welsh to Cate, who responded. Cate then hugged the petite woman and thanked her—one of the few words Elijah had been able to pick out of the conversations he'd overheard all day.

Elijah opened the door and stepped into the twilight. Cate followed him and he set the latch. He reached back and took her hand. Though they both wore gloves, the contact felt intimate. What did he expect? They were embarking on a journey alone. Intimacy would be unavoidable. He just had to strive to keep their interactions chaste.

Ifan had provided directions to the alley via Cate. Elijah guided her down the empty street and crossed the other side. Voices sounded from farther down, and Elijah quickened their pace. He turned right into the alley and exhaled a small breath of relief.

Two horses, held by Ifan and Berwyn, stood ready. Elijah helped Cate to mount the smaller of the two. Ifan said something to Cate and she thanked him as she'd done his wife earlier.

Elijah stepped forward and offered his hand to Ifan. "Dee-allch," he said, hoping he wasn't mangling the Welsh word for thank you.

Ifan gripped his hand firmly. "Croeso."

Elijah thought that was probably "you're welcome." He turned to say good-bye to Berwyn and lost his balance as the boy hugged him. He said something in Welsh. Elijah ruffled his hair in response and when the boy stepped away, gave him a warm smile.

Elijah climbed astride his horse and led Cate from the alley. They made their way quietly down the street and out of the small town. He directed them toward the hills, which were in the opposite direction of their ultimate destination: Kentchurch in England. Leaving town via the wrong road was just one of the many techniques Elijah was using in order to avoid detection.

They rode in silence for quite a while, the cool night air enveloping them in a comfortable cocoon. At least that's how Elijah felt. He'd loved being out at night in Australia. The sounds and scents were so different there. Here, he could smell the sea, which wasn't too far off, and hear the faint signs of nocturnal creatures moving about their business. They were fortunate to be traveling in midsummer, when it wasn't too cold, and just as lucky to have the moon guiding them.

"How long will we ride?" Cate's voice broke into his thoughts. He hadn't forgotten she was there. On the contrary, he'd been even more attuned to her presence. It seemed as though they could be the only two people in the world. He'd felt like that often in Australia, where the spaces were so open and the population so sparse.

"Until the moon starts to set." He'd told her they'd sleep under the sky until morning, at which time they'd alter course and head toward England. To her credit, she'd not only accepted the hardship, she'd exhibited an enthusiasm for it, having never slept outside before.

More than an hour later, they came upon a stream. "Time to stop." He heard her intake of breath and looked over at her to see her hand covering her yawning mouth.

She offered a weak smile. "Sorry. I'm glad to take a rest."

He nodded, then scanned for a place to camp. The hills rose beyond the stream to their left, where the terrain grew increasingly uneven as it marched toward the Snowdon Mountains. To their right were low shrubbery and intermittent crops of rocks. He spotted a particularly large group that would shield them from the path and decided to make camp there. He led Cate and her mount to it and dismounted.

He helped Cate down, his hands encircling her waist as she pulled her leg over and slid to the ground. "Give me a moment to mask our departure from the road then I'll water the horses, " he said.

"What are you going to do?"

He plucked a branch from a shrub. "Cover our tracks." He completed his task quickly and returned to Cate.

"I'll go with you. I'd like to wash my face." She looked at him with curiosity. "Is that all right?"

"It would be best if you could keep the disguise for now. Can you do that?"

She exhaled, but smiled at the end. "I can."

He guided the horses to the stream, whispering gratitude and encouragement. When he returned to her a few minutes later, she immediately set about removing her horse's saddle to grant the animal a rest.

Elijah marveled at her capability and initiative. "You know what you're doing."

"My parents made sure I was educated, regardless of my sex."

He thought he might like her parents. Provided her father wasn't a member of some secret organization who was likely behind Matthew's death. Elijah dispelled the thought. He didn't want to think about that right now.

"Let me know if you require assistance with the saddle once you have it loose."

"Thank you." She shot him a look that said she appreciated the offer.

Elijah saw to his own horse. When he was finished and had fed both animals from their packs, he pulled a flagon of ale from his saddlebag and took a long drink. He held it out to Cate, who took it and satisfied her own thirst.

Cate crossed her arms and rubbed her hands up and down her biceps as she studied the sky.

"Are you chilled?" Elijah asked. They had a light blanket, which he removed from the bag. He wrapped it around her shoulders, his fingers grazing her arms. The touch reminded him why he'd worked so diligently to keep her at a distance the past few days. Since Stratton Hall. Since they'd been so fortunately interrupted. Not that his body agreed. No, his body was quite frustrated with her proximity and the fact that he couldn't finish what they'd started.

She looked up at him, her eyes nearly as dark as the night surrounding her. "Thank you."

"I'm sorry about your face." There were smudges in the grime, but she was still dirty. It did nothing to detract from her beauty—at least to him—or his desire for her. "Tomorrow night we'll stop somewhere we can tidy up." He hoped. There were few villages along their route, and they'd likely have to depend upon the kindness of a stranger. He glanced up at the sky. "We're going to lose the moon shortly. Let's find a place to sleep."

"Together?" she asked.

"There's only the one blanket, though I don't really need it."

"You don't?"

"I'm accustomed to sleeping with just my coat for warmth, but then summer nights in Australia are warmer than summer nights in Wales."

"Are they?" she asked with keen interest. "Tell me how else they're different. You've seen and experienced so much that I never will."

He heard the envy in her voice and felt a pang of regret for her. She was well aware of how her sex impacted her ability to enjoy certain experiences and it really wasn't fair. He could see her enduring—enjoying, even—many activities that would be unseemly for a woman. He'd already seen her deal with highwaymen and an attack that had left her friend wounded. Yet, here she was, undaunted.

With a gentle—and quick—touch against her lower back, he guided her to the rocks and sat down with his back against one. "Sit with me."

She sank to the ground beside him and pulled the blanket from her shoulders. Cozying up to him against the rock, she draped the cloth over them both. "For now," she said, correctly guessing that he meant to protest.

He should insist she scoot away from him, but sharing body heat would be a necessity as the temperature dropped even further over the next few hours. He'd known they would have to sleep against each other, but he'd hoped she might slumber before he gathered her close. And potentially spent a sleepless night.

She settled next to him. "Tell me about Australia."

He lifted his arm and put it around her shoulders and stopped himself before he could stroke her—or think about why the action came so naturally. "It's very big. At least, it felt that way because there were so few people."

"Did you meet any of the Aboriginals?"

"You know their name," he marveled. "I shouldn't be surprised, given your intellect."

"Thank you. Tell me about the people."

He chuckled softly, enjoying her enthusiasm. "Yes, I met some of them. They are people, just like us, with families and traditions. But they live quite differently. They hunt and gather their food. I learned to hunt as they do."

She turned her head to look at him briefly. "You did? That must have been quite thrilling."

"It was." He recalled the time he spent with a young man from a nearby group. "Using a spear takes some getting used to."

"A spear! I can see you wielding such a weapon. I'd already envisioned you as a fierce soldier. What else?"

He wanted to ask how else she'd envisioned him, but decided that path led to trouble. Particularly when he thought about the myriad ways he'd envisioned her. "The food is different. I miss the macadamia nuts." He'd brought some on the voyage, but they were long gone. "And various fruits."

Her eyes sparkled with interest. "What are they like?"

"Sweet and delicious." *Like your mouth.* This was a potentially dangerous conversation. He wondered if there was such a thing as a safe conversation when he was nestled under the stars with the most alluring woman he'd ever known, and he grasped for something to fill the pause created by his errant mind. "The stars are different in the southern hemisphere."

"Are they? I didn't know that."

"My favorite constellation is called the Southern Cross. It's used in navigation in southern seas."

"It's so strange to think you were so far away. Did you miss England?"

"No."

She turned in his arms and studied him for a moment. "You answered that very quickly. And definitively. You were happier away from here."

He couldn't lie. "I was."

"You wish you could go back." The words were spoken softly, but with an edge of disappointment.

"In some ways. In other ways, I look forward to being here." He did? He'd resigned himself to his new role, even if he didn't like it. But he realized he hadn't really felt a purpose, a *drive* beyond fulfilling his duty. The army had taught him that nothing was more important than duty. And yet here he was, with Cate, and he felt as though he did have a purpose—finding this sword with her and avenging his brother's death. Avenging? Did he really plan to punish the men who'd killed him? Perhaps not personally, but he would see them suffer for their crimes under the law.

"You do?" Her lips curved into a smile. "I'm glad. But I wish I could go back with you. What do you miss most about it?"

"My horse."

She laughed. "I see. So it isn't really about the place at all, but about what you feel a connection to. I'm encouraged by this revelation. You don't seem particularly close to your mother, and with your father and brother gone, I wondered if you cared about anything or anyone. Save Wade. It's clear he's important to you and you to him."

"You're right about that," he said quietly. Wade was about the only person he cared about. Until now. He looked into her eyes, lost the sense of time and place, felt her shift as she turned into him and laid her hand against his chest, leaned his head down . . .

He pulled back, knocking his head back against the rock.

Her face creased with concern. "Are you all right?" Her hand came up and cradled the back of his head.

A shock of lust so strong it nearly took his sight, slammed through him. "We should sleep. Tomorrow will be a long day of travel."

She didn't retract her hand. "How far will we get?"

"Not near enough to Kentchurch, but we'll find a place to spend the night." He reached up and took her hand from his head. "You mustn't be so familiar."

"It's a bit late for that, isn't it?" she asked with more than a dash of irony.

"No, it is not. By necessity, we must sleep close tonight, but do not take anything else from it. There will not be a repeat of what happened at Stratton Hall."

She exhaled. It was a sound of longing and disappointment, and it nearly cut completely through his resolve. How he wished they could get to Kentchurch tomorrow. The sooner he deposited her with her parents, the better.

She shrugged out of her coat.

"What are you doing?"

"I'd like a pillow."

He pulled the coat back up over her shoulders. "Use mine." He removed his garment and folded it for her before laying it on the ground.

"Won't you be cold?"

"No." He was actually quite overheated at present and predicted it would be some time before he cooled.

She looked at him with doubt, but eventually stretched out on the ground. He took the blanket off his legs, though he'd been quite thankful for it as a shield a moment ago. He settled the cloth over her and she drew it up to her shoulders. "Aren't you going to lie down?"

"Not yet. I will soon."

She gave him a saucy look. "I won't bite. Unless you ask me to."

"Cate, for the love of God, please stop."

"Why? Is there any reason we can't pursue our mutual attraction? And don't tell me you aren't attracted to me."

"I can list many reasons, the primary one being the fact that you're a virgin."

"Who said I was?"

Hell and the devil. She wasn't a virgin? He suspected that bounder Iscove was to blame. Elijah vowed in that moment to make hunting him down his very next project—as soon as he brought Matthew's murderers to justice. "You shouldn't say such provocative things—true or not."

She sighed. "I am a virgin, unfortunately. And probably destined to die one since I doubt I shall marry."

"You could marry." She was intelligent, beautiful, and moneyed. She *ought* to marry, regardless of what she'd said to him the other day following the highwaymen's attack.

She arched a dark brow, barely perceptible in the fading moonlight. "Why would I? My life is exactly as I like it right now. Save the fact that you won't bed me."

She really was trying to kill him. "Good night, Cate," he practically growled.

"Good night, Elijah. Don't hesitate to inform me if you've changed your mind."

He couldn't bring himself to acknowledge her audacity with an answer. But that didn't stop his brain from conjuring all manner of ways in which to satisfy her curiosity. How in the hell was he going to endure the next few days in her company?

CHAPTER 15

*U*pon waking, Cate had been disappointed to find that Elijah was no longer beside her. She'd been vaguely aware of him next to her in the night, of his warmth and presence. It had been both comforting and arousing, but she'd been so tired, she'd simply slept through it. And now he was gone. Or rather, saddling the horses.

"Good, you're awake." His tone was sharp, closer to his military voice than the voice of the man she'd come to know and like very much. The man she knew cared about her more than he wanted to, and perhaps even more than he realized.

She stretched her arms to the sky. "Yes. I slept surprisingly well. Did you?"

He threw her a dubious glance, but didn't answer. She took that as a no and wondered if she'd been the cause of his discomfort. She hoped so. He was being frustratingly stubborn.

Once the horses were saddled, he offered her some cheese and bread to break her fast. "Eat quickly so we can be on our way."

He'd gone back to his autocratic ways.

She devoured the food, not because he'd instructed her to, but because she was hungry. Then she slipped off to take care of her personal needs. When she returned, he stood beside her horse with an impatient look.

"Are you going to be a bear all day?" she asked.

"Miss Bowen, I am not a bear."

"Oh, you're going to 'Miss Bowen' me now." She huffed out an exasperated sigh. "Can't we just go back to the way things were?"

He helped her onto the horse, but kept his touch brief and brisk. "And how is that?"

"Don't be obtuse. You do that often. You pretend not to hear or to misunderstand. Or sometimes you simply ignore questions altogether. You're a frustrating man."

"Isn't that already on my list? I daresay I've lost track." He was trying to be stoic, but a glint of humor showed through in his tone and the subtle arch of his brow.

"Yes, it is. I'm adding provoking. And stubborn. And foolish."

"That's quite a list. I do hope you're writing it down. Come, let's move to the road then I'll come back and cover the evidence of our camp."

Cate walked her horse to the road and held his reins while he went back and erased their presence. She was exceptionally grateful to be sharing this journey with him—both for his company and his expert protection.

He took the reins from her and climbed onto his horse. The morning sun was bright and hot, warming the dark coat covering her back. Generally, she would argue that men's clothing was far more comfortable; however, today she would trade the layers on her upper body for a light day dress.

They rode in silence for quite some time, varying their speeds as the terrain allowed. Finally, at midday, they stopped for respite. As they sat down for a light repast packed by their Welsh hostess, she considered whether she wanted to continue to vex him or choose a safer topic. It didn't matter since he spoke first.

"I know you said you'd come to Septon House with me, but I've decided that won't be necessary. I think it's wiser if you remain with your parents after we find the sword."

He'd *decided*? She wasn't to be consulted? Cate gritted her teeth and tried to catch his eye, but he was fixated on something in the distance. She turned to see what he was looking at, but saw nothing and determined he was simply avoiding looking at *her*. "I want to see this through with you."

"It isn't your problem."

It wasn't, but that didn't mean she didn't care. "It is if Septon is involved. I need to know if he caused your brother's death." She'd tried not to think of her father or Septon being a part of this mysterious Order. Every time she did, her insides congealed and she felt as if she was going to toss up her accounts.

"I would argue your logic. Septon's involvement still has nothing to do with you. Unless you somehow participated." Now he shot her a glance. "But you did not."

"Would you accept that I just want to help you? That I care what happened because he was your brother?" She didn't think she was making an impact on him. "It's unfair of you to deny me the opportunity to see this to the end. If I were a man, you would accept my help."

"If you were a man, many details about our association would be different." His gaze dipped to her costume. "Despite how you are garbed, you are, however, *not* a man."

She was irritated with him, but the bead of appreciation in his assessment sparked hope within her. "How nice of you to notice," she murmured.

He finished his last bite and stood abruptly. "We need to go." He held his hand out to help her up.

She brushed crumbs from her lap and accepted his assistance. "That's how it's to be, then? I express my wishes, but it doesn't matter? You aren't my father or my husband. If I decide to follow you to Septon House, you can't do anything to stop me."

"You are correct; however, I can express my concerns to your father about your safety. I can only hope you adhere to societal norms and actually listen to your father, who will certainly instruct you not to go." He frowned at her. "But I am fairly certain you wouldn't obey him or a husband either. It's probably best you prefer to remain unwed."

Was he saying she would make a terrible wife? Any other woman would be outraged, but he was right. And what's more, she had no quarrel with that. "My thoughts exactly. It's also why you should accept my invitation. You won't be spoiling me for any man."

"Please stop bringing that up." He led her horse to a small rock and cast her a derisive glance. "Mount up yourself."

She did as he bade while he once again disguised any evidence of them having stopped, and soon they were back on the road. She guided her horse alongside him. "I've been giving this considerable thought. What else is there to do on such a journey, especially when one's companion is frightfully close-mouthed?"

"I'm not close-mouthed. We are simply trying to make a good pace, which doesn't allow for much conversation. What are you giving considerable thought? Never mind. I don't think I care to know."

"Your rejection. You have a high moral code. Is it from the military?"

He looked at her askance. "Probably."

"As I've said before, you won't be ruining me or spoiling

me. I want to be with you and I don't wish to marry you. Provided we can avoid pregnancy, there truly is no reason we can't indulge our desires. You do know how to avoid pregnancy, I take it?"

"Good Lord, woman, you would try a saint's patience. Please cease in asking me such questions!"

"Perhaps I'll seduce you in your sleep tonight."

He drew his horse to a halt and turned to look at her. She stopped and faced him. A few feet separated them, but it might have been a canyon. "You will not seduce me. And you will not prattle on about our desires. Yes, I know how to prevent pregnancy. I had a mistress in Australia and I've stopped in many ports around the world. I'm quite adept at not leaving my seed where I don't wish it to be left and at protecting myself from all manner of disease. However, you shall not be privy to such techniques, as I have no intention of using them with you."

"You're being foolish. We want each other and—"

"Yes, I want you," he thundered. "But I'm not going to have you. Not tonight. Not ever. I have no interest in marriage, and my code of honor would insist I marry you."

She blinked against the ferocity of his outburst. "Even though I don't wish to marry you?"

He ground his teeth together. "Your wishes do not signify."

Anger flared in her belly, driving away the desire. "I see. You are safe from my advances and my further interest. The surest way to earn my disdain is to discount my preferences. Congratulations, my lord."

She turned her horse and kicked her into a gallop. As for the dust they kicked up from the road, she hoped Elijah might choke on it.

∾

*I*t was dusk and Elijah knew Cate had to be bone tired—he was. However, she didn't show it. She sat as straight in her saddle as she had earlier in the day. Either she was exceptionally well-seasoned or her pride would rival that of any soldier he'd met.

As expected, they hadn't come across a village and likely wouldn't until it was fully dark. They needed to rest. Thankfully, tomorrow's journey would be relatively short. With luck, they would be at Kentchurch by noon.

A collection of buildings and smoke from a chimney signaled respite ahead. Elijah only hoped the inhabitants would allow them to lodge in their barn. He slowed his horse and waited for Cate to ride up beside him. They hadn't spoken since after lunch, when he'd used every weapon in his arsenal to discourage her attentions, including belittling her, which he knew would drive her mad. It had worked. Her outrage had been quick—and glorious, truth be told. He did enjoy watching the color rise in her cheeks and the sparks ignite in her magnificent eyes. He was going to miss her when they parted ways.

She took her time coming abreast of him and when she did, she said nothing. She spared him a quick glance and nothing more.

"I'm going to ask if we can lodge in these people's barn. Just wait in the yard while I speak to them."

"What if they don't speak English?" Her question was oversweet and the look she gave him would've curdled cream.

He hadn't considered that. "We're close enough to the border. I'm sure they speak English." He *hoped* they spoke English.

She pursed her lips at him but said nothing further.

They rode into the yard, and he dismounted. He stretched

his legs as he made his way to the door. He cast a look back at Cate, but couldn't read her expression in the diminishing light.

He set his knuckles against the door just as it came open.

A ruddy-faced man in his fifties raised a lantern and looked Elijah up and down. "What can I do for you?"

"Good evening, kind sir. We've traveled quite a long distance and we simply can't continue tonight. I wonder if we might lodge in your barn?"

The farmer glanced back at Cate on her horse. "Of course, of course. My wife will clobber me if you sleep in the barn, however. She'll insist you sleep upstairs in one of our children's old rooms. I'm Charlie Hewitt. Is it just you and your companion?"

Blast. He hadn't planned on having Cate come into contact with anyone. How was he to explain a woman dressed like a man?

Elijah glanced back at her and realized he had to think fast. She'd dismounted and was striding toward them. Her gait was confident, purposeful, but unmistakably feminine.

"Mr. Hewitt, I am Jones and this is my bride-to-be. I'm afraid your kind hospitality has forced my hand. We are on our way to Gretna Green. Please excuse her disguise. It was necessary in order to sneak her away from her overbearing cousins."

Mr. Hewitt had two impressively bushy gray brows, which currently resided somewhere barely south of his hairline.

Cate joined Elijah at the door. "Good evening."

"Anne, this is Mr. Hewitt. I was just telling him how we escaped your malevolent cousins so that we may wed at Gretna Green."

Her gaze reflected the merest hint of surprise, but Elijah doubted Hewitt had caught it. In fact, Elijah was surprised *he* had caught it, but then he'd come to know Cate quite well in the last several days. That was a sobering and somewhat troublesome realization.

Cate smiled. Thankfully the grime on her face didn't disguise its brilliance. "Good evening, Mr. Hewitt. I deeply appreciate your hospitality." She slid her arm around Elijah's waist, shocking him with the contact, but he kept his composure. "You are most kind to help us on our journey to happiness." She tipped her head into Elijah's side and he wondered if she was overselling the ruse.

An attractive, white-haired woman appeared behind Mr. Hewitt. "What have we here, Charlie?"

"A young couple on their way to Gretna Green." Hewitt's gaze had turned a bit skeptical. Elijah held his breath.

"Oh!" Mrs. Hewitt stepped forward and the lantern light showed her to be slightly plump, with an apron tied about her waist. "How romantic. Do come in." She gasped when she caught sight of Cate's face. "Whatever happened to you, dear?"

"I tripped when we stopped for lunch." Cate had once told him that she and Grey were used to disguising their identities. It appeared she was quite good at fabrication of all kinds. Elijah added ingenuity to her list of traits.

"Well, you'll want to get cleaned up before supper. We've already eaten, but there's plenty for the both of you." She reached out and grabbed Cate's hand to drag her into the house. "Come in, come in."

Cate lifted one shoulder as she gave Elijah a wordless look and followed Mrs. Hewitt inside.

"Let's get your horses settled," Hewitt said as he ambled toward the beasts.

Elijah trailed him. "So long as you're sure this isn't an imposition."

"It isn't, but I'll trust you to do right by that young lady.

Her reputation is already gone and from the looks and sound of you, you're gentleman enough to know what would happen to her if you don't wed."

"I am, and I place Anne above all else." Elijah tried not to let the man's words bother him. Cate *was* a lady, and her reputation—if she'd had one at all—would be in shreds if anyone knew of her activities. But for now she was Anne . . . Someone on her way to Gretna Green.

After they took care of the horses, Elijah cleaned up in the barn. When he entered the house for supper, he stopped short at seeing Cate. She stood at the table, helping Mrs. Hewitt to set it, her hair clean and damp, hanging down her back. She wore a simple, homespun gown that was a bit too short and too loose around the waist, but the bodice hugged her breasts perfectly. And her face was clean. He'd thought the mud hadn't disguised her beauty, but he'd been wrong. He'd almost forgotten how the curve of her lip and the saucy tilt of her nose took his breath away.

"Mr. Jones," Mrs. Hewitt said, "please join us. I'll bring some mutton stew and fresh bread." She disappeared through a doorway into the presumed kitchen, leaving them alone. Elijah wasn't sure where Mr. Hewitt had gone after stabling the horses.

"They've allotted us rooms upstairs," Cate said, laying the utensils on the table.

Rooms, plural. That was for the best. Spending the evening pretending that they were to be wed was going to try his resolve. He was glad he'd be able to seek refuge alone when it concluded.

"I'm sorry for the ruse, but he offered us lodgings in the house and I had to think of a way to explain why a woman would be dressed as a man."

"You devised the perfect reason, just as you concocted the perfect escape plan in Harlech. You ought to have been a spy.

I believe subterfuge and deception are two of your best skills."

"Thank you. I think."

Mrs. Hewitt returned with two bowls of steaming stew. She set them on the table. "Just let me get the bread."

"May I help you, Mrs. Hewitt?" Cate asked.

"That isn't necessary. Please, sit. You must be famished. Mr. Hewitt is pulling some ale. He makes it himself and I daresay it's the best you'll find this side of Hereford."

"Sounds wonderful, thank you."

Elijah held a chair for Cate to sit and took the one opposite her with the second bowl of stew. For a minute, they simply ate, both eager to appease their hunger. Mrs. Hewitt brought a basket of thickly sliced bread and a dish of butter. Behind her, Mr. Hewitt carried a tray with four cups. After setting the bread and butter down, Mrs. Hewitt took a seat while Mr. Hewitt distributed the ale.

"Tell us about how you met and fell in love," Mrs. Hewitt said before taking a drink of ale.

Good God, this was going to be worse than he'd thought. Elijah's gaze connected with Cate's and they wordlessly decided that she would talk. He might be good at devising plans, but that didn't extend to spinning romantic tales.

Cate finished a bite of bread and washed it down with a swig of ale. "It's quite a story." Her dark eyes lit with mischief and Elijah stifled a groan. Perhaps he ought not have let her take the lead.

"Magnus came through town with his acting troupe a few weeks ago." *Magnus?*

"You're an actor?" Mrs. Hewitt asked, her bright blue eyes intrigued.

Apparently. Or perhaps not. "I'm more the director and organizer of the group."

"I see." Mrs. Hewitt sounded less enthusiastic than before.

"Oh, he still acts," Cate said, smiling. "He played Sir Andrew Aguecheek in *Twelfth Night*—that's when I first saw him."

"And it was immediately love, wasn't it?" Mrs. Hewitt smiled at Mr. Hewitt. "It was that way with us too."

Mr. Hewitt coughed gruffly.

"Yes, I was instantly smitten." Cate threw him a playful glance. She was enjoying this tale far too much. "Of course, Magnus didn't see me in the audience, did you, Magnus?"

What the hell sort of name was Magnus, anyway? "No." He could hardly wait to hear how he met her and undoubtedly fell at her feet.

She gave him a coquettish look. "I admit I was rather forward. I waited for him after the performance to tell him how much I enjoyed the play. We shared a mug of ale at the pub and by the end of it had decided to marry."

Elijah coughed to cover the bark of laughter that rose in his throat. What utter *tripe*.

"Why are you eloping?" Mrs. Hewitt asked, looking between them. "Mr. Jones mentioned your overbearing cousins. Were they not in favor of the match?"

Elijah surprised himself by interjecting. "Not at all. Miss Thimblebottom is an orphan, you see." He cast Cate a look to see what she thought of *her* name, but her expression was relatively placid. Save her eyes, which were charged with deviltry. "She is—rather *was*—at the mercy of her selfish relatives, who sought to marry her off to a local gentleman she did not fancy."

Mrs. Hewitt gave Cate a sympathetic pat on her hand. "Was he awful?"

Cate nodded. "Oh yes. He smelled of elderberries and cheese. Rancid, stinky cheese. And he was quite old. He could be my grandfather. I might have been able to suffer all of that; however, he was also fond of barking at the children in the village—an irony since his chief desire in taking me as a wife was to have children." She shuddered and again Elijah had to quash his amusement.

"Mr. Jones here rescued you," Mrs. Hewitt said.

"Indeed." Cate smiled at him as she resumed eating.

Mr. Hewitt leaned toward Elijah. His face, lined with age, formed deeper creases. He spoke in a low tone. "Are you certain you wish to marry her? You aren't merely playing the gentleman to save a young lady?"

Cate's spoon halted on the way to her mouth—only briefly, but Elijah caught it. She'd overheard Mr. Hewitt.

"I am quite certain I wish to marry her. Miss Thimble-bottom is the soul of kindness and gentility and I am more in love with her than I ever imagined possible."

Cate turned to look at him. Her eyes glowed with wonder.

Elijah averted his gaze, suddenly uncomfortable. He was playing a role. Hell, she was the one who'd cast him as an actor. Still, something about the words had stirred him. Love was an emotion he'd barely experienced. Those he'd loved as a child had either killed the emotion in the case of his mother, or abandoned it in the case of his father, when he'd drunk himself to an early grave.

"Well, that is just terribly romantic." Mrs. Hewitt dabbed at her eye. "What of your acting troupe, Mr. Jones?"

"They are continuing on. I have an assistant who is managing the company while I am away. You can see why we are traveling so quickly since I must return to my duties." Apparently he was better at weaving lies than he'd thought.

As they finished their meal, Mrs. Hewitt asked questions about the sorts of plays they performed, whether they might come anywhere near there, and if Cate wanted to try her hand on the stage.

"I think I might," Cate answered. "I believe I possess a certain talent for pretending to be someone I'm not."

"Indeed you do," Elijah said softly. He smiled at her to complement their ruse, but found it wasn't difficult. She might provoke him to fits of anger and frustration, but she also drove him to feelings of contentment, and of course, desire.

After supper, Elijah yawned purposefully and asked if they might find their beds. Mrs. Hewitt showed them upstairs, which sported two small, identical rooms across the hall from each other.

She leaned close and whispered something to Cate before bidding them both good night and disappearing down the narrow stairs.

"What did she say?" Elijah asked.

"She said Mr. Hewitt insisted on us having separate rooms, but that she was well aware that we were up here alone and she wasn't one to judge." Cate arched a brow at him and crossed her arms. The movement pushed her breasts up against the top of her gown, drawing his eye to the tantalizing flesh.

He jerked his gaze back to her face. "Where are your clothes? You'll need to wear them again when we leave in the morning."

She stood in the doorway of her chamber. "They're hanging in my room. This gown once belonged to one of Mrs. Hewitt's daughters. I'm only borrowing it for the evening."

He wanted to say she looked lovely. That he'd never seen her look more beautiful. But such comments would only encourage her to continue her campaign. "Good night, then."

He turned and went into his chamber before he could do something foolish. He closed the door and set about ripping his clothes off in rising frustration. His mind wandered over her arguments. She didn't expect marriage. She wanted a sexual encounter. With him. With no strings that would bind them together. They were in the middle of nowhere with their identities completely cloaked. If there was ever a time to accept her invitation, it was *now*. *Here*.

He stood in the center of his room, wearing nothing but his breeches and boots.

With a vicious oath, he went to the bed and sat. He tugged off his boots, barely resisting the urge to throw them against the wall. He decided to toss his stockings since they wouldn't make noise, but the effort was annoyingly dissatisfying as they simply landed in a silent tangle on the other side of the room.

He stretched out on the bed and tried not to think of Cate. Those damnable dark eyes of hers floated through his mind. Along with those eminently kissable lips that liked to challenge and amuse him. Her attempts to persuade him lingered, coaxing his body into a raging lust. His cock lengthened and grew thick in his breeches. His hand went to his fall.

He could pleasure himself or allow her to do what she wanted.

Throwing his arm over his eyes as if he could block her from his brain, he groaned. And then he pushed up from the bed. With purpose, he strode from the room and crossed the small corridor to her chamber. He didn't bother knocking, just opened the door, stepped inside, and closed it behind him.

Moonlight streamed past the flimsy curtain that barely covered the small window and illuminated her wide-eyed expression as she sat up in the bed.

His body was strung tight. "We will do this precisely my way and it will be only this night. In the morning, we will not speak of it again and you will not demand any more of me. Are you agreed?"

She stared at him in silence. He held his breath, cursing himself for being a fool. She nodded slowly. "Yes."

Anticipation pulsed through him. "Tonight, you are mine."

CHAPTER 16

*C*ate could scarcely believe what he'd said. The possession and desire in his voice were unmistakable and so arousing she could barely stand it. With hands that were suddenly trembling, she pushed back the coverlet. She wore an insubstantial, ill-fitting chemise provided by Mrs. Hewitt. It gapped at her chest, revealing far more flesh than was seemly, but that didn't matter, did it? None of this was seemly and she didn't want it any other way.

She wanted to ask why he'd changed his mind, but even more, she didn't want to give him an opportunity to change it back.

His eyes were pale in the moonlight, the lids hooded, giving him a brooding, almost predatory look. She was his prey. And she was eager to be. She shivered.

He came to the bed and she realized the first button of his fall was undone. That simple incongruity gave him an air of carelessness that she'd never seen before. He was a soldier, dutiful, honor-bound, absolutely scrupulous.

She scooted to the edge of the bed. Her head was on level with his hips. The evidence of his desire stood thick and rigid in his breeches. She'd touched Iscove's, stroked it. Reveled in its softness and marveled at her power as she'd brought him to completion, his seed spilling over her hands. That he hadn't been able to do the same for her had been frustrating, but she had no doubt that Elijah would.

Wetting her suddenly dry lips with her tongue, she reached out and caressed the bulge. He sucked in a breath. His hand stroked her jaw and he tipped her head up. The second her gaze connected with his and registered the stark lust in their depths, liquid heat gathered between her thighs. Her breasts felt heavy, full, eager for his touch.

She unbuttoned the remainder of his fall, her eyes never leaving his. The connection between them grew hotter, as if it lived and breathed. She slipped her hand inside his breeches and ran her fingers along his length, wishing his small clothes weren't in her way.

"Cate, how in the hell do you know how to do that? No, don't tell me. I don't want to know who else you've touched like this."

"It wasn't like this." It had been completely dark. Here, there was the moonlight and she could see him well enough to appreciate the muscles delineating his chest, the pale swath of hair that marched toward his groin. "This is much, much better."

He groaned as she pushed his breeches down over his hips. He helped her strip them down his legs then kicked them off before clasping her hand. With a swift tug, he pulled her to stand before him. The top of her head came to just beneath his chin. She pressed a kiss to his collarbone, licked her tongue along his flesh.

He tangled his hand in the back of her hair and pulled her head back, tipping it to give him access to her mouth. Which he took ravenously. His kiss was hard and deep, his tongue sweeping into her with brutal, delicious strokes. He held her fast, plundering her while his other hand pushed her hips to his. His erection pressed into her belly and she longed to feel him flesh to flesh.

As if he read her mind, he let her go long enough to rip the chemise over her head. Cool night air soothed her heated flesh, but not in the way she wanted. She burned for something only Elijah could give her.

He turned them, switching their positions so that he was next to the bed. He sank down on the mattress and pulled her forward to stand between his thighs. Wordlessly, he ran his palms atop her collarbones and stroked them down over her breasts, just barely grazing her nipples. Already stiff, they pulled with want and she gasped with disappointment when he didn't increase his touch. His hands traveled lower, skimming over her ribs and belly and then outward to her hips. He clasped her outer thighs and ran his fingers over her buttocks. Every touch, every caress ignited a new fire of need. Her legs went soft, but she didn't buckle.

His hands came forward and brushed between her thighs, widening them slightly. His knuckles rubbed against her folds and her hips jerked. But he didn't continue. She nearly groaned in frustration. Instead, his hands came back up and cupped her breasts, lifting both.

She'd closed her eyes as he'd conducted his scrutiny, but she opened them now and watched him. His gaze was locked on her breasts, his dark gold lashes fanning out over his eyes.

His thumbs flicked over her nipples, sending shocks of desire straight to her core. She swayed toward him, wondering how long she could continue to stand unaided. His fingers worked over her, tugging at her nipples, then caressing them with soft strokes. His palms massaged her. Again and again, he taunted each breast. The need built inside of her, gaining strength.

He curled one hand around her back and splayed his

palm against her spine. His mouth came down on her breast, at once devouring and worshipping her with his lips and tongue. She moaned as she reached new heights of longing. He held her captive to his mouth—one hand on her back and one holding her breast as he feasted.

She closed her eyes and cast her head back. Everything she had was focused on what he was doing to her, the incredible sensations she'd never imagined. She thrust her fingers into his thick hair and clutched him to her, desperate that he never leave her.

He moved to her other breast, taking her into his mouth. He gentled, suckling her so softly, but then he drew his teeth over the nipple and heat flooded her core. She wanted him there, between her thighs. She parted her legs, almost without thinking, and pushed her hips forward, seeking.

The hand on her back moved lower, glided over her buttocks. His touch was light, taunting, then harder, his fingers digging into her backside as he clasped one side.

Keeping his mouth on her breast, he removed his grip and slipped his fingers between her legs. He went slowly, his fingertips grazing over her folds, just skimming against her flesh. It wasn't nearly enough. She pushed forward again.

"My eager Cate," he murmured against her. "Kiss me now." He pulled his head from her and she bent to put her mouth on his.

He thrust his tongue up into her as his finger made a similar intrusion. She moaned into his mouth as his thumb worked her clitoris. She'd read that this should be a particularly sensitive spot and it was. He seemed to know precisely what he was doing as he used his thumb and finger to push her to the edge.

He kissed her deeply, commanding her with every stroke of his tongue, every nip of his teeth. He broke away from her and looked into her eyes. "Do as I say now. You trust me, don't you?"

She nodded, unable to speak.

He pushed her back and brought his legs together. Then he pulled her forward once more so that she straddled him. He scooted back. "Kneel on the bed."

That would open her thighs and reveal him to her in the most intimate way. For the first time, she faltered. Perhaps sensing her hesitation, he put one hand behind her right knee and gently pulled it forward.

She did trust him. And she couldn't stop this. She didn't want to.

She put her knees on either side of him and he leaned back. Cupping her backside, he moved her with him until she was directly over his face. Then he urged her down until his tongue licked at her folds. Sensation, new and devastating, slammed into her. With an aching moan, she clamped her eyes shut. Watching him do that was even more overwhelming. She didn't know how much more she could stand.

He massaged her backside as he deepened his kiss. He lifted each side of her, creating sensations she never imagined. His lips and tongue did to her sex what they'd done to her mouth, exploring and tasting her with fierce precision. His hands came over her hips and settled against her thighs, widening her even farther. Then his thumbs were against her, assisting his mouth, opening her for greater access. His tongue speared deep into her and the tension building inside of her reached a dizzying height. She clutched at his head, as much to ground herself as to encourage him. Something was coming if he would just . . .

He slipped his finger into her again at the same moment his mouth closed over her clitoris and sucked hard. She pushed down against him, her muscles clenching as everything exploded. She completely lost control, her body convulsing in great, riotous waves. He didn't let up. His finger stroked into her more quickly now and his lips and tongue continued their onslaught. She cried out over and over again, whimpering as shock after shock crested over her.

When the storm began to fade, he lifted her left leg over him and pressed her back against the mattress. She opened her eyes to see him rising over her.

"Oh my God." That was all she could think to say. She was utterly robbed of speech, of coherent thought, of everything but bone-deep satisfaction.

He reached down and stripped his small clothes away and she suddenly realized they weren't finished. *He* wasn't finished. At least she didn't think he was. She glanced down, saw his cock rising against his belly, and had her answer.

His mouth fell over her breast again, suckling her deep and reigniting her lust. How could she want him again so quickly? And how she wanted him. As if he hadn't just pleasured her.

"Cate, are you still with me?"

She'd closed her eyes again, but opened them now to see him staring at her intently. His hands were braced on either side of her head and he knelt between her legs.

"Yes." The sound of her own voice, dark and seductive, was foreign to her.

He kissed her again, not quite as deeply as the last time. He tasted different and when she realized why, she felt a moment's shyness. No, this was an adventure she'd craved, and she wouldn't balk. She reached up and curled her hand around the back of his neck, holding him as captive as he'd done her before. She speared her tongue into his mouth, kissing him with the stark urgency he'd shown her.

He responded in kind, pushing her into the bed with the pressure of his kiss. When she was dizzy again with desire, he lifted his head. "Widen your legs and bring your knees up."

She did as he commanded, utterly enslaved by his attentions. He'd said this would be one night only and she had the sense he was giving her everything he had, that he was committed to making this a night she would remember for the rest of her life. That made her both sad and excited.

He reached between her legs then and touched her, his fingers soft at first like before and then opening her and gliding over her with expert strokes. He pressed on her clitoris and massaged. Her muscles coiled again as the tension rebuilt.

Then his cock was there, nudging against her opening. He went very slowly. Due to her athletic activities, there was no membrane to block his entry, but she still felt the intrusion as something new, something she was unused to. He spread her folds and slid inside, pushing himself until he couldn't go any farther.

He didn't move at first, as if he were giving her the chance to grow accustomed to his presence. She appreciated it because she loved this new feeling. He made her feel full and hungry at the same time. He withdrew slightly, then rocked forward again. She clutched his shoulder for an anchor, already sensing that what she'd felt before was about to be intensified a hundredfold.

She brought her legs up even more, which seemed to give him even greater access. He groaned just before taking her mouth in another searing kiss, and then he began to move. His strokes were long and slow at first, methodical in their penetration. It was exactly what she expected from a man like him—measured, controlled. But, oh so devastating.

He moved faster, piercing her with delicious thrusts. She started moving too, lifting her hips to meet him.

He broke the kiss and his breath came hard and fast as he quickened the pace even more. "Look at me, Cate."

His gaze was intense, brutal even, as he drove into her. She stared up at him, entranced. Her body coiled tight as another orgasm thundered toward her. He slammed into her again and again, each time sending her inexorably closer to the limit. She closed her eyes as it broke over her. She cried out as she spasmed, unable to control her body and what he'd done to her.

And then he was gone.

"Elijah!" She reached for him, but he'd moved to the side of the bed and had his back to her.

He grunted. Then a long moan. She lightly touched his back, realizing what he must be doing. He'd said he knew how to prevent a pregnancy and she was grateful. Still, she couldn't help but wish he could've finished as she had.

His back rose and fell with his breathing. She gave him a moment to collect himself.

"Does that feel the same?" she asked.

He turned and tossed his smallclothes onto the floor, having used them to clean up.

"Leaving me, I mean."

He turned and settled his back against the wall, then drew the coverlet up to his waist. "No."

Now she felt doubly sorry. "I appreciate you doing that. You mentioned multiple ways to prevent a child. Do you also use a condom?"

"You know what that is?" He shook his head. "I shouldn't be surprised. You are the most educated female I know."

She sat back against the small iron headboard of the bed and pulled the coverlet to her waist as well. Their legs were intertwined beneath and she was aware of his heat and the light hairs grazing her flesh. "I'll hope you think that's a good thing."

His gaze was tinged with humor. "It's certainly different. But yes, on you, it's . . . attractive." He sounded surprised by that realization, but she didn't care. She was just glad he felt that way.

"So you do use condoms?"

"I have, yes. But I don't have any with me, or I would have employed one."

She crossed her arms beneath her breasts, heedless of her nakedness. "How does it feel?"

He arched a brow at her, probably disbelieving he was having this conversation. "Not as good as bare flesh. However, it's better than having to remove myself."

She winced. "Does it ruin it for you?"

"No, it just . . . dulls the intensity a bit."

Sitting here talking with him in the moonlight, naked, having just engaged in intercourse . . . Any other young woman would be horrified. But then any other young woman wouldn't have done it. Nor would they be contemplating doing it again. She tried not to stare at his chest, so broad and superbly carved. She longed to run her hands over him as he'd done her, to learn the planes of his body so that she might commit him to memory.

"What about . . . doing it again?" she asked. "I was surprised to find satisfaction twice so quickly. Is it the same for you?"

"Not quite. I need a little respite between."

"How much?"

He laughed and she loved the sound, wished he did it more. Lines crinkled around his eyes. He looked younger, more relaxed. Indeed, she'd never seen him look this at ease.

She turned in the bed and scooted next to him against the wall, crossing her ankles beneath the coverlet. Her feet dangled over the edge of the bed, though not quite as far as his did, of course.

"Why are you so against marriage?" She hadn't intended to ask, but this was the most intimate they would ever be. And she wanted to know. In truth, she wanted to know everything about him, but he was so frightfully secretive. "I know you'd rather keep it to yourself, but we've agreed to keep tonight inviolate, so if you'd care to unburden yourself, I'd like to listen."

He glanced down at her before looking toward the window with a pensive air. "I don't know anyone who is happily married. It seems a waste of time and one's energy."

Cate thought of her parents, who were insanely happy. Their love was not only palpable; it was infectious. "Was your parents' marriage one of obligation?"

"I'm not entirely certain, but I know my father loved my mother once."

"She didn't love him?"

He shrugged and the atmosphere turned cool. "I don't believe she loves anyone. Maybe my brother." He shook his head. "I don't know. And it also doesn't matter. She's scarcely a part of my life."

"Few people are," she said softly, beginning to understand the lonely boy he must have been, the lonely man he'd grown into. "Some marriages are successful. My parents are happy."

"Most are not. Look at your cousin Stratton and his wife." His features darkened, and she could tell he regretted bringing them up. It led to thoughts of Septon, which had to remind Elijah of his potential involvement in Matthew's death—*if* Septon was a member of the Order of the Round Table.

"I don't know that I agree with your assessment that 'most' are failures, but, as you say, it doesn't signify. It only matters that *your* marriage is successful."

He looked at her askance, determination lighting his eyes. "I am not, nor will I ever be, married."

"So you keep saying," she murmured. She turned toward him and tentatively touched his chest. He drew a breath, just slightly sharper than a normal intake. She flattened her palm against him, felt his heart beating. "Perhaps you'll change your mind if you meet the right woman."

"I might ask why a woman like you, one who has no inclination for marriage either, is so interested in my marital plans."

Why was she? Unlike him, she hadn't decided that she would *never* marry, just that she needn't and that it was highly unlikely. Had she unconsciously decided that marrying him would be acceptable? She entertained the thought—being his countess, sharing his life, his bed . . .

Sharing. That was the word that gave her pause. It was why marriage in theory didn't appeal to her—because in most cases there was no sharing. Her parents' marriage was not the norm, and Elijah had given her no reason to think he would be like her father. He'd already tried to curb her activities on more than one occasion, and that was enough for her to acknowledge he wasn't the man for her. And she would probably never meet one who was.

"You look as though you're trying to solve the problems of the world," he said.

She blinked at him. "No. Just thinking about what you said. You're correct. I have no inclination for marriage. I do, however, have an inclination for you right now." If she was only to have one night with him, she wanted to make it count.

She pulled him down for a kiss, splaying her hand over his chest and digging her fingers into his flesh. Moving her hand up, she found his nipple and grazed her fingers over the tip. He angled his head and speared into her mouth, his hand tangling in her hair as he held her close.

She pulled away from him and moved her attention to his

chest. She traced her palm over his muscles, reveling in his hardness. Were men as sensitive to touch as women? She plucked at his nipple, then leaned over to lick it.

He fisted her hair, holding her to him. Then he dragged her onto his lap. She turned, facing him, and kissed a path to his other nipple before using her teeth to score his flesh.

He sucked in a sharp breath as his hand found her breast and tweaked her nipple. He pinched it firmly, then drew it out before letting go and starting over again.

She trailed her mouth up his collarbone to his neck, licking and sucking his flesh. He pushed the coverlet away and situated her on her knees, straddling him. His hands skimmed down her sides and settled on her thighs, massaging her flesh as she kissed the underside of his jaw. He'd shaved before dinner, and his flesh was smooth with a faint scent of the soap he'd used.

Whatever time he'd required to restore himself had elapsed. His cock rose between her legs, rubbing against her and firing her desire. She pushed down, grinding her flesh against his. He lifted slightly, meeting her, teasing her.

She widened her legs and rocked her hips. His cock slid up against her clitoris, jolting her with sensation, then back along her sex, taunting her with the promise of what was to come.

She cupped his neck and kissed him. All the while, she rotated against him, working herself into a fevered state of need. His fingers dug into her thighs, guided her to increase her speed.

She moved faster, desperate to have him inside of her. She broke the kiss as she reached down and stroked his cock.

"Cate." He sounded strained. "It's too soon."

"Not for me." She felt moisture at his tip and her need rose even higher. "I want you inside me again."

He groaned, his hands moving up to her hips and tightening around her flesh. He held her up as she guided him to her opening. Sliding him in wasn't as easy as she'd thought. He wetted his fingers on his tongue and stroked her opening. He paid special attention to her clitoris, coaxing and arousing her until she began to climb. His finger pushed inside, stretching her, pleasuring her. Then his cock was there instead and he slid into her with a sure, swift stroke.

"Cate." His hand cradled the side of her neck, pushed the mass of her hair back over her shoulder and tucked it behind her ear. "You can control this. Ride me. If you want."

She did. She rose, pulling herself almost completely off his shaft, then sank down again. The sensation of him filling her was so spectacular. White lights danced behind her eyes. She opened them, wanting to see him as she moved over him. *Ride me*, he'd said.

She lifted again and pushed down even more swiftly. She ground her hips into his, loving the feel of him against her and inside of her. He was everywhere she wanted him to be. His head tipped down and took her breast into his mouth. He nipped and licked at her, one hand holding the back of her neck, the other gripping her hip as she pleasured herself —and hopefully him.

Pressure built in her core as she moved faster and faster. She tried to establish a rhythm, but it was so hard with what he was doing to her breasts and the pleasure cresting within her.

His hips came up, helping her. Their bodies came together in a frenzied dance, but then he gripped her waist and held her still. He pulled her up and then pushed her down again, slowing the pace for several agonizing moments.

"Elijah," she breathed, knowing her orgasm was so close, but also realizing he was keeping it from her.

"Just wait." He continued his careful assault, moving her

slowly, but oh so blissfully. He set a new rhythm where she rocked up and down, like a boat bobbing on the sea. "You are so beautiful." He kissed her throat, laving her flesh as he drove up into her—relentless, but with such measured care.

She didn't know how long she floated, with her body stretched tight in the space between immense pleasure and profound satisfaction. Then he stroked her clitoris, pressing hard against her, and everything shattered. Animal sounds came from her throat, but she was powerless to stop herself. Her body was no longer her own—she was wholly, completely, and rapturously at his mercy.

He pulled her completely off him then and roughly set her aside. Damn, she'd almost forgotten he had to leave her. She looked over at him, his hand stroking along his cock. She added hers, taking over for him, sliding her fingers over him from base to tip. She licked her lips, ready to take him in her mouth, but liquid spurted forth and he cried out. "Cate!"

She worked her hand harder, pulling everything from him that he could give. His hips moved off the bed as he stroked into her hand, greedily taking what she offered.

When it seemed he was finished, she slowed her movements. He slumped back and slid down the wall. She pulled him over and guided him to fall onto her pillow. He closed his eyes. She ought to clean them up, but she was suddenly so tired.

She curled next to him, her arm slung over his hips. He turned his head and kissed her hairline. "Cate." He said her name so softly, she almost didn't hear him. What was unmistakable, however, was the note of longing in his voice.

Cate fell asleep smiling.

CHAPTER 17

*E*lijah floated in a dream. Cate looked up at him with her seductive eyes just before her head bent over his cock. Her mouth was hot and wet and so tight around him. Her hand clasped his base and held him as her lips moved over him.

"Stroke it." He moved her hand up as she rose, showing her what to do. God, she was heaven on earth.

She increased her speed, sucking him to the back of her mouth so that he grazed the top of her throat. Her fingers and tongue worked him with an expertise that blew his mind into a thousand pieces. He plunged his hands into her hair and thrust into her mouth. His balls tightened, signaling the onslaught of his orgasm. He groaned as he came, his seed spurting into her mouth. He fell back against the mattress as the shockwaves crashed over him.

Shit. This was a dream. But he was next to Cate. Had he just embarrassed himself? His eyes flew open, he saw her crouched over him, realized it *wasn't* a dream.

"Jesus, Cate." He swung his legs from under her and sat up

on the edge of the bed. Early morning light filled the room, and he blinked against the intrusion.

She sat up and looked at him quizzically, her hair a tangled, ebony mass. "What's wrong?"

"Did you just . . . ?" What a ridiculous question. Of course she had. He had. *They* had. He'd meant to satisfy her curiosity last night. And maybe his own lust. Definitely his own lust. He was a beast.

"Are you angry?" She tipped her head to the side, looking more curious than anything else. "I thought you would like that."

"No. I mean, yes. I do like that. Did like that." Hell, he wasn't making any sense. "That is actually one of my favorite activities. No, I'm not angry. Just surprised."

The corner of her mouth lifted. "You did seem to enjoy it."

More than he ever had in his life. "You were quite good at it."

"Well, you did guide me, so I'm glad I was a quick study. But then I always have been."

All of it had been real. Even his telling her what to do. He massaged his forehead, certain he'd never in a thousand lifetimes be able to banish the memory of her mouth and hands pleasuring him to within an inch of his life.

Yes, she'd been an astonishingly quick study. Last night had exceeded every fantasy he'd ever had—and not just about her. But now it was over. He'd said one night and that come morning, they wouldn't speak of it again.

Good thing he didn't plan on talking.

He tugged her against him and kissed her, sweeping her hair from her face and pulling it down her back. He kissed her like it was the last time, because it probably was. Turning, he pressed her down onto the bed and shifted himself over her.

She twined her arms around his neck, but he pulled them

free and pinned them on either side of her head. She opened her mouth, but he kissed her with a "shhhh" sound whispering over her lips.

He moved his lips to her jawline, licking a path to her ear. He nipped at the lobe and dashed his tongue along the outer shell. She shivered.

How he loved her responsiveness. With every touch and kiss, she moved or made a sound, did something that told him she liked it, that she was unbearably aroused. He'd taken great care to explore her body, thrilling in every crest and hollow of her flesh. From the creamy swell of her breast to the gentle dip of her waist to the soft recesses of her sex, he'd been utterly captivated by her.

He found his way—slowly—to her breast. The nipple hardened as he teased her. He suckled her, all while he kept her hands pinned to the bed.

Her legs fell open, inviting him to nestle between her thighs. Did she know what she did to him? Impossibly, he felt his cock stirring. How could he be ready again?

He let go of her hands and cupped her breast, holding her to his mouth while he devoured her flesh. She instantly plunged her fingers into his hair and urged him on. Moving his hand down, he found her sex, already slick and ready. He stroked her clitoris, rousing her, taunting her until her hips began to move against him. He slipped his finger into her, felt her muscles contract around him, and his cock sprang to life.

He wasn't sure he wanted to make love to her again. It was a lot to ask of her. But he could give her pleasure. He pumped his finger in and out as he lowered his head and sucked at her clitoris.

She gasped, pushing up into him. "Elijah!"

He pushed her legs apart and licked at her folds, loving the taste and feel of her in his mouth. Her thighs quivered and her muscles tightened. He put two fingers into her, stretching her and thrusting hard and fast. She bucked off the bed, her movements becoming more frenzied as she sought her release. He licked into her and pressed on her clitoris as she came apart. Her cries filled the small space, fed his own lust, but he wouldn't satisfy it. Hell, he was already past satisfied.

He eased away from her, turning to reach for his breeches where they lay on the floor. Pulling them on, he stood and buttoned the fall before turning to face her. "We need to be ready to leave as soon as possible. We're supposed to be in a hurry to get to Gretna Green, and I don't wish to impose on the Hewitts' hospitality more than necessary."

She sat up and smoothed her hair back from her face, trying to calm the tousled mess. He glanced around and was relieved to see a glass so that she could tidy her hair. "That's it. You really meant that come morning we wouldn't talk about what we did."

He bent and picked up his smallclothes, glad he had another set in his chamber along with a fresh shirt. "Yes, I meant it."

"Can I at least thank you for a night I shall never forget?"

Her words sounded so final, but that's what he wanted, wasn't it? That's what he'd said it would be—one night and nothing more. He struggled between feelings of euphoria from their activities, self-recrimination due to his lack of discipline, and misery because he was certain never to experience a night like that again.

"Elijah," she said softly, holding her hand up toward him in all of her naked glory.

He turned from her. "You need to get dressed. I can't . . . look at you like that anymore. I'll see you downstairs."

Feeling like a bit of a cad, he took himself from her presence. Their hostess had left water and basins in their rooms.

He hadn't needed it last night after cleaning up in the barn, but he made use of it this morning. However, his efforts to scrub Cate's scent from his body were futile. Even if he couldn't smell her, he could feel her and probably always would.

What had he done?

He hurried to finish his ablutions and took himself downstairs before he heard Cate leave her room. As if he could avoid her—they had at least today together. It was possible they could part ways as early as this evening, depending on how long it took to find this blasted sword.

The sword. Without it, he would never have met her; his new life as the earl would be as dull and predictable as he'd expected it to be. Actually, he wouldn't even be the earl. Without the sword and someone's lust to obtain it, Matthew would still be here.

His shoulder muscles bunched with tension as he arrived downstairs. He couldn't lose sight of his goal—pursuing Matthew's killers. She'd distracted him, pleasantly so, but that was all it had been. Now he needed to refocus his mind.

Mr. Hewitt shambled from the kitchen. "Thought I heard you on the stairs. I trust you slept well?" He gave no inkling that he was aware of what had transpired above stairs, thank goodness.

"I did, thank you. I'll just go see to the horses."

"I'll give you a hand." Hewitt joined him and they went to the stables.

A little while later, they walked the horses to the front of the house just as the door opened. Cate stepped outside, a slice of bread in her grip. Elijah's stomach grumbled in response.

With Cate outfitted in her men's garb, Elijah could almost pretend last night had never happened. Except for the feminine jaunt to her step. And the tilt of her head. And the familiar jut of her chin.

He had to stop thinking about it, about *her*.

Mrs. Hewitt gave him some cold ham and a slab of bread, which he quickly devoured. Then they thanked their gracious hosts, who bade them good luck on their journey. Mrs. Hewitt hugged Cate and wished her a lifetime of happiness while Elijah stood ready to help her mount.

He touched her as little as possible, but just clasping her waist sent a riot of memories through his mind and stirred his lust. Leaving her as quickly as possible, he climbed atop his own horse and led her from the yard.

Keeping up the pace, which didn't allow for conversation, was thankfully easy. Even when they intermittently slowed to rest the horses, he kept his distance so she couldn't speak with him. More than a few times, he caught her looking at him and each time his insides smoldered with want.

As they neared Kentchurch, he realized he needed to engage her in conversation. Their association may have been reaching its end, but they still had to recover the sword. He slowed a bit and rode beside her. He couldn't see her face clearly with the shadow cast from the brim of her hat. "Do you have a plan once we reach Kentchurch?"

"I'm afraid I don't. I've been thinking of little else." He found this surprisingly disappointing. He'd been lusting after her all morning and she'd been—rightly—focused on their goal. He was an ass.

"You've no idea where to look? Ifan didn't give you any clues?"

"He didn't know. I wish the map had been more specific. Why send us to Harlech when the sword was never there?"

"Perhaps they didn't want it to be that easy. It is a treasure, after all." He thought about the tapestry and how it had taken careful thought and deduction to determine they should go to Harlech in the first place. "Is there anything else on the tapestry that could help us?" Damn, he was especially angry with himself for letting the villains steal it.

She tilted her head, and he could see that she was frowning. "Not that I can think of, but I suppose the clue could be hiding in plain sight like Harlech was."

"Let's see if we can puzzle it out."

She shot him an appreciative glance that evoked a warm response straight from his chest. "All right. There's Harlech, the ocean, the battle scene with Glendower, the shield, and the flaming sword."

His shield had been a hidden clue. "Are there any other shields?"

She thought a moment. "Yes, but none with a distinct coat of arms that I can recall."

He couldn't recall anything either. "Any flags or banners?"

"Not that I remember. Damn, this is hopeless."

"It isn't. There has to be something. What about the back, are you certain there was nothing there?" He'd seen her looking at it several times.

"No, though it wasn't very neatly done, as it should've been."

Elijah remembered Garber making the same observation. In his mind's eye, he saw the most glaring imperfection—an odd shape in the upper right quadrant of the back. It had almost looked like the letter X, but one line was slightly longer than the other and it hadn't exactly been an X . . . "I think there was a small sword sewn into the back," he said the words as they came into his brain—like a jolt of awareness that felt . . . right.

They hadn't been traveling very fast as they'd talked, but she pulled her horse to a stop and stared at him.

He halted and looked over at her, excitement spreading through him like a fast-moving fire.

"It looked like a mess of thread, almost like a misshapen X," she said slowly, thoughtfully.

"Yes, in the upper right quadrant."

She tipped her head to the side. "What do you suppose that means?"

"I'm not sure. But if we think it indicates the location of the sword, perhaps it's directional."

"Meaning it's somewhere in the northeastern part of the estate?" she asked.

He couldn't tell if she was feeling as enthusiastic as he was and her lack of excitement was dampening his. "It's at least *something* to go on."

"Yes, it is." She narrowed her eyes and looked determined. "How shall we proceed? We can't very well ride onto the estate and ask to search the northeastern corner. If it's even still there after four hundred years." Her frown returned and he realized she wasn't allowing herself to be optimistic.

He nudged his mount closer so that he could touch her wrist. "We're going to find it. Whether it's there or someplace else. It's your life's work."

"It was my dream." *Was.*

"Don't let it go." Her dreams were what made her so unique. So beguiling. So Cate. He pulled away and steered his horse forward. "Let's hurry."

They rode the rest of the way in silence. When the Kentchurch Court tower loomed in the distance, he slowed and flicked her a glance. "Follow me."

She nodded, and guided her horse behind his as he led her past the entrance to the estate. Once they were well past the main house, he left the road and veered north. He figured they were likely on estate grounds, so he kept a sharp eye out in case they encountered anyone.

When they reached a small copse of trees, he dismounted

and tied his horse to a tree. She did the same. As she tethered her mount, she asked, "Why are we stopping?"

"I think it's better if we continue on foot. I want to walk up that hill over there and see what's in the northeast corner."

She nodded and after finishing their task, they made their way to the top of the small hill. It provided a good vantage point from which he could survey the area. Right away he noticed one particular partially-ruined stone building.

Cate pointed at the round structure. "What is that?"

"I believe it's a dovecote."

She lightly shook her head. "Of course it is. I haven't seen one in a while."

"Unsurprising as they've somewhat fallen out of favor." He looked at her askance. "They were, however, quite popular in the fifteenth century."

Now her eyes lit in the way he'd been anticipating earlier. "Yes, they were."

They started down the hill simultaneously, the decline and their excitement quickening their pace to a near run. At the base, he motioned for her to slow while he looked around, ensuring there was no one about.

He led the way to the round, stone building that had once housed several hundred doves, but whose roof was now caved in. She went up to it and flattened her palm against the stone. "Do you suppose it's really that old?" she asked.

"Likely." He slowly walked around the building, scanning for any sign of, well, anything. An inscription in a stone near the ground caught his eye. He squatted and pulled off his glove to run his fingers over the numbers. "Fourteen eighteen."

A shadow fell over him and he looked up, but couldn't see her face with the sun shining behind her head. "That's not that long after the battle at Harlech. But where do we look?"

He stood and now he could see her expression. It was a mixture of apprehension and enchantment. "Let's take our time here."

"You look outside," she said. "I'm going in."

She pivoted before he could respond, and the words "be careful" died on his tongue. He needed to stop thinking of her as someone he needed to care for. They would part soon, and it would be much easier to let her go if he remembered that they shared a fleeting association and nothing more. Only he was fairly certain that was a lie.

~

*C*ate tried to slow her thundering heart. She'd been disappointed so many times. This dovecote could be the resting place of Dyrnwyn or she could walk away from it empty-handed. Again.

Elijah also seemed eager, but was that true or was she simply seeing what she wanted to see? He was trying to be supportive at least, and she appreciated that.

She paused at the arched doorway and inhaled deeply. Summer scents of grass and wildflowers reminded her of days spent outside with her brother when she was younger. He'd learned to dig for treasure—animal bones, coins, whatever he could find—at a very young age and had taught Cate to be observant and curious. She employed those tools now as she studied the entry and looked for a clue.

Nothing leapt out at her from the weathered gray stone. She stepped inside and was amazed at the number of small nesting boxes built into the walls. Hundreds of doves would have nested here. The birds had provided food, of course, and feathers for mattresses. She imagined the smell of the waste in here would've been most foul, but then it would have been removed and used for the garden in all likelihood. Could Dyrnwyn be in such an inauspicious place?

Cate moved farther inside, careful not to step on any of the stones that had likely made up the roof, but now littered the dirt floor. Once there had been a hole in the top for the birds to come and go, but there was no telling what that part of the structure had looked like.

Grass had sprung up between the stones, since plenty of light now made its way inside the building. Cate was surprised at how large it was—a good ten paces across—and supposed it would seem even more so if not for the remains of the roof cluttering the space.

Her brother's words came back to her. He always said to "be methodical." And so she was. Starting at the left of the door she moved clockwise, studying the stone nesting boxes for any indication. It seemed a futile effort. There was nothing but a steady line of empty boxes marching around the circle. She went from top to bottom, but made a note to have Elijah review the upper portion since his height would give him a much better advantage. So she spent extra time on the bottom half. About a third of the way through, her eyes began to water and she realized she'd forgotten to blink.

Taking a sustaining breath, she blinked several times and bent down to look at the lower stones in this section. Was that a blemish in the stone above that box near the bottom? She blinked again and squatted low to investigate it further. A blemish or a mark . . .

Her heart began to pound as she drew off her glove and touched the symbol. And yes, it was a symbol. It perfectly matched the "mistake" on the back of the tapestry—the X that wasn't really an X but more like a poorly drawn sword.

"Elijah!" Belatedly, she realized she ought not to have yelled, but she hadn't been able to contain herself.

She didn't turn, but heard him come into the dovecote.

"What is it?"

"Here. It's here." She scooted to the side to give him access. "Look at the symbol."

He knelt beside her, putting one knee onto the dirt. She waited, breathless, for his reaction.

And she wasn't disappointed.

He grinned at her and her heart skipped. "You found it."

"I found *something*." She urged herself to be cautious and pragmatic. But it was so damned hard, especially with him here to share the moment. "Is the stone loose?"

He slipped his fingers into the box and grasped the stone, pulling at it. "I think it might be." He extracted his knife from his boot and put both knees on the ground to give himself a firmer stance. Using the blade, he carved around the stone in an effort to pry it loose. With a bit of effort, the block came free. He caught it and set it aside.

Now the nesting box was twice as large as the others. He leaned close to look at it and then pushed his hand inside. "It's hollow back here."

Cate inhaled sharply. Her stomach dropped into her feet. "Is it empty?"

He pushed his arm in farther and his face tensed as he rooted around. "No, there's something there. I can grasp it, but when I pull it up, I can't get it free. I need to remove more stones in order to extract it."

"What is it, a hilt?" She held her breath.

He smiled. "No, but you didn't expect them to bury it without some sort of protection, did you? It's a box and it's heavy." He withdrew his hand and went to work carving away the stone above the one he'd already removed.

Anticipation flushed through her. "I wish I could help you or that we had a better tool."

"I'll get it." He worked slowly and steadily, removing his coat to work faster. Cate fought the urge to pace as well as the desire to stare at him in his shirtsleeves and perhaps encourage him to remove his waistcoat too. She shook herself and called herself a ninny.

When he'd finally removed three more stones, he sat back on his heels. "Can you see it?"

She leaned over beside him and put her hand to her mouth. There, tucked into a hole behind the nesting boxes was a box maybe a foot wide. She curled her fingers around the aged wood and tried to pull it up, but he was right, it was heavy. "I can't get it."

"May I?" he asked.

"Please." She sat back and watched as he liberated the box, appreciating his endeavors. She couldn't make out the muscles working beneath his sleeves, but imagined them quite clearly.

He set the box on the ground between them. The wood was old, but in excellent condition. While the container was a foot wide, it was at least four feet long. There was a clasp in the middle.

"There's no lock," she said, somewhat stupidly. After everything they'd been through, she expected another obstacle.

"Are you going to open it?" he asked.

"I'm afraid." She looked at him helplessly as dread snaked up her spine.

"Don't be." He gazed at her with encouragement. "This is a moment to celebrate, no matter what you find. You've come this far—farther than anyone else before you."

"I hope so. If it's not inside, it's safe to say someone did get here first."

He shook his head. "You are an exasperating woman. Open the damned box before I do."

She couldn't resist smiling at him and wondered if he'd provoked the reaction on purpose. With a silent prayer, she released the clasp and gently opened the lid. As light found its way inside the box, her breath lodged in her throat. There, nestled in a bed of red linen, was a sword.

It was a humble-looking weapon, long, but with a very simplistic cross-guard. The pommel was also simple, except for a small red jewel glimmering in the center. The blade was aged, but not dull, and it looked as though it could be over a thousand years old.

"Dyrnwyn," she breathed. With suddenly trembling fingers, she curled her hand around the hilt.

The cock of a pistol rent the still summer air.

"Cate, I must thank you for finding the sword. Now, I'm afraid you must give it to me."

CHAPTER 18

*E*lijah picked up his knife and leapt to his feet. His pistol was tucked into his coat, which was an unfortunate meter away. Not that it would've helped since they were well and truly outnumbered as six masked brigands filled the dovecote.

He couldn't tell which one had spoken, but his attention was immediately grabbed by one of the men—again they were masked—when he snatched Cate by the arm and hauled her up beside him.

The villain held a pistol to her temple. "I won't miss at this range, and ye're not getting another piece o' me." He had to be one of the men Elijah had injured the other day. "Drop yer knife."

Though it went against every impulse in his body, Elijah let the blade tumble to the ground and clenched his hand into a tight fist. "Let her go. You only want the sword."

The villain sniffed Cate's hair. "She's awfully pretty."

Elijah snarled and barely kept from launching himself at the man.

"Stop. Do let her go." It was the crisp, refined voice of the man who'd spoken initially.

Cate turned her head toward him. "Kersey?"

Fury blistered through Elijah as he looked at the man who'd spoken and watched as he removed his mask. "I ought to have known you would recognize my voice, cousin."

"What are you doing?" she asked, anger filtering into her surprise. "Are you part of this mysterious Order that wants the sword?"

If he was, and it seemed so, he was also behind Matthew's death. Rage clouded Elijah's vision and stole his reason. He rushed forward and his fist connected with the man's jaw in a satisfying blow.

Instantly, two men were on him, pulling at Elijah's arms and dragging him away from Kersey.

"Don't make me hurt the gel," the man holding Cate said.

Elijah froze, his chest heaving and his pulse racing. "If you harm her in any way, I'll kill you."

"You have my word she'll be unharmed." Kersey went to the box with the sword and bent down.

"As if I'd trust you," Elijah spat. "I hope you have a plan to be very far away from me for the rest of your life because when I get my hands on you, you'll wish you'd never threatened her."

Kersey looked up at him, his eyes narrowed in irritation. "I'm not threatening her, you oaf. You're the one putting her in danger. These men are the worst sort. I've instructed them not to hurt either of you, but as you can see, they're a bit difficult to control. Do Cate a favor and just be quiet. Please."

Elijah longed to pummel the man senseless, but the situation was exactly as Kersey described. Elijah tried to strategize a way to reverse the power in the dovecote, but the numbers were against them.

"If anything happens to her, your life won't be worth

anything." Not that it was worth much now, because Matthew's killer had a name and a face. Elijah's quest for answers suddenly became a need for vengeance.

Kersey exhaled. "I've already said she'll be unhurt, provided you cooperate. And your cooperation requires you to remain silent. If you cannot, I shall have the men take you outside where you won't be a nuisance."

With supreme effort, Elijah pressed his lips together to keep from continuing his verbal assault, since that was the only weapon currently available to him. Or it had been, until Kersey had taken that too. Elijah couldn't risk being taken from Cate's presence—he wouldn't leave her alone with Kersey or any of the other criminals.

With a final glare, Kersey returned his attention to the sword. Elijah would bide his time and look for a way to turn the tables. He couldn't let Kersey escape with the sword—or get away with murdering his brother.

"Kersey, what are you doing?" Cate asked. She shook with anger, fear, and probably shock. Kersey was the last person she expected to be after the sword. "You were behind the theft of the tapestry."

"Guilty." He touched the hilt of the sword, his fingertips tracing the jewel at the center of the pommel.

"How did you know to come here?"

He glanced up at her. "With the tapestry in my possession, it wasn't difficult to find someone in Harlech to share information about it. However, once we arrived here, we had no idea where to search. I figured you would show up eventually, and so I waited."

He'd had to rely on *her* to find it. She stiffened, all of her muscles tensing with fury. "It's my discovery. *Mine.* You can't take it from me." Desperation ate at her insides. She couldn't lose the sword now.

"I can, and I will." He gazed at her with pity, which only infuriated her more. "I sympathize with your plight, but I'm afraid I can't let you have the sword."

Cate longed to hit him as Elijah had. "You can't 'let' me? All these years you've suffered from a terrible reputation that I didn't think you had necessarily earned, but this . . . This far exceeds anything I thought you capable of."

"Are you speaking of the drinking and whoring, or the rumor that I killed my wife?" The question dripped with scorn. He sounded like a man who knew he was reviled and didn't care. But she knew he did—at least, she thought he did. She'd seen him after his wife had died. He'd been broken.

"You didn't kill her."

"No, I didn't kill her." He flashed her a cold smile. This was a side of him she'd never seen or imagined. "But I *was* a horrendous rake, thanks to my father's tutelage."

"You didn't have to be like him," she said softly.

"And what should I have been like with no one else to guide me?"

She wanted to say her father would've, but he hadn't been allowed to spend enough time with Kersey. She felt sorry for him, but struggled to understand why he was chasing the sword. "Why do you want the sword? You aren't an anti-quary. I didn't even realize you were interested in any of this."

"Why, because I'm not part of your family's precious scholarly circle? I know how much your father looks down on my father and his attempts to build a medieval library of his own."

She scowled at him. "Because your father is a feckless ass. It's a diversion, just like his women."

"Why does your family have the right to decide who's

important enough to collect books or trinkets?" The derision in his tone permeated Cate like frost in midwinter.

"We don't." She struggled to understand his animosity. "So you want the sword in order to be taken seriously?" She completely understood that goal, since it was hers.

"Among other things."

Then perhaps you should start by realizing Dyrnwyn is not a "trinket." She bit her tongue, lest she provoke him into changing his mind about protecting her from his men. "And are you a member of this Order?"

"I'm surprised you know of it. I thought it was secret."

She lifted her chin. "I know many secrets. What I don't know is why you would want to join that group. Was it to gain credibility?"

His lips spread into an enigmatic smile. "For now, that shall remain a secret that you don't know."

His taunting tone grated her nerves to a fine powder of frustration. "Will you tell me what you plan to do with the sword?"

He shrugged, and she was again overcome with the desire to strike him. "It belongs to us—the group."

It bloody well did *not*. "It belongs to the people of Britain. It should be in a museum. What will your 'group' do with it?"

"Another secret I shan't disclose." He turned his focus to the sword. His fingers curled around the hilt and he lifted it from the box. Her heart clenched as she watched him hold it and realized she hadn't even had the chance to.

He stood and brandished the sword, gazing at it in stark admiration. "Look at the steel of the blade. It's tinged blue. If I turn it thus"—he twisted it in the sunlight and it seemed to glow—"it looks as though it might spark into flame." He looked at her reproachfully. "You didn't think it would *actually* burst into flame, did you?"

Cate didn't answer. She was too distraught that she was

about to lose the fruit of her life's work. She imagined Glendower lifting it in battle, Gareth accepting it from Rhydderch Hael on his wedding day. "It's . . . everything I ever wanted." She looked at him hopelessly. "Please let me have it so I may give it to Penn for the museum."

His features darkened. "Of course you want to give it to your brother. No, this discovery is mine now."

"At least let her hold it," Elijah said, his deep voice cutting through the dovecote like an arrow speeding toward its prey.

She looked at him and saw something in his eyes—a suggestion maybe. If she could take the blade, perhaps she could use it . . . "Yes, will you let me? I didn't have a chance."

Kersey thought for a moment, his gaze skeptical. "All right, but if you try anything, I'd hate for Norris to pay the price."

One of the men holding Elijah drove his fist into Elijah's lower back, eliciting a grunt from him. Cate tensed, but Elijah gave her a reassuring stare.

"I won't do anything. Just let me hold it for a moment." She held her hand out and eventually Kersey transferred the sword to her. It was heavy, weighing her arm down.

Kersey gave her a sly smile. "I think you *do* hope it will burst into flame."

That would've been extremely helpful. However, for it to do that would mean that she was a descendant of Gareth or one of the other knights, as Glendower apparently had been. And she was fairly certain she was not. The blade grew even weightier. Her arm sagged and she had to tip the blade down. She grunted in frustration and pain.

Kersey snatched it back from her. "Clearly it's too heavy for you." And yet he wielded it with no trouble at all. "I know you think I'm a villain, Cate, but I'm not. I'm simply taking what I deserve."

"What does Cate deserve?" Elijah asked sharply.

Kersey frowned at her. "I am sorry that it has to be like this." He looked to the two men who weren't occupied with either Elijah or Cate, but who had pistols directed at them. "Tie them up."

The men stowed their weapons and one went to Cate. He pulled her arms behind her back and bound her wrists, while the man who'd been holding her kept his pistol trained on her. Cate didn't bother fighting, especially when she looked over at Elijah. He struggled, and it took two men, but they wrestled him to the ground and bound both his hands and feet.

Kersey cast Cate an apologetic glance. "A necessary frustration, I'm afraid. I can't have you following us."

"I'm going to find you, Kersey." Elijah's promise was low and venomous.

Kersey pivoted to stare down at Elijah. "I wouldn't bother threatening me, Norris. These men don't like leaving loose ends. If you can't swear to let this entire matter go, I think you'll find they won't leave you alone. You'll be the one pursued, not me."

"He won't cause you any difficulty," Cate said, throwing Elijah a pleading glance. For now, they needed to say whatever necessary to survive. She didn't want him endangering his life—not for this.

The men holding Cate lowered her to the ground and tied her ankles together.

Kersey tucked the sword back into the box and hefted it under his arm. "And now I'll bid you adieu, fair cousin." He hesitated, frowning down at her. "Perhaps it would appease your disappointment if I left the tapestry with you. I have no further need of it." He nodded toward one of the men. "Fetch it."

"Ye sure that's a good idea?" the man who'd originally held Cate asked.

"Don't question me," Kersey snapped.

The other man returned with the tapestry and set it on the ground.

Kersey tapped the sword box with his free hand. "Your assistance in this momentous discovery is greatly appreciated." He inclined his head toward his band of villains and disappeared from the dovecote.

The two men standing nearest looked at Elijah as though they wished they could eviscerate him, but in the end they took themselves off. However, the man who'd been holding Cate went over to Elijah and knocked the butt of his pistol against his temple.

"Stop!" Cate tried to wriggle across the dirt to get to Elijah.

The villain only laughed as he left the dovecote, leaving them alone.

It took a great deal of effort, but Cate eventually reached Elijah's side. She turned her hips and brought herself to a kneeling position. She leaned close and looked at his head, wishing her hands were free. A small rivulet of blood leaked from his blond hairline. "You're bleeding."

"Am I?" He turned his head, his blue-gray eyes boring into hers. "Are you all right?"

They were so close—close enough that she could kiss him. But he'd been clear about putting last night behind them. "I'm so sorry. You shouldn't even be here."

"Why not? The tapestry belongs to me, and Kersey is responsible for my brother's death. Our paths are irrevocably intertwined. You are the one who needn't be here. I know you wanted the sword, but I should've insisted you go home to Monmouth."

There he went, being autocratic again. "You did, if you recall. But I wouldn't change anything. You and Wade would've been overcome at Harlech, and you wouldn't have been able to communicate with Berwyn, which is what led us to the sword." They also wouldn't have spent last night together—and that was something she could never bring herself to regret.

"Can you sit behind me so that I can try to use my fingers to pull at your ropes?"

She turned and flopped onto her backside behind him, then scooted up against him. "Will that work?"

"It will take some time." His fingers plucked at the rope between her wrists. "Hold as still as you can."

"Do you really mean to go after Kersey?"

"Yes. But first, I'm taking you home to Monmouth. And this time, I'll brook no argument."

She knew better than to offer one, but that didn't mean she was going to follow his directive. Monmouth was scarcely ten miles from here and it would be good to discuss everything they'd learned with her father. She wanted—no, she needed—to know what part he played in all of this, if anything.

Elijah worked his fingers slowly but methodically as he endeavored to separate the knot holding her wrists together. "I should have asked Kersey if he'd been working with Septon, since they're both part of the Order."

"You're assuming Septon is part of the Order."

"You seemed convinced that he was."

It did appear to be the only explanation for Septon's secretive behavior over the years. However, to think that he could be in league with Kersey and stealing the sword made her nauseated. "I would still like to know what Kersey plans to do with Dyrnwyn." She was frustrated that he wouldn't say.

"Perhaps he plans to sell it. What other motive could he have?"

Cate thought it over, but couldn't come up with one. She

also couldn't come up with a reason for him and Septon to be working together. "Kersey hates Septon. I can't envision them aligning over this."

"Money is a powerful motivator and will unite the least likely of people—even foes."

"Just because they're in this Order together doesn't mean they share a common goal. Ifan mentioned corrupt members. Perhaps Kersey is one of them, while Septon is not." And if her father was in the Order, she had to assume he wasn't corrupt either. To imagine anything else would completely alter her world.

"You must believe what you will, but don't expect me to do the same." With a final tug, he loosened the rope.

Cate pulled her wrists apart until the rope fell away. She brought her hands in front of her, stripped her gloves off, and massaged her tortured flesh for a moment before starting in on the knot between her ankles. "Will you cast my father as a villain then too?" She finished untying the rope and thrust it away before pushing up and kneeling beside Elijah.

His eyes met hers. "We don't know that your father is even a part of the Order."

She focused on untying the rope at his wrists. "Just as we don't know Septon is. All I'm asking is for you not to cast blame before we know all of the facts. We don't even know that Kersey had anything to do with Matthew's death."

"You can't think he was blameless in that—not when it's obvious this group of miscreants has been carrying out his commands for quite some time with the goal of obtaining the sword."

She didn't know what to think. Her mind was still grappling with the fact that Kersey had been behind all of the attempted thefts. She pulled the knot loose and swept the rope away. Plucking up her discarded glove from the dirt, she used it to dab at the blood that had caked along his temple. "We should find some water. Do you suppose our horses are still outside?"

"I doubt it," he said. "Kersey didn't want for us to follow him, but he knew we wouldn't remain bound forever. Honestly, I wonder why he let us live, particularly when his comrades seemed so keen to commit violence."

Cate shuddered. "Kersey may be a thief, but I can't yet call him a murderer."

Elijah turned his head and her hand fell away. "*I* can."

~

*E*lijah ground his teeth as he jumped to his feet. He helped Cate stand, then stalked from the dovecote. Angry energy coursed through him as he strode to where they'd tethered the horses. As expected, they were gone.

He turned to see Cate approaching, her expression wary. He stared at the tapestry in her arms, and wondered why Kersey had given it to her. Guilt? That single act changed nothing in Elijah's mind. Cate might doubt Kersey's involvement in Matthew's death, but Elijah did not. The blackguard would pay for his crime.

Elijah had started this journey intent on finding out what had happened to Matthew. But with every truth they uncovered, the matter had become clear and was even more nefarious than he'd thought—Matthew had been coldly killed to find this sword, his entire existence negated by another's greed.

Elijah had sought to bring the criminal to justice, but now, knowing that the perpetrator was a nobleman, he realized just how difficult that would be to accomplish without solid proof. He thought through all he knew, and it seemed likely that Kersey had been the one to secure Dalby a position at Stratton Hall in exchange for his continued help with the maid at Cosgrove. The connection seemed obvious now that Elijah knew Kersey had been after Dyrnwyn all along.

If Elijah could persuade Dalby to testify against Kersey, justice might yet be possible. But first he had to find Dalby, and if he did, would the man agree to speak against the heir to an earldom? Or worse, was he truly unaware of Kersey's involvement? He'd claimed not to know the identity of the person in charge.

Prosecuting Kersey seemed unlikely. The man would get away, and who knew what he would do next? He had to be stopped, and Matthew's death would be avenged. Elijah would be doing society a favor by getting rid of him.

Cate walked to him, her brow creased. She reached up and touched his jaw. "You look particularly furious. If Kersey had something to do with Matthew's death, we'll have him arrested."

"*If?* Need I remind you that his hirelings are responsible for attacking us on the road as well as shooting Grey? He's demonstrated his ability to condone violence." He realized he sounded brutal, but he didn't care. She needed to acknowledge her cousin's depravity. "You can't deny he's a criminal."

She blanched and let her hand fall from his face. "I know, but he's my cousin. I just . . . I need some time adjust my thinking."

Elijah thought of his own family and didn't understand her misplaced loyalty. "We can't choose our relatives." He turned from her stricken expression. "We need to find transportation. I'm not certain I want to alert the Scudamore family to our presence." A thought occurred to him and he faced her again. "What would we have done with the sword if Kersey hadn't shown up? We found it on their land, doesn't it belong to them?"

She looked utterly defeated. "Yes, I suppose it does. I

wonder if they knew it was even there. I doubt it, otherwise they surely would've removed it from the dovecote, don't you think?"

"That seems logical. What do you want to do?"

"Until we recover the sword, it seems moot to tell them about it." She glanced away briefly. "Unless you plan to see Kersey arrested for its theft."

"I will certainly add it to his crimes once we track him down." He pivoted. "Let's start walking—we should be there in a few hours." They couldn't ask for assistance. It was one thing to make up an elopement story for a country farmer and his wife and another to outright lie to a member of the gentry—people Elijah might very well see in his new role as earl.

She tucked the tapestry beneath her arm.

"Do you want me to carry that?" he asked.

She shrugged. "I suppose it does belong to you."

It did. And now that he'd recovered it and would be returning her to her parents, they would part.

He took the tapestry from her. The moment he'd been anticipating the last several days was nearly here. It was time to end their association. Time to let her go.

CHAPTER 19

*W*alking up the familiar road toward her home gave Cate a welcome jolt of warmth. Though the journey from Kentchurch had been long and hot, her mind felt as if she'd traveled even farther and was even more exhausted than her body.

Elijah strode beside her, but had kept his attention focused stoically forward. She'd never seen him truly angry before. Could she blame him? He'd finally determined who'd killed his brother—or at least he thought he had. Cate worried about what he might do.

Yet she was also furious with Kersey for stealing the sword. And yes, he might very well have killed Matthew Hollister.

She peered over at Elijah. His profile was so familiar now. As was his voice. His scent. His touch. Was it just last night that he'd made love to her and changed her life irrevocably? He'd said it would be just the one night, but she still felt a connection between them. In the dovecote sharing their excitement at finding the sword, watching his fury as Kersey's man had threatened her, she'd thought he'd felt it too. She longed to talk to him about it, but to what end? She didn't think he would want to be the husband she needed, someone who would support her passion for antiquities and adventure. No; as far as she knew, he didn't want to be any kind of husband at all.

"Turn here," she said, leading him up the main drive to Hollyhaven. She'd always loved the charm of her home with its stone façade and mullioned windows, and she'd never been happier to see it.

As they neared the front of the house, she turned to face him. "Before we go in, I would ask that you allow me to explain our circumstances to my parents. They will not be . . . enthused that we are traveling alone together."

"I can't imagine they would be." His tone was dark, irritated.

"They're not going to make any demands upon you. I wouldn't let them, anyway. They'll understand how we came to be in this situation once I tell them what happened to Grey." Cate felt a pang of remorse. She couldn't help but think of what Elijah had said. If not for Kersey, Grey would be uninjured and would've discovered the sword along with Cate.

He gave a slight nod. She walked up to the door and put her hand on the latch when it came open, startling her.

"Cate! I saw you through the window." Her mother, Margery Bowen, clasped Cate in a tight hug. When she pulled back she looked down at Cate's clothing. "Goodness, why are you dressed like a man?"

"It's quite a tale, Mother. Allow me to introduce my traveling companion, Lord Norris."

Mother scrutinized him quite thoroughly. "Good afternoon, my lord. Do come in, both of you." She opened the door wide and stepped aside so they could move into her father's office, which was situated to the left of the entry hall, with a view of the front drive. "Rhys, it *is* Cate, and Lord Norris."

Father came forward, his dark brows practically meeting over his eyes as he looked at Cate with concern. "I'm glad you're home. Septon is here, and he had me quite worried."

Cate turned her head and saw the moment Elijah's gaze found Septon across the room. His complexion darkened by a shade and his eyes turned to ice. She rushed to stand beside him. "Father, come meet Lord Norris. He escorted me from Harlech."

Father assessed Elijah in much the same way her mother had. He offered his hand. "Thank you for seeing my daughter home safely." He turned and gestured for Septon to come forward. "You've already met, have you not? Septon told us he'd made your acquaintance when Cate stopped in at his house party."

"Indeed." Elijah's tone carried frost to match his eyes. "And what are you doing here, Septon? Instead of at your house party."

Septon pursed his lips. "I was worried about Cate. There's an item missing from my collection. After interviewing my staff, I determined that she'd been in my private library." The look he delivered Elijah said he knew that he'd been there too, but for whatever reason, he didn't say so. Cate was grateful, since convincing her parents that they needn't demand anything of Elijah might actually be more difficult than she'd let on outside.

"I presume you took it?" Septon asked Cate.

"Yes." She tossed Elijah a look that she hoped he would interpret as instructing him to remain quiet. Fortunately he did. "I was going to return it." Thank goodness she'd kept it on her person instead of storing it in her saddlebag, or it would be gone now. She pulled the folded page from her coat and handed it to Septon with a wince. "I apologize for its current state."

Septon frowned at the parchment, but didn't comment. When he looked up at her, his gaze was expectant. "Well, did you find it?"

She knew what he meant by "it." "Yes. But it's gone. Kersey stole it from me." The crushing defeat of losing the sword washed over her again.

Septon flinched, and her father inhaled sharply. Her mother touched his arm.

Septon shook his head. "Blast. Have you any idea where he is now?"

"No," Elijah said. "But there are many things we don't know. For instance, I should like to know whether or not you are a member of the Order of the Round Table."

Septon paled. "Please sit."

"I prefer to stand." Elijah's response came fast and clipped. "I beg you to answer the question."

Septon looked him in the eye. "Yes, I am a member."

Cate's chest constricted. She longed to take Elijah's hand, but didn't dare. Instead, she looked to her father. "Are you?"

Father, thankfully, shook his head. However, he didn't look surprised by any of this.

"You are aware of the Order, however?" she asked.

"I am."

Suddenly it was all too much. All of the secrets. All of the lies. Cate looked from her parents to Septon and back again. "What else have you kept from me? This Order, that poem by Anarawd . . . " Her father's nostrils flared, but she didn't bother hiding the bitterness in her voice—she couldn't. "I'd wager Penn knows all about them."

"Cate, we didn't lie to you," Father said.

"But you kept secrets. Why, because I'm a woman? I'm a woman who tracked down the flaming sword." *And who should have it in her possession.* Fury and disappointment blazed inside of her. She glared at first her father and then Septon. "But maybe you already knew where it was."

"Actually, no, we did not," Septon said. "The Order strives to keep Arthurian artifacts secret and safe. We don't necessarily go looking for them. We do what we can to leave them buried, which is why that de Valery document was locked away in my *private* library."

Cate rankled beneath his condescending tone. "Well, Kersey was looking for the sword, and he's a member of your bloody Order."

Septon glanced at her father. "No, he's not."

Cate's neck prickled. "He indicated he was."

"He most certainly is not," Septon said firmly. "I am aware of every member, and he is not one of them. Perhaps you misunderstood."

She thought back to their conversation. He hadn't actually confirmed his membership, but neither had he denied it. He'd certainly been *aware* of the organization and its secrecy.

If Kersey hadn't taken the sword for the Order . . . "Why did he want the sword, then?"

"I can't say," Septon said.

He couldn't have chosen three worse words to utter in that moment. "Of course you can't. If you'll excuse me, I'd like to transform myself back into a woman, not that any of you would ever mistake me for being a man."

Cate pulled the hat from her head and stalked from the drawing room, not even caring that she was leaving Elijah to the wolves.

∾

*E*lijah felt an urge to applaud Cate's exit. He was, however, too upset over what he'd just heard.

Cate's mother, Margery, moved close to her husband. "I'll go after her in a moment," she said quietly.

Elijah looked at Septon. "Are you certain Kersey isn't part of this Order?"

"Absolutely. I am one of the highest ranking officials," Septon said. "As I said, I know of every new member—and there are very few."

Perhaps that explained why Septon hadn't known of the men who'd come to Cosgrove. If they were part of Kersey's band—which Elijah believed—and Kersey wasn't part of the Order . . . Well, who the hell were they? And why had Ifan said they *were* the Order? "I'm very confused by this secret organization. Kersey and his crew wore masks. They followed us from Septon House, held up Cate's coach, attacked us and stole the tapestry at Harlech, then stole the sword from us at Kentchurch. Kersey may not have outright confirmed his membership in the Order, but he didn't deny it either."

Septon wiped a hand over his mouth. The lines etched into his aged face deepened. He sank down onto the settee. "He committed all of those acts?"

Elijah registered the man's reaction and recalled that his paramour, Lady Stratton, was Kersey's mother. Did Septon have a close relationship with Kersey? Elijah didn't imagine so, given that Lady Stratton had apparently abandoned her son to be with Septon. "Not personally. I can't prove that he was one of the highwaymen we encountered or if he was in the group at Harlech, since they were all masked."

"Then how do you know Kersey is responsible?" Cate's father stepped toward Septon and clapped him on the shoulder while he asked Elijah the question. Mrs. Bowen went around and sat beside Septon. She rested her hand along his forearm. Their behavior was that of a family. Elijah had never felt more alone. And that only increased his ire.

Elijah needed them to understand everything Kersey had done. "He's been after the sword all along—he and his band of mask-wearing miscreants. I can say with certainty that the men with him at Kentchurch were the same men who held up Cate's coach and attacked us at Harlech. They shot Cate's maid, for heaven's sake."

Bowen snapped his gaze to Elijah's. "Is she all right?"

"She will be, but her leg is wounded. She and my valet were forced to stay in Harlech so she could recuperate. That is why Cate and I are alone."

"You reference my daughter by her first name," Bowen said, his tone darkening. He and his wife exchanged concerned looks. "Do I need to be aware of something?"

Elijah's gut tightened. He was suddenly uncomfortably aware that he'd known their daughter in the most intimate of ways, and that he had no intention of doing anything about it. Christ, he was an utter scoundrel. "You do not." He barely gritted the words out. "It's true that we've become . . . familiar on our travels, but not in the way you might suspect." The lie burned his tongue. But what could he do? Admitting anything would require they marry and even if he wanted to, she didn't.

"Kersey shot Cate's maid?" Septon asked, his voice high and thin.

"As I indicated, I can't say for sure, as they were masked," Elijah said. "At the very least, the man responsible was in Kersey's employ."

Septon hung his head. "I can scarcely believe any of this. I know Kersey has been troubled—and I blame myself—but I never imagined he could be capable of such violence, or such greed."

Elijah's lip curled. "Believe it. I need to find him."

"To recover the sword?" Bowen asked.

"Yes." *And to ensure he suffers for killing my brother.* Elijah didn't say the last. He needed their help to find Kersey, and if they knew what he planned, he suspected they wouldn't give it. "Do you have any idea where he might've gone?"

Mrs. Bowen looked at first her husband and then at Septon. "He wouldn't go back to Stratton Hall, would he?"

Septon shook his head. "No, I don't think so. But I do have an idea." He exhaled, sounding weary. His complexion looked gray, which, coupled with his gray hair and gray eyes, made him look completely listless, as if the very life were being sucked out of him. "There have been rumors of a faction forming within the Order." He looked at Bowen. "Timothy Foliot seeks to be the next Prime Chevalier"—he glanced at Elijah—"that is, the Order's highest office. I knew he was ambitious, and I've begun to suspect that he might resurrect Camelot."

Bowen crossed his arms over his chest. "Camelot is the group that seeks to find all Arthurian artifacts and return them to their rightful owners and it's made up of the heirs of the knights, yes?"

Septon nodded. "They've cropped up now and again over the centuries. They always seek to 'cleanse' the Order, to rid it of anyone who isn't a direct descendant of the knights. And their primary goal is to find every artifact. Dyrnwyn would be high on their list."

"You think Kersey is part of this Camelot group?" Mrs. Bowen asked.

"It pains me to say so, but it makes sense, especially if he was vague about being part of the Order." He massaged his temple. "I also remember seeing him with Foliot once. It was a year or more ago—at a party. They were at the faro table together. I didn't think anything of it, but now it seems quite dubious."

Elijah didn't really care about any of this nonsense regarding the Order. He only cared about the sword because Cate wanted it. Cate *deserved* it. And he'd get it for her—sending Kersey to his grave in the process. He moved to stand in front of Septon. "Where is Kersey?"

Septon looked up at him, his gray eyes full of remorse. "I'm afraid I can't say."

Elijah's temper snapped. He prided himself on his control and objectivity, both of which he'd honed in the military. However, in this moment, his ability to see past his hurt and rage was nonexistent. "The hell you can't. Tell me where he is."

"Lord Norris, there's no call to be rude," Margery said softly. She stood from the settee and fixed him with a stare that reminded him too uncomfortably of Cate.

Septon held up his hand briefly. "It's all right. He lost his brother, Margery. And his own life has been endangered several times. Furthermore, Cate's life was endangered. If they injured her maid, it is only by the grace of God that Cate is safe."

"It wasn't God, it was me," Elijah bit out. "I have kept her safe and I will continue to do so." He realized his mistake as soon as he said it. Both of her parents looked at him with new interest. He ignored the unease swirling in his gut and plowed onward. "Tell me where Kersey is. I will retrieve the sword and ensure he doesn't hurt anyone again."

"That sounds ominous," Rhys said.

"He can't go alone," Margery interjected.

Septon stood. "I agree. We'll go with you."

Bloody, bloody hell. Elijah didn't want them to come with him. He wanted to face that prick Kersey alone. And they knew it. That was why Septon wouldn't reveal the location.

Elijah would be forced accept their company. He wanted to shout with frustration, but he worked to rein in his anger. "We'll leave in the morning."

Septon nodded. "Agreed." He reached out and clapped his hand against Elijah's bicep. "I'm so sorry for what you've lost. I'll do whatever necessary to see that Kersey finds justice, that your brother's death is vindicated."

What he'd lost.

What had he lost? A brother who had never known how important he'd been to Elijah, whom Elijah hadn't even realized he'd loved until just recently. Until maybe this moment. Emotion burned the backs of his eyes. Elijah wanted to share Septon's sentiment, but the older man wouldn't go to the lengths that were necessary to truly find vindication because Kersey was like a son to him. And Elijah meant to kill him.

~

*C*ate sat in her bedroom and brushed her hair. She'd dined in her room, still too upset with everyone to spend the evening with them. She wondered how long Elijah had stayed with her parents and Septon, and what they had discussed.

Mother's maid had come to help Cate with her bath, but hadn't said a word about anything that had gone on downstairs. And Cate hadn't asked. Instead, they'd talked about Grey and her injury. Cate also told the maid about Wade and suggested that he and Grey might even marry. Back in Harlech, Rhona had joked about having to read the banns. Cate thought it was not only possible, but likely that Grey and Wade had fallen in love. Their caring behavior toward one another following Grey's injury had said everything.

What would their union mean for Cate and Elijah? They were supposed to go their separate ways after finding the sword, but that hadn't gone at all according to plan. Cate resisted the urge to throw her brush against the wall. Taking a deep breath, she continued to brush her hair. And think about Elijah.

Would he leave her now and go after Kersey? Had Septon or her father even known where he'd gone? She shouldn't have left earlier, but she'd been fed up, exhausted, and just plain distressed. Losing the sword—that had ironically rested just ten miles from where she'd grown up—was a calamity she didn't know how to recover from.

A light rap on her door interrupted her thoughts. "It's Mother."

Cate had been expecting her at some point and was actually surprised she'd waited this long. "Come in."

Mother closed the door behind her and stepped into the chamber. She was still dressed in her dinner gown. Her blond hair—unmarred by even a single strand of white—was swept into an elegant style.

She smiled as she touched Cate's cheek. "I missed you, dear." She perched on the end of the bed. "Are you all right? I didn't want to disturb you. I suspected you wanted to be alone for a while."

Cate turned away from the small glass on her dressing table to face her mother. "Thank you. I appreciate that." *Liar.* "I lost the sword." Emotion clogged her throat.

Mother leaned forward and took her hand. "I'm so sorry. I know how captivated you've always been by it. Are you terribly angry with everyone?"

Cate thought about all of the secrets that had been kept from her over the years and her ire rekindled. "Yes, I'm angry. Our sex is eternally cheated."

Mother sat back on the edge of the bed. "In some ways, yes. Your father doesn't discount us, however." She looked at Cate intently. "You don't think he's unfair, do you?"

Not compared to everyone else, including Septon. "No. But my entire life I've sought to discover Dyrnwyn and no one took me seriously. No one thought I would find it."

Mother cocked her head to the side. "I don't think that's fair. I encouraged you."

"Yes, but now it seems as though information was purposely kept from me so that I *wouldn't* find it."

"Yes, it does seem that way." Mother pursed her lips. "And unfortunately you're right. I'm certain that's what Septon did, and your father didn't help by not telling you about the Anarawd poem. Perhaps if you knew about the Order's goals you would've changed your mind about searching for Dyrnwyn."

Cate considered this for a moment. "No, I wouldn't have. I don't agree with their goals. Artifacts—Arthurian or other-wise—should be shared with the world. We have much to learn from them."

Mother smiled, the flesh around her eyes crinkling into small fans. "You and your brother are exactly alike. Penn doesn't give a damn about the Order either."

Any burst of pride Cate might've felt was crushed beneath the confirmation that she'd been right—Penn had been privy to information that had been kept from her. "Did Penn know about the poem too?" she asked quietly.

Mother exhaled, perhaps with a touch of regret. "Only because he was here when we found it. It was just after he'd come to live here, when his mother had become ill. You hadn't been born. I hadn't even married your father yet."

She knew her parents had met when she'd brought him her de Valery manuscript to analyze, but it seemed there was more to the story. "You found the poem together?"

Her mother smiled softly. "We did. It was quite an adven-ture. I'll tell you about it some time. It's where we fell in love."

Like the adventure she'd just taken with Elijah? But no, they hadn't fallen in love. At least, he hadn't. Cate wasn't sure what she felt. She only knew that thinking of him made her feel as hollow as thinking of Dyrnwyn. Maybe more so. She shook the melancholy thoughts away. "Why did you call the Order 'infernal'?"

Mother rolled her eyes. "The Order caused us some problems during that adventure, but it all worked out in the end, even if Septon did make us promise to keep the poem secret —that included swearing Penn to secrecy too. The poem is a contemporary work of Arthur and his knights. It proves they existed as men in our history. But you probably figured that out, my brilliant girl."

Cate warmed beneath her mother's praise. *She* never discounted Cate's abilities. "I did. Why does the Order want to keep it secret? It's an important historical artifact." Like the tapestry and the sword.

"Because they believe the thirteen treasures of Britain— which are apparently also as real as the men—would cause turmoil and bloodshed as people clamored to claim them." Her eyes narrowed briefly. "And I suppose they're right, since this Camelot faction has gone after the sword."

"What Camelot faction?"

"Septon explained after you left that there's a group within the Order that seeks to return all Arthurian artifacts to the actual knights' descendants. They are somewhat militant in their methods and it seems as though Kersey has joined them." She pressed her lips together. "Your father is quite upset."

Because Kersey was important to him for some reason. Father had always gone out of his way to ensure they spent their summers together—until Lady Stratton had left her husband. Then Lord Stratton had kept Kersey from all of them, despite Father's efforts. It had hurt him greatly not to be able to see Kersey, and Cate had wondered why. "Is there a reason why Kersey is so special? Is this another secret?"

"Now *that* is very complicated. Yes, it's a secret, and unfortunately one I am not permitted to share." This time, the regret in her tone was unmistakable. "It affects too many people and it may just be that it stays a secret forever."

Cate was horribly intrigued, but knew that once her mother had made a decision, it was nearly impossible to change her mind. "I hate that you won't tell me."

"Does it help to know that Penn doesn't know it either? I promise that if this information is ever going to come to light, you will be the first person I tell." Mother smoothed her hands down her skirt. "Now, tell me about Lord Norris before your father and Septon set out with him in the morning."

"They're all leaving together?" Presumably to find Kersey.

"Yes. Septon didn't want to disclose Kersey's potential location. He's afraid of what Norris might do. The earl blames him for his brother's death."

Cate's heart ached for Elijah's loss. "And he may be justified in doing so. Kersey certainly had the motive, given his pursuit of the sword, and he had a connection with someone in the previous Lord Norris's household who tried to steal the tapestry. He seems more than a bit guilty."

"Do you think he is?"

"I don't know." Cate wished she did. "He did keep me from being harmed at Kentchurch. His hirelings are a mercenary lot."

Mother paled a bit. "I hate that you were in danger. I believe we're going to have to reassess your future travel with Grey. I'm just glad Norris was with you in this instance."

Cate was glad he'd been there too. Indeed, she didn't want

to contemplate him *not* being there. "Elijah has been an excellent traveling companion."

Mother's eyebrow arched, and Cate realized she'd just first-named him in front of her. "He called you Cate downstairs." *He had?* "It seems you share a certain level of familiarity. Your father and I have allowed you far more freedom than any young woman ought to enjoy—and I don't regret that. Society's silly rules mean as little to me as they do to you. However, your safety and well-being *are* important to me. Do you want to talk about your relationship with Norris?"

What could she say? She certainly didn't want to reveal the depths of their familiarity—rather, intimacy. And she was confused. She wanted him desperately, could barely envision going back to her life of just a few short weeks ago, but what was the alternative? He wasn't ever going to marry, not that she was sure she wanted him as a husband, and she doubted they could maintain a romantic relationship, particularly since he'd plainly stated that last night would not be repeated. "I don't think so."

Mother's green-brown eyes studied her. "If you change your mind, you know where to find me. Don't forget that I was once a young unmarried woman like you. I've told you before I never wanted to marry, that falling in love with your father wasn't something I'd planned."

Yes, Cate knew that. It was why she didn't think she needed to marry either. "It was really that easy? You fell in love with Father and decided marriage was worthwhile?"

"I'm not sure it was easy." Her lips curved up. "In fact, I'm fairly certain I made your father a bit mad with my insistence that we needn't marry." Cate wondered how far their relationship had progressed on that adventure and decided there were parts of Mother's story she didn't need to hear. Apparently Mother agreed because she said, "Well, that's neither here nor there. I just hope you know that I will always support you, provided you don't do anything exceedingly foolish." She gave Cate a pointed look that carried a wealth of meaning.

"I always endeavor never to bring you shame or embarrassment. All I've ever wanted was to make you and Father proud. It's why I wanted so badly to find the sword."

"Oh, Cate." Mother left the bed and pulled Cate from her chair to enfold her in her arms. Cate welcomed the comfort, squeezing her mother tight as she'd done in her girlhood.

"I love you so much, and we couldn't be more proud of you."

"I love you too." They broke apart a moment later. "Thank you."

"Get some sleep. The men will undoubtedly be off fairly early."

The men. "I should like to accompany them," Cate said.

Mother's gaze turned shrewd. "I figured as much. I would too. However, your father and Septon are adamant that we not go. Who's to say what we might do after they leave . . . "

Cate grinned. "*Where* are they going? Or are you supposed to keep that from me too?"

Mother's forehead creased. "In fact, I wasn't supposed to say anything, but I don't see why you can't know, so long as you don't tell Norris."

"I won't even see him." *Unless she stole into his room in the middle of the night.* The thought summoned heat and anticipation throughout her body.

"Kersey will likely take the sword to the man heading this Camelot group within the Order. His name is Timothy Foliot and he resides in Glastonbury." Of course he did. Glastonbury was one of the places most associated with Arthur. In fact, Glastonbury Abbey was one of the many supposed burial sites of Arthur and Guinevere.

"Do they plan to simply travel to his home and demand he relinquish Dyrnwyn? Kersey had at least five men, and Foliot could have even more." Cate wished that Grey and Wade were with them to increase their numbers.

"Septon has a plan that involves the Order. I'm not aware of the specifics. He seemed fairly certain that Kersey would go to Foliot and that he would go alone. It seems Foliot is very particular about who is allowed to visit him."

How Cate longed to go! "Does that include a ban on women?"

"Perhaps, but I don't think that's why your father doesn't want us to go. He sees this as dangerous and I don't disagree. We should probably remain here." She sounded disappointed, but she'd made a decision and Cate couldn't hope to change her mind. Which meant she had to come up with another plan if she wanted to be the one to reclaim the sword.

She said good night to her mother and considered her options. Her earlier thought jumped back into her head: *unless she stole into his room in the middle of the night.*

Perhaps she could convince Elijah to leave with her. If Kersey was traveling alone, maybe they could overtake him. He'd presumably stopped somewhere for the night. She calculated the time in her head and determined they could be as little as four or five hours behind him. If they left after the household was abed and traveled along the river to Chepstow, they could catch up with him *before* he reached Glastonbury. It seemed their chances for retaking the sword would be far greater if they stopped him from arriving at his destination.

Cate's gaze strayed to her armoire, which held the men's clothing she'd removed earlier. Mother's maid had offered to take the garments away, but Cate hadn't been willing to part with the memories they represented. Now she was glad she hadn't, for they would be most useful.

She turned to the clock on her mantel. Just past ten. She had at least a few hours to wait.

Would Elijah go with her or would he agree with her father and Septon that it was too dangerous for her? Could she persuade him to take one last adventure together, knowing it might be their last?

Emotion burned in Cate's chest, making the loss of the sword pale in comparison. Maybe it wasn't the sword that had upset her most. Maybe it was the threat of losing Elijah. Somewhere between realizing her lifelong goal and spending a week with a charismatic earl, her priorities had changed. Not only was she worried she couldn't return to her life before Elijah—she feared she didn't want to. And where would that leave her?

CHAPTER 20

*E*lijah stared at the ceiling of his bedchamber and tapped his foot against the base of the bed. He doubted he'd sleep, but he should at least try. Hell, he *was* trying, but it was useless. Between his fury at Kersey, his frustration with Septon and Bowen, and his unsatisfied desire for Cate, he had no hope of finding rest.

He wondered where she was. He had no idea where her chamber might be located, not that he would go to her. The only thing worse than first-naming her to her father would be sneaking into her chamber under his very nose.

And now he had to journey with both Bowen and Septon. He pounded his fist into the mattress in renewed resentment. Why wouldn't they just tell him where Kersey was going?

Because they didn't want him to resort to violence. He hadn't voiced his intent, but they'd—accurately—surmised what he planned. There had to be a way he could do what he needed without them interfering.

The sound of his door latch turning jolted him from the bed. Light from a single candle flickered into the room. He rushed forward as the door closed and swung the intruder around.

"Cate." She was garbed in her men's costume, clearly ready to depart. "What the devil are you doing here?"

She looked him up and down. "Good, you're at least partially dressed." He wore his breeches and a shirt that hung loose around his hips.

He would argue that being dressed in her presence wasn't good at all, but they were past such flirtation, if they'd ever even been there at all. Wait, of course they had. They'd flirted with for quite some time before . . . *before.*

"Why does it matter?" he asked as she steered back into the chamber.

"Because we're leaving."

He stopped and turned to face her. "Where are we going?"

"To get Dyrnwyn back."

"I don't know where it is." His pulse quickened. "Do you?"

"Yes. Get dressed."

She knew where to go. His shoulders dipped in relief. But it was brief. He looked at her skeptically. "Who else is coming with us?"

She looked at him as if he were daft. "Who do you think? Did you suppose I would just come into your bedchamber in the middle of the night to fetch you whilst everyone else awaited us downstairs?"

He fought the urge to smile. How he loved her humor and intellect, even cloaked in sarcasm. Now he fought the urge to kiss her. She smelled of honey and lilac, as if she'd just bathed. The scent was intoxicating and such a welcome distraction from the turmoil of the last hours. It felt so good to let his anger and sadness and fear melt away . . . He blinked. "You can't come with me."

She put her hand on her hip. "Of course I can. We've

taken every step of this journey together. I don't mean to let you finish it alone."

"It's too dangerous, Cate. I can't let you come."

Though the candlelight offered meager illumination, he could see the fury kindling in her gaze. "You can't 'let' me come? As it happens, you have no say. If you don't 'let' me come, you don't go anywhere. Do you know where to find Kersey?"

Hell and the bloody devil. "You're a menace of a female."

"Thank you. Now get dressed." She went to the window and lifted the curtain to peer out into the night. "We need to borrow horses from the neighbor down the road. I don't want to chance waking the stable lad. He'll tell my parents, and I want at least a few hours' lead time."

"You've thought this through quite thoroughly." He couldn't keep from admiring her. It seemed he'd done that from the moment they'd met. She might be exasperating and infuriatingly tenacious, but he actually loved that about her.

Loved?

How could he know what that felt like? Because he did. He'd figured it out earlier when he'd thought about what he'd lost to Kersey. He'd never be able to tell Matthew what he'd just realized—that he'd loved him.

But with Cate it was different. She wasn't family, they didn't have a shared history—she was just someone who'd stumbled into his mundane life, bringing color and vivacity and . . . love.

She turned from the window and frowned. "Why aren't you getting dressed?"

He had to touch her, hold her, make love to her one more time. He quickly went and locked the door. "Come here."

She moved toward him, a perplexed look wrinkling her brow. "What is it?"

He took her hand and pulled her against him. "I decided one night wasn't enough."

Her eyes widened with surprise and it was the last thing he saw before he kissed her. Their mouths connected with heat and passion. It was as if the last day hadn't happened. They were back in their little room in the farmhouse.

He molded his hands to her backside as he pressed her against him. She twined her hands around his neck and her hat fell to the carpet behind her, loosening her hair so that it tumbled past her shoulders. Her fingers crept up into his nape and pulled at his hair.

He lifted her and coaxed her legs around his waist. She locked her ankles, bringing her hips flush against his so that his cock rested perfectly against her sex. He thrust his hips, taunting them both, and she moaned.

"Too many damn clothes," he muttered into her mouth.

She pulled one arm from his neck and tried to wriggle out of her coat.

He tossed her onto the bed and she let out an arousing little squeal. "Kneel up."

She did as he bade, quickly removing her boots with his assistance. He set about stripping away her coat, waistcoat, and cravat.

There was something inexplicably enticing about her wearing men's clothing. "I am profoundly grateful you are a woman, but I must admit I enjoy seeing you in this costume." He whipped the cravat from her neck and dropped it on the bed. The shirt fell open, exposing the creamy flesh of her neck.

"What makes it so alluring?" She fingered the collar. "Is it the shirt?" Her hand fell to the breeches and she unfastened one of the buttons. "Or is it these?"

His mouth had gone dry. "All of it. Rather, none of it. I

prefer to rip every garment from you so that I might enjoy your naked flesh."

She unfastened another button. "What's stopping you?"

"The fact that you have to put it all on again. For that reason alone, I will use caution." He exhaled, but it did nothing to calm his raging lust. He found the hem of the shirt and whisked it up over her head. She wore a garment that covered her breasts—a sort of modified chemise with a drawstring at the bottom. He reached for the string and pulled it, freeing her breasts.

She slipped her arms through the straps and he helped to lift it over her head. "Thank you for being careful. Rhona spent an hour making that."

He scarcely heard what she said because he was too busy staring at the dusky hue of her nipples. Bending forward, he sucked one deep into his mouth, using his tongue and teeth to tease her. She gasped as she wound her fingers into his hair and held him against her. "Elijah, please."

She pulled at his shirt and tugged it over his head, forcing him to pull away from her for a brief moment. Her hands splayed over his shoulders, clutching at him as he went back to his feast. He cupped her, holding her to his mouth. He unbuttoned the rest of her fall and pushed the breeches down. She wore nothing beneath them and his fingers skimmed over her bare hip.

"Off," he groaned, coming up to take her mouth in another fierce kiss.

She worked to pull the breeches from her legs and kick them aside. He barely gave her time to readjust on the bed before he pushed her back into the pillow. Still kissing her, he brushed his hand between her thighs and pushed them wide. She complied, opening herself to his touch. He found her slick folds and stroked her, concentrating pressure on her clitoris.

She deepened the kiss, curling her hand around his nape and driving her tongue into his mouth. He responded by thrusting his finger into her. Her fingers bit into his neck.

She put her other hand on his backside and pressed him down. He moved his hand and rocked into her, sliding his cock over her entrance. She fumbled with the buttons of his fall. "Off," she said, repeating his command.

He sat back and unbuttoned his breeches. She followed suit, sitting, and as he drew the garment off, she turned him and pushed him back as he'd done to her. "My turn," she said.

She kissed him, thoroughly but briefly, before trailing her mouth down to his chest. She used her tongue to blaze a path of need straight to his groin. Her dark hair cascaded over him as she moved down. He wrapped his hand into the thick strands and held it aside so he could watch her.

She threw him a wicked smile just before her lips closed over his cock.

"God, Cate." He thrust up into her mouth. She licked and sucked, using her hands and tongue to drive him to the brink. Then she left him—but only for a moment. Soon she was straddling him.

"Is this all right?" she asked tentatively. She dragged herself over his moist cock and white lights danced before his eyes.

"It's exceptional." He almost couldn't speak. He gripped her hips and worked her over him, rising up into her and creating a friction that made her moan low in her throat.

He found her channel again and stroked his fingers into her, opening her. She widened her legs over him and pressed down. Grasping his cock, he positioned himself. "Lift up."

She braced her hands on his chest and lifted. He slid into her, meaning to go slow, but she slammed down on him, taking him fully inside of her.

Her fingers dug into his chest as she ground down against

him. He clasped her hips again and pulled her up, showing her how to move. She rocked forward again, taking him deep, then rose, then fell once more.

He skimmed his hand up her ribcage and found her breast, cupping the mound and then pulling on the nipple. Her movements grew faster and he urged her forward so he could take her breast in his mouth. He leaned up and suckled her. She rode faster, and he felt his orgasm building already. No, he wasn't ready. He needed her to come and then he'd turn her over . . .

She quickened the pace, rising off of him and sliding down again with increasing speed and intensity. He'd watched her ride a horse, knew her muscles could do exactly what they needed to do to bring herself to come.

But that didn't mean he wouldn't help. He fell back on the bed and brought his hand down between them. He found her clitoris and stroked her hard. Her muscles clenched and he knew she was lost. She clamped down on him, squeezing as she cried out.

"Cate, you have to—" But it was too late. She was too tight, felt too damned good. He thrust up into her and came. He knew he had to pull her away, to get out . . . but he couldn't do anything but pump into her again and again. And she didn't stop. She rode him over and over, her hips finally slowing as she fell forward over his chest.

He caught her and turned, withdrawing from her quickly. Not that it mattered. The damage could already be done. And shit, then where would they be?

Married?

He could think of worse predicaments. Particularly since he was in love with her.

Would she consider it? She'd been clear about not needing or even wanting to marry. She cherished her independence above all else. He couldn't see her succumbing to the constraints of becoming his countess. Her love for antiquities was far more than a mere hobby, and he didn't think he could compete with it.

Hell, it was an entirely moot consideration. After he killed her cousin, she wasn't going to want anything to do with him.

He pushed up and went to tidy himself before getting dressed. Once he had his breeches on, he turned to see her sitting up and brushing her hair back over her shoulder. She was magnificent in the candlelight—her skin glowing like polished bronze, her dark eyes gleaming with satisfaction.

"Do you need help getting dressed?" he asked.

She looked at him intently as if she might say something more meaningful than whether or not she could tie a cravat —clearly she could—but in the end she only reached for her breeches.

He turned from her, not to give her privacy, but to save himself from seeing what he'd never see again. He dressed quickly and went to the armoire to collect his pistols along with the bag of powder and ammunition. "We're going to need more weapons."

"I have my pistol." She pulled on her waistcoat. "And I can nick another from my father's library. Kersey will supposedly be traveling alone, but we should be well armed in any case."

"How do you know he's alone?"

"Septon said the person he's going to prefers it that way."

Elijah set his hat on his head. "So much the better for us."

"Precisely." She looked up at him, a bead of uncertainty in her gaze. "Before . . . Why wasn't one night enough?"

Because you're an incomparable woman and I love you like I've never loved anyone before. The words scorched his tongue, but how could he say them when there was no future between them?

"You spend days campaigning for me to take you to bed, and you want to question why?" He arched a brow at her. "I'm a man. You came into my room in the middle of the night. It was an opportunity I couldn't ignore." How callous that sounded. Yet how accurate. Men were beasts.

Little lines of disappointment gathered between her brows and he felt like more than a beast. She stepped toward him. "Does that mean that after today we are well and truly finished?"

"I don't know how we would continue. I can't very well take you as my mistress."

"No, I suppose not, at least not in the traditional sense." She avoided looking at him, averting her gaze to the floor. "I can't see myself living in some house in London waiting on you."

He envisioned one of those exotic birds again, but this one was caged and longed to be free. "No, I can't see you doing that either." He touched her jaw. "Cate, we both knew how this would end—with each of us going our separate ways."

She clapped her hat on her head and started for the door. "We should go. Everyone should be asleep, but be as quiet as possible." Her tone was short, clipped, verging on irritated.

That was for the best. Leaving her would be much easier if he thought she didn't like him anymore.

～

The sun was just barely peeking over the horizon as they crossed the bridge from Chepstow into England. After borrowing horses from a neighbor—Cate had paid the stable lad not to tell anyone until morning—they'd picked their way along the Wye River in the dark. The moon had guided them for a short time before setting and then they'd slowed until the predawn light had offered enough illumination to continue at a decent pace.

All during the journey, they'd kept their conversation to necessity. There was no more discussion of the future—or lack thereof—or of the past, which was heavy in Cate's mind. She'd been surprised when he'd taken her to bed again, but elated. Being with him had fulfilled her in more ways than she'd imagined. It had been more than a physical act—at least to her. It seemed that to him, she was precisely what she'd offered: a shag without any burden attached. And she couldn't go back now and say she wanted more.

Though it had been on the tip of her tongue.

Did she want more? He was right—she didn't want to be his mistress ensconced in some townhouse, waiting on his every move. No, she wanted to be his partner, as she'd been during this entire adventure. She thought of what her mother had said, how she and her father had fallen in love in a similar fashion. Could that be what Cate was feeling? Did she love Elijah?

A bright warmth burst in her chest. Yes, she loved him. He'd treated her with more respect and care than any other man of her acquaintance. Yes, he'd tried to command her about, but only because he wanted to keep her safe. He was a man of pride and principle, and she wouldn't have him any other way.

But her feelings didn't matter since he would never love her. He'd said before that he didn't even know what love was.

When they reached the other side of the river, she rode up beside Elijah. "I hope Kersey isn't an early riser. We need every moment to catch up with him."

They'd discussed the timeframe when they'd set out. Assuming Kersey had stopped somewhere for the night, they should be able to overtake him.

"Yes, the later he leaves the better," Elijah said. "I'd guess he stayed somewhere in or near Bristol."

"That's my thought as well." Cate shot him a sidelong glance. He stared straight ahead. She would miss his profile.

They continued in silence, riding for quite some time until they skirted Bristol. She slowed her horse to a walk. Elijah did the same. "What is it?" he asked.

"I think I should tell you where we're going now."

Elijah's eyes flickered with surprise. "That would be helpful."

"Kersey is going to a house near Glastonbury to see a man named Timothy Foliot. I'm not certain of his route, but if we cut across the Mendips, we might be able to gain a little more time."

"That's rougher terrain," Elijah said.

"Riding around them will add hours. And if he's going that way, we'll be able to cut him off and ambush him in return."

His eyes lit with appreciation. "I'd like that."

Something about the set of his mouth indicated that appreciation might not be the right emotion. She knew he was angry with Kersey—and he had every right to be. But was there more to it? Since their encounter with Kersey and his men at Kentchurch yesterday, Elijah had carried an air of something . . . sinister.

"What do you want to happen with Kersey?" she asked tentatively.

"I want you to regain Dyrnwyn."

"What of him? Are we going to take him to the local constable?"

Elijah's gaze hardened. "What will that accomplish? We'll have him brought up on charges of theft? What else can we say he did?"

Cate opened her mouth, then snapped it closed. They had

no proof other than their own account of what had happened at Kentchurch. And his only true crime was stealing the sword, something she'd planned to do too. "The theft will be enough."

Elijah edged his horse closer. "His men held up your coach, attacked us at Harlech where they shot Grey, *and* they murdered my brother. You think prosecuting him for theft would be enough?" His lip curled, revealing his even, white teeth and making him look more primal than she'd ever seen him.

"What else would you do?" She feared she knew the answer.

He sat straight and walked his horse away from her. "You don't have to come. I'll leave you wherever you'd like and continue on my own."

She moved to catch up with him. "No, I'm coming with you." If only to ensure he didn't do something he might regret. She felt betrayed by Kersey—her own cousin—and he'd engaged in dastardly behavior. But *he* hadn't shot Grey, nor did they know for certain whether he'd had anything to do with Matthew's death. She couldn't forget the way he'd kept her from harm at Kentchurch. His men would've happily killed her and Elijah, but Kersey had ensured they were safe. She clung to the notion that there was goodness in him.

She spent the next several miles trying to think of how she could convince Elijah to at least delay his judgment. Or better yet, to allow the law to determine Kersey's punishment. He could potentially be hanged for theft, yet she doubted they'd sentence a nobleman to that end. More likely he'd be transported or imprisoned.

The terrain grew more uneven as they rode into the hills. They followed a modest path, which ultimately led them to the Cheddar Gorge.

"There!" Elijah pointed to a single rider ahead of them, galloping east along the edge of the canyon. He kicked his horse into a dead run and gained on the rider, while Cate worked to keep up.

As they neared the rider, she saw that the man was indeed Kersey. He looked back over his shoulder and urged his horse faster. Elijah pulled a pistol from his pocket and fired. He missed, but it frightened Kersey's horse enough that it reared and threw Kersey to the ground.

Cate struggled to reach her cousin, but Elijah got there first. He slid from his horse and stalked toward her cousin, just as he clambered to his feet. The sword was in his hand.

Drawing her horse to a halt, she jumped down. "Kersey, stop, please."

His back to the canyon, Kersey held the sword in front of him. He'd lost his hat in the fall, and the cool breeze tossed his dark hair. "How in the bloody hell did you find me?"

"Septon knew where you were going," Cate said.

Kersey looked past them. "Where is he?" he spat the question.

"Not here," Elijah said softly. "You get to deal with me." He pulled his second pistol from his other pocket and transferred it to his right hand. Hatred burned in his gaze.

Fear curled through her. "Elijah, don't."

"He killed my brother."

Kersey flinched in surprise. "I didn't. I had nothing to do with his death. I only wanted the tapestry so that I could find the sword. No one was supposed to be hurt."

Elijah strode toward him. "But people *were* hurt—Cate's maid, my brother. Your secret Order will stop at nothing to get what it wants."

Kersey's eyes narrowed. "I told you, that wasn't me."

Elijah pointed his pistol at Kersey's chest. "Even if you didn't pull the trigger of the pistol that shot Grey or cause

Matthew's coach to crash, you were behind both of those occurrences. At least be man enough to own what you've done."

"Elijah, don't!" Cate grabbed his arm and the pistol fired. Thankfully, the shot went wide.

Kersey lunged toward him with the sword. Cate pulled her hand away as Elijah rushed forward. He lowered his body to avoid the arc of the blade. She held her breath until the sword cleared his back. He brought his hand up to dislodge the weapon from Kersey's grip, and suddenly the blade erupted with pale flame from hilt to tip.

Cate gasped as Kersey's eyes widened. Elijah jerked back. Kersey pushed at him, and Elijah pulled his waist so they fell together at the edge of the cliff.

Everything seemed to happen in a dream. Their motions were slow, the sounds around her muted. Kersey had Elijah pinned to the ground, the flaming sword raised. With one blow Cate was going to lose what she wanted more than anything—not Dyrnwyn, Elijah.

She moved closer, her heart in her throat. "Kersey, take the sword and go."

CHAPTER 21

*E*lijah clasped Kersey's wrist and tried to wrestle the sword from his grip. He was aware of Cate, that she'd moved closer and said something. Had he heard her right?

She said it again. "Kersey, take the sword and go. Please."

Elijah struggled to look past Kersey and saw the anguish in her face.

"I don't care about the sword. Just don't hurt Elijah. I couldn't bear it if you did."

Kersey's arm sagged and Elijah took advantage of the opening. He flipped Kersey to his back, bringing them perilously close to the edge of the cliff.

All of the rage pent up inside of Elijah—from Matthew's death, from Cate being in danger, probably all of the anger he'd buried his entire life—gathered into a combustive mass. Elijah tightened his grip on Kersey's right hand, so close to where the ground fell away. He wrapped his other hand around Kersey's throat, intent on ending this right now.

Kersey's eyes widened as he tried to pry Elijah's fingers from his neck. Failing, he reached up and grappled for

Elijah's shoulder, but Elijah only squeezed harder. Kersey next tried to wrench his wrist from Elijah's grip. Their arms swung out over the canyon. Kersey's grasp loosened. Elijah took in Kersey's bright red face, bulging eyes, and felt Cate pulling at his shoulder.

"Elijah!"

Kersey began to weaken, his body ceasing to fight. Elijah could kill him, but the sword . . . Kersey's fingers uncurled from the hilt. It was going to fall . . .

Elijah let go of Kersey and dove for the blade, its flame going out the moment Kersey relinquished his grip. Stretching, Elijah reached for the sword before it disappeared into the canyon below. His hand closed around the hilt, but he was too far out . . .

A firm hand clasped his calf, kept him from tumbling over the side. Blood rushed to Elijah's head as he hung suspended for what seemed like forever.

Multiple hands dragged him back up, pulled him onto the grass and dirt. He collapsed onto his back, his lungs heaving. He stared up at the blue sky dotted with puffy clouds. It was so serene, so beautiful. Vaguely, he was aware of the sword resting in his hand. He glanced over at the blade lying against the ground and saw Kersey sprawled nearby. His eyes were closed, and he breathed as heavily as Elijah. Maybe more so, because Elijah had nearly choked the life from him.

What had he done?

Elijah closed his eyes briefly and saw red from the sun burning the backs of his lids. Sweat dotted his brow and he wiped it away, letting his hand fall over his forehead. Had he really meant to kill Kersey? He was a soldier, trained to fight and kill. Though he'd never had to, he'd been ready to do his duty. Was avenging his brother worth the weight of killing someone? Kersey had behaved despicably, but it wasn't Elijah's responsibility to play judge.

A hand grazed his jaw. Elijah snapped his eyes open and squinted up into Cate's face. She was paler than he'd ever seen her; her eyes looked hollow.

He reached up and touched her cheek. "I'm sorry. I didn't want him to get away with all he'd done. My brother, Grey, you . . ."

"Why did you go after the sword?" Her gaze flicked to the blade, her brow creasing. "It doesn't mean anything compared to you. If I'd lost you . . ."

She could still say that after what he'd tried to do? "You aren't angry with me?"

"No. You were protecting yourself, protecting me. But you were foolish to go after Dyrnwyn. I meant it when I told Kersey that I don't care about it. Not anymore. I've spent my whole life chasing a dream without realizing what it was I really wanted. You're the dream, Elijah. You're the treasure."

He clasped the back of her head and pulled her down, kissing her fiercely. She cupped his face and kissed him back.

A moment later, she pulled back and smiled down at him. "I love you."

"Not nearly as much as I love you."

She sucked in a breath. "You do?"

"Of course I do. Love has been a fleeting thing in my life. Never have I felt it as strongly and as surely as I do with you. It took me a bit to realize what it was, but I think I've loved you since Septon House. At least." He smiled.

"I love it when you smile. Promise me you'll do it more."

"It's hard not to in your presence."

A groan interrupted them. Elijah's smile faded.

"Kersey." Elijah sat up and moved to the other man's side, letting go of the sword.

Kersey's eyes were open, their gray pupils reflecting the blue sky. He didn't look at Elijah or Cate, who had moved to his other side. "Now what?" he croaked.

Elijah cringed, realizing the man's voice was affected because of him. "Thank you for keeping me from falling over the cliff."

Kersey threw him an uncertain glance. "Maybe I was just trying to save the sword."

"I don't think so. You could've made your way down into the canyon and found it."

"Maybe." He shrugged against the ground. "You could've done the same after you'd finished me off."

He could've, but he hadn't. "I wasn't thinking about that when I dove for it, actually. And I suspect you did the same with me. I guess when we were pushed to the edge, we both acted nobly."

"Nobly. Ha." There was no humor in the dark chuckle that followed Kersey's words. He squeezed his eyes shut as he tried to sit up. Cate and Elijah helped him, supporting his back and shoulders. He looked around, his gaze settling on the sword. "What are you going to do with it?"

Elijah waited for Cate to answer. It was her decision to make.

"I don't know. I'd like to give it to Penn for the museum, but it rightfully belongs to the Scudamores." She looked at Kersey in puzzlement. "Actually, it might rightfully belong to you. Kersey, it *burned.*"

His gaze darkened to steel and he shot a glance at the blade. "I know."

"This means that you're worthy, that you must be a descendant of one of the knights."

Elijah watched a play of emotions across Kersey's face—astonishment, frustration, and maybe hope.

"I don't even know what that means. Is my father not my father?" Yes, that had been hope in his eyes.

Elijah heard the wistfulness in his tone and suddenly felt

a kinship with this man who wished his parent wasn't his parent.

"I don't know either, but I'll help you find out," Cate said.

Kersey looked at her with disbelief. "You'd help me? After everything I've done?"

She nodded. "I would. You said you weren't responsible for killing Matthew."

Weariness sagged through Kersey's frame. "That was the Order. The men who were assigned to me—the ones you saw at Kentchurch—they were cutthroats. They were instructed to go to any lengths to obtain the sword. They pretended to be highwaymen and stopped your brother's coach to rob him of the tapestry."

"The tapestry wasn't even with him," Elijah said.

Kersey's lips formed a grim line. "I know. They tried a similar trick with you and Cate after they knew you'd found the tapestry. Since Cate's vehicle was in front, they held it up as a means to lure you away from the map, which we knew was in your coach. However, they didn't count on you being such a dangerous adversary."

Discussing this was sparking Elijah's ire again. "How could you condone them threatening Cate?"

Kersey's gaze turned dark and fierce. "Every step of the way, I ordered them to keep her safe. I vowed to kill anyone who harmed her."

Kersey's vehement protection of her mollified Elijah's anger. Somewhat.

"What about Grey? Were you there?" Cate sounded as though she was holding her breath.

"I was in Harlech, but not at the castle. I never would've allowed them to shoot anyone." He wiped his hand over his face. "They were furious that I wouldn't let them kill you at Kentchurch. They were ready to mutiny. It's why I snuck away from them this morning."

"That's why you're alone?" Cate asked. "Septon said you'd be traveling alone because Foliot prefers privacy—he wouldn't have wanted you to have company."

"They were his hirelings, so he wouldn't have minded." Kersey stared at her, his lip curling. "What does Septon know of any of this?"

"He and my father were supposed to accompany Elijah to find you and recover the sword." Cate glanced at Elijah. "But we decided to come alone."

"They'll follow you though, won't they?"

"Probably."

Kersey tried to stand, but it took him a second to find his feet. Elijah leapt up and helped him. "I need to go," Kersey said. He looked to Elijah. "If you'll let me."

Cate touched his forearm. "Why?"

"I can't see Septon." He looked around for his horse, saw it grazing a few dozen yards away.

"Wait," Cate said, "I still have more questions. Why did you join the Order? It only admits scholars and descendants of the knights. You didn't even realize you were a descendant until today."

He arched a dark brow at her, looking more like the rake he was purported to be. "Are you saying I'm not a scholar?" He relaxed his features. "Of course I'm not. I wonder if Foliot somehow knew I was a descendant—he recruited me quite specifically." He shook his head. "I can't ask now, and anyway, my membership isn't exactly with the Order."

"It's with the Camelot group," Cate said.

Surprise flickered in Kersey's gaze. "You know of it?"

"Septon told us. Kersey, why not stay with us?" Cate asked. "We'll explain to my father and Septon."

"No, I don't want anything to do with Septon. I thought I wanted revenge . . ." He shook his head again. "Never mind."

He gestured toward the sword lying in the grass. "Take it, Cate. Do what you think is best."

He strode toward his horse. Elijah sent Cate a supportive glance and then hurried to catch Kersey. "I know what it's like to be driven by resentment and revenge. I've taken care of the revenge part, but the resentment will always be with me. It's up to you to decide how much power you give it over your life."

Kersey turned with a grunt.

"You're going to try to discover your heritage now?" Elijah asked.

He looked at Elijah over his shoulder. "It's all I have left."

Amazed at the compassion he could manage to feel for this man, Elijah clapped him on the arm. "You might be surprised to find what you have—what you're capable of."

Kersey nodded toward Cate. "Take care of her. She'll drive you to drink, but I daresay she'll be worth it."

Elijah smiled. "I know she is."

Kersey lifted his hand and waved at Cate, then mounted his horse and rode away.

Elijah watched him disappear over a hill and turned back to Cate, who was already striding toward him.

He clasped her in his arms and pulled her close. His chin grazed the top of her head as he stroked her back. "He's a troubled man."

"Aren't you all?"

Elijah barked a laugh before tipping her chin up to kiss her. "Kersey says I'm in for more of it with you."

"That depends on what you intend. Will I be your occasional lover, your contracted mistress"—she made a face—"or something more . . . permanent?"

Her gaze was so adorably hopeful, he couldn't help but smile.

"I should like you to be whatever you desire, Cate. You

are a woman of independent thought and quite capable of deciding what you want. If it were up to *me*"—he clasped her waist—"I would make you my countess, but I fear that isn't in your plan."

She rested her palms against his chest. "It wasn't. And I would be doing myself a grave disservice if I didn't tell you exactly what I require to agree to wed you."

He arched a brow at her, feeling skeptical, but also suspecting he knew what she might say. "What is that?"

"I am an adventuring antiquary. I belong to a ladies-only group of antiquaries. I like to dirty my hands and solve mysteries. Above all, I love to learn. If you can't accept, no, that's not quite right. If you can't *endorse* my passions, I'm afraid a formal union won't be possible—whether we love each other or not."

He stared down at her and pretended to consider what she was saying. "That's a lot to expect of a man. I'm not certain . . ."

She pulled her hands back and lightly smacked them back into his chest. "Careful what you say."

He squeezed her waist. "You didn't let me finish. I'm not certain your list is complete. At least, I hope your passions might extend to me."

"Of course they do. In fact, you might be my favorite passion."

"Well," he drawled, "how can I argue with that? I accept your terms." He grew serious, astounded at the sudden direction his life was about to take—and the fact that he was quite content about it. Hell, he was ecstatic. He stared down into her incredible, dark eyes. "Cate, long ago I chose a life that wouldn't allow for a long-term home or a family. But when the earldom was thrust upon me, everything changed. I resented it at first and planned to continue on as I've always done—alone. But then I met you and *that* is really when it all changed. I could never settle for what I thought I wanted, not when you've shown me a happiness I never imagined. A love I never dreamed existed." He paused at her indrawn breath. "Will you consent to be my countess?"

"Oh, Elijah. Yes." She cradled his cheek. *"Yes."*

He lifted her up and spun her around before setting her back on the ground and kissing her soundly.

He raised his head and looked down at her beloved face. "You've made me so happy. Have you any idea how much more palatable Cosgrove will be now that you'll be there? And before you say we may not spend much time at Cosgrove, let me also say how much I look forward to adventuring with you."

"You're marrying me to ease your boredom?" she teased— he could tell by the sparkle in her eyes and the way her lips spread in a wide, heart-tugging smile.

"It is one of many reasons." He cocked a brow at her. "Perhaps I should draft a list . . . "

She laughed. "We'll do it together." She shook her head. "Elijah, I never expected to marry anyone. Falling in love with the right man was a necessary element and until you, I wasn't sure it was possible. But you made it more than a possibility; you made it everything I need. *You* are everything I need."

He brushed his lips against hers. "You are a treasure beyond words, Cate."

"And you are my heart's desire." She stood on her toes and kissed him.

EPILOGUE

*C*ate sat in her father's study with Elijah, awaiting Septon's arrival. It had been three days since they'd recovered Dyrnwyn. Septon had followed them alone—Cate's parents had preferred to remain at home in case Cate and Elijah returned. He'd gone home to Septon House after failing to find them and receiving word that they were safe in Monmouth. Cate had invited him back to Hollyhaven, and he was due to arrive any time.

"Are you certain about what you're doing?" Elijah, beside her on the settee, touched her hand.

"Yes." Cate glanced at her mother sitting in an adjacent chair. She'd been delighted to learn that Cate and Elijah would be marrying. The banns had already been posted, and the wedding would take place in just three weeks. Cate didn't want a large, fancy occasion. She just wanted Elijah.

Wade and Grey had also decided to marry, though it had taken a bit of convincing on Wade's part. Grey was already a widow and wasn't certain she wished to wed a second time. However, when they'd arrived at Hollyhaven two days ago, Cate could tell her maid was changed. As a woman in love,

Cate recognized the same state in Grey and told her so. They were to be married the week after Cate and Elijah.

Father and Penn stood at the large table that dominated the room. Dyrnwyn sat on top of it. They'd studied the sword relentlessly since she and Elijah had brought it back. Cate had written to Penn immediately and he'd arrived late yesterday.

"I still think it's a mistake to give it over," Penn said, his brows dipping low over his blue eyes.

He'd stated his opinion at least a hundred times, but Cate refused to be swayed. She'd thought about it and discussed it with Elijah endlessly. They'd agreed that this was the right decision—though he'd left it entirely up to her. She suppressed a smile as she glanced at her future husband, thinking again how lucky she was to have found him.

The butler, Thomas, entered and announced Septon.

A palpable tension seemed to grip the room. Cate squeezed Elijah's hand.

Septon's gaze immediately fell on the sword. His intake of breath was like a pistol shot. He moved toward the table slowly, his eyes never moving from the blade.

"You've studied it?" he asked softly.

"Yes," Penn answered. "Though it doesn't do what it did for Kersey."

Septon's brows nearly flew off his face. He swung around and turned to Cate. "What did it do?"

Cate stood and went to the table, Elijah at her side. Her mother joined them so that they all circled the sword.

"It burst into flame when he wielded it. He's a descendant of one of the knights."

Septon's eyes were huge. His hand covered his mouth. He looked down at the sword and shook his head. "I had no idea."

Cate exchanged looks with her family. They had

wondered if this was another secret Septon had known. Evidently not.

"Where is he?" Septon asked. "Lady Stratton is quite concerned for him."

Cate was glad to hear it. Kersey needed affection more than anyone she'd ever met—even more than Elijah. "I don't know, but I daresay he's trying to discover his true heritage. He's hopeful that Stratton isn't his father."

Septon shot a quick glance at her father, whose expression was stoic.

"You're not interested in prosecuting him for anything?" Septon asked, looking from Cate to Elijah.

"No," Elijah said. "It seems Foliot is really behind it all."

Septon nodded grimly. "I went to his house when I tried to find you and the sword. We had a brief exchange. He was enigmatic, as I'd expected. I wager the Order is in for some dark times."

"Can you simply expel him?" her mother asked.

"It's not that easy. He has many followers. And he's a descendant, while I am seen by many to be an interloper."

Penn scoffed. "What a bunch of nonsense. Disband the entire thing and give everything over to the people. I'll be happy to catalog and research the lot before I put it in the museum."

A few days ago Cate would have agreed with her brother, but after seeing what the sword could do and what lengths men would go to in order to possess it, she had changed her mind. She turned to Septon. "I want you to take the sword. Not for the Order, but to keep it safe and secret. Can you do that without giving it to the Order? As you said, it may be in for some troubled times."

Septon nodded. "I can. I will." He ran his finger along the hilt. He looked at Cate intently. "May I?"

"Of course," Cate said.

He lifted it from the table and turned it in his hand. "It doesn't feel different than any other sword."

"Not now, but if you try to use it, the blade will become heavy, unwieldy. I tried to employ it myself and couldn't even lift it." She exhaled. "It only responds to those who are worthy."

"And that's Kersey," Septon said. "Remarkable."

Penn frowned. "I could just as easily hide this sword away as Septon. In fact, it might be better if I did since Septon is associated with the Order."

Her father's eyes lit. "He has a point, Septon. Why not give it to Penn?"

Septon gave the sword a long, keen look before turning his gaze to Penn. "Will you promise not to publicize it? And not put it in the museum?"

He appeared satisfied, if not terribly pleased. "If I must."

"Then it's settled," her mother said, "Penn will take it."

"Should we inform the Scudamores about it?"

"I don't think so," her father said. "The fewer who know of its existence, the better."

Septon nodded. "I agree. This is why the Order has tried to so hard to keep the Thirteen Treasures hidden."

"Then why is the Heart of Llanllwch in the Ashmolean?" Elijah asked. "Shouldn't it be stowed away somewhere?"

"The Order keeps it under guard, and believe me, people have tried to steal it." Septon glanced at Penn. "Haven't they?"

"Indeed. It's also incredibly popular. You'd have a difficult time convincing the university to hide it away."

Septon looked from Cate to Penn and back to Cate again. "Might I spend some time with the sword?"

"Yes, please," Cate said. "We've taken a rubbing of it, and I've made some drawings of what it looked like when we found it and when it burst into flame."

"Penn, would it appease you to have the tapestry for your museum?" Elijah offered. "I'd be happy to donate it."

Donate it? Cate retook his hand and smiled up at him. "You could make them pay for it."

"I could, but I have other items I can sell—provided my wife allows me to. She's quite opinionated when it comes to our collection."

Our collection. Her heart swelled. "That's a marvelous idea. But I wonder if we shouldn't give it to the people of Harlech instead—display it in the church there."

"I can arrange for that," Penn said. He looked to Elijah. "If you'll allow me."

Elijah nodded. "Thank you."

Penn returned his attention to his sister, his expression bemused. "Cate, are you sure you're prepared to relinquish the sword and the tapestry in the same day? I know how desperately you wanted them."

Cate looked up at Elijah, her heart swelling with love and pride. "I have everything I want right here."

Don't miss the next exciting book in the series, Lord of Fortune when a dashing adventurer (Penn!) partners with an enigmatic woman to search for treasure and battle a dangerous secret society in the lush countryside of Regency England and Wales.

THANK YOU!

Thank you so much for reading Romancing the Earl! It's the third book in the Legendary Rogues series. I hope you enjoyed it! Don't miss the rest of the series:

The Legend of a Rogue
Lady of Desire
Romancing the Earl
Lord of Fortune
Captivating the Scoundrel

Would you like to know when my next book is available and to hear about sales and deals? Sign up for my VIP newsletter at https://www.darcyburke.com/readergroup, follow me on social media:

Facebook: https://facebook.com/DarcyBurkeFans
Twitter at @darcyburke
Instagram at darcyburkeauthor
Pinterest at darcyburkewrite

And follow me on Bookbub to receive updates on pre-orders, new releases, and deals!

Want to share your love of my books with like-minded readers? Want to hang with me and get inside scoop? Then don't miss my exclusive Facebook groups!

Darcy's Duchesses for historical readers
Burke's Book Lovers for contemporary readers

Need more Regency romance? Check out my other historical series:

The Untouchables
Swoon over twelve of Society's most eligible and elusive bachelor peers and the bluestockings, wallflowers, and outcasts who bring them to their knees!

The Untouchables: The Spitfire Society
Meet the smart, independent women who've decided they don't need Society's rules, their families' expectations, or, most importantly, a husband. But just because they don't need a man doesn't mean they might not *want* one...

The Untouchables: The Pretenders
Set in the captivating world of The Untouchables, follow the saga of a trio of siblings who excel at being something they're not. Can a dauntless Bow Street Runner, a devastated viscount, and a disillusioned Society miss unravel their secrets?

The Phoenix Club
Society's most exclusive invitation... Welcome to the Phoenix Club, where London's most audacious, disreputable, and

intriguing ladies and gentlemen find scandal, redemption, and second chances.

Wicked Dukes Club
Six books written by me and my BFF, NYT Bestselling Author Erica Ridley. Meet the unforgettable men of London's most notorious tavern, The Wicked Duke. Seductively handsome, with charm and wit to spare, one night with these rakes and rogues will never be enough...

Secrets and Scandals
Everyone has secrets and some of them are a scandal . . . six sexy, damaged heroes lose their hearts to strong, intelligent women in the glittering ballrooms and lush countryside of Regency England.

Love is All Around
Heartwarming Regency-set retellings of classic Christmas stories (written after the Regency!) featuring a cozy village, three siblings, and the best gift of all: love.

If you like contemporary romance, I hope you'll check out my **Ribbon Ridge** series available from Avon Impulse, and the continuation of Ribbon Ridge in **So Hot**.

I hope you'll consider leaving a review at your favorite online vendor or networking site!

I appreciate my readers so much. Thank you, thank you, *thank you*.

AUTHOR'S NOTE

I chose to set this story in and near Wales both because of the subject matter and because my grandmother, Selma Rita King Finney was born in Cardiff in 1916. I still have family there and was fortunate enough to visit several years ago. It's a beautiful land with charming people, and while the Welsh language is difficult to pronounce, I find it lovely—probably because I can still hear my great-uncle Alec singing it.

The thirteen treasures of Britain are mythical objects that appear in various legends. They have been used in countless stories and in many ways (Harry Potter's Deathly Hallows are somewhat based on them). I adapted them for the Legendary Rogues series and added the Heart of Llanllwch for purely narrative purposes. The flaming sword tapestry is completely fictional. The fate of Owen Glendower is unknown—he disappeared after Harlech fell and is thought to have died at Kentchurch, where he may have lived in hiding with his daughter Alice and her husband John Scudamore.

The Order of the Round Table is a completely fictional group, but is based on the myriad secret societies that have existed for centuries. Edmund de Valery and Anarawd are fictional characters as are the documents they produced.

Of course there is no proof that King Arthur, his knights, the Round Table or any of Arthurian legend is real. I'd like to think it's a little bit history, with a dash of embellishment, and a lot of great storytelling.

ALSO BY DARCY BURKE

Historical Romance

Legendary Rogues

The Legend of a Rogue

Lady of Desire

Romancing the Earl

Lord of Fortune

Captivating the Scoundrel

The Phoenix Club

Invitation

Improper

Impassioned

Intolerable

The Untouchables

The Bachelor Earl

The Forbidden Duke

The Duke of Daring

The Duke of Deception

The Duke of Desire

The Duke of Defiance

The Duke of Danger

The Duke of Ice

The Duke of Ruin

The Duke of Lies

The Duke of Seduction

The Duke of Kisses

The Duke of Distraction

The Untouchables: Spitfire Society

Never Have I Ever with a Duke

A Duke is Never Enough

A Duke Will Never Do

The Untouchables: The Pretenders

A Secret Surrender

A Scandalous Bargain

A Rogue to Ruin

Love is All Around
(A Regency Holiday Trilogy)

The Red Hot Earl
The Gift of the Marquess
Joy to the Duke

Wicked Dukes Club

One Night for Seduction by Erica Ridley
One Night of Surrender by Darcy Burke
One Night of Passion by Erica Ridley
One Night of Scandal by Darcy Burke
One Night to Remember by Erica Ridley
One Night of Temptation by Darcy Burke

Secrets and Scandals

Her Wicked Ways
His Wicked Heart
To Seduce a Scoundrel
To Love a Thief (a novella)
Never Love a Scoundrel
Scoundrel Ever After

Contemporary Romance

Ribbon Ridge

Where the Heart Is (a prequel novella)
Only in My Dreams
Yours to Hold

When Love Happens

The Idea of You

When We Kiss

You're Still the One

Ribbon Ridge: So Hot

So Good

So Right

So Wrong

ACKNOWLEDGMENTS

This was one of those books that felt like it would never, ever end. And I'm pretty sure my family thought so too! I can't thank you enough for your understanding and your support —I love you more than I can ever say!

I have to give a HUGE thank you to Leigh Duvan for reading and providing exactly the feedback I needed. This book rocks because of you. I can't wait until it's my turn to read!

Another MASSIVE thank you to the Dream Teamers. Your encouragement, enthusiasm, and generosity with your time is incredibly humbling, and I just can't say it enough: *thank you.*

I couldn't manage without my incredible tribe of writer friends: Elisabeth, Joan, Rachel, Erica, Emma, and Janice. There are plenty more of you out there and I hope you know how much I appreciate the ways you touch my life.

As always, thanks go to an incredible production team, without whom this would look like the equivalent of a high school assignment bound in a Pee Chee folder. Team

Romancing the Earl includes the fabulous Eliza Dee, the lovely Martha Trachtenberg, and the amazing Jaycee DiLorenzo.

"...A fast paced story that was exciting and interesting. This is a definite must add to your book lists!"

-Kilts and Swords

"Once again Darcy Burke takes an interesting story and...turns it into magic. An exceptionally well-written book."

-Bodice Rippers, Femme Fatale, and Fantasy

LORD of FORTUNE

"If you love a deep, passionate romance with a bit of mystery, then this is the book for you!"

-Teatime and Books

"I don't think I know enough superlatives to describe this book! It is wonderfully, magically delicious. It sucked me in from the very first sentence and didn't turn me loose—not even at the end ..."

-Flippin Pages

CAPTIVATING the SCOUNDREL

"I am in absolute awe of this story. Gideon and Daphne stole all of my heart and then some. This book was such a delight to read."

-Beneath the Covers Blog

"Darcy knows how to end a series with a bang! Daphne and Gideon are a mix of enemies and allies turned lovers that will have you on the edge of your seat at every turn."

-Sassy Booklover

ABOUT THE AUTHOR

Darcy Burke is the USA Today Bestselling Author of sexy, emotional historical and contemporary romance. Darcy wrote her first book at age 11, a happily ever after about a swan addicted to magic and the female swan who loved him, with exceedingly poor illustrations. Join her Reader Club newsletter for the latest updates from Darcy.

A native Oregonian, Darcy lives on the edge of wine country with her guitar-strumming husband, incredibly talented artist daughter, and imaginative son who will almost certainly out-write her one day (that may be tomorrow). They're a crazy cat family with two Bengal cats, a small, fame-seeking cat named after a fruit, an older rescue Maine Coon with attitude to spare, and a collection of neighbor cats who hang out on the deck and occasionally venture inside. You can find Darcy at a winery, in her comfy writing chair balancing her laptop and a cat or three, folding laundry (which she loves), or binge-watching TV with the family. Her happy places are Disneyland, Labor Day weekend at the Gorge, Denmark, and anywhere in the UK—so long as her family is there too. Visit Darcy online at www. darcyburke.com and follow her on social media.

facebook.com/DarcyBurkeFans

twitter.com/darcyburke

instagram.com/darcyburkeauthor

pinterest.com/darcyburkewrites

goodreads.com/darcyburke

bookbub.com/authors/darcy-burke

amazon.com/author/darcyburke